He'd waited t   s
moment, this opp   a
a thousandfold i   e
reality was so mu   n
anything his mind could have ~~laura~~ed
against his own, pressed in perfect complement. He
moved his free hand to her face, and pulled her against
him, tangling his tongue against hers, kissing her deeply.

He felt the intake of her breath against his mouth,
could sense the eager, hammering cadence of her heartbeat in his mind. He could smell the hot musk of her
blood as it raced suddenly, wildly in her veins; and his
body reacted. He felt a tingling warmth in his gums, a
tightening in his groin, and he leaned toward Lina,
pressing her back against the couch until she lay beneath him, enveloping his hips between her thighs. She
clutched at his hair as he drew his lips away from hers.
The tips of their noses brushed; her breath fluttered
against his lips and she whispered his name, fully aware
of the hardening length of him, the swell of his growing
arousal pressing through his pants against her.

For a moment he hesitated, uncertain and frightened
that he would forget himself, that his body would forget
the difference between bloodlust and desire . . .

BOOK YOUR PLACE ON OUR WEBSITE AND MAKE THE READING CONNECTION!

We've created a customized website just for our very special readers, where you can get the inside scoop on everything that's going on with Zebra, Pinnacle and Kensington books.

When you come online, you'll have the exciting opportunity to:

- View covers of upcoming books
- Read sample chapters
- Learn about our future publishing schedule (listed by publication month *and author*)
- Find out when your favorite authors will be visiting a city near you
- Search for and order backlist books from our online catalog
- Check out author bios and background information
- Send e-mail to your favorite authors
- Meet the Kensington staff online
- Join us in weekly chats with authors, readers and other guests
- Get writing guidelines
- AND MUCH MORE!

Visit our website at
http://www.kensingtonbooks.com

Dark Thirst

Sara Reinke

ZEBRA BOOKS
Kensington Publishing Corp.
www.kensingtonbooks.com

ZEBRA BOOKS are published by

Kensington Publishing Corp.
850 Third Avenue
New York, NY 10022

All Kensington titles, imprints, and distributed lines are available at special quantity discounts for bulk purchases for sales promotion, premiums, fund-raising, educational, or institutional use.

Special book excerpts or customized printings can also be created to fit specific needs. For details, write or phone the office of the Kensington Special Sales Manager: Attn. Special Sales Department. Kensington Publishing Corp., 850 Third Avenue, New York, NY 10022. Phone: 1-800-221-2647.

Zebra and the Z logo Reg. U.S. Pat. & TM Off.

ISBN-13: 978-1-4201-0053-2
ISBN-10: 1-4201-0053-X

First Printing: July 2007
10 9 8 7 6 5 4 3 2 1

Printed in the United States of America

Prologue

Brandon sensed the Grandfather coming before he ever appeared in the doorway; like the way the electrical charge from an encroaching storm would shiver through his form, Brandon felt the hairs along the nape of his neck raise, and he knew.

His gift of telepathy, something that came inherently to other members of the Brethren, had never been strong within him. The Grandfather had always told him it was because he was damaged, that like his ears and voice, his extrasensory perception was long-since ruined. His brother, Caine, had always told Brandon it was because he was weak—in body, mind, and spirit. *No better than a woman,* Caine would sneer, his own mental prowess already formidable despite his relative youth. *Or worse than that—a human. You're as weak and wretched as the fetid meat of humanity, brother.*

Brandon was in his room with his youngest brother, Daniel, who was four years old. Daniel was sitting in a broad patch of sunbeam beneath Brandon's window, coloring books and crayons spread around him in a messy circumference. Brandon knelt, watching the boy draw wild, looping circles in red, blue, and green, his mouth open in a wide smile, moving nonstop with chattering words Brandon could not hear.

When he felt the odd, ominous, prickling sensation in the air, tingling around him, Brandon lifted his head. Daniel didn't notice it; he was too young yet, and it would still be many long years before his mind allowed him such uncanny awareness. The boy saw the Grandfather, however, as he stepped into the doorway beyond Brandon's shoulder, and his dark eyes widened, the happiness in his face fading abruptly to fright.

They were the last of their kind, Brandon and his family, two hundred and twenty-three of them living in close quarters in neighboring horse farms in central Kentucky. Humans might have called them vampires, were they aware of their existence, but to Brandon and his people, they were simply called the Brethren.

The Grandfather seldom visited the younger members of the clan—and never Brandon. He was always too busy or otherwise preoccupied, and he had never made any secret of the fact that he considered Brandon a disgraceful blight among the Brethren.

Brandon had been Daniel's age when he had come upon a trio of burglars in the middle of the night as they had robbed the downstairs parlor of the great house. He had been four years old when they had attacked him, beating him mercilessly in attempt to keep from being discovered. He had been only a child when his throat had been cut—rendering him mute for life—and his head battered, leaving him deaf in both ears. Just as Daniel's ability to sense his fellow Brethren had not yet fully matured, Brandon's healing abilities as a member of the Brethren—the accelerated capacities that would seem to grant them immortality—had not been developed enough. They had kept him from death, but had left him ruined, at least in the Grandfather's stern regard. Brandon was a constant symbol of weakness to most of his family, and particularly to the Grandfather; one to be disdained and ignored.

That afternoon, however, he didn't intend to ignore

Brandon. But at first, Brandon couldn't fathom what the Grandfather might want.

Is he lost? Does he want to see Daniel? he wondered rather naïvely and stupidly. He rose to his feet, lowering his eyes to the floor in polite deference to his elder, at a complete loss as to the reason for his presence.

And then he saw the paper in the Grandfather's hand, a single sheet, with a distinctive logo atop the page that Brandon recognized even from across the room.

Oh, God.

He had been diligent about getting the mail every day, taking Daniel with him and making a trek out of it as they went together down the two-mile-long, winding drive leading from the great house through the rolling acres of the Grandfather's Thoroughbred farm, to the roadside mailbox at their gated entrance.

He cut his eyes quickly, frantically toward his bedside clock and saw it was only one o'clock in the afternoon. *The mail must have come early,* he realized in dismay, feeling his stomach twist inward upon itself, tightening into a tense, painful knot. *Oh, God, it came early.*

"Take Daniel to his room," the Grandfather said. Brandon couldn't hear his voice, but he could read his lips. Worse than this, he could sense him plainly in his mind; the Grandfather was the strongest telepath in the Noble family, but he seldom forced his thoughts upon the younger Brethren unless he meant to be taken at murderous severity. *Take him now, Emily.*

Brandon's younger sister, Emily, strode briskly past the Grandfather and across the room. She reached for Daniel, but the little boy shied behind Brandon's hip, his small fingers clutching anxiously at the belt loops of Brandon's jeans. Brandon looked down and saw him whimper his name, frightened.

It's alright, Brandon tried to convey in a gentle smile, as he brushed his hand against the cap of his brother's hair to draw his fearful gaze. Even though his telepathy was weak, he could speak to Daniel with his mind, but it was strictly forbidden by the mandate of the Grandfather. Not until Brandon's bloodletting. Normally, Brandon was helpless to use his telepathy unless another Brethren member deliberately opened his or her mind to him. Otherwise, his extrasensory perceptions were as deafened as his ears, and it felt as if a heavy cowl lay draped constantly within his mind, stifling him.

It will be different once you've gone through the bloodletting, his twin sister, Tessa, had tried to tell him. *Your powers will strengthen, just like mine did. You'll see.*

However, Brandon suspected the Grandfather and Caine were right; his abilities were damaged from the same injuries that had cost him his hearing and speech. He didn't want to see if they would strengthen after his bloodletting. He didn't want to go through the ancient, brutal ceremony—even if it meant he'd be able to communicate freely with his mind.

Daniel was too young to control his own mental abilities, and his mind was always open. Brandon ordinarily shared his thoughts with Daniel freely and without rebuke as a result, but he could sense that today, such defiance—and particularly in the presence of the Grandfather—would be a foolish mistake.

He stroked Daniel's hair again and nodded once toward Emily, smiling in encouragement. *Go with her,* he tried to say in the simple gesture. *I'll be okay.*

Daniel looked unconvinced, but he wasn't too young to understand one didn't disobey the Grandfather. He slipped out from behind the shelter of Brandon's long legs and hooked his hand against Emily's outstretched, awaiting palm.

Brandon glanced toward the doorway and found their oldest brother, Caine, watching from the threshold, his brows narrowed, his dark eyes glittering meanly, the corner of his mouth hooked in wicked triumph. Like most of his siblings—except for his twin sister, Tessa, and

Daniel—Caine considered Brandon unfit to hold a place among the Brethren. In that moment, as the two brothers locked gazes, it didn't take a genius to figure out who had discovered that the mail had been delivered early and who had brought the letter from Gallaudet University to the Grandfather's disapproving notice.

Brandon had wanted to go to the all-deaf school for years, even before he had earned his high school equivalency. The Grandfather hadn't allowed him to go to elementary or high school, however, and had permitted Brandon's instruction only under the supervision of a private tutor. Jackson Jones, Brandon's teacher, who was also deaf, had told Brandon about the college in Washington, D.C.; it was Jackson's alma mater, and to Brandon, it had seemed a place of impossible promise and wonder.

Of course, the Grandfather had no intention of allowing Brandon to leave the Brethren to go to college. He'd made this vehemently clear. Brandon had known it. He had applied to the school anyway. He had planned on leaving on his own, running away, abandoning the Brethren and going just the same.

Although there was no way the Grandfather could know all of this simply from the letter, Brandon knew that he did. He could see it in the man's cold, unflinching gaze, the way his coal-black eyes seemed to bore into Brandon's skull, to grasp him firmly and hold him fast, without the Grandfather laying as much as a finger on him. He knew and he was enraged.

Oh, God, Brandon thought, as the Grandfather swung the door close behind Emily and Daniel, slamming it with enough force so that although Brandon couldn't hear the sharp report, he could feel it resounding in the floorboards beneath his feet. Caine remained in the chamber, as if by unspoken invitation, and his smile grew wider at the mounting dismay in Brandon's face.

The Grandfather was more than three hundred years old but had the prowess and build of a man no more than in his mid-forties. He was strong; like all of the Brethren Elders, he commanded the well-honed strength of more than twenty human men. He had a heavy sheaf of white hair that fell nearly to his hips, standing out in stark contrast to his black shirt. Ordinarily, the Grandfather always wore sport coats and suits, no matter the occasion or weather. Today, he had abandoned his tie and jacket and turned back his shirt sleeves to his elbows.

Oh, God, Brandon thought, his body paralyzed with fright, his mouth gone dry and tacky with it, his shoulders trembling uncontrollably.

What is this? the Grandfather asked, with a demonstrative waggle of the letter from Gallaudet. His mouth did not move; his voice fell with cold remonstration through Brandon's mind.

Grandfather, Brandon thought, blinking down at his toes. *Please, I can—*

The Grandfather's hand whipped around, a blur in his peripheral vision before it plowed into the side of his face. The blow sent Brandon flying. He slammed into a bookshelf, knocking the wind from his lungs, and crumpled to his hands and knees on the floor. He blinked at the polished hard wood beneath him, at the tiny pinpoints of sudden light that danced in his line of sight. Droplets of blood peppered down from his nose, spattering between his hands. His mind was swimming; the Grandfather had struck him hard enough to leave him witless.

He felt the floorboards tremble beneath his palms at the Grandfather's approach, and he cowered, just as the Grandfather's hand closed fiercely in his hair, forcing his head back. *Close your mind to me, boy,* the Grandfather said. *That gift is reserved for a full-fledged and fed Brethren. You disgrace your bloodline—and me—to use it otherwise, even in your pathetic and limited capacities.*

He released Brandon's hair, and Brandon crumpled to his hands and knees again, trembling. *Get up,* the Grandfather said, and Brandon obeyed, stumbling to his feet. A glance promised he'd find no rescue from his brother; Caine remained rooted in place by the doorway, his arms folded across his chest, watching in silent, thinly veiled amusement.

Did you think I wouldn't find out about this? the Grandfather demanded, shoving the letter into Brandon's face. Brandon had a momentary, dazed glance at the words,

"Congratulations! You have been accepted to Gallaudet University, the world's only university for deaf and—"

and then the Grandfather jerked it away again.

Brandon wore a notebook on a chain about his neck, in an engraved brass case his father had ordered custommade for him. Writing notes in its small, three-by-five pages was the only means by which he was allowed to communicate in the house, by the Grandfather's directive. Although Brandon knew sign language, the Grandfather had strictly forbidden it, and threatened to sternly punish anyone else who learned it.

Brandon reached for the notebook. His hands were shaking as he flipped back the brass lid. He carried a matching gilded pen tucked at the hinged end of the notebook. He pushed it out with his thumb and began to write, struggling vainly to think of some appeal the Grandfather might consider, some explanation that might spare him from what was about to come upon him in undoubtedly brutal measure.

Please, Brandon wrote. *Grandfather, please, I'm sorry.*

The Grandfather snatched the notebook and jerked it. Brandon gasped as the chain cut sharply into the back of his neck and then snapped with the force of the Grandfather's pull. The notebook sailed across the room. He had a split second to blink at it, startled and dismayed, and then felt the whip of sudden wind as the Grandfather struck him again, sending him crashing across the room. He fell against a table, his feet skittering over the crayons

Daniel had left scattered on the floor, dancing against half-finished drawings of houses and horses. The edge of the table caught him squarely in the gut, and he stumbled backward and fell, gasping futilely for breath.

All of your life, you have been spoiled, the Grandfather said, and again, his hand fell against Brandon's hair, wrenching him to his feet. *Your father has coddled you because of your weakness, and I have let him for far too long.*

Again, his hand smashed against Brandon's face, and again, Brandon crumpled to the floor. He could feel blood coursing from his nose. He could taste it in his mouth, bitter and salty, but he did not fight or resist his grandfather. Jackson Jones had taught him the martial art of aikido, in addition to reading, writing, and sign language. Although Brandon had never officially tested, Jackson had told him that he was proficient enough at the sport to likely attain at least a first-degree black belt. But he couldn't fight the Grandfather; wouldn't fight him. Whatever further punishment the Grandfather intended for him would pale in violent comparison to anything meted out if Brandon dared to defend himself.

The Grandfather clamped his hand against Brandon's throat and shoved him back against the wall, rapping his head painfully. He hoisted the younger man aloft and held him there, strangling against his palm, with Brandon's feet dangling helplessly a good foot off the floor.

You disgust me, boy, the Grandfather seethed in Brandon's mind. His eyes had turned black, the dark of his irises seeping outward, swallowing any hint of his corneas from view. His canine teeth began to drop as his face flushed with fury. *You are a disgrace to your family—a disgrace among the Brethren. I thought you could bring me no greater shame than the night you abandoned your bloodletting—let your sister, Emily, take your place in the hunt, but this . . . !*

I'm sorry . . . ! Brandon thought, struggling vainly, wheezing soundlessly under the crushing weight of the hand collapsing his windpipe. *Grandfather, please . . . I . . .*

The other Brethren laugh at us, the Grandfather said, leaning toward Brandon, watching the young man's face flush purple with the strain for air. *They laugh at the Nobles, that we abide by you, keep you among us, keep you from those rites of passage that are customary and expected of a Brethren your age. And now you think you can just leave these walls— abandon a birthright that has been fought and sown for you for more than one thousand years—so that you can harbor the paltry ambitions of the human stain?*

He opened his hand, and Brandon crumpled to his knees, clutching at his throat and dragging in whooping mouthfuls of air.

I do not know why I bother with you, boy, the Grandfather said. *Or why I continue to let the least among us tax my patience the most.*

I am sorry, Grandfather, Brandon thought, still gasping to reclaim his breath.

There will be no university for you, the Grandfather said coldly, and he ripped the acceptance letter from Gallaudet into pieces. Brandon blinked at them, his eyes flooded with involuntary tears as the shreds fluttered to the floor around him. *Not now, boy, not ever.*

Brandon hung his head, still shuddering for breath. *I'm sorry,* he thought, over and over. *I'm sorry.*

Give me your hand, Brandon.

Brandon held up his right hand and felt the cool press of the Grandfather's fingers as he wrapped them about. *You will go through the bloodletting,* the Grandfather told him.

Brandon blinked down at the floor, numb, hurting, and dazed. He nodded. There would be no fighting it, no protest now. His father—who had kept him from it for so long—would be helpless against this, a direct mandate from the Grandfather.

If you ever run from me, know this, boy, and mark it well, the Grandfather said. *There is no corner of this earth, no measure of time that can keep you hidden from me. I will find you. I will return you to this house, and I will punish you a thousand-*

fold what you have suffered today. And when I am finished, I will cast you into the Beneath, boy, and leave you there to rot.

Brandon nodded, trembling.

When your hands are healed, you will succumb to the blood-lust. You will know your first kill.

Brandon looked up, startled, bewildered. *My hands . . . ?*

And then the Grandfather closed his hand into a fist, crushing the bones in Brandon's right hand, splintering them inward beneath his brutal, forceful grasp. Brandon jerked against him, screaming soundlessly in bright, brilliant agony. When the Grandfather turned loose of him, he pitched forward, cradling his shattered hand against his belly, gasping for breath as his mind threatened to abandon him.

Give me your other hand, Brandon.

Brandon blinked up at his grandfather, his eyes stricken and terrified. *No,* he thought, shaking his head, desperate. *No, Grandfather, please don't . . . !*

He was left-handed. He wrote with his left hand, signed primarily with his left hand, held a toothbrush, fed himself, scratched his ass—everything with his left hand.

This fact wasn't lost upon the Grandfather. "It would be cruel," he said aloud, pinning Brandon with his icy gaze. "The height of cruelty, in fact, to damage them both, would it not? You wouldn't be able to write. You wouldn't be able to defy me with the sign language I've banned— that you continue to use, in spite of this. I'm neither blind nor stupid, boy. I know of your transgressions. You hide nothing from me."

I'm sorry, Grandfather, Brandon thought, trembling in pain and fright. *Please, I—*

The Grandfather caught him by the throat, firmly beneath the shelf of Brandon's chin, forcing his head back. "Even your worthless modicum of telepathy would be even more so, because I would forbid anyone to open their minds to you. Who would dare defy me and try, with you as testimony to my reprisal?"

His hand tightened, crushing Brandon's windpipe, and Brandon whimpered soundlessly, breathlessly. "You would heal, of course," the Grandfather said. "But it would still take months—grueling, agonizing months in the meantime. You would be crippled."

I'm sorry, Brandon thought again, his mouth open as he gasped vainly for air.

"As I said, it would be cruel," the Grandfather said. "And I am not."

He released his grip on Brandon's throat. Brandon crumpled forward, choked for breath, wheezing. He huddled against the floor, trembling, waiting for the Grandfather to leave. He'd had his fun; he'd made his point with brutal emphasis, and Brandon waited for it to be over, to feel the floorboards beneath him tremble as the Grandfather walked away.

When several long, excruciating moments passed, and the Grandfather didn't move, Brandon looked up at him, hesitant and wary.

"I will let your brother decide," the Grandfather said, and he glanced over his shoulder toward the doorway.

Oh, God, Brandon thought, as Caine stepped away from the threshold, moving at the Grandfather's beckon. He strolled slowly across the room, moving like a cat closing in deliberately on some helpless prey. His face betrayed no emotion, but his dark eyes gleamed with unmistakable glee.

"Surely Caine might find some compassion in his heart for you in your plight," the Grandfather said. "My mind is so clouded with rage at the moment, I'm afraid I might mistake vindictiveness for justice."

Caine looked down at Brandon, his expression impassive and unmoved. He held out his hand, expectantly. "Give me your hand, brother."

Brandon locked gazes with him, his brows furrowed. *Fuck you, Caine.*

The Grandfather struck him, slapping with enough force to snap his head toward his shoulder. *You will show your brother respect,* he told Brandon sharply. *He has earned it, and you will demonstrate it—the same respect you offer me, or any other member of our Brethren who have embraced the bloodlust and made their rightful, honorable place among us.*

Brandon looked up at Caine, his vision bleary, fresh blood spilling from his nose. Caine held out his hand again patiently. *Give me your hand, brother,* he said once more, his voice mockingly gentle inside Brandon's mind. There was no fighting him; no defying the Grandfather. Brandon held up his left hand, his entire body shaking with terror.

"If you plead with me, I will listen," Caine said, closing his fingers slowly, firmly around Brandon's. "I'm not cruel, either, or without mercy." He smiled at Brandon. "Beg me for it, Brandon."

Brandon spat a thick mouthful of blood against his shoes. *Fuck you, Caine,* he thought again.

Caine crushed his brother's left hand, shattering the bones in his fingers and palm, making Brandon shriek again in soundless, breathless pain. When he was finished, the Grandfather draped his hand fondly against Caine's shoulder and they walked away, leaving Brandon huddled against the floor, surrounded by the shredded acceptance letter, his broken hands tucked against his belly, his breath escaping him in sodden, sob-choked gasps.

Chapter One

Thirteen months later

The nine-millimeter pistol tucked down the back of Angelina Jones' baby-blue sweat pants kept wanting to slide down the crack of her ass as she marked a vigorous jogging pace. She could have pulled it out and carried it in her hand, but she didn't want people to get the wrong impression, despite the fact her oversized sweatshirt had the word *POLICE* clearly emblazoned across the front.

Of course, she could have simply left the damn thing at home. She wasn't on the clock; she was taking her morning run, and going to her older brother Jackson's condo building to water his plants while he was out of town. It wasn't as though she needed the pistol for anything, but for Lina, leaving the gun behind would have been akin to forgoing her shoes or shirt. She didn't feel right without its comforting heft somewhere within her immediate reach. She was a cop. She didn't stop being one just because her shift came to an end. She never considered herself "off duty," and she always carried her gun.

She wore her chin-length spray of wild, loosely curled hair stuffed beneath a navy blue baseball cap, with her iPod headphones tucked into the recesses of her ears. She was listening to a medley of her favorite running tunes— right now, her feet were dropping in heavy rhythm to match that of a Kanye West song. She hummed along under her huffing breath. It was barely dawn; the sky was gray and infused with pale, early morning sunlight. The air was cool, crisp, and somewhat damp, and enveloped her every stride like a mist. Her Reeboks slapped and splashed through shallow puddles pooled in depressions along the sidewalk. She shouldered past commuters hunched and hurrying for subway depots or bus stops. She danced back from the curb as taxi cabs careened recklessly past, slopping dirty gray water up from the gutters.

The music was an indulgence for twenty-six-year-old Lina, having grown up under the watchful eye of her mother, Latisha, who had not condoned or tolerated anything even remotely deemed "ghetto."

"Dr. King didn't fight and die so you could run around gang-banging," Latisha had told Lina and Jackson more times than Lina could count. "Miss Rosa Parks didn't keep her seat on that bus so you could listen to gangsta-rap garbage and dress little better than hoodlums."

Latisha had dropped out of high school in her junior year to have Jackson, but that had not prevented her from eventually obtaining her GED and then earning a nursing degree. She'd juggled two to three jobs throughout Lina's childhood, just to make sure Jackson could go to a special school for deaf kids once his hearing had grown too bad for him to remain in the public system, and so that they could have a home in a safe, quiet suburb, rather than something in the crime-ridden downtown area. She had busted her ass, and more than Dr. King or Miss Rosa Parks, Latisha Jones had been a hero to her daughter.

Lina had the day off for a change. She had considered jumping in her car at the first crack of daylight and heading east, driving until she hit the ocean, and then spend a leisurely long weekend squelching her toes in cold, wet sand and enjoying the pounding thunder of surf against the lip of the seaboard. It had been a tempting thought, especially considering she had no one to spend the weekend with. Jude was gone. He'd left her for a white woman—a circumstance so ridiculously cliché that when he'd first told her about it, Lina had laughed out loud for nearly three whole hours before her grief and disappointment finally took over.

She had thought about abandoning the city for the beach but hadn't in the end, because she had agreed to be a bridesmaid in her friend Melanie's wedding. Even though under ordinary circumstances, Lina would rather take repeated, forceful blows in the gut than wear a dress and heels, she'd known Melanie since elementary school, and had been helpless to refuse.

Jude was going to be at the wedding. It would be the first time Lina had seen him in three months, and it wasn't a reunion she was looking forward to. *I'm sure he'll have Ashlee in tow,* she thought. Ashlee was the white woman, Jude's new girlfriend, and Lina wondered—not for the first time—if she could wear her pistol's shoulder harness beneath the purple satin confection of her gown and still be inconspicuous.

Even if she could find a way to beg out of the wedding— which she was sorely tempted to try—Lina was still trapped in the city. She had promised Jackson she would take care of his plants. *His stupid damn plants,* she thought, as she stepped too heartily into a puddle and slapped her sock with water. She sucked in a hissing breath through her teeth, but her pace did not as much as falter. Kanye segued into some Black Eyed Peas, and she broadened her stride to match the new beat pounding in her ears.

Jackson had gone to stay with their mother in Sarasota, Florida. Two weeks earlier, Latisha had gone through a radical mastectomy to remove a cancer-ridden left breast, and several of her lymph nodes. Lina and Jackson had flown down together to be with her for the

surgery, but work had brought Lina home again shortly
thereafter. Jackson was a teacher at St. Bartholomew's,
a parochial school for hearing-impaired children. He
had lost his own hearing in what had proven a steady,
cruel decline since early childhood, and by the age of
eighteen, had been completely deaf. He had been able
to arrange for a lengthy sabbatical from his instruction
to help Latisha through her recuperation, and wouldn't
be home again for another three weeks.

Lina reached Jackson's building and darted up the
broad, granite front steps. She ducked into the foyer,
keeping her earphones in place, her music cranked. She
made an immediate left and entered the emergency
stairwell, where she began her ascent, scaling two steps
at a time. She could have taken the elevator, but this was
better for her—Jackson lived on the top floor, eight stories up. He used the space more as a greenhouse than a
home, tending to an assortment of exotic plants that he
loved like children. Lina didn't get it, but she knew if
anything happened to those rotten plants in his absence,
she would never hear the end of it.

By the time she reached the eighth floor, the Black
Eyed Peas had given over to Mary J. Blige. Lina hummed
along to the singer's honey-sweet timbre as she opened
the stairwell door and walked down the carpeted corridor toward Jackson's corner apartment. Jackson kept a
spare key taped beneath his welcome mat, but Lina had
a copy of her own. She fished her key ring out of her
sweatshirt pocket, unlocked Jackson's double deadbolts,
and stepped inside.

On the first day of her duties, Lina had found a note
taped inside the door Jackson had left for her. *Hey, Scarecrow,* he'd greeted, and then had launched into a lengthy
diatribe about the care and feeding of his goddamn
plants. *Like I'm a moron and can't figure out how to put water
in a pitcher, then pour,* Lina had thought.

She'd crumpled the note in her hand and thrown it

away. If he'd wanted her to pay a lick of attention to his instructions, he should have known better than to call her "Scarecrow." It was a nickname Jackson had given her in childhood. Lina was pretty enough, she supposed, but the moniker was pretty appropriate, though she hated to admit it. She had long, strong limbs, narrow hips, no waist to speak of and not much of a bosom. She was lean and lanky, all muscles and flat planes; even Jude had pointed out her lack of feminine wiles. "You're hard, Lina," he'd told her as he'd left her. "Inside and out, everything about you is hard."

She supposed his new girlfriend was soft and compliant. *Inside and out,* she thought with a thin, humorless smile.

Jude had left some of his things at her apartment after their split, and had flooded her answering machine and cell phone voice mail regularly demanding their return. Lina had boxed up the pair of expensive Italian leather dress shoes, silk tie, pair of gold cufflinks, and designer-brand socks and stuffed them in the back of her closet, along with his pride and joy—a black Dolce and Gabbana suit. Jude had loved that suit more than anything—including Lina, apparently. He'd reserved its use for closing arguments in larger cases and special occasions when he wanted to appear at his most immaculate, affluent best. The last such instance had been for his firm's New Year's bash. They'd returned to her apartment in the aftermath. He'd broken up with Lina less than a week after that, and the outfit had remained in Lina's possession ever since.

She imagined she was sitting on a hoard worth at least two grand, and figured she'd find a use for the stuff sooner or later. Giving in to Jude's thinly veiled threats and returning them wasn't an option. *You snooze, you lose, asshole,* she thought. *Next time, pack your shit up before you break up with someone.*

Jackson's threshold opened onto a spacious living

room. The entire eastern side of the room was nothing but windows, a veritable paradise for a plant enthusiast like Jackson. Lina imagined his landlord could have charged seven times the monthly rent Jackson shelled out for that place, and he would have paid it gladly, eagerly, if only for the windows alone. Beyond them was a long, narrow terrace awarding a great view of the city. Lina and Jude had made love on that terrace before, unbeknownst to Jackson.

But she didn't want to think about Jude.

He was more than a clotheshorse, although that was evidenced enough by the crap he'd left behind in her apartment. Jude had turned out to be her polar opposite, a meticulously prissy man obsessed with perfecting his appearance. He used to tell her that it was because of his job; as an attorney, it was important to look good, in the esteem of not only clients, but judges and juries, too. But he had been a lawyer longer than he'd been a narcissist, and Lina didn't believe the two had to necessarily go hand-in-hand.

When she had met Jude, she'd been a wide-eyed rookie on the police force, and he'd been a fresh-faced assistant district attorney. Back then, he'd worn polyester-blend, no-brand suits from JC Penney and had cared more about justice than whether or not his hair was perfectly sculpted. But time—and the lure of the private sector—had jaded him. Jude had gone to work for Quinn, Mistretta & Miles, a partnership of personal injury specialists, and from there, had racked up a sizable fortune at the benefit of automobile accident, medical malpractice, and workplace liability victims.

He sold his soul, Lina thought with a humorless smirk. *And guess what? The devil wears Dolce and Gabbana, not Prada.*

She walked across the living room, still humming along with Mary J. as she headed for the kitchen. A breakfast bar was all that separated the two. If it wasn't for the small bedroom and bathroom down a nearby corridor, the condo would have passed as an oversized efficiency, in Lina's estimation. But Jackson loved it, and he was the one who had to live there, she figured. *Him and his stupid damn plants.*

She flipped on the kitchen lights and walked toward the sink to grab the watering pitcher. She halted in midstep as soon as the bright fluorescents flooded the room, glaring against the immaculate white linoleum floor, glazed against the polished surfaces of the stainless steel appliances.

Somebody's been here.

There was an empty glass sitting in the dish drain that had, as of last week, been empty. Three empty beer bottles were turned upside down to drain in the plastic rack, and a plate had been propped against them to air dry.

Lina's left hand moved for her iPod while her right moved toward the small of her back, reaching beneath her sweatshirt hem for the butt of her pistol. She turned off the music, cutting Mary J. off in mid-croon. She pulled out the gun, settling her index finger lightly, reflexively against the trigger as she thumbed off the safety, and reached with her other hand to pull the headphones out of her ears. With the plugs gone, the music off, she heard what she had been oblivious to since walking in the door—the sound of water running from the bathroom, the shower in use.

Somebody's still here.

Lina frowned, walking slowly, cautiously out of the kitchen and down the corridor toward the bedroom. No one was supposed to be there. Jackson would have told her if he'd given anyone permission to use the apartment. He didn't have a girlfriend at the moment, or many close friends for that matter—certainly no one he would have awarded a key to the apartment, or to whom he would have revealed the location of his hidden key.

Somebody was trespassing; somebody who clearly knew Jackson was out of town, and thought his or her presence would go unnoticed.

Think again, asshole.

She stepped carefully into the bedroom, holding the gun between her hands, the muzzle aimed before her as she cut her eyes about, surveying. The bedclothes were turned back on Jackson's queen-sized mattress; someone had been sleeping there. A peculiar little notebook rested on the bedside table; no bigger than an index card, it was housed in a decoratively engraved brass casing, with a long chain affixed, as if someone wore it about his or her neck. She saw an oversized duffel bag on the floor, with a tangle of clothes, a pair of jeans, a discarded T-shirt, and a beige barn jacket crumpled beside it.

She saw no evidence of anyone having gone through Jackson's drawers or closets, but that didn't mean they hadn't, and had simply cleaned up after themselves. Her frown deepened as she crept toward the bathroom, and she paused, her breath drawing abruptly still as the shower suddenly cut off.

She heard the soft dripping of water and the creak of the shower door hinges as it swung open. She heard movement, the rustling of a towel. The door was halfway ajar, and she saw steam curling out in a warm, moist cloud. She sidestepped toward the door and used her shoulder to ease it open further, awarding her an unobstructed view of the bathroom beyond, and its occupant.

Its naked occupant. Its naked *male* occupant.

He stood with his back to her, rubbing a towel against his dark hair. He was white, tall, lean, and built magnificently. Lina stood, momentarily dumbfounded, blinking in stupefied admiration at the well-etched musculature of his back and shoulders, his sculpted buttocks and legs. The sight of him sent a shiver through her, along with the startling realization that it had been three months since Jude had left her; three months since she had been with a man, or even caught a glimpse of one in such a state of undress.

She shook her head, forcing herself out of her reverie.

What the hell is wrong with me? She cleared her throat, narrowing her brows and putting on her most stern, businesslike facade. "Police officer," she said. "Put your hands up and come out of there."

He didn't turn, startled by her voice, as she might have expected. He didn't comply with her command either. He didn't do anything, in fact, except keep toweling his hair dry, as if she hadn't even spoken at all.

"Hey, buddy," Lina said, her frown deepening. *God, does he not speak English? Is he drunk or on meth or something? That's all I need.* She considered ducking out and calling for backup, but decided against it. In addition to being a cop, and armed, she was also a second-degree blackbelt in aikido. Jackson had taught her, being a fourthdegree black-belt himself.

"I'm a cop, buddy," Lina said, more loudly this time, as the guy still didn't as much as flinch. "*Soy policia, hombre.* I've got a pistol in my hands and I'm telling you to put your hands up. Turn around to face me—nice and slow. Do it now."

He bent over, rubbing his calves with the towel. *Why in the hell did he have to go and do that?* Lina thought, because it awarded her an admittedly pleasant view. She shook her head again and reached forward, tapping him with her fingertip.

"I'm talking to you, asshole," she said, poking him in the back. "I said put your hands—"

He whirled, startling her, moving so quickly, she had no time to react. She felt the blade of his left hand strike the side of her pistol, battering it from her grip and knocking it toward the bathroom sink. His right hand darted forward, with the heel of his palm presented in an aikido-style punch, and Lina parried the blow instinctively, swinging her own arm up to block. The force of his punch sent her staggering backward, and she crashed down onto her ass.

Again, she moved out of instinct, punting out her right

leg and smashing the heel of her Reebok squarely into
his knee. He uttered a soundless grunt of air and stumbled sideways, catching himself against the sink vanity.

Lina scrambled to her feet a split second before he
came at her again, swinging at her with a volley of swift,
sudden, powerful punches. Whoever he was, he was
trained in martial arts, and he was goddamn good at it,
too. She had never seen anyone move so fast before in
her life, not even Jackson.

She swung her arms again and again in a blind panic,
ducking and weaving, trying desperately to prevent him
from landing one of those powerful, brutal blows to her
face. She tried frantically to fend him off, sending her
own punches flying whenever she could, striking at his
eyes, his throat, and the vulnerable plate of his breast-
bone. She kicked at him, driving her feet around again
and again in sweeping roundhouse kicks, but he danced
around them, blocking them with his hands, using his
legs and feet to counter her best attempts.

He forced her toward the bed, and she floundered
when the backs of her knees met the mattress. She sat
back, using her momentary loss of balance to her advantage. She swung her legs up, punting him with both feet
squarely in the midriff, pummeling the wind from him.
He doubled over, gasping sharply, and then tripped over
the tangle of clothes piled on the floor. He fell forward
and against her, knocking her back onto the bed. Lina
struggled but he recovered enough from her kick to
grasp her firmly by the wrists, pinning her arms helplessly against the mattress.

She thrashed beneath him, bucking her hips, struggling to draw her knee between them to drive into his
groin. "I'm a police officer!" she screamed. "Get off me,
you son of a bitch! Get off me!"

She locked her legs around his midriff and heaved
mightily, managing to throw him sideways. They rolled
together on the bed, and she wound up on top of him,

straddling his hips. "You're under arrest!" she shouted, her voice hoarse and winded, her baseball hat long-since tumbled from her head, her dark curls splayed in a disarray about her face. She clasped her hands against his wrists and leaned over him, putting her full weight against him, struggling to hold him down. "I said you're under arrest, goddamn it!"

He fell still beneath her, blinking up into her face, and for the first time, she saw him—dark eyes, dark hair, strikingly handsome, no more than in his early twenties at the most. There was a faint but distinctive scar running beneath the shelf of his chin, a thin, pale line cutting nearly from ear to ear. She loosened her grasp around his wrists and her mouth dropped in stunned surprise.

"Brandon?" she gasped.

He nodded once, looking rather sheepish all of a sudden, and moved his hand, his fingers sweeping in erratic patterns in the narrow margin of open air between them. Sign language.

Hi, Angelina, he finger-spelled.

Chapter Two

Angelina Jones.

My God, the last time I saw her, I was a goofy damn kid, Brandon thought. She left him as breathless and dumbstruck now as she ever had then.

She would come to visit Jackson sometimes on the farm in Kentucky. She would stay with her brother at his guest house, and during the day time, she would entertain herself while Jackson tended to Brandon's tutelage. The last time Brandon had seen her, he'd been sixteen years old, and he had harbored a tremendous crush on her.

He remembered playing basketball with her at a portable hoop Jackson had set up in his driveway. Jackson had been sitting on his stoop, nursing a sore knee, while Brandon and Lina had played together. It had been the first day of her visit, his first opportunity to have seen her in more than a year, and he had been simply awestruck by the then-twenty-one-year-old beauty.

Her dark hair had been twisted back in exotic braids that Jackson called *corn rows*. They lay against the contours of her scalp to the nape of her neck, where they dangled together in short plaits fastened with multicolored plastic beads. She wore a white, sleeveless, formfitting halter shirt that plastered itself against her breasts, and left her midriff bare. He remembered that her nipples had stood out clearly through the thin Lycra, and how that realization—and the subsequent memory of it—had seen him spend many long moments alone in the bathroom masturbating for several months to come. The fact that the Brethren were strictly forbidden to ever become sexually involved with humans seemed irrelevant to his imagination.

She'd worn black spandex biking shorts that had hugged the sleek curves of her buttocks and outlined the muscles in her long, strong thighs. Her caramel skin, lighter in hue than her brother's, had grown glossy with sweat, and her dark brown eyes had flashed with mischievous energy as she'd squared off again and again against Brandon.

She was a good basketball player—damn good. And rough, too. She plowed into him time and again, using full-body blocks to hinder his shots or force him out of bounds. On more than one occasion, she'd jostled him, and he'd been able to feel her breasts, the wondrous and momentary press of her nipples through her shirt and the sweat-soaked fabric of his own. Again, this had proven all the inspiration his teen-addled hormones had needed, and by the end of the game, he'd been gasping, exhausted, and utterly, hopelessly in love with her.

Not to mention beaten by her.

"Nice game, kiddo," she'd told him, tousling his hair playfully with her fingertips to draw his gaze so he could read her lips.

Kiddo. It had hurt his feelings, but he could hardly blame her. She'd been a student enrolled in the law enforcement program at Eastern Kentucky University. He'd been sixteen years old; to her, little more than a child.

When Brandon's older brother, Caine, had caught a glimpse of Lina, he had leered at Brandon, his brows narrowed. "I think the Grandfather should pick her for your bloodletting," he'd told Brandon, because the bloodletting ceremony had only been days away. "I think he should make you tear her apart and drain her dry."

Brandon had been horrified. He knew what happened
when one succumbed to the bloodlust. He'd seen too
many other bloodletting ceremonies and still remembered the horrific shrieks resounding through the night
that he'd heard as a little boy, long after he'd been sent
to bed, before he had been robbed of his hearing. He'd
seen the monsters that his father and uncle had become
on the night Brandon had been attacked by burglars,
their jaws so distended, they'd snapped loose of their
hinges, their fangs hooked and gleaming in the moonlight, each nearly as long as a grown man's index finger.
Brandon remembered drowning in his own blood, his
throat cut, his head so battered, his ears had been irreparably damaged, and he had been more frightened of
his father—of the thing Sebastian Noble had become—
than any pain he'd suffered.

And then he had seen what they did to the burglars,
the monsters who had been his father and uncle. He had
seen what was left of them when they were through.

He hadn't meant to flee his own bloodletting. All he'd
known was that he didn't want to be like that, a monster—
this terrifying, blood-crazed, ravenous thing. He had stolen
money from his father—three hundred dollars taken from
Sebastian's wallet—and he'd given it to Jackson.

What's this? Jackson had signed, puzzled.

*So you can take Lina to the casino boat in Indiana on
Friday,* Brandon had signed back, trying to be noncha-
lant, hoping his hands wouldn't shake too badly. *My
father told me to give it to you. The Grandfather is having some
kind of party, and he thought you might like the night off since
she's in town.*

Jackson had looked somewhat skeptical but had
taken the money. More importantly, he'd taken Angelina and they had not been on the estate that Friday
night for the bloodletting. And while his family members had succumbed to the bloodlust and turned into
the sabre-toothed, demonic things that had so terrified
Brandon as a child, he had stolen into Jackson's house

and hidden there until daylight, fighting the desperate, terrible urges within him.

Jackson had kept a key under his doormat then, as now, and Brandon had hidden in the darkness, pressed in a corner of the guest house's dining room. Ordinarily, the Brethren fed in discreet fashion, using their keen telepathic abilities to subdue victims into quiet, unresisting states. But on bloodletting nights, when a young member fed for the first time, the Brethren attacked and killed every farmhand living on the grounds and took no pains or efforts to keep them from terror or pain. The rolling acres turned into fields of slaughter, the night punctuated by shrieks and screams as every man, woman, and child was slain—all except for the Grandfather's farm manager, Diego, and a handful of human men the Brethren referred to as the Kinsfolk.

The Kinsfolk kept the Brethren supplied with victims upon which to feed. They were well paid for their efforts and discretion, and the Brethren farms were kept stocked with a plentiful and endless supply of workers— most illegal immigrants fresh off the transit from Mexico and lured by promises of working some of the most prestigious and renowned thoroughbred racing farms in the world. Few spoke much English, and they were all paid under the table, so they were never missed. Brandon had always felt badly for them.

They are cattle, the Grandfather had said. *Fresh meat for the celebration of slaughter.*

On the night that was supposed to have been his bloodletting, Brandon had huddled in his corner, his fingers tangled in his hair. He could feel the others searching for him, reaching out with their minds, using their telepathy to try and sense him. They would punish him if they found him; worse, they would realize what he had done in sending Jackson and Lina away, and only make him butcher someone else. They would force him into the bloodletting, and so Brandon had tried with every desperate measure he could muster to keep his mind, his thoughts hidden from them.

Can't sense me, he'd whispered in his mind over and over, his eyes closed, his face greased in cold sweat, his gums swollen and hurting so badly from where his teeth wanted to drop, he could scarcely press his lips together. *Can't sense me, you can't sense me, I'm not here, I'm not . . .*

His younger sister Emily had killed in his stead, because the number had been set—there were supposed to be two new initiates that night, his twin sister, Tessa, and Brandon. The number had been set, and there had been no undoing it. It was the way of the Brethren and so Emily had made her first kill.

The Grandfather had been furious with Brandon. The beating he'd received over the letter to Gallaudet might have seemed tame by comparison, except Brandon's father, Sebastian, had seen him spared from it somehow. He'd protected Brandon for as long as he could, until the day the Grandfather had learned about the acceptance from the university, and pummeled Brandon nearly lame. Sebastian had protected Brandon up until that point, and part of the appeasement for Brandon's offense that he'd offered the Grandfather had been the immediate dismissal of Jackson Jones, Brandon's beloved tutor.

Brandon had been devastated. He'd been able to have only a brief good-bye with Jackson, and he'd clung to his friend, weeping inconsolably. He could still remember the press of Jackson's large palm against his hair as he'd tried to draw the boy's gaze. *It's alright,* he had signed to Brandon, smiling gently at him, the way Brandon had smiled at Daniel on the afternoon his Grandfather and Caine had crippled his hands for a time. The sort of smile you offered when you knew it wasn't going to be alright, but you hoped someone else might believe it, anyway—for your sake, as much as their own.

Brandon still didn't know what pretense Sebastian had offered Jackson, but he hadn't fired him exactly. Whatever he'd been told, Jackson left quickly, by the

Monday following the bloodletting. He'd pressed a note against Brandon's palm as their brief embrace had parted, and later, alone in his room, Brandon had opened it to find Jackson's home address and e-mail.

Whatever you need, whenever you need it, Jackson had written. The note had been gold to Brandon, the most precious thing he'd owned. He kept it hidden from his father, the Grandfather, even Tessa—everybody—for the next five years.

He'd never seen Angelina again. Jackson mentioned her sometimes in passing, brief comments in e-mails, but Brandon had never delved any more deeply. Seeing her in Jackson's apartment, realizing it was her strong thighs clamped firmly on either side of his naked hips—those same thighs he had so lusted after in his adolescence— left him breathless all over again. *My God, she's still beautiful,* he thought.

Brandon Noble.

My God, the last time I saw him was five years ago in Kentucky, Lina thought. He'd been a skinny, scrawny kid then, sweet and somewhat shy, her brother's student in a private tutoring gig. Brandon was deaf and mute, both handicaps apparently the result of an attack against him when he had been very young, some sort of burglary gone horribly awry. The scar she'd seen on his neck— the one she'd recognized him by—had been a result of that assault. Jackson had told her that someone had tried to cut Brandon's throat.

Brandon Noble was the grandson of Augustus Noble, and while the name meant exactly jack-shit to Lina, it apparently meant a great deal in the worlds of liquor distilling and thoroughbred horse racing. According to Jackson, the Noble family had amassed a sizable fortune through these endeavors. They owned the Bloodhorse Distillery, one of largest independent producers of bourbon in the world. Additionally, several Triple Crown contenders had been sired from their stables, and nearly every year without fail, a horse from the Noble farms had been favored in odds at the Kentucky Derby. Brandon Noble was rich—not just country-club rich, or even uptown wealthy. He was Paris Hilton rich—like buy-your-own-small-island wealthy, the sort of money a working-class cop like Angelina Jones could only dream of having access to. *Hell, and even then, I wouldn't know what to do with it.*

Brandon's father had hired Jackson ten years ago to come and live on the family's enormous farming estate in Woodford County, the pristine Bluegrass region of Kentucky. Jackson had been Brandon's teacher up until five years ago, when he'd abruptly left Kentucky and returned home to the city. He'd never said why exactly; she had gone to visit him, and he had brought her to a riverboat casino in Indiana on Friday night. By Monday, he had left Kentucky and the Nobles for good. Jackson had asked her if she could run a background check on several members of the Noble family, including Augustus and the boy's father, Sebastian. They had all come up spotless, impeccable, and Jackson had never said anything more.

Is Brandon alright? Jackson asked, his words appearing as type on a small panel on his digital phone. *Have they been looking for him? Have they called the police?*

Though they were only words affixed on the screen, Lina could sense her brother's inexplicable anxiety behind them. She frowned, a keyboard in front of her as she typed back a reply. *He's fine, Jackie. I don't know if anyone's looking for him or not. He hasn't told me. It's not like he's a kid running away from home. He's a grown man now, twenty-one years old. He can leave the house if he wants to.*

Had Brandon Noble *ever* grown up. Gone was the gangly, uncertain boy she remembered meeting on the occasions she'd had to visit Jackson. He had grown up and filled out, becoming a lean, strong, and extraordinarily handsome young man.

He's been practicing his aikido, she added. *He damn near kicked my ass.*

Really? Jackson typed, and Lina had no problem imagining the sudden, delighted edge behind the words. *Put him on the phone. Let me talk to him.*

Brandon sat behind Lina on one of Jackson's couches. He had dressed, donning the T-shirt and jeans that had been on the bedroom floor. His dark hair lay in uncombed, damp waves about his face, and he sat with his shoulders hunched, his expression mournful and ashamed. When Lina motioned to him, he rose to his feet and came reluctantly to the phone, as if anticipating remonstration.

He had kept trying to write her little notes in the brass notebook she'd seen beside the bed. A small pen fit neatly at the hinged end of the pad, and he would slide it out with a deft flick of his thumb, and then scrawl hastily against a page. He'd rip notes out and hand them to her, his handwriting quick, but surprisingly neat. *I'm sorry,* the first one had said. *Jackson doesn't know I'm here. I asked at the school and they told me he was out of town.*

She stood back and watched him at the phone as Jackson typed something to him. After a moment, Brandon's expression softened and he smiled. He opened his mouth and laughed soundlessly; the blade that had cut his throat as a child had severed his vocal cords completely. He reached for the keyboard and his fingers flew in reply.

He told me once where he kept the spare key, Brandon's second note had read. *I didn't think he would mind. He's told me before I could come anytime. He said—*

At that point, Lina had caught his hand and stayed him in mid-scribble. *I can read sign, Brandon,* she said, holding her fingers pressed together and upright, her thumb tucked in against her palm, forming the letter *B* in sign language. She brushed her hand in this position against her cheek; this was Jackson's pet sign for Brandon, an abbreviation of his name. At this gesture, Brandon had blinked at her, and she had been moved with pity at the comprehension and relief in his face. Jackson had told her once that Brandon's family had forced him to use the notebook to communicate with them, that while one of his sisters and his father had taken the time to learn some basic sign language, no one else had—by strict instruction of Augustus Noble.

I can read sign, she had motioned again, and he'd nodded, abandoning the notebook from that moment onward.

I think they're part of some kind of cult, Jackson had told her of Brandon's family, when he had originally asked her to conduct background checks on them. *There are several families out there and they all own neighboring horse farms—the Nobles, the Davenants, the Trevilians, and the Giscards. They're all in the family business together and no one ever seems to leave. It's like the goddamn Twilight Zone.*

Lina didn't know about that. She imagined having a family business that raked in the millions of dollars the Nobles and their neighbors boasted would be plenty of incentive for their kith and kin to stay close at hand. She had been willing to entertain the notion of cult activities, however, even though Jackson had given her nothing more specific to go on than his own suspicions. She'd heard of certain Mormon sects—unsanctioned or recognized by the official church—that still practiced polygamy and lived in very tight-knit communities of the sort Jackson had described. It wasn't unfathomable that Brandon Noble's family had been involved in such a thing.

She watched Brandon turn to her. *He'd like to speak with you again,* Brandon signed, his long, elegant fingers dancing in the air. Jackson had told her once that his father, Sebastian Noble, had been a friendly enough man, but that the grandfather, Augustus, must have surely been "one mean son of a bitch," as Jackson had put it. Jackson hadn't known firsthand. He'd never met Augustus Noble, not even once during his tenure at the farm.

I want you to look out for him, Scarecrow, Jackson typed to her in instruction. *Don't tell anyone he's there, OK? And if anyone asks, if anyone comes looking for him, don't say anything. OK?*

Lina frowned. She glanced over her shoulder at Brandon, who had gone to stand by the terrace doors, admiring the view. *What aren't you telling me, Jackie?* she typed. *What's going on here that you don't want me to know about?*

There had been more to Jackson's leaving Kentucky than any suspicions of a cult. She knew her brother well enough to realize that. He had kept in touch with Brandon; regular, constant contact, as if despite his absence, he had felt some sort of responsibility for the younger man, some concern for his well-being.

Is he in some kind of trouble? she asked.

No, Jackson typed. That was it. No further explanation. The two letters, red LED characters, glared up at her from the screen. After a long, nearly accusatory moment, they disappeared, and he wrote anew. *Promise me you'll look out for him. Just until I get back.*

Lina's frown deepened. *The hell with this,* she thought. *Melanie's wedding is this weekend, Jackson,* she typed, her fingers striking sharply against the keypad. *I'm supposed to be a bridesmaid, remember?*

Take him with you, then, Jackson replied.

Oh, there's something Jude would love, she thought, and she typed: *I can't be babysitting some kid who is more than old enough and able to take care of himself.*

Please, Lina.

Lina blinked down at the screen, at her brother's simple, poignant plea. And he'd called her by name, too, not *Scarecrow,* which meant he was serious. *Damn it,* she thought.

He needs you, Jackson wrote. *I need you.*

Please.

She sighed heavily, tucking her hair behind her ears. "Alright," she whispered, and she typed it into the keypad. *OK.*

She brought Brandon to Joe's Wok, four blocks from Jackson's condo. She'd had her mouth set on Joe's tonsil-searing kung pao chicken since waking that morning, and she'd be damned if she missed out on it.

So, she signed to Brandon as they sat across from one another in a booth. *You going to tell me what's going on?*

He blinked at her. He'd been stirring a single packet of sugar into his green tea, but the spoon paused now, and he regarded her, all large and uncertain eyes. Lina looked back at him, momentarily pinned by his gaze. Over and over, this would happen, and she had no accounting for it; he would do no more than look at her, and it was as if he reached out and caught her squarely by the chin, holding her firmly. Every time it would happen, she'd feel a strange, but not entirely unpleasant warmth spreading through her, sort of the way a shot of good whiskey will seep through your bones once it hits your belly. As long as he looked at her, holding her gaze, she found herself unable to think, speak, damn near breathe.

And then he'd look away, as he did right now, and it would be like someone had physically cut a taut line between them. Lina would nearly jerk at the release, and whatever odd paralysis had seized her so briefly would be gone.

Jesus, I'm acting like a teenager all squealy over Orlando Bloom, she thought, shaking her head. *What the hell's the matter with me? He's a kid—five years younger than me!*

Jackson wouldn't tell me, she continued, using the pet sign for her brother's name. It was nice sometimes, sign language—one of the few times in life when you could speak with your mouth full and not seem impolite, as she was at the moment. *I don't imagine you will, either, but I'm giving you the chance anyway.*

Brandon set his spoon aside and looked down into the steaming pool of tea in his small, porcelain cup. *I don't want to go back to Kentucky,* he signed. *I don't want to be like my family.*

He seemed to be phrasing this carefully, the motions of his hands as he signed growing somewhat terse and rigid. She didn't know what he meant exactly; there was the major drawback to signing—it was hard to gauge subtle inferences from gestures, as one could from spoken voices.

You don't have to go back to them, she told him. *Not if you don't want to. You're an adult now, Brandon. They can't stop you. I don't know what they've told you, but if you're afraid they'll cut you off, stop giving you money, they—*

It was the only thing she could think of, the only reason he'd feel his family had any sort of power of him—the threat of stripping him from the will, of taking away some manner of allowance or inheritance. Brandon's eyes widened as she signed this, and his hands darted up, moving in sudden, brisk interruption.

I don't give a shit about their money, he signed angrily. *Is that what you think? That's not what this is about.*

"Then what is it about, Brandon?" she asked, leaning forward. Something was going on, something Jackson knew about but wouldn't tell her.

He shook his head. *You wouldn't understand,* he signed.

Lina frowned, settling back in her seat again, folding her arms across her chest. "But I suppose Jackson does?"

To her surprise, Brandon shook his head again, lowering his gaze toward the table. *No,* he signed. *He doesn't understand, either. He thinks he does, but he has no idea.*

She reached for him, draping her hand against his, drawing his gaze. "Has no idea about what?" she asked, and again, when he looked at her, she felt as if an invisible hand had grasped her, holding her still, leaving her breathless.

About my family, he said. *About what will happen when they find me.*

Chapter Three

Brandon hadn't taken his medicine that morning. His head hurt, but that was the least of his worries at the moment. His head had been hurting him nearly nonstop since he'd left Kentucky, a dull, persistent, throbbing ache nestled behind his eyes, shuddering through his temples. He figured it had something to do with stress; Christ knew he had plenty to feel tense about. Especially that afternoon, he realized to his sudden and absolute dismay.

His hands had healed. Although the bones had knitted whole once more in less than three months, it had taken nearly a year before Brandon had regained full mobility and dexterity in them, and even now, they still pained him on occasion. The healing was an endowment that came with being of the Brethren, just like his telepathy and the bloodlust. But unlike his telepathy or healing abilities, the bloodlust was something Brandon had found he could control.

Every day, twice each day, he took 150 milligrams of Wellbutrin, popping the small, lavender pills to help suppress his urges, to keep the horrible, brutal desire within him under some semblance of control. He still couldn't be around humans in close proximity for too long without being aware of them—smelling their individual, musky scents, imperceptible to them, or sensing the ebbing and flowing inner tides that comprised their bloodstreams. But at least with the drugs, that was all there was; a momentary discomfort, an acute awareness that bordered on heightened. He felt no urge to act upon these sensations. He still felt somewhat inhuman himself.

But he'd forgotten to take his morning dose. Lina had caught him getting out of the shower, and in the aftermath, he'd simply forgotten. It had not occurred to him until well past midday, as he and Lina sat together over lunch in a Chinese restaurant. As he had sipped his green tea, the warmth had caused a dull, throbbing ache to stir within his gums, and he had realized. He had remembered.

Oh, shit.

You can't deny what you are, his older brother, Caine, had once told him. *You can't run away from it. There's no escape. The bloodletting ceremony only marks your transition from childhood to man. The bloodlust will come upon you regardless. There's no denying its inevitability.*

That isn't true, Brandon thought as he looked down at his untouched plate of food. *It can't be true. It can't be.*

And yet, without the Wellbutrin within him to dampen his urges, dull his desires, every time Lina would look at him, he could feel the bloodlust rising within him; a gnawing, insistent pang in his gut, a scraping, scratching, insistent sensation behind his eyes, in the recesses of his sinuses, a tingling ache in his mouth where his canines stirred, swelling within the confines of his tender gums, wanting to descend.

Jackson had helped him arrange for the prescription without any of the other Brethren knowing—especially the Grandfather. Jackson had believed Brandon would benefit from the drug's antidepressant capacities. Brandon had wanted the tablets because he'd hoped that they would lessen his desperate urges to feed, much as they were reported to diminish sexual urges. It had worked;

for more than a year now, Brandon had felt in control of himself, his body, and mind. Until that afternoon, that moment in the Chinese restaurant.

He sipped his water, slipping a chip of ice into his mouth and massaging it against his upper palate to try and relieve the throbbing pain in his gums. Cold helped better than warmth. The hot tea had only aggravated the oversensitive tissue. *I need to get out of here. I need to take my medicine.*

Caine would have taken the symptoms in his mouth and mind as evidence that he was right, that there was no refuting Brandon's place among the Brethren, whether he wished it or not. Brandon didn't want to believe him. He was desperate for any other recourse but this, to be like Caine, his father, the Grandfather. Even Tessa, his sister—his twin, the one who had once known him more deeply, truly, fondly than anyone else in the world—had succumbed to the bloodlust.

There had once been a time when Tessa had been his staunchest ally, when his twin sister had defended him fiercely against any abuse or mockery, even against Caine or the Grandfather. But that had been before her bloodletting. She had made her first kill, and on that same night, had been married off to Martin Davenant. She had left the great house and gone to live on the Davenants' estate, as had been expected of her, and from that moment on, she'd been a relative stranger to Brandon, someone who wore the face and form of the sister he still loved deeply, but whose heart and mind had become alien to him.

Brandon thought of her in the restaurant, as he stirred absently at his lo mein with the narrow tips of chopsticks. She had text-messaged him for days after he had left, and his absence had been discovered. His father had given him a cell phone last year for Christmas, so that he could use the text-messaging feature to keep in touch with Tessa, and it had become inundated with messages she had left for him.

Brandon, where are you? Please call home.

Brandon, talk to me, please. I love you.

The most heartbreaking had been: *Brandon, please, you're scaring Daniel. He thinks the Grandfather has put you in the Beneath.*

And the last message from Tessa two days earlier had been an ominous warning: *They're coming to find you, Brandon. Please call me.*

He had thrown the phone away after this one, tossing it into a dumpster before he had reached St. Bartholomew's School and learned that Jackson was gone. He had found himself wishing ever since that he had kept the cell phone. He missed his sister; he was lonely and uncertain and more than a little frightened, and had no idea what in the hell he was going to do.

He glanced at Lina. *I need to get out of here,* he thought. *The longer I'm with her, the more she's in danger.*

He could smell her, the warm, musky fragrance of her blood, and he could sense it within his mind, the pulsating course of it as it rushed through her form. He could sense these things and they caused the bloodlust to rouse within him. His heart rate suddenly quickened, his breath growing faster, sharper; his groin trembled with sudden, reflexive excitement, and his mouth ached with arousal of its own.

I have to get out of here.

It was a myth that humans could become like the Brethren and endowed with their longevity if bitten. It was also a myth that the Brethren could not walk about in daylight, that they slept in coffins, were ghastly pale, cast no reflections in mirrors, and could be warded away with garlic or crucifixes. Humans who were bitten by the Brethren were *food.* Brandon had always slept in a bed, the same as anyone else in his family. Garlic was no more than a seasoning to him, the same as anyone else. And he didn't know what Caine would do if he couldn't see himself in the mirror; impeccably vain, Brandon's oldest brother was known to spend more than an hour in the bathroom each morning, brushing his waist-length sheaf of heavy black hair, or otherwise grooming and preening himself into what he considered presentable form.

But the Brethren could will a human into compliance, as vampires were often portrayed in the movies. Just as they could sense each other's thoughts and presences, they could do so with humans when they wished. It was how they fed, as a general rule. The ceremony of the bloodletting—when the bloodlust was yielded to fully, wildly, recklessly, and the feeding became frenzied, horrific— was an occasional indulgence. Like any good predators, the Brethren had existed for as long as they had, living undetected among their prey, because they understood discretion was the better part of valor—and survival.

Brandon had not undergone the bloodletting yet, and the antidepressants usually kept the urge to feed—and even his modicum of mental ability that came with that urge—at bay. But he had forgotten his medicine that day, and he was vulnerable. Worse than that, Lina was vulnerable. He could feel this every time she met his gaze. He could feel the bloodlust stirring in his body, his mind reaching out to hers.

He tore his eyes away from Lina's and took a long drink of water. He sucked several pieces of ice into his mouth, and winced as the shocking coldness pressed against his swollen, throbbing gums.

I have to get out of here now.

He stood, sliding out of the booth. Lina blinked at him in bewildered surprise, a forkful of kung pao chicken poised midway to her mouth. She said his name, and he watched her lips flutter and fold themselves around the consonants and vowels, auditory nuances he could not remember and would never hear again. *Brandon . . .*

I have to go, he signed at her. He reached into his pocket, fishing out his wallet. He thumbed through the bills folded together inside—three hundred and sixty-three dollars, every dime he could scrape together before he'd left Kentucky—and tossed a ten spot down onto the table. *I'm sorry,* he signed, because she looked flabbergasted and confused, and he needed to say something, some kind of explanation. *I'm sorry, Lina, but I just . . .*

His hands faltered. What could he tell her? *I'm a vampire, Lina—you know, like in those piece-of-shit horror movies—only I take drugs so I won't want to rip your throat out. I've forgotten my pills, and right now, it's not a good idea for you to be around me, because I could damn well kill you.* She would think he was nuts.

He walked toward the door, shoving his hands down inside his coat pockets and hunching his shoulders against the cold that greeted him. He turned to his right, following the crowded sidewalk, heading back toward Jackson's flat. He would collect his things, leave some money to repay Jackson for the food and beer he'd used while there, and go. He didn't know where, but figured he would decide once underway. *It doesn't matter—anywhere,* he thought. *Just as long as I'm moving. Maybe they won't find me then.*

He felt a hand fall firmly against his sleeve, and he whirled, startled. Lina stood behind him, her brows narrowed, her mouth already in motion.

". . . but I promised Jackie I'd look out for you until he gets back in town," she snapped. "I don't know what's going on with you as far as your family goes, but if you're in some kind of trouble, you need to tell me. I'm a police officer and I can help you." She gave his arm a little shake for emphasis. "I can help you."

He shook his head. *No, you can't.*

He turned to walk away again, because he was all too aware of the scent of her blood; she was excited and aggravated, and it had heightened the rate at which her heart sent blood pounding through her slender form. The awareness of it left a startling pain searing through his mouth, where his gums were swollen and tender and his canine teeth wanted to descend, dropping to their full, distended lengths. He had to get away from her. He needed his medicine.

She didn't understand, didn't recognize his torment, or her own risk because of it. She caught his arm again and he turned, taking her by surprise as he closed his hands firmly, suddenly against her elbows. He had a fleeting second of rationale, and then his mind felt murky, submerged in sudden, vivid heat. *The bloodlust.*

Her eyes widened and she gasped as he jerked her forward, pulling her against him. He kissed her deeply, fiercely, pressing his mouth against hers and tasting her. He didn't mean to. His body didn't understand the difference between sexual arousal and the excitement of the bloodlust. His mind couldn't yet distinguish one overwhelming need from another and without the drugs to contain them both, he yielded. All Brandon knew was that he was seized with an absolute and urgent hunger brought on by this woman's proximity to him, the intoxicating scent of her body, her blood and he needed release desperately. He kissed her, pressing his tongue against hers, tangling his fingers in her hair. He let his left hand slide down to cup against her breast, touching her through her sweatshirt, and he moved his hips against hers, grinding his sudden, straining arousal against her apex in firm, insistent promise. In that moment, he meant to rip her clothes from her and bury himself inside of her, taking her right there on the street corner in broad daylight.

Lina didn't give him the chance. She caught his hand against her breast, folding her fingers about his, and then bright, excruciating pain seared up toward his shoulder and neck as she craned his wrist at a sudden, unnatural angle. He gasped sharply for breath as she hyperextended his arm, and he crumpled to his knees, helpless and immobilized.

"What the hell was that?" she demanded, hooking her free hand beneath his chin and jerking his face up to look at her. She looked wide-eyed and stricken, as stunned by his impulsive advance as he was. "What's wrong with you? Why the hell did you do that?"

I'm sorry! I'm sorry! he signed, drawing his fist in quick, frantic circles above his heart. He grimaced as she momentarily flexed her grasp against him all the more, and then she stepped back, letting him go. Brandon drew his aching wrist against his belly and stumbled to his feet, trying to catch his breath.

Don't you ever do that again! Lina signed at him furiously. *Who do you think you are? If you do that again, I'll break your goddamn arm! Do you understand?*

Brandon nodded, hanging his head, aghast and horrified. *Jesus Christ, I could have killed her,* he thought. He had completely lost control when he'd kissed her. His reason had abandoned him and there had been nothing but the hunger, that overwhelming, excruciating need for release. That his body had reacted to it sexually—and not by tearing her throat open—was due to his unfamiliarity with the bloodlust, his inexperience as a hunter, and not through any conscientious restraint on his part. *Caine's right—I can't control what I am.*

He pressed the heel of his hand against his brow, shaking. *God help me, I could have killed her.*

"Lina?"

She was still breathless and utterly stupefied by Brandon's kiss, and at first, didn't even realize that someone was calling out to her. *He kissed me,* she thought.

If ever there had been an understatement, she figured that would be it. Brandon Noble hadn't just offered her a fleeting peck on the cheek or lips—the sort of thing exchanged by cordial strangers—or even some sloppy, open-mouthed, disgusting offering made by a drunk guy in a singles' bar. He had kissed her deeply, the way a man kisses a woman in prelude to lovemaking, the way Jude used to kiss her.

Who am I kidding? she thought. *Jude never kissed me like that. No one has.*

"Lina?"

She felt a hand fall against her shoulder, and she turned, swatting it away in start. Her bewildered surprise only mounted when she realized who stood behind her, who had come up to her on the sidewalk. *Oh, Jesus, now I know I'm dreaming. Somebody pinch me quick.*

"Lina, I thought that was you," said Jude Hannam, her former lover, his mouth stretched in a broad but somewhat uncertain smile. There had once been a time when that smile, gracing the bottom half of his handsome, angular face, had made her heart tremble. That was, of course, before Brandon Noble had kissed her.

There had been such passion in Brandon's mouth, the way he had grasped her arms and yanked her near, the way his hand had fallen firmly against her breast, kneading her, leaving her breathless with shock and delight. His tongue had tangled against hers, and there had been such urgency in his kiss, nearly desperation, as if he'd wanted to tear her clothes off and make love to her on the sidewalk at 42nd Street.

And for a moment, I wouldn't have minded that, she thought. That was the most bewildering, frightening notion of all. In that moment of his kiss, with his hand against her breast and his hips against hers—with the considerable swell of his arousal pressing through his jeans and against her groin—she had wanted him with that same desperate insistence she'd felt in his mouth.

What the hell is wrong with me?

"Jude," she said, blinking stupidly. He wasn't alone; perched at his hip, near enough to be a buxom, bleached-blond, albino conjoined twin was Ashlee, the token white woman—arm candy. She looked as perfect as Lina remembered, all pale, creamy hair, enormous breasts and flawless makeup, her wide eyes a shocking shade of blue attainable only courtesy of tinted contact lenses. Lina wondered just how long they'd been standing there, and how much of her exchange with Brandon they'd witnessed.

"Uh, hi," Jude said, his smile growing somewhat awkward and strained. He glanced from her toward Brandon. "Everything okay here?"

The first words out of his mouth hadn't been, *Give me back my Dolce and Gabbana suit,* so Lina suspected he had indeed witnessed the kiss, and the ensuing wrist lock, and was appropriately befuddled. She imagined in Jude's estimation, Lina should spend the rest of her life in chaste solitude, mourning his loss.

"Everything is fine," she replied carefully, glancing at Brandon. "We . . . we were just . . ." She fumbled for something, anything to say, and Brandon met her gaze, his brows raised inquisitively. "This is one of Jackie's students," she said. "A former student, that is—Brandon. Brandon, this is a . . . a friend of mine, Jude Hannam." She finger-spelled Jude's name for Brandon in further clarification.

"Nice to meet you," Jude said, leaning forward and extending his hand to Brandon. He studied the younger man curiously, almost suspiciously. "Brandon, is it?"

Brandon nodded as he accepted the shake.

"He's deaf-mute," Lina said, not missing the not-so-subtle fashion in which Jude abruptly pulled his hand away and wiped his palm against his pantleg, as if the conditions were contagious.

"Oh," Jude said. "Well, yes, then." To Brandon, he added, "I said it's nice to meet you." He said this in a loud voice, with exaggerated mouth movements, as if he hoped that, by shouting, Brandon might be able to hear him. That obligatory courtesy over with, Jude returned his attention to Lina. "You remember Ashlee Ferris, don't you?"

Lina's brows narrowed slightly. "How could I forget?" she said, sparing the blonde a brief but withering glance. She didn't really want to stand there and force a conversation with her ex-boyfriend and his *fuck-du-jour,* and especially since she was still feeling decidedly light-headed and somewhat aroused from Brandon's kiss. Looking at Jude, talking to him, thinking about him were the farthest things from her mind.

"So are you going to be at Melanie and Joel's wedding tomorrow?" Jude kept cutting his eyes back and forth between Lina and Brandon. He spoke with a bright tone in his voice and a friendly enough smile on his face, and Lina wondered why in the hell he was offering such idle chitchat.

"Uh, yeah," she said. "I'm a bridesmaid. I sort of have to be there."

"Yeah," he said with a shrug and a sheepish laugh. "Me, too. I'm invited, I mean. I already RSVP'ed. I didn't know if you'd changed your mind."

"Melanie was my friend before Joel was yours," Lina replied coolly. She knew how childish that sounded, but she didn't care. *If either of us should have been grown-up enough to back out of this, it was you, Jude.*

A glance out of the corner of her eye told her whatever burr had flown up Brandon's ass in the restaurant, clearly upsetting him, was stirring again. He'd begun to fidget, shifting his weight uncomfortably, shoving his hands down into his jacket pockets. He looked at her, his brows raised, imploring, almost like a toddler in need of the restroom. Something was wrong, and if he tried to cut and run again, she'd have the added trouble of trying to dislodge herself from Jude's unwanted company to give chase.

"Look, we've got to go," she said to Jude, not missing the immediate and visible relief that flooded over Brandon's face. "We . . . we've got stuff to do, and . . ."

"He's staying with you?" Jude asked.

"With Jackie," she replied quickly. The details were none of his goddamn business. She hooked her hand against Brandon's elbow and steered him about, walking quickly away from Jude and Ashlee. "See you, I guess."

"Sure, tomorrow," he called back.

Terrific, Lina thought with a scowl.

Chapter Four

Lina was still reeling by the time they'd hiked back to Jackson's condo. Not much could have emotionally buffered her against running face-to-face into Jude once more, but Brandon's kiss had taken care of that nicely.

Brandon walked out of the bedroom. He cut her a glance, but looked away quickly as he ducked into the kitchen. Neither of them had said anything more about the kiss. In fact, on their way back to the apartment, they hadn't said anything at all. He seemed tense and anxious around her, as if the kiss hadn't been intentional at all, and was something he was ashamed of in retrospect.

How can you kiss someone like that accidentally?

She wondered if he was sick, maybe suffering some kind of momentary delirium. In the restaurant, he'd seemed decidedly uncomfortable, and hadn't touched his food. His face had grown flushed, glossed with a light sheen of perspiration, and he'd grown somewhat restless, squirming in his seat as if agitated. His fingertips had kept brushing lightly, almost gingerly, against his upper lip, as if he felt pain there.

An allergic reaction maybe? she wondered. *Something in the food?*

She heard the kitchen sink run as he filled a glass of

water. She watched out of the corner of her eye and saw him draw his hand toward his mouth, tilting his head back as he then drained the cup. He was taking something, some kind of medicine. *For what?* she thought.

She'd heard of people who had impulse-control disorders, the unfortunate results of head injury or trauma. They were helpless to control their urges, no matter how reckless, because that portion of their brain no longer held them in check. Some of the people she'd busted in her career had cried this excuse. Brandon had been injured as a child—that was why he was deaf and mute. His throat had been cut, and he'd been severely beaten in the head.

Could he be like that, then? He can't control himself without medicine?

Whatever the reasons for his kiss, Lina had no excuse for her reaction to it. She'd liked it, plain and simple. It had been too long since Jude had left her, and she'd had a man—any man—treat her like a woman, someone desirable and beautiful, and not just a comrade, one of the guys. She usually liked it that way; preferred it, in fact. But ever since Jude had left, Lina had to admit that she'd missed feeling attractive and feminine to a man. She'd missed feeling like a woman.

She had liked Brandon's kiss because it had stirred that within her again. It had made her realize how deeply, profoundly lonely she really was. It had left her wanting more.

Brandon gave her a wide berth as he walked into the living room, as if he was hesitant to draw too near to her again. Lina wondered if Jackson knew about any sort of impulse-control disorders Brandon might be suffering. *There's no way,* she thought. *He would have told me.*

Her cell phone rang, thrumming against her belly from inside her sweatshirt pocket and she blinked, snapping out of her reverie. She pulled the phone out and flipped it open. "Lina," she said in greeting, and cleared her throat slightly to rid her voice of the damned little warble thoughts of Brandon's kiss had left in it.

"Hey, *chère*." The voice on the other end of the line was deep and rich, with a slow, Southern cadence that lilted gracefully around the French pet name.

Lina smiled, grateful for this unexpected distraction and rescue. "Hey, Rene," she said, turning slightly away from Brandon. "How are you doing?"

Rene Morin was her partner. Or at least, he had been up until a year ago. They'd responded to a seemingly run-of-the-mill domestic dispute call that had proven to be anything but. One of the suspects involved had turned out to be a mule for one of the city's leading drug dealers, and when he'd bolted from the scene, ducking out of a window and onto a rickety fire escape leading down from the twelve-story tenement building, Rene and Lina had given chase.

Rene had beat her out the window and begun his descent first. When the suspect had paused several floors below them and pulled a semiautomatic handgun from the waistband of his pants, it was Rene at whom he took aim. The first shot ricocheted off the metal beams of the fire escape between them. The second had punched through Rene's leg, shattering his knee cap and leaving a ruined, gaping maw of bloody, exposed meat where the joint had once been.

She still dreamed of the sound of Rene crying out, his voice startled at first, and then ripping sharply with pain. He'd crumpled sideways, collapsing a full story down the fire escape. How he hadn't tumbled over the side and pitched helplessly to the pavement below was nothing less than a miracle. Lina had scrambled after him, screaming into her mike that she needed backup immediately; there was an officer down. They were the most terrifying words she'd ever uttered.

"I'm hungry," Rene said. "And I'm bored. Let's get some food, whatever you like, *chère*, my treat."

He was from Louisiana, and even though he'd lived more than ten years in the city, he'd never lost his unusual but pleasant combination of antebellum drawl and delicate French accent. His family was Cajun, and his father had made a modest fortune off investments in the oil industry in the Gulf of Mexico. This was a fact Rene kept hidden from most people; few on the police force had realized just how wealthy Rene was, and even Lina had been his partner for the better part of a year before he'd confided in her. "I was born poor white trash," he'd said. "Now I'm just poor white trash with money."

Rene had been estranged from his father for most of his life, he'd told Lina, but still had been named the solitary heir when he'd died. She didn't quite understand Rene's fierce need for secrecy when the matter came to his wealth, but suspected he hadn't wanted to fend off endless attempts to beg or borrow from him, or people wanting to be his friend simply because of the money. He was a guarded, private person, friendly enough with an irrepressible Southern charm, but not close to many at all. Lina had always felt pleased and proud and somehow absurdly touched that Rene had allowed her past his heavy internal defenses, that together, they'd learned to mutually trust and depend on one another.

Rene lived alone in an enormous, old, partially dilapidated building on the south end of town; he'd fixed up the top floor somewhat into an expansive loft filled with antique furniture, drapes, and screen partitions to mark the boundaries from room to room. No walls. "Walls leave me nervous," he'd explained to her once. "They make for small spaces."

He'd hated the hospital in which he'd spent several months following the shooting because the rooms were too confining. He'd reminded her often of some exotic animal pacing restlessly at the zoo. Only Rene had been unable to pace. The gunshot wound that had ruined his knee had cost him his leg. It had been amputated at mid-thigh.

She had been assigned to work with someone else ever since the shooting, but the guy was not and would never be her partner. That distinction would always belong to Rene Morin. She worried about him, all alone in that shadow-draped, open space he called his home. For a man who hated walls, he loved locks—and had plenty of them and state-of-the-art security—between himself and the outside world in his crumbling old high-rise. She didn't worry for his safety from anyone else but himself. He had lapsed into a deep, relentless depression since the loss of his leg and his police career. He had been fitted with a lightweight, titanium prosthetic that allowed him to lead a relatively unhindered, mobile life, but he hated it.

"Looks like *Robocop*," he had told her once, mournfully gazing down at the slender rods of metal and intricate network of hinges bridging the open space between his thigh and shoe. He'd spared her a wink and a humorless smile. "Maybe I can pick up cell phone signals with it, no?"

She worried that he had grown addicted to the pain killers prescribed to him for his leg, and that he had begun to drink heavily on top of that. Even now, despite the relatively early hour, she thought she detected a slight slur to his voice.

"I can't, Rene," she said, glancing across the room as Brandon walked toward the corridor leading toward the bedroom. "I . . . I'm kind of babysitting."

"Babysitting?"

She stepped carefully toward the hallway and watched Brandon through a mirror over Jackson's chest of drawers. The mirror faced the doorway, and through it, she could see the younger man collecting his things, stuffing discarded clothes into his duffel bag. He began to flip the covers back into place, making the bed.

"Yeah, one of my brother's former students is in town," she said. "Jackie asked me to look out for him."

Brandon looked up toward the mirror and she ducked away before he caught sight of her.

"Bring the *petit* along, then," Rene said. "I'll buy for him, too."

Lina had killed the man who had hurt Rene. She'd hurried to reach Rene, scrambling down the fire escape when she saw him fall, and the suspect had turned his pistol toward her. She had leveled her own gun and opened fire. She hadn't even hesitated. She'd caught a glimpse of Rene, his leg bloodied, his face gone ashen and twisted with pain; she'd heard his voice, his ragged, gasping cries of pain, and she'd blacked out. She didn't remember squeezing the trigger. She had been so seized with outrage and terror . . .

That son of a bitch shot Rene!

. . . that she'd acted out of pure, adrenaline-infused instinct. She'd fired twice, before the suspect could even lob off a shot at her. Both bullets had punched into his chest, knocking him backward and sending him toppling to the alley below.

There had been an inquest into the shooting, but she hadn't minded the administrative leave. She had spent the time keeping constant vigil at Rene's bedside. He didn't have any family left, no one else to comfort him but her.

"Maybe tomorrow, Rene," she said.

"You alright?" Rene asked, not missing the peculiar edge to her voice. He knew her too well; they were like an old married couple, the other guys on the force used to joke. Sometimes, it was as if Rene could read her mind.

"Yeah," she replied. "Yeah, it's just . . . I ran into Jude a little while ago. I think it just frazzled me."

"Jude Law, eh?" Rene asked with a thin laugh. The time constantly spent at his bedside after he'd been shot was part of the reason Jude claimed to have left her. It was then, he'd said, that he began to feel "abandoned" by Lina, resentful of the devotion she showed to her partner, and about that time that he had begun his clandestine affair with Ashlee for whom he'd eventually leave Lina. Ashlee had apparently paid attention to Jude—the sort he'd been lacking from Lina while she spent all her time at the hospital with Rene.

Selfish prick, she though of Jude, not for the first time or, she was sure, the last.

There was no love lost between Jude and Rene either. "Jude Law" was Rene's less-than-affectionate nickname for Lina's ex, a sarcastic play not only on his occupation, but on his penchant for cheating, too. "So how is the old *salaud?*" Rene asked.

He had lapsed in and out of drug-induced unconsciousness for much of the first week after his shooting. Lina had sat at his bedside, holding his hand and stroking his hair, listening as he murmured restlessly, deliriously in French. She'd had no idea what he was saying, but he'd sounded so fragile and frightened. A nurse had overheard him one day, and had offered an attempt at translation.

"I think he's saying he's hungry," she said, frowning slightly. "I haven't taken French since high school, but I think that's what it is, over and over. He's saying he needs to feed."

"Lina?" Rene said, more concerned this time.

She blinked, snapped out of her memories. "Yeah, I . . . I'm fine, Rene. I'm just . . . . .this isn't a good time. I'll call you tomorrow, okay?"

"Alright, *chère*," he said after a long moment in which she was sure he was frowning, suspicious despite her reassurances.

Chapter Five

I still can't believe she didn't kick my ass, Brandon thought, as he and Lina walked together toward the front entrance of the Metropolitan Zoological Gardens. *She should have kicked my ass. She had every right to. I would have let her.*

She had recovered from his kiss and they'd said no more about it, even though Brandon continued to feel like shit.

It was a gorgeous day, the sky flawless, the sun bright, and Lina had suggested they visit some of the city's attractions. The chilliness had yielded to warmer temperatures, and he'd left his jacket behind, comfortable in a T-shirt and jeans. The zoo was their first stop on Lina's proposed sight-seeing expedition. It was world class, she'd explained to him on the taxi ride over. "Ranked one of the top zoos in the country, I think," she'd said.

He had offered to drive, rather than have them take a cab, and she'd blinked at him in surprise. "You have a car?"

He'd nodded. *I didn't sprout wings and fly to get here,* he'd signed in reply. He'd taken her outside, across the street from Jackson's apartment building to a paid parking lot. It was an untended kind, with a slotted metal box. You parked your car and put money into the numbered slot that corresponded with your parking space.

Brandon had been dismayed when he'd brought Lina to space number 4, and found it empty.

I don't understand, he had signed, looking around, bewildered. *I parked it right here.*

"Are you sure?" Lina had asked.

Yes, I'm sure, he'd said. He'd picked the parking place because he knew he'd remember the number—four, just like Daniel's age. *I parked it and I paid for it—five dollars for the week, like the sign says.*

"A week?" Lina had asked. "It's five dollars a day, Brandon."

If he'd had a voice, he'd have groaned aloud.

"How long has it been since you left it here?" she asked.

Three days, he'd replied, tangling his fingers in his hair in dismay. *Christ, I'm an idiot.* He could tell she thought so, too; he didn't need any keen gift of telepathy to discern this. *She thinks I'm a country bumpkin fresh off the turnip truck. Jesus Christ.*

"What kind of car was it?" she'd asked.

It was a Mercedes, I think, he'd signed, and then frowned. *No, wait. It was one of the Audis.*

Lina had blinked at him, her brows rising. "*One* of the Audis?" she'd repeated, and he'd nodded, not understanding her incredulity.

My grandfather only uses them during the spring meet, to take them to the track, he'd signed. *He probably hasn't even noticed it's missing yet.* She'd rolled her eyes and shook her head, walking away at this, leaving him bewildered and somewhat wounded by her reaction.

Brandon had never been to a zoo before. Everything he'd seen thus far in the city had been striking and new to him, because he'd lived his entire life sequestered on the horse farm. He'd only ever seen pictures in books, on television, or online of skyscrapers and exotic wild animals, and as he and Lina passed beneath the towering granite archways heralding the main entrance to the zoo, he stopped in mid-stride, looking up, his eyes wide with wonder.

God, I wish Daniel could see this, he thought, and for a moment, loneliness and sorrow closed in around his heart, tightening.

The Grandfather's Audi had been towed away and impounded. Lina had used her cell phone from the parking lot to call the tow company listed on a nearby sign, but the news had not been good. If he wanted the car back, it would cost him three hundred dollars—nearly all of the money he had. In the meantime, the Audi would remain the guest of Baker & Sons Towing, or "Assholes, Incorporated," as Lina had officially dubbed them.

Lina caught him by the hand, offering his arm a little shake to draw his gaze. "You okay?" she asked, and he nodded. "You with me?"

He nodded again and when she smiled, he was helpless but to smile with her. "Come on," she said, tugging him.

Large groups of schoolchildren visited the zoo that day, and everywhere he turned, it seemed Brandon found painful reminders of Daniel, from the way they scurried from one exhibit to another, their little mouths spread widely in broad, happy grins, or the way they reached for parents and teachers, with both hands outstretched and skyward in universal beckon.

My little brother, Daniel, is like this, he signed to Lina, as a cluster of children darted past and around them in a scampering, giggling throng. He finger-spelled his brother's name first, and then demonstrated his pet sign for him, a signed letter *D* brushed against his cheek, so she'd understand future references. *Everywhere and into everything. Nonstop motion.*

"How old is he?" she asked, and he held up four fingers, making her smile.

He knew she was curious about his family. The fact that he'd been tight-lipped and reluctant to offer much, if anything, by way about them had only made her more curious. She'd seen the life he'd led on the farm. She was perfectly aware of how wealthy his family was. She probably also had suspicions and concerns about them, even if she'd said nothing directly to him. Jackson would have told her, because Jackson had harbored plenty of his own.

And he doesn't even know half of it.

"Do you have any other brothers and sisters?" she asked.

He nodded. *I have a younger sister, Emily, and an older brother, Caine,* he said. *And Tessa, my twin.*

"Twin?" Lina's brows raised in surprise.

Brandon smiled crookedly. *We're not identical or anything,* he said, and after she blinked at him for a moment in start, she laughed.

"I didn't realize you had such a big family," she remarked. "You must miss them a lot."

I miss Tessa, he admitted, because that was at least somewhat true. He didn't miss the stranger she'd become since her bloodletting, but he missed the old Tessa—*his* Tessa—his best friend. *And I miss Daniel. He would love it here.* His hands hesitated as that aching heaviness settled once again within him. *I took care of him. We spent a lot of time together.*

As in the better part of practically every day. More than just a brother, Daniel had been Brandon's friend and constant companion. *Pretty much my shadow,* he thought with a sad smile, remembering how he'd been able to sense if Daniel tried to sneak up on him along a corridor in the great house; how his brother's presence had always felt warm and bright in his mind, like a sunbeam filtering into a darkened room through a part in heavy draperies. How he'd go along with Daniel's efforts and feign obliviousness—right up until the moment he'd draw to an abrupt halt and whirl about, his hands raised, his eyes wide—the deaf-mute equivalent of shouting "Boo!" Daniel would squeal with sudden laughter Brandon couldn't hear, and his mouth would unfurl in a wide, wondrous smile.

He blinked, shaking his head. *God, I don't want to think about you, Daniel,* he thought, pinching the bridge of his nose momentarily, feeling the dim grumblings of a fresh headache stirring in the recesses of his skull. *I'm sorry, but I can't. Not today. It's too soon, and I . . . I miss you too much.*

"What about the others?" Lina asked.

They had reached a large, fenced enclosure that housed a family of timber wolves. The exhibit had been landscaped with tall grass and dense underbrush to provide as natural a habitat as possible for the animals, and Brandon had to look carefully before finding any signs of them as they lay tucked and nestled in the shade beneath a thick growth of trees.

Wolves are highly social animals, the placard in front of the exhibit read. *They spend their entire lives in organized packs of two to twelve individuals. The social structure within these close-knit communities is a strict hierarchy based on the dominance of the strongest, or "alpha," male. Younger members must constantly assert themselves in order to improve their status among the pack hierarchy.*

Sounds like home, he thought.

"You said you had an older brother?" Lina asked.

Caine, he signed, but gave no corresponding pet sign to accompany the mention. He had nothing fond to offer his brother, by way of reference or otherwise. *My brother's name is Caine.* He was willing to let it lie from there, but he could feel her eyes on him, and knew she waited for something more.

Brandon couldn't remember a time when Caine had been anything but cruel or malicious toward him. Even in childhood, Caine had seemed to derive a sadistic sort of glee from tormenting his younger siblings, and Brandon in particular. "You'd better keep from trouble, or the Grandfather will toss you down into the Beneath," he'd say, with a wicked grin and a mean glint in his dark, narrow eyes. "The Abomination lives there and it will eat you, liver, lights, and all."

"He's lying," Tessa would tell Brandon, but despite her brave words, there had always been fear and uncertainty in her eyes. "There's nothing down there but the wine cellar and lots of old, moldy boxes."

Caine had tried to frighten their youngest brother, Daniel, with those same stories years later, but Brandon had intervened.

Stop it, Caine, he'd written on a page from the notebook he wore around his neck.

Caine hadn't even looked at this angry note as Brandon had shoved it toward him. He'd locked gazes with Brandon, his coal-black eyes glittering, and had deliberately crumpled it in his fist, unread.

"They say the Abomination is ancient," he said, cutting a glance toward Daniel. "The first one of us, born at the dawn of all things, and having roamed the earth for all of the millennia since."

Shut up, Caine, Brandon wrote, ripping the paper loose and thrusting it at his brother. He put his arm around Daniel's small shoulders and turned him about, ushering him away, but Caine followed, stepping deliberately into their path to block their way, and again, crushing Brandon's note in his hand, tossing it to the floor.

"It's long-since gone mad down there in the Beneath," he told Daniel, who shied behind Brandon's hips, his eyes round and frightened. "It creeps around in the darkness, scrabbling and scratching at the dirt, living off the blood of rats. It—"

Brandon seized Caine by the throat, shoving him backward, smashing him against the wall. He held him pinned there, gazes locked, but Caine had simply found his effort amusing. "Will I one day tell stories about you creeping about in the Beneath, little brother?" he asked, the corner of his broad, thin mouth hooking wryly. "That's where the Grandfather thinks you belong. Will it be your turn soon to drain the life from vermin to sustain yourself, your mind broken, the rest of eternity spent in darkness and madness?"

Brandon had shoved his hand directly in front of Caine's face, his middle finger upthrust. It was a gesture even Caine, ignorant of sign language, could understand. *Fuck you, Caine.*

Caine had only laughed at him. Daniel had begun to cry when Caine walked away, and Brandon knelt before his youngest brother, cupping Daniel's face between his hands.

"I don't want the Grandfather to put you in the Beneath, Brandon!" Daniel had cried, his face flushed, his voice hiccupping with tears.

Brandon had stroked Daniel's dark hair back from his face and smiled at him. *He won't, Daniel,* he'd thought to his brother, because Daniel's mind was always opened to him. *I promise.*

Daniel had thrown his arms around Brandon's neck, and Brandon had lifted him against him as he stood, easily bearing the little boy's slight and insignificant weight as he wrapped his legs around Brandon's waist. Brandon couldn't hear him, but could tell he was still crying by the gasping breaths he took against Brandon's neck and the way he trembled against him. Brandon had turned and realized to his start that Tessa stood in the parlor doorway behind them. She'd heard every word Caine had uttered, but still she had said nothing. Brandon locked gazes with her, his brows furrowed. *Fuck you, too, Tessa,* he'd thought, and he'd walked away.

Caine and I are not particularly close, he signed to Lina as they stood together in front of the wolf pen at the zoo.

"I gathered that, yes," she said with a nod. "Any particular reason?"

He shook his head. How could he tell her? *Caine hates me because I'm not like him,* he thought. *I'm weaker than he is, different somehow. I'm not like any of the others, none of the Brethren and they hate me for it. I constantly remind them that none of them are nearly as perfect as they like to think they are, that we have vulnerabilities, too, just like humans—and that scares the hell out of them.*

He moved his hands, palms up, fingers spread, sweeping them first upward and then down toward the ground. *I don't want to talk about it.*

He shoved his hands into the pockets of his jeans, effectively ending his side of the conversation, and turned, walking away from the wolves.

* * *

They spent the rest of the afternoon at the zoo, and then strolled together through the neighboring Water Tower Park. This expanse of rolling hillocks, shaded tree groves, and winding footpaths surrounded an enormous water tower with a white limestone facade fashioned to resemble Greco-Roman architecture. The top of the tower was crowned with statuary—nine women looking out across the city, the Muses from Greek mythology, Lina explained.

"My mom used to bring me and Jackie here every summer for day camp," she said, smiling somewhat wistfully as they walked along. "She couldn't ever afford to send us to a real camp, the sleep-away kind, but I never minded. I loved it here. I learned to play basketball at those courts right over there . . ." She pointed. "That's where I got one of my nicknames, Hoops."

Hoops, he finger-spelled, wanting to be sure he hadn't misunderstood her.

She laughed, looking embarrassed. "Yeah," she said. "I can't remember who started that. I think it was Dewaine Cosier. He had the biggest thing for me. And I was always whipping his ass at H-O-R-S-E."

Can't imagine that, he signed, and she laughed. "The river is over that way . . ." she pointed. "And my mom used to work right over there." She pointed again, this time to an enormous building in the distance, across the street from the park. It was just barely visible over the tops of the trees. "Memorial General Hospital. She'd drop us off every morning on her way to work, and pick us up again in the afternoon coming home. She worked there her entire career, can you believe it? The whole time she was a nurse, until she retired. You can still go in that building and find people who know Latisha Jones. Everybody loved her."

Her smile faltered, and in his mind, Brandon could sense a sort of melancholy shadow fall upon her. He touched her arm to draw her gaze, and signed, *They told*

*me at St. Bartholomew's that she's sick. That's why Jackson
went to Florida.*

Lina nodded. "Breast cancer," she said. "She had surgery to remove it, and I got to be there for that. She starts her chemotherapy this week. I . . . I'm glad Jackie can be with her."

I should be, too, she thought, and Brandon heard this in his mind. He sensed Lina's thought distinctly—and all of the sorrow, shame, and remorse that came with it. It was the first time in his life that he had ever unintentionally overheard someone else's thoughts. It was a telepathic ability he hadn't realized he possessed, something so unexpected and seemingly impossible, he wondered if it had really happened at all.

She looked at him and feigned a smile he knew she didn't feel because, to his amazement, he could sense this, too, as plainly as he had her thoughts. "But Mom will be alright. She keeps telling me that. And I keep trying to believe her."

He didn't miss that her eyes had glossed suddenly with tears or that she blinked furiously down at her feet, still forcing a smile as she tried to hide them. Her sorrow punched straight through any incredulity he felt at that momentary awareness of her thoughts, and he felt immediately ashamed of himself for his own selfish wonder.

The Brethren were unaffected by cancer. Their metabolisms and healing capacities were so far accelerated beyond those of humans that nothing short of immediate, cataclysmic trauma—like a bullet to the head, or the stereotypical stake through the heart—could kill them. Any other ailments were dispatched of by their heightened immune systems before any ill effects could be had.

I wish I could share that with her, Brandon thought, likely the only time he'd ever wished the curse of being one of the Brethren upon anyone else. *If I could give that to your mother, Lina, I would.*

Come on, she signed, beckoning with her hand so that she didn't have to look up at him. *Let's get out of here. I'm starved.*

* * *

She promised him pizza for supper, because apparently, the city had a signature style that was known and renowned and was by no means the variety to which he was accustomed. "Oh, my God!" she'd exclaimed, when he'd told her, sure, he'd had pizza before. He might not have realized a person paid daily not weekly for parking in the city, but he'd grown up on a farm, not the moon. *Papa John's will deliver anywhere if you pay them enough,* he'd signed.

"That's not pizza," Lina had said, and then she'd promptly hailed a cab. "That's it. We're going to Danny O's." He'd finger-spelled the name back to her, and she'd nodded. "You'll need a knife and a fork and a pitcher of beer for this, at least," she'd offered with a conspiratorial wink. "And probably two of each."

Along the way, she'd leaned forward, tapping on the plexiglass separating the driver and the backseat of the cab. He watched her mouth move in profile, unable to decipher what she was saying. He glanced down at her ass, admiring the way the wasteband of her sweatpants fell even lower when she was sitting, and how he had a fairly nice glimpse of the top of her tan-colored nylon panties. Obviously, Lina liked thongs, a realization that left him fidgeting in his seat, and sudden, dim warmth stirring in both his groin and mouth.

Oh, shit. He glanced at his watch. He was due to take his Wellbutrin again. He'd brought it with him this time, not wanting to risk another incident like the kiss earlier. He shifted his weight, reached into his pocket and pulled out a small packet of foil. He'd hoped he could take the pills without Lina's notice, but she turned at the sound as he ripped back the foil, and watched him dry-pop the tablets.

"What's that?" she asked.

Oh, shit.

It's . . . medicine, he said, taking the middle finger of his right hand and rubbing it in small circles against his left palm, a sign reminiscent of an old-fashioned medicinal mortar and pestle. *For my hands. They still hurt me sometimes.*

Her brow rose. "Still? What happened?"

Nothing, he signed, cupping both hands into O-shapes and then pushing them lightly outward, opening his fingers. He noticed the cab driver watching him curiously through the rearview mirror. He'd been doing that all along, ever since they'd climbed into the cab and Brandon had started signing. Brandon shook his head at Lina, uncomfortable with the audience and wanting to abandon the entire topic. *It's nothing.*

They made a stop along the way to the pizzeria. Brandon felt a peculiar shiver stir the hairs along the nape of his neck as the cab pulled to a halt in front of a large building. He peered through the window, up at the building's looming, stern, black-stone facade and the feeling only mounted, a strange and not entirely unfamiliar sensation, as if someone whispered lightly inside his mind. It was faint, indistinct, but unmistakable still the same.

Someone is here, he thought, his eyes widening, his throat suddenly constricting. *Oh, Jesus. One of the Brethren is nearby—close enough for me to sense them.*

He turned to Lina in alarm, and gasped sharply as she got out of the car. *What is she doing?* he thought, his heart suddenly hammering. *Lina, come back! We have to go! Jesus Christ—they're here!*

He tried to open the door, hooking his hand desperately against the release and shoving his shoulder against the window. He blinked in bewildered fright as nothing happened, and looked frantically toward the driver.

"Forget it, kid," the driver told him, his lips flapping in the rearview mirror. "I'm not letting both of you out so you can stiff me on a fare."

But you don't understand! Brandon wanted to cry to him. He whirled again, pressing his hands against the glass. *Lina! Lina, please, you don't understand! They followed me here! They found me—we have to go!*

He watched in mute, helpless horror as she thumbed the panel of an exterior intercom box, trying to reach someone inside the building. Apparently, she wasn't having much luck, because she turned after a moment and walked back to the car.

"Oh, well," she said, sitting down and closing the door. "He's not home. My partner. Well, he's my former partner, anyway, but he . . ." Her bright smile faltered, her brows lifting in concern. "What is it?" she asked, noticing his ashen pallor, his distressed expression. "Brandon, what's wrong?"

The cab was moving again, pulling away from the black building. As it did, the sensation within Brandon's mind, faint to begin with, began to dwindle all the more. He pressed the heel of his hand against his brow and frowned, turning to look behind him toward the building. *I . . . I must have been imagining things,* he thought. *That has to be it. I'm jumping at shadows. If it had been the Brethren, they would have sensed me, too. They would have come for me, taken me.*

"Brandon?" Lina said, touching his hand, making him jump, wide eyed and startled. "What is it? What's wrong?"

Brandon glanced toward the rearview mirror, and found the cab driver watching him again, his thick eyebrows drawn, his eyes narrowed. *Goddamn freaky kid.* Brandon heard his thoughts plainly. If he hadn't been so unnerved by what had just happened, the peculiar sensations that were now fading in his mind, Brandon might have been more astounded by this. *Probably strung out on drugs,* the man thought. *Hyped up on meth or some shit.*

If only you knew half of it, mister, Brandon thought and then he signed to Lina, touching his thumb to his chest and wiggling his fingers quickly, briefly. *Nothing's wrong. I'm fine.*

Chapter Six

Danny O's was a small, smoke-filled pizzeria and pub, close enough to Metropolitan University to be packed to overflowing capacity that night with students eager to party. Lina held Brandon's hand as they ducked together through the throng.

The main bar area was absolutely crammed. She could hear the muffled refrains of live music coming from the far end of the room. She shouldered and jostled her way toward the adjacent room, where she hoped they might find a free table or booth from which to order pizza. In nothing short of blind good fortune, they stumbled past a booth just as a group of four guys, all already drunk and stumbling, abandoned it.

"Hey, girl," one of them said as he eased past her, eyeing her up and down, brushing entirely too closely for her liking. His hand slipped against her, sliding along her arm, reaching nonchalantly for her breast. Just as she moved to jerk back to swat his hand away, she caught a blur of movement out of the corner of her eye, and then the young man cried out sharply, dropping to his knees.

"Goddamn it!" he gasped, his voice shrill and breathless as Brandon held him pinned in a wrist hold.

I didn't even see him coming, she thought in amazement. *How in the hell did he move so fast?*

"Hey, get your fucking hand off him, asshole," one of the other guys said, stepping toward Brandon, his fists bared. These were big, strapping guys, the kind who looked like they spent more time at the gym than attending classes, and Lina was immediately alarmed.

Oh, we do not need this. We do not need a goddamn bar brawl . . . !

"What are you, deaf?" the guy said, reaching out and slapping one large, heavy hand against Brandon's shoulder. "I said get your fucking—"

Brandon's free hand shot out, clamping against the man's broad throat, crushing hard enough to snuff the words from his mouth. The guy's eyes bulged from their sockets and he uttered a breathless squawk as his face grew abruptly, alarmingly flushed.

"Brandon," Lina said, reaching for him. *Jesus Christ, these guys outweigh him by a good thirty pounds each! How is he doing this?* "Brandon, let them go."

None of the other young men came to their friends' aid. They drew back, their eyes suddenly wide and hesitant. Lina touched Brandon's shoulder, and he whipped his head around to look at her. The severity in his gaze, the frightening, hardened look startled her, and she drew back uncertainly. *God, what's wrong with his eyes?* It looked as though his irises had grown, expanded somehow, nearly drowning his eyes completely in darkness. *Brandon,* she signed, her hands trembling. *Please let them go.*

He blinked at her, and his expression softened. All at once, his eyes looked normal again, and he glanced toward the two young men, opening his hands, releasing them. He stepped back, eyeing them warily, folding his hands into light, ready fists.

"Jesus, man, what's your problem?" the guy with the injured wrist whined as his friends helped him stagger to his feet. "You're fucking nuts, you know that?"

The other couldn't speak yet; he clutched at his throat and uttered hoarse, gagging sounds as he struggled to reclaim his breath. Both of them leaned heavily against

their companions as they shoved a path through the
crowd toward the exit.

Lina and Brandon stood beside the empty booth. The
momentary commotion had attracted a small circumference of nearby curious onlookers, but now that the tension
had dissolved, so too had their audience. *What the hell was
that?* she signed. She kept looking at his eyes. *I must have
been imagining things,* she thought. *The way his irises had
seemed to grow.*

He shrugged somewhat sheepishly, and forked his
fingers through his hair. *Aikido,* he finger-spelled, and
Lina frowned.

Bullshit, she thought. Brandon might have used aikido
maneuvers, at least in the wrist lock, but that didn't explain
what had just happened. *It doesn't even begin to,* she thought.

He was trying to feel you up, Brandon signed pointedly,
and her frown deepened.

I can take care of myself, she signed back, her movements sharp and stern. *Don't do that again, do you understand? You can't just walk around wrist locking people. This is
the city, Brandon, not the Bluegrass backwaters. You're going to
get yourself in some serious shit.*

He blinked at her, abashed. *I'm sorry,* he signed.

Two hours and twice that many beers apiece later, the
incident with the college guys was pretty much forgotten. A large pizza with all the works—fondly dubbed an
"Around the World" special at Danny O's—sat virtually
untouched between them.

"When I was growing up, I didn't feel a part of anything really," Lina told Brandon. They were leaning in
toward each other, each with one hand draped against
the table, their knuckles nearly brushing. She was pleased
to see that the alcohol had helped Brandon loosen up a
bit, his restrained, reserved facade softening. His smiles
came more readily and less guarded, his posture relaxed.
Every once in a while, he would take the tip of his fore-

finger and run it lightly, almost shyly against the back of her hand, making her smile.

Why? he asked, touching his fingertips to his forehead and then drawing them down, forming the signalphabet letter *Y* in inquiry.

"My mom was hell bent that Jackie and I weren't going to grow up gangbangers in a ghetto somewhere," Lina said. "She busted her ass pulling double shifts at the hospital, then working holidays and weekends at a clinic over in Smoketown. All so we could live in the suburbs. And it worked. Neither one of us wound up in gangs or doing drugs. Everyone thought we were too white." She laughed, because sometimes even hurtful things could be amusing in retrospect. "The only problem was, the white kids didn't want much to do with us either. Even though we went to their schools and lived in their neighborhood, we were still black. We were still different."

She had uncurled her fingers and watched as he did the same. Their fingertips brushed lightly together before hooking briefly, gently.

"My mom's uncle had red hair and blue eyes," she said, and when he blinked in surprise, she nodded. "He wasn't white. It was just something latent in the genes, Mom said. I remember her telling me when she was a little girl, people would come to the house and want to know who the white man was in their living room. And when the circus would come through town, Mom said she couldn't go, because blacks weren't allowed—but her uncle would take my mom's two older cousins with him and go, because they all looked white. Nobody could tell the difference, at least, not in the dark under a circus tent." She smiled sadly. "Sometimes when I was a little girl, I wished I could pass for white, too. Then at least, I'd feel like I belong somewhere."

He slipped his hand away from hers to sign. *How about now?*

"Now I don't give a shit," she said, laughing, taking a sip of beer. "Now I don't think of myself as black or white. I'm blue. You know, the police uniform."

He smiled and she laughed again. *So how'd that happen?* he asked.

She shrugged. "How'd I wind up a cop? It was that or be a nurse, like my mom. And since I couldn't pass chemistry, which I would have needed for nursing school, I majored in law enforcement." She drained the last of her mug dry and glanced about for the waitress, signaling for another. "Plus my grandpa was a cop. He retired after thirty-some-odd years on the force. My mom's the youngest of five kids, all of them girls but one, and my uncle, Francis, was killed in Vietnam. So because there were no sons to carry on the family tradition, and Jackie couldn't do it because of his ears, it kind of fell to me." She smiled. "I don't mind. It's a good job. I like what I do. I'm good at it."

Have you ever killed anyone? he asked, and her smile faltered, her mind cutting back to that terrible night on the fire escape, to Rene's face twisted with pain, and the buck of the pistol against her palm as she opened fire.

"Yeah," she said. "Yeah, I did. Once."

I couldn't do that, Brandon said. *I couldn't kill someone.*

"Sure you could," she said, her eyes distant, Rene's anguished cries still echoing in her head. "Sometimes people have it coming." She blinked, shaking her head once, forcing the dark memories from her mind. "Anyway, that's just part of the job. It's not the whole job. And now my grandpa and I can sit around and tell each other war stories when I go to see him. He lives in a nursing home near my mom in Florida."

The beer had addled Brandon more so than her, and while he was in such pleasant spirits, she decided to take a chance. "How about you?" she asked, and he blinked at her, inquisitive. "Is your grandpa still alive?"

Christ, yes, Brandon signed. *Nothing short of a bullet in the head would kill him.*

This struck him as particularly amusing, and he laughed, his shoulders shuddering.

"You don't get along . . . ?" Lina asked, prodding gently.

He laughed again and shook his head. *No,* he signed. *No, we don't. I'm a bit of a disappointment to the Grandfather.*

"I'm sure that's not true, Brandon," she said, leaning forward and touching his arm. But when he looked at her, any trace of humor faded from his face, and his eyes grew sad and somewhat wounded. She realized that it was true, at least in Brandon's eyes. *One mean son of a bitch* is the term Jackie had used to describe Augustus Noble, and all at once, Lina didn't doubt it for a minute.

The waitress returned with two mugs of beer. *I got this,* Brandon signed to Lina, raising his hips so he could fish his wallet out of his pocket. She watched him give the waitress a ten spot and wave away her offer to make change. As the girl left, Lina watched Brandon's eyes roam out across the crowded bar. His expression grew troubled, nearly wistful.

I wish I could be like them, he signed, his hands moving absently.

Puzzled, Lina looked around. "What do you mean?"

Going to college, he said. *Going out, making friends, having fun.*

"Brandon, you can do that," she said, reaching for him again, drawing his gaze. "Who told you you couldn't?" She didn't need him to tell her, though. She already knew. *One mean son of a bitch.*

I was accepted into Gallaudet, he said, and she blinked in surprise.

"Really? That . . . that's wonderful, Brandon," she said, pleased for him, but puzzled by the turn in conversation. "Does Jackie know? That's where he went . . ." When Brandon nodded in interjection to let her know that he knew this, yes, she leaned across the table toward him. "Is that why you left your home? Jackie . . . he's told me things about your grandfather. He told me he wouldn't let anyone learn sign language to speak with you. He wouldn't let you go to any kind of school for deaf kids." *Would he not let you go to college either?* she thought.

Gallaudet was an extremely prestigious university; any family would be proud to have a student accepted there. *But the Nobles aren't just any family, are they?*

Brandon tilted his head back, draining half his beer in two, long, deep swallows. He set the glass down and belched softly against the back of his hand, then wiped his fingertips against his left palm a time or two, signing apology. *My grandfather broke my hands when he found out I'd applied to Gallaudet,* he said, and Lina felt her chest tighten, her throat constrict, the wind in her lungs abruptly faltering.

What? she thought, stricken.

Well, not all on his own, Brandon signed. *He broke the right side. My brother, Caine, took care of the left.*

He's joking, Lina thought. *He's got to be. He couldn't have meant . . .*

She looked him in the eye and he met her gaze evenly. *Oh, my God.* She thought of him downing the mysterious little pills in the cab. *It's medicine,* he'd told her. *For my hands. They still hurt me sometimes.*

He's not joking.

Brandon hadn't said his fingers had been broken; he'd said his hands. That wasn't the sort of injury one simply splinted and waited to heal. *We're talking surgery, screws and pins, physical therapy, months and months of it, if not years,* she thought. *And all that time, he couldn't talk to anybody. Jesus Christ, he couldn't sign or write . . . !*

She blinked at him in stunned horror. *What kind of monster would do that to you, Brandon?*

My family isn't like yours, he signed to her at length. He wouldn't meet her gaze; he fixed his large, dark eyes on a point somewhere on the tabletop and kept them there. *You didn't feel like you fit in anywhere as a kid, but I still feel like that. My family is different. They're not like yours. They live their whole lives in cages, like that wolf pack at the zoo, and they do things a certain way because that's how it's always been done. And nobody ever says anything otherwise, because if you do . . .*

His hands fell still and he folded them together. He

didn't finish but he didn't have to. *Because if you do, they break your hands,* Lina thought, aghast. *Jesus Christ, who are these people—the backwoods mafia? If they do something like that just for wanting to go to college, what will they do to someone who runs away?*

She looked at Brandon, heartsick and frightened for him. *What are they going to do if they find you, Brandon?*

Brandon remembered the morning after the Grandfather had beaten him, broken his hands. His mother had come to him the night before, when he'd been so wracked with pain, he'd been nearly delirious. She had spoken to him in his mind; she was a powerful telepath, and her words had caressed him, calming him, soothing him. *Brandon . . . take these. Take these, darling. They will help you with the pain . . .*

She'd pressed something between his lips, some kind of pills. The medicine had indeed dulled the pain, but they'd knocked Brandon out, too. When he'd come to again, the pain had returned in full, excruciating measure, and his mind had been cloudy and dazed.

He remembered watching Caine enter his room, his long, dark hair caught back in a ponytail against the nape of his neck, his dark eyes cold as he stared impassively at his brother. Their younger sister, Emily, was with him.

Poor Brandon, she purred inside of his head, her face twisted with feigned sympathy. *How are you feeling?*

Brandon lay supine in bed. His hands were swaddled in heavy bandages to try and immobilize the shattered bones. From his elbows to his fingertips, his arms were propped up on pillows. The slightest hint of movement sent unimaginable pain lancing through his entire shoulder girdle and down his arms; it would seize his chest and tighten through his groin, and he would suck in hissing breaths through his teeth. He said nothing to his brother or sister. He wasn't allowed to use his telepathy, and they knew it; they were deliberately baiting him, trying to get him in trouble.

We've brought you something, Caine said, his hand darting out as he threw something at the bed, a rumpled pile of fabric. It slapped against Brandon's lap, cream-colored silk with ruffles and lace, stained in places with dark patches that still smelled distinctly like blood to Brandon's sensitive nose.

It's the dress Emily wore to her bloodletting, Caine said, smiling thinly. *She thought you'd like to borrow it for yours.*

Brandon heard Emily giggle in his mind and frowned. *Fuck you,* he thought.

Oh, shame on you—I'm telling, Emily said. They knew what caused him the most pain, and so when she hopped into bed with him, pouncing against his lap and straddling his hips, it was not with the innocent good cheer her bright grin so deceptively presented. She jostled him, and he twisted, gasping sharply, his mind nearly fading beneath the sudden, molten swell of agony.

Get off me, Emily, he thought, making her smile widen.

You're not supposed to be using your telepathy, Brandon, she said, waggling her forefinger at him in a scolding gesture.

Get off me, he said again, his frown deepening.

That's no way to be, Caine said. *Emily's been thinking about you. Look what else she brought.*

Emily held up a thin scrap of fabric she'd been clutching in her hand; a pair of satin panties trimmed in lace, dyed to match the dress. *I thought these would suit you, too,* she said, and when she fluttered them in his face, he jerked away, sending fresh new spears of pain radiating from his arms at the motion. *They're still fresh.* She shoved the panties against his face. *See? They still smell like pussy.*

Get off me! he snapped in his mind, and Emily twisted like he'd physically thrown her away from him. She tumbled sideways off the bed and crashed to the floor. Caine darted forward to help her as she sat up, her hand pressed to her brow, her eyes wide, angry, and somewhat bewildered.

What's going on in here? Brandon heard their sister, Tessa, say. He blinked toward the doorway, his mind and gaze both blurred with pain, and saw her there. Her brows were narrowed, her dark eyes angry as she glared at Caine and Emily. "Leave him alone," she said aloud. "Get out of here or I'll tell Father."

Emily limped to her feet, leaning heavily against Caine for pitiful effect. "Go ahead," she said, glowering. She nodded once toward Brandon. "You're as pathetic as he is, you know that?"

"Not quite," Caine said. Like Emily, he kept shooting dark, wary glances at Brandon, his expression inexplicably puzzled, as if Brandon had bitten them or something. "One of them at least has some balls."

Emily and Caine left. Brandon had closed his eyes, but he felt them go, their icy presence in his mind receding. He'd been left alone with his twin, but had found no comfort there, even though Tessa tried to offer it to him. *Brandon,* she whispered gently inside his head.

He knew it wasn't entirely her fault, the fact that she'd changed since her bloodletting. As a woman among the Brethren, she'd been expected to assume her role as a new adult, a new wife. Brethren women didn't question their mates; they especially didn't challenge the Elders. Whatever freedoms and liberties Tessa had enjoyed in the great house as Sebastian Noble's daughter had ended the moment she'd become Martin Davenant's wife.

Martin says it should be at least a few months before your hands are healed enough to take off the bandages, Tessa said. He felt the mattress settle slightly as she sat beside him. *It won't be that bad. Martin said I could stay for a while. I'll be here and you can talk to me with your mind, just the two of us, like when we were kids, remember? I won't tell the Grandfather. I'll help you eat, wash your face, get you dressed . . .*

She tried to touch his face, but he turned away. *Brandon, why do you keep doing this?* she asked, sounding weary and exasperated. *It's time to stop. Just go through the bloodletting and be done with it. You'd heal faster, anyway, if you fed—weeks instead of months.*

He felt the heat of tears in his eyes and pressed his lips

together in a thin, defiant line. *No,* he thought, shaking his head.

Why do you keep fighting it? Tessa asked. *The bloodlust is part of who you are. Why do you keep fighting what is your nature, Brandon?*

Because it's wrong! he'd cried desperately. *We're all monsters! That's our nature! How can you not see that, Tessa? How can nobody else see it but me?*

Brandon turned away from the window in the cab, glancing toward Lina, who rode beside him on their way back from Danny O's to Jackson's apartment. She was worried about him; he knew it, and now she was only worried all the more, because he'd drank too much and said too much. He'd revealed far more than he should have.

Tessa had recoiled at his mental cry on that morning in his room a year ago, just like Emily and Caine had. Her hand had darted to her face, her fingertips pressing against her brow, and she'd backpedaled, her face twisted in a wince. She'd left him alone, but it hadn't mattered. She had abandoned him years before that, on the night of her bloodletting, whether she had meant for it to happen or not. Brandon had been alone—utterly alone, with no hope for rescue, none for escape.

He and Lina weren't even halfway back to Jackson's yet, not fifteen minutes from the bar, but already, his accelerated metabolism had kicked in, dissolving the intoxicating effects of the alcohol in him. He no longer felt giddy or comfortable or relaxed, and knew within a few more minutes, he'd feel no differently than he had before he'd indulged in his first sip.

Jesus, I told Lina too much, he thought, turning away again, looking out the window, wishing desperately he could just take the entire night back and start it over again from scratch. *She doesn't need to know the truth about the Brethren. She doesn't even need to suspect it.*

Chapter Seven

Lina awoke the next morning with bright sunlight in her face, hazy and glaring through Jackson's floor-to-ceiling windows. She grimaced, sucking in a breath through her teeth and brought the blade of her hand up to shield her eyes. She'd slept on the couch, enduring a night with what felt like a thick metal bar and at least a dozen poorly cushioned springs digging into her body at various uncomfortable points. She sat up slowly, her hair a mess, her face set in a groggy scowl as she massaged a wicked crick that had formed in her neck. *Jesus, Jackie, you'll spend $1,500 on a goddamn houseplant, but you won't even buy a sofa that's less than twenty years old?* she thought grumpily.

She squinted toward the windows, making a mental note to spend the next night at Jackson's apartment either with her back to the east, or taking up Brandon's offer to trade places with him and sleep in the bed. She'd refused the night before, still unnerved by his kiss outside of Joe's Wok, and not completely convinced that Brandon wouldn't try to sneak out and run away if he spent the night on the sofa.

What would be so wrong with that? she thought that morning, just as she had the previous night. There was more to his circumstances than he was saying—more, apparently, than even Jackson knew. *He's in some kind of trouble, and I bet it would make my life a hell of a lot easier if he did just skip town.*

But she'd given her word to Jackson, and more than this, there was something about Brandon Noble she found intriguing. More than just that wondrous, stupefying kiss from the day before, and more than just the fact he was strikingly handsome, there was something about the kid she liked. Or at least, that piqued her curiosity.

She saw him standing out on the terrace, a silhouette in motion against a backwash of new sunlight. She rose to her feet and walked to the sliding glass doors, watching as he stepped forward and pushed his hand out slowly, deliberately in the open air. Again, he moved forward, and circled his hand, palm facing upward, and then he reached toward the balustrade, sweeping his arm around to the side, palm out.

He was performing *kata,* a rhythmic, choreographed presentation of *aikido* maneuvers. She slid the door open and stepped outside to join him. The immediate press of the cool morning air frosted her breath around her face and raised goosebumps along her bare arms.

He pivoted his hips, drawing his hands toward him in tight circles, and as he turned, he caught sight of her. He immediately came to a halt, his eyes widening, his balance wavering. He stumbled slightly, and his expression grew sheepish. *Good morning,* he signed, bringing the blade of his hand from his lips to rest against the cup of his other palm and then sweeping his open right hand upward, mimicking the sunrise.

Good morning, she signed in reply.

I didn't mean to wake you . . . he began, but she shook her head, staying his hands.

"You didn't," she said. "Mind if I join you?"

He seemed surprised, but nodded, stepping sideways in invitation. Lina walked beside him and settled her feet into a ready stance. "You may have to go slow at first. I haven't done this for a while," she admitted, glancing at him so he could read her lips. "Don't tell Jackson."

He laughed soundlessly. *Deal,* he signed. His hair lay in an unruly, dark corona about his face, tumbling past his ears and drooping over his brow in haphazard waves. When he smiled like that, Lina felt something visceral within her tremble.

They moved together, stepping in tandem, their hands punching and sweeping slowly, precisely in the air, their bodies moving in fluid rhythm as they pivoted and turned with each motion of the *kata.* Lina pulled every breath in deeply through her nose, feeling it fill her core, tightening through her torso, just as Jackson had taught her. *God, I'd forgotten how good this feels,* she thought. She ran by daily habit, and there was a stark contrast between that rapid, ruthless pounding on her body, the exertion on her form, and this gentle, deliberate series of movements that stretched and stirred her muscles languidly.

When they were finished, they segued seamlessly into sparring maneuvers, practicing striking and elbow-thrusting techniques together. What began in the same slow, methodical fashion as their previous *kata* quickly grew rougher and more heated, the punches faster and more forceful, the elbow pushes and armlocks more aggressive, until both of them were sweating despite the early morning chill, and any semblance of routine was gone. They fought, pure and simple, and Lina couldn't help but grin as she ducked and blocked her way around a constant volley of blows.

I haven't done this in ages, she thought, cutting her head to the left, feeling the snap of wind against her face as Brandon thrust the heel of his hand past her cheek. She remembered that yesterday, when she'd surprised him in the bathroom, he'd attacked her vigorously, relentlessly, with a speed and tremendous power like nothing she had ever seen before. She wondered now if that had been her imagination, brought on by the panic she'd felt in the moment. While Brandon fought her earnestly, and didn't seem to be pulling his punches, blocks, or kicks, it was with nowhere near the speed or strength she remembered.

She met his gaze, locking eyes with him, and swung her

hand up, folding her fingers around his wrist, the heel of his thumb. She stepped forward and pivoted, sweeping his arm around in a wrist lock. He let her flip him, dropping his shoulder and tucking his head as he hit the patio floor. She let him go and he rolled smoothly, getting his feet beneath him and rising again.

He rubbed his hand momentarily, almost unconsciously, and she hesitated. "You alright?" she asked.

He nodded, unfazed, and flapped his hand to her in beckon. They grappled again; this time, when she snapped a punch at his face, he caught her in a wrist hold, folding his hand expertly around hers, his fingers settling against the crook of her thumb joint. It happened so unexpectedly and he moved so fast, she didn't have time to counter him, much less escape. He closed his hand and twisted, hyperextending her wrist and sending a sudden, shocking pain up her arm. Lina cried out sharply, dropping to her knees.

Brandon immediately released her and danced backward, his eyes flown wide. *I'm sorry!* he signed, drawing his fist in circles against his heart. He reached for her, meaning to help her to her feet, but she shook her head, holding out her hand to keep him away. "Don't," she said, gasping. "Just . . . just don't."

Goddamn it! she thought, cradling her aching wrist. She stumbled to her feet, her eyes smarting with tears. He'd grabbed her quick and hard; it felt like he'd damn near crushed the bones in her wrist beneath his hand.

She turned and found him watching her, his brows lifted, his expression somewhat mournful and uncertain. *Game over,* she signed, drawing her fists together, striking her knuckles, and then shaking her hands, as if to loosen a cobweb caught on her fingertips. *At least until you learn your own strength,* she added mentally.

He nodded, looking even more abashed, as if he'd been privy to her thought somehow. He looked down at the ground, his shoulders hunching, like he braced himself for a rebuke. *I'm sorry,* he said again, still tracing circles against his heart with his hand.

Lina had seen Brandon naked the day before—she knew he was lean, but nearly all muscle. That still didn't account for that crushing grip he'd awarded her wrist, or the speed with which he'd reacted. It had seemed impossible, damn near inhuman. *Maybe I wasn't imagining things yesterday after all.*

His dismay at having hurt her seemed genuine, and she found herself charmed. She reached out, smiling slightly, tousling his hair to draw his gaze. When he blinked at her, all round, dark, and remorseful eyes, her smile widened. "I'll live," she told him. "Don't worry." She flapped her hand in beckon as she walked toward the sliding glass door. "Come on."

She signed to him as he fell in step, walking with her back into the living room. *I have to go to a wedding tonight,* she said, drawing her hands together, crossing one atop the other in front of her. *You'll have to come with me.*

I can stay here, Brandon offered in sign language.

Lina winced inwardly. She didn't want to explain to him in too much detail that she didn't quite trust him not to run away if left on his own, or that she had promised Jackson she'd keep an eye on him. *No, why don't you come?* she signed. *They'll have an open bar, dinner, dancing. It will be fun. You'll see.*

Fun, indeed, she thought. *My dickhead ex and the bimbo he dumped me for will be there. Remember them? Not to mention at least a hundred of our mutual and mostly former friends. Fun, fun, fun.*

Brandon drew to a halt, his expression puzzled and somewhat troubled. Again, it was as if he'd read and was reacting to her thoughts, something Lina found increasingly disconcerting. *I don't have anything to wear,* he signed at length, with a demonstrative sweep of his hands to indicate his T-shirt and sweatpants.

Lina nodded. "I know," she said. She thought of the back of her closet at home, the Dolce and Gabbana suit and boxload of other items that had once belonged to Jude. Brandon was of a similar tall, lean build. And it seemed such a shame to let the clothes go to waste. She smiled again and dropped him a wink. "I think I have something that will work."

She brought him to her apartment, and he blinked in wide-eyed surprise as she pulled the suit out of the back of her closet. It was wrapped in plastic, but she lay it against her bedspread, raising the dry cleaning bag so he could get a better look. He studied the suit for a long moment and then glanced at her, a speculative brow raised.

Hold it up to you, she signed. *Let's see if it fits.*

He caught the crook of the hanger against his hand and lifted the blazer off the bed. He held it up to his chest, looking down, frowning thoughtfully. To Lina's inexperienced gaze, it looked like it would be a perfect fit. Her smile widened. "It's yours, then," she said, when he looked up at her.

He blinked in surprise. *I can't take this,* he signed, after setting the coat back against the bed. He handled it gingerly, as if afraid to wrinkle the fabric. *Do you know how much this suit is worth?* he asked. *It's a—*

She caught his hands before he began to finger-spell *Dolce.* He'd told her he had been raised on a farm, not the moon, and apparently, his family's money had awarded him some fine fashion sense. She could nearly see the question forming in his mind: *How in the hell did a woman on a cop's lousy salary wind up with a fifteen-hundred-dollar designer suit in her closet?*

Trust me, you don't want to know, she thought with a smirk. "I know what it's worth," she said, adding, "Jackshit to me, because I can't wear the damn thing. It's been taking up space in my closet for too long now and I'm sick of looking at it. It's yours."

She left the bedroom, walking down the short corridor into her living room, and he followed. "I have a hair appointment I have to go to," she said, turning around so he could read her lips. "It's just up the street. I have to get my hair set before the wedding tonight. You'll have to stay here while I go."

Melanie, her friend and the upcoming bride, had made an appointment for Lina, along with the other brides-maids, at a very chic, expensive salon downtown. How-ever, Lina had promptly canceled it and made one of her own, with Keyah Reynolds at the A Cut Above beauty parlor, where she'd been a regular customer for the last five years. Keyah was an older, heavyset black woman who doted on Lina like a mother and had seen her through countless relaxers, extensions, dye jobs, curler sets, and shampoos—not to mention her breakup with Jude.

Lina didn't like the idea of leaving Brandon alone while she went, but figured he stood less of a chance of bolting if he was at her apartment, in an area of town unfamiliar to him, and without any of his belongings, or a way to return to Jackson's to claim them. She also had a double-key dead-bolt on her front door, and Jackson's apartment had the turn-bolt style. Brandon could easily let himself out at Jack-son's if the urge to flee hit him, but at Lina's, once he was in, he was stuck fast unless he knew how to pick locks.

She sure as hell wasn't taking him to the beauty shop with her. Keyah oversaw a group of a half-dozen other stylists, and Lina could only imagine—and cringe—to think of their reception of Brandon if she brought him with her—a good-looking white boy, tall and lean, built like a brick shit-house.

Christ, I'd never hear the end of it. She winced to think of all the "look-who-has-jungle-fever-now" cracks she'd have to endure.

"I have closed-captioning on my television," she said, because Brandon looked around her living room, his eyes round and somewhat hesitant. "There's food in the fridge and beer, too. Help yourself. I won't be gone long. Maybe a couple of hours. I'm going to change my clothes before I go." She eased past him and headed toward the bedroom again. She glanced over her shoul-der as she walked away. "Make yourself at home."

Chapter Eight

Make yourself at home, Brandon thought. *Right.*

Lina had just left to go to her hairdresser's, and he stood alone in her living room, feeling awkward and uncomfortable in her absence. Being at Jackson's was one thing, but this was something else entirely. He knew Jackson as well as any family. Lina was still very much a stranger to him.

That's not true, he told himself. *And you know it.*

He walked around the room, curious, trying to relax. Her entertainment center was lined with framed photographs, and he stood for a while, admiring them. One was of Lina surrounded by a group of women, all of them laughing as they enjoyed a night on the town, dressed in miniskirts and slip dresses, holding brightly colored drinks with little paper umbrellas poking out the tops.

Another showed Lina in her police uniform, a close-up shot of only her face and neck, the front of her shirt. There was a man in the picture, with his arm hooked around her neck. He, too, wore a police uniform; Brandon could see the edge of his name tag in the shot: *R. Morin.* He was white, his dark blond hair cut short beneath his hat. He was turned toward Lina in profile, with nothing really distinguishable about his face because he was planting a huge kiss on her cheek. She laughed in the photograph, her mouth spread in a broad, beautiful grin.

Another picture was of a tall, wiry, older black woman; Lina's mother, apparently. Lina and Jackson stood on either side of her in the picture, arms around her, all of them dressed in shorts and T-shirts, standing beneath a stand of palm trees and smiling.

He lifted in hand another of Jackson, a soft smile lifting the corners of his mouth. It was an older picture, taken at the farm in Kentucky. Brandon recognized the brick facade of Jackson's guest house in the background, the portable basketball hoop in the driveway.

I remember the first time I saw that hoop, Brandon thought fondly. *Hell, and a basketball, too, for that matter.*

Jackson had come to work on the farm as Brandon's teacher when Brandon was ten years old. Brandon remembered standing side by side with Tessa in the yard behind the great house, watching a yellow rented moving truck roll slowly past, following the narrow private lane twining through the horse farm, back toward the staff housing on the back acreage. A small car was towed behind it, an older model, nondescript brown sedan with dents in the fenders and an out-of-state license plate.

It was springtime and warm, the dogwoods all in bloom, the air heady and thick with the perfume of their blossoms. Brandon remembered watching the truck, puzzled but unalarmed, wondering if Diego, the farm manager, had hired another person to join the ranks of the Kinsfolk. The Mexican migrant workers who minded the farm never arrived with moving trucks; to have more than the clothes on their backs and a few meager possessions was a rarity.

Caine came outside to call them for breakfast, but Brandon didn't even notice his sister turn at the sound of his voice. He was too busy watching the truck, his hands hooked over the top plank of the white rail fence surrounding the yard. When Caine approached, smacking Brandon in the back of the head hard enough to knock him face-first into the fence, Brandon sucked in a hissing, startled breath. He felt the grain of the wood mash against his bottom lip from one side, the edge of his teeth from the other. He stumbled back, his hand darting against his mouth, even as Tessa rushed to his defense, shoving Caine back. Her brows were narrowed, her small hands clamped into angry fists, and her mouth moved in a soundless, furious barrage.

Caine seemed unoffended and amused by her fire, and when he turned his dark, narrow gaze from her toward Brandon, Brandon shrank back, shying against the nearest fencepost, lowering his eyes to his toes. He drew his fingertips away from his lip and saw blood smeared.

When Tessa led him into the kitchen, he watched the silent flurry of activity that ensued. The large space, encompassing an adjacent informal dining room as well, was crammed with people, everyone moving and jostling about, their mouths flapping as they laughed and talked. Brandon had seven uncles, his father's brothers, all of whom lived in the great house with their respective families. Although Sebastian Noble had only one wife, several of his brothers had two and three apiece, and a half-dozen children besides. More than seventy people total called the great house home, and that morning, at least half seemed to be jockeying for elbow room and breakfast around the tables while his mother, Vanessa, and his aunts flanked the industrial-sized stove and microwaves, fixing eggs, toast, bacon, and cups of milk.

While the men of the Brethren took care of business and finances, the women tended to homes and families. Wed in their mid-teens to Brethren males often two or three times their age in arrangements preordained by the Elders, women were the Brethren nurses, housekeepers, cooks, and teachers. They had no say in the rules or governing of the clans, no place or voice among the Council. They sated their bloodlust after the Brethren males had taken their turns, typically feeding on the least-desirable human stock. The seeming chaos of that morning was nothing unusual or new to Brandon's mother, Vanessa, and she maneuvered through it gracefully, juggling a bottle for baby Emily, a dishrag, and plates of scrambled eggs.

Tessa shoved her way across the room toward Vanessa, her mouth moving as soon as she and Brandon were across the threshold and into the small, adjoining mudroom to stomp the dew off their shoes. To judge by the disapproving glance Vanessa shot toward Caine, Tessa had tattled on his bullying in the yard. Caine stood across the room, arguing back in his own defense, from the looks of his surly, scowling facial expression as he spoke.

"You always take his side!" Brandon could read his brother's lips clearly. "You never listen to me, you or Father! You only ever pay attention to him!"

He jammed an angry forefinger emphatically toward Brandon, and Brandon cut his eyes to the floor. All the while, toddler Emily ran full tilt and revved up around the kitchen, her mouth hanging open in a happy, soundless squeal as she chased three of her smaller cousins, all in diapers, all leaving trails of fallen Cheerios in their wakes.

While Tessa wrangled Emily, hoisting her in a bear hug and hauling her toward the table, Vanessa drew Brandon aside and squatted in front of her son. Although he tried to keep his shame-faced gaze pinned on his toes, she hooked her fingertips under his chin, forcing his head up. She dabbed at his lip with a wet washrag and he didn't miss the shadow that momentarily clouded her dark eyes, or the way she shook her head slightly as if to say, *Not again, Brandon.*

Such calamity was nothing less than a daily occurrence for Brandon. The bullying from his older brother was nothing new, and it seemed Brandon presented his parents with a never-ending array of cuts, scrapes, bruises, and abrasions meted out by Caine. Caine seemed to de-

light in tormenting Brandon, in using his fists and feet to
drive his younger brother farther and farther into the
shy, meek shell that he'd erected around himself over the
years. That morning had been an atypical public display;
ordinarily, Caine took care to make sure no one was
around to bear witness, and Brandon's injuries were
often discounted as simple, clumsy mishaps he'd brought
upon himself.

Even though she'd scolded Caine, Vanessa's movements were jerky and abrupt, her expression displeased,
as if she considered Brandon partially to blame as well.
She had her hands full with her four children, and all
Brethren women were expected to help with the rearing
of their kin, so she had little time or patience for
shenanigans between her boys. "Why can't you stick up
for yourself for once, Brandon?" she said. "Your brother
would leave you alone if you did. You're supposed to
meet your new teacher this morning and now you're all
banged up and—"

Something from behind them in the melee that was
the Noble family breakfast assembly distracted her, and
she first turned, then pulled away from him, marching
over to break apart a tussling match that had broken out
between two of Brandon's cousins.

Brandon didn't know what a *teacher* was, and didn't
want to risk further frustrating his mother by asking. His
mouth cleaned up, he sat, shoulders hunched, eyes
downcast at the table. He didn't eat his breakfast, feeling
sullen and unhappy, and didn't miss his mother's exasperated glance as she scraped his untouched egg and
bacon into the trash can.

Brandon's father, Sebastian, came to his room to get
him shortly after breakfast. Tessa and Caine were downstairs on the first floor with the other school-aged Noble
children for their daily tutelage, while Emily and the
younger children played together in the nursery. Usually
Brandon—unable to speak, hear, or read and write
beyond the kindergarten level—spent the day in the

nursery, too, but Vanessa had proven sore with him for not eating his breakfast and had directed him to his room with a stern look and a demonstrative finger pointing up the main staircase.

Brandon was delighted that Sebastian came to his rescue. It was an unexpected treat. Although Augustus Noble owned the Thoroughbred farm, most of his time and attention was diverted toward the Bloodhorse distillery. Sebastian, however, oversaw the day-to-day business affairs of the farm. He kept an office in the main horse barn, and that's where most of his time was spent. While Diego, the farm manager, tended to the care and upkeep of the animals and grounds and supervised the staff, Sebastian managed the bookkeeping and records. It was a full-time obligation, one that left him little time for playing with his deaf-mute and lonely son.

Brandon cherished those rare occasions when Sebastian was able to make time for him. They would spend hours in the barns, watching as the Kinsfolk and farm hands brushed and curried the Grandfather's prized Thoroughbreds, grooming each until their dark, satiny coats gleamed in the summer sunshine. The Grandfather had practice fields upon which the horses would be exercised daily. There was always a tremendous amount of activity surrounding the barns and exercise yards, plenty to fascinate and entertain Brandon. He loved the smell of the horse barns, the sweet fragrance of fresh hay intermingling with the spicy, musky scent of horse dung and sweat. Sometimes his father would let him feed treats to the horses, handfuls of dried corn or special feed pellets, and Brandon delighted in the sensation of their loose, velveteen lips tickling against his outstretched and upturned palm, the slight, delicate scrape of their teeth as they nibbled the food he offered.

Brandon's handicaps hadn't mattered to Sebastian; he'd been able to speak to his son through his mind, and most times, even this had proven unnecessary. All it took was a smile or a nod, a simple hand gesture in beckon or a doting pat and Brandon understood him perfectly.

That day, however, they hadn't gone to the horse barns or the exercise fields. Sebastian had taken Brandon in his pickup truck and they'd driven together toward the staff houses. Sebastian had pulled to a stop in front of one of the modest brick bungalows reserved for the Kinsfolk to use, in a portion of the farm where the Brethren weren't allowed to feed during the bloodletting ceremonies. Brandon was surprised to find the yellow moving van parked here, the back door raised and left standing wide. A clutter of brown cardboard boxes surrounded the metal loading ramp of the truck and the yard. The little brown sedan had been unhooked from tow behind the van and now sat parked in the driveway.

You're supposed to meet your new teacher this morning, Vanessa had told him. Brandon blinked at his father in hesitant confusion, and Sebastian had smiled, motioning with his hand as he climbed out of the truck. *Come on.*

Brandon followed, standing shied somewhat behind his father's hip as they walked into the bungalow together. Trapped in his world of helpless silence, Brandon had become painfully withdrawn over the years, timid and shy. The Brethren seldom met strangers as it was, because few outside of farm staff were ever allowed onto the farms, much less into the great house, and when Brandon first caught sight of Jackson standing in the living room of the guest house, he'd nearly been paralyzed with anxious fright.

He hadn't known Jackson's name, of course. Although he could communicate in rudimentary fashion with his family, such things as introductions were lost upon him. All Brandon had known was that the man shaking hands with his father was black—the first African American he'd ever seen up close and outside of television—and enormous, quite possibly the largest man Brandon had ever seen. Tall and thick and strapped with muscles, the man had been bigger and broader than Sebastian and had towered over Brandon. His head was shaved bald, his coffee-colored skin gleaming, and although his face had been kind, his mouth stretched in a broad smile, Brandon had still shrank behind Sebastian, hooking his fingers desperately against his father's pant leg, frightened when he'd offered the boy an outstretched hand.

Sebastian patted Brandon's head, easing him reluctantly forward, nodding in encouragement toward the black man's proffered hand. *This is your new teacher, Brandon,* Sebastian told him inside of his mind, not illuminating matters in the slightest for the boy. *His name is Mr. Jones.*

Brandon had accepted the shake, wide eyed and hiccuping for breath. When the man had closed his fingers around Brandon's hand, he nearly swallowed Brandon's whole.

While Sebastian and the man had spoken together again, Brandon had retreated once more behind the shelter of his father's leg. The longer they stood there, however, the more curious Brandon became, and his gaze eventually wandered, traveling slowly, inquisitively along the boxes and bags stacked around the modestly furnished room. Several had already been unpacked, and Brandon saw books and boxes of crayons atop the coffee table. He drew away from his father and went to look more closely, wondering if the large, dark man with his father had children. The idea of a new possible playmate appealed to him. None of the Kinsfolk had children, nor did few, if any, of the farm hands. The Grandfather disapproved of having children outside of the Brethren on the property.

He peeped inside a box left opened beside the coffee table and found it filled with coloring and activity books, hardbound storybooks, boxes of crayons, packages of markers, and more. He looked at the books on the coffee table, lifting each curiously in turn. He recognized the pictures on some of the covers, stories he remembered from his childhood, before he'd lost his hearing. He couldn't read well enough to maneuver his way through the books on his own, and of course, no one could read to him now, but he still remembered them fondly, and flipped through the pages of *Where the Wild Things Are*—once his favorite—almost forlornly. Sebastian still read to his children every night; Tessa and Emily would tussle for position on his lap, while Caine would sit on the floor by his feet. Brandon would sit with them, and would watch his father's lips move, his mouth opening and closing without understanding much of what he offered. Even with such close proximity, he would feel utterly alone in those moments, as if he watched his family helplessly through a picture window, unable to join them.

A ball on the floor by the coffee table drew Brandon's gaze. He set the book aside and picked it up, studying it carefully. He'd never seen a ball like this; it was made of thick, orange rubber, and felt somewhat heavy to him. Its surface was pebbled, rough and fascinating beneath Brandon's fingertips, scored with grooves that marked it like the segments of a peeled orange. It smelled funny to Brandon's keen and sensitive nose, like the rubber sole of a tennis shoe. Brandon dropped it and smiled hesitantly as it bounced back up again, slapping against his hands.

Sudden movement out of the corner of his eye startled him, and he shrank back, dropping the ball as the black man stepped into his line of sight. He was smiling, but Brandon shied, looking around in wide-eyed anxiety for his father, frightened that he would be scolded for snooping in the man's belongings.

To Brandon's dismay, he realized the living room was empty. Sebastian was gone, and with a sudden shudder of bright, strangling terror, Brandon darted for the nearest window. He shoved the drapes aside and watched his father's truck drive away. *He's leaving me!* Brandon had thought, confused and frightened. *Why? What did I do? Where is he going?*

He turned around and pressed himself back against the window sill, wondering if Sebastian was punishing him for not eating his breakfast or for the scuffle that morning with Caine. When the large black man approached him, Brandon scrambled back along the wall, pressing himself into a corner of the room, his breath hitching, tears welling in his eyes. The big man realized his distress and stopped, his brows lifting, his expression gentle. He folded his long legs beneath him and smiled again. He moved his hands in the air, not casual gestures, but motions that seemed deliberate and purposeful to Brandon, even though he had no idea what they meant. He watched, momentarily transfixed, as the man's long fingers seemed to cut and dance in the air, and when the man drew his hands still, Brandon blinked at him uncertainly.

The man continued to smile, not seeming the least bit impatient or irritated. He stood and went back to the coffee table. He opened a box of markers and Brandon saw him lean over, writing something quickly against a sheet of construction paper. He stood again, and came back to Brandon's corner, forcing the boy to recoil in bright new alarm.

The man genuflected again and then patted his hand against his chest. He held the sheet of construction paper out toward Brandon, pointing so the boy could see the neat, block letters written there. *Mr. Jones.*

It took Brandon a moment of conscientious effort to decipher the words, combining the letters in his mind. He looked from the page to the man, and again, the man patted his chest and then tapped his fingertip against the sheet demonstratively.

His name, Brandon realized with a smile. *That's his name.*

This is your new teacher, his father had said. *His name is Mr. Jones.*

The man smiled with him, but when he rose to his feet, Brandon's fear instantly returned. Unbothered, the man walked away again, leaning over to lift the strange orange ball in hand. He turned to Brandon and held the ball out, offering it to him, his brows raised as if in invitation or inquisition. Brandon shook his head, shying back again. He'd been able to figure out the man's introduction, but this was something more complicated and he didn't understand.

Mr. Jones held out his free hand to Brandon and flapped at him in beckon. *Come on.* He turned around and walked across the living room, heading for the front door. Brandon watched him bounce the ball as he went, dribbling it in tandem with his stride, a seemingly effortless act that again, left Brandon mesmerized with momentary wonder.

Mr. Jones walked outside, leaving Brandon alone in the living room. After a minute of timid hesitation, Brandon's curiosity got the best of him, and he scurried outside.

He found the man standing in the driveway, in a circumference of blacktop cleared among the stacks of boxes waiting to be brought into the house. He stood facing a tall metal post that had been mounted on wheels. A broad fiberglass backboard crowned the top of the post, and affixed to this was a loose-webbed basket that dangled down over the ground. It was not a permanent fixture on the grounds, and Brandon figured the man had brought it with him in the moving van.

Mr. Jones bounced the ball easily on the ground in front of him. He looked over his shoulder and smiled to see Brandon. He nodded toward the basket, encouraging Brandon to come closer. Brandon watched as he caught the ball between his hands and then threw it effortlessly away from him, arcing it skyward from head level. It sailed toward the pole, and then bounced off the backboard, dropping neatly down through the basket. It bounced against the driveway, and Mr. Jones jogged forward to retrieve it.

Brandon smiled in curious wonder until the man turned, holding the ball out toward him. *You try it,* the gesture seemed to impart, and Brandon took a hedging step back, shaking his head. He was terrible at games, slow moving and clumsy. He was seldom, if ever, invited to play in such activities among the other Brethren children because no one wanted him on his or her team.

Mr. Jones nodded, walking toward him, holding out the ball, apparently unwilling to take no for an answer. Brandon continued shaking his head. Mr. Jones pressed the ball between Brandon's hands and then stepped aside, nodding once toward the basket. *Try it,* he seemed to say.

Brandon blinked up at the post. He realized the only way to discourage the man was to prove he couldn't do it. Thus, he tossed the ball, stumbling forward with the effort. The ball fell short, bouncing against the blacktop without even grazing the rim of the basket. Brandon dropped his gaze to his toes, hunching his shoulders, certain the man would scold him. A moment passed, then two, with nothing, and Brandon risked a wary, hesitant peek. He watched Mr. Jones walk over to retrieve the ball and then bring it back. He held it out, smiling, not a hint of aggravation in his face. *Try again,* that smile seemed to suggest.

Brandon tried for the better part of the next half-hour, unable to accomplish what Mr. Jones had done effortlessly and in one try. No matter how many times he missed or how frustrated Brandon became with himself, Mr. Jones didn't show even a fleeting hint of irritation or impatience. He kept offering the ball to Brandon time and again, always with that gentle smile and an encouraging nod to *try once more.*

Finally, just as Brandon was about to stumble with fatigue, not to mention burst into demoralized, unhappy tears, he launched a shot toward the basket and blinked in utter astonishment as it sailed through the hoop. It fell through the basket and bounced against the ground, and Brandon gaped between it and Mr. Jones, his mouth spread in a broad, amazed grin. Mr. Jones grinned back at him and held out his hands, his fists closed, his thumbs raised. *Good job!* this told Brandon, as clearly as if Mr. Jones had spoken the words and Brandon had been able to hear them.

Brandon moved to retrieve the ball and try again, but Mr. Jones waved, staying him. He watched, puzzled, as the man cupped his hand lightly in the shape of a "C," as if he held a glass, and then mimed bringing it to his mouth. He glanced at Brandon, pointed, and then did this again. Brandon understood him and blinked in pleased surprise. The man had asked him if he wanted something to drink.

Brandon nodded eagerly, hot, tired, and thirsty, and Mr. Jones had smiled, flapping his hand in beckon as he'd walked toward the house. *Come on.*

Brandon stood at the breakfast bar dividing the guest house's kitchen and dining room. He watched as Mr. Jones dug among a large box on the countertop, searching for plastic tumblers. The man then rummaged through a large plastic cooler that he'd used to tote along some refrigerator staples, including a large bottle of lemonade. He poured some into two cups and offered one to Brandon, who gulped at it greedily.

He realized the man was watching him with kindly interest, sipping at his own lemonade, and Brandon paused, feeling awkward and uncertain. He blinked at the man, using the cuff of his hand to wipe a mustache of lemonade from his top lip.

Mr. Jones set his cup down and covered his ears with his hands. Brandon looked at him, frowning slightly, puzzled. Mr. Jones patted his hand against his heart and then covered his ears again. He did this twice more before Brandon understood his meaning.

He . . . he's like me, he thought in stunned amazement. It was the first time it had ever occurred to the boy that anyone else in the world might have suffered a handicap. But that seemed to be what this man was trying to impart with his gestures, that he, too, was deaf.

Brandon smiled, and Mr. Jones smiled, too. He lifted his cup in hand again and as he took a drink, he dropped Brandon a wink, pointed at him and then tapped his fingertip against his brow. *You're a smart kid,* he seemed to say, and Brandon flushed with happy pride.

You're supposed to meet your new teacher this morning, Vanessa had told her son, and Brandon wondered dimly if *teacher* was another word for *friend.*

As he stood in Lina's apartment, holding a picture of Jackson that well could have been taken on that very day so long ago, Brandon smiled. Jackson had indeed proven a friend to him. *My best friend, in fact,* he thought. Like Brandon, Jackson had not been born deaf. A congenital condition had caused the gradual but unavoidable loss of his hearing. Jackson had not been mute, however. From what Brandon understood, according to his father and Tessa, Jackson spoke remarkably well. This was how he had taught Brandon to read lips.

Jackson had been at the farm for about a year, Brandon recalled, and one day happened to witness Caine and some of the older Brethren cousins bullying Brandon. It was nothing unusual; the group had sneaked out of the kitchen during the melee that was breakfast at the great house, and waited for Brandon to leave, crossing the yard for the fence line and roadway beyond to walk up to Jackson's house. Sometimes Sebastian would give his son a ride, but Brandon had come to so enjoy Jackson's company that more often than not, he wouldn't wait for his father and would set off on his own, the earlier the better.

As Brandon had tromped across the backyard that morning, he'd been carrying an armload of books Jackson had loaned him. He neither saw nor sensed Caine and the others as they ducked around the side of the house and converged on him from behind. All he knew was that at one moment he was walking along, excited to demonstrate his reading progress to Jackson, and the next, he felt something hook the front of his shin—his brother's foot—sending him stumbling.

He fell to his knees, the books spilling across the grass. Now he'd realized his company, seeing a half-dozen pairs of legs stepping into a quick, tight circumference around him. He'd reached for *Treasure Island* and Caine had stomped his sneaker down heavily atop the cover, pinning it to the ground.

Brandon looked up and watched Caine's mouth flapping at him: *What's all this, dipshit?*

Jackson had been teaching Brandon to read, write, and sign, all of which the boy had picked up with phenomenal success. He'd been so desperate to communicate and so eager for the opportunity that he'd gladly devoted himself to the hours of necessary practice, both with Jackson and while home on his own at the great house.

Caine leaned over and snatched *Treasure Island* in hand. Brandon scrambled to his feet. *Give it back, Caine,* he wrote on a page in the little brass-adorned notebook his father had given to him only months earlier. Sebastian had been flushed with pride upon the presentation, pleased with Brandon's progress.

Brandon reached for the book, but Caine held it aloft, beyond his reach, his brows narrowed, his mouth hooked in a thin, malicious smile. "Take it from me."

Again, Brandon reached for it, and again, Caine drew it away. "You want it?" he asked. "Go fucking get it." He shoved his free hand against Brandon's shoulder and pushed him roughly to the ground. Brandon landed on his bottom, his legs splayed, and he watched in wide-eyed horror as Caine chucked the hardbound book, throwing it like a frisbee with a deft flick of his wrist, sending it sailing up onto the roof of the back porch.

Caine laughed at the dismay on Brandon's face, and the cousins all joined in. At that moment, Jackson had appeared, striding briskly into the cluster of boys and seizing Caine roughly by the arm.

"What are you doing?" Jackson asked him. "Leave Brandon alone. Why did you throw that book?"

"Let go of me!" Caine cried. He jerked his sleeve loose from Jackson's grasp and danced backward, his dark eyes flashing hotly, his cheeks ablaze with twin patches of angry, humiliated color. He snapped something at Jackson, spittle flying from his lips, his small hands balled into fists. Brandon hadn't understood what he said at the time; it was a word he'd never seen spoken before, but he'd recognized the sounds, at least in part. It had started with an *N* and ended in an *R*.

Jackson's hand swung around, and he slapped Caine across the face, snapping the boy's cheek toward his shoulder. It was a restrained blow, considering the man's strength, but it sent Caine stumbling sideways nonetheless. He blinked at Jackson in stunned surprise, and Brandon blinked along with him, as did all of their cousins. Then Caine's face flushed brightly with new rage, and he shouted again before turning and bolting for the back door.

Brandon had been terrified. When the other boys were gone, fleeing after Caine, he looked up at Jackson, stricken. Jackson had struck Caine. He would be fired now, of that Brandon had no doubt. Caine would tell their mother, who would in turn, tell Sebastian, and Sebastian would fire Jackson.

They'll make him leave. I'll never see him again. Brandon's eyes filled with tears with this realization. *He's my friend, and they'll make him leave!*

Jackson squatted in front of him, his expression softening. *You OK?* he signed, pointing first to Brandon and then finger-spelling the pair of letters. Brandon nodded. His eyes were still flooded however, his expression aghast, and Jackson smiled at him gently, pressing his palm against his cheek as if to reassure him.

Don't worry, he signed to the boy. *It's alright.*

He began to gather the fallen books, motioning to Brandon to help. When they were finished, Jackson stood, helping Brandon to his feet. He led the boy into the house. Sebastian had been waiting for him in the kitchen, with Caine at his side and in tears, hiccuping and yowling.

Sebastian had sent Brandon out of the kitchen, but Brandon had lingered in the doorway, hiding at the threshold, struggling to glean any hint of their conversation. He couldn't see enough to read lips and follow along from his vantage, however, but was amazed when, at length, Sebastian gave Caine a sharp shake by the shoulders, his expression stern as he offered some kind of remonstration. Caine seemed as surprised by the rebuke as Brandon, and he tried to sputter out some reply.

"Apologize to Mr. Jones!" Sebastian said, turning his head enough for Brandon to watch his lips move clearly. "Then straight upstairs to your room to wait for me while I get out my belt!"

Brandon's eyes had widened more. Their father seldom threatened to spank them, much less actually saw it through. Whatever Caine had done, whatever he'd said out in the yard, it must have been horrible indeed.

"Why are you taking his side?" Caine had bawled. "He hit me, Father! Brandon fell! I didn't do anything to him. He's lying to—"

"I said apologize!" Sebastian snapped, giving Caine another swift shake. Caine started to cry again, and he mumbled something in Jackson's general direction. His brows were furrowed all the while, his mouth turned in a sullen, disagreeable frown.

What did Caine say? Brandon asked Jackson, as the two had walked together back toward his house. He'd watched as only moments earlier, Jackson had climbed carefully up onto the roof of the back porch to retrieve *Treasure Island*.

Never you mind, Jackson signed back.

They walked along in silence for a moment, but Brandon's curiosity remained piqued. *I know it was something bad*, he signed. *Daddy's going to spank him for it.*

I wish he wouldn't, Jackson replied, looking momentarily unhappy. *But that's his call to make, not mine. You do the crime, you do the time, Brandon.*

So what was Caine's crime? Brandon asked.

Jackson paused. *He called me a* nigger, he said, finger-spelling the word. Because this meant nothing to Brandon, he added, *It's a very bad word. A hateful word. People use it sometimes about black people like me, and it's wrong.*

What does it mean? Brandon asked.

Jackson squatted, folding his long legs so he could look Brandon in the eye. *It means you're ignorant and afraid,* he signed. *You don't understand people who are different than you because their skin is darker than yours, for example, and it's easier to be frightened of them, hateful to them, than to try and learn to like them.*

He stood again, ruffling Brandon's hair affectionately. *Come on,* he said. *You have a spelling test this morning.*

Brandon had groaned silently, trudging along in step with his teacher.

Does your brother pick on you like that often? Jackson signed to him. *I saw him push you down.*

Brandon didn't answer at first; he simply shrugged. Jackson had seen him with enough skinned knees, busted lips, bruises, and scrapes to figure out the answer for himself anyway.

That had been the first day that Jackson had showed him aikido, introducing him to the ancient martial art with a few simple moves, some basic stances. It had been something new to fascinate Brandon, and he'd dived into studying and practicing with the same relentless enthusiasm he'd shown Jackson's other tutelage.

Of course, the lessons had helped because Caine had not stopped picking on Brandon at all. Nor had he bothered to clean up his mouth.

You and your damn dirty nigger boyfriend, Caine had sneered once at Brandon, only months before Jackson had left the farm for good. Brandon had snapped at this; it had been one taunt too many for one morning, and as

Caine had reached out to shove Brandon's shoulder, Brandon had caught his hand and wrenched it in a wrist lock. He craned Caine's arm behind him, pinning his hand against the small of his back, and then he'd shoved Caine face-first against the nearest wall, holding him here.

If you call him that again, I'll break your goddamn arm, he'd told Caine in his mind, summoning the pathetic little telepathic ability he called his own to make himself heard. *I will rip your fucking shoulder out of the socket and shove your hand up your ass, Caine, I swear to God.*

Brandon moved to set Lina's picture of Jackson back on the entertainment center, but the cardboard arm on the back of the frame buckled. *Shit!* he thought, snatching at the photo as it tumbled from the shelf, but it fell past his fingers and hit the floor. The frame broke apart, the glass pane popping loose, the cardboard backing falling away. Nothing looked shattered or irreparably broken, and Brandon squatted, collecting the pieces, hoping he could somehow prop it all back up without Lina noticing.

Five years ago, Caine had laughed at Brandon's threat, but he'd still rubbed his wrist gingerly when Brandon had turned him loose. He also hadn't summoned the balls to say anything else about Jackson, at least for that day. It had been a fleeting, minor victory, one Brandon still savored.

Brandon blinked in surprise to discover a second picture had been tucked into Lina's frame; the one of Jackson had been placed atop it, covering it from view. Brandon lifted it, curious, and was surprised anew to see Lina standing with a man in the photo—the young black man they had met on the street the day before outside the Chinese restaurant.

This is a . . . a friend of mine, Jude Hannam, Lina had said.

In the picture, Lina and Jude were obviously more than just friends. Jude stood behind her, his arms wrapped around her as he grinned broadly and nuzzled her neck. Lina's hands draped against his forearms, and she was laughing.

Brandon had no accounting for the sudden, strange ache the picture caused in his gut, the tight, somewhat suffocating feeling of dismay that seized him. *He's her boyfriend. Or he was, anyway. And not too long ago either.* A small date had been digitally imprinted on the bottom corner of the photograph; it had been taken less than a year ago.

He felt disappointed somehow, unhappy, and frowned as he gathered up the broken picture frame. *What the hell's the matter with me?* he thought. *It's none of my business. Besides, he was with someone else yesterday, a blond woman.*

And, he reminded himself firmly, Lina was a human, and intermingling with humans outside of the Kinsfolk was severely restricted among the Brethren. Only the Elders and more trusted older members of the group, like Brandon's father, had been allowed to interact with humans beyond the boundaries of the farm, and only then, in extremely limited—and fiercely controlled—capacity.

Humans were considered little more than meat, with their short lives and imperfections, their diseases and infirmities, what Caine or the Grandfather would have called their "wretched and inherent failings." Sex with a human was never allowed, and was considered an abomination. If Brandon hadn't thus far earned himself a lifelong banishment to the depths of the Beneath, he would sure as hell do so by acknowledging any tender emotions for a human woman. Not to mention what the Brethren would do to him if he happened to make love to Lina, and it was discovered.

Like she'd let me make love to her anyway, he thought, as he returned the frame ever-so carefully to the shelf, placing Jackson's picture again atop the one of Lina and Jude. *I'm just a stupid damn kid to Lina, one of Jackson's students.* He thought of their basketball match together years earlier, and of how she'd tousled his hair in playful dismissal in the aftermath. *I wouldn't have a hope in hell.*

Chapter Nine

Lina burst through the apartment, running late and nearly frantic. She clutched a plastic shopping bag in her hand, and her tumble of freshly rolled curls bounced out from beneath the edges of a triangular silk scarf Keyah had wrapped around her head to protect from the light drizzle that had started falling. She found Brandon sitting on her couch, a book in his hand, one of her police textbooks, some yawnfest about civil law.

That kid would read the back of a cereal box for pleasure if he didn't have anything else around, Jackson had told her once, fondly.

"I'm really, really late," she said when he looked up at her. She pointed to the wall clock for emphasis. "I have to be at the church in an hour. Can you get dressed here? Do you mind?"

He shook his head, closing the book between his hands, tucking the edge of the page down in a slight dog ear to mark his place. He studied her as he rose to his feet, his gaze curious, lingering at her hairline, and she remembered the scarf, to her mortification. "It's . . . it's raining," she said, reaching up to pull it off. "I didn't want my hair to frizz." She stopped herself; the embarrassment of all of those curls flopping out, unruly and untame, framing her head like Medusa's snakes, would be worse than simply keeping the slip of fabric in place.

She hated being late almost as much as she hated primping and fussing with her appearance, which is what she had left to do. She'd stopped by the drugstore on her way home from the beauty shop, and picked up some new lipstick, eyeshadow, and liner, all in complementing shades of plum and purple that she hoped would match her bridesmaid's dress. *And not make me look like a hooker,* she added mentally. She seldom wore makeup; maybe an occasional dabbing of lip gloss or cover-up, and Melanie had drawn her aside a week or so ago with a pleading expression on her face.

"Please tell me you'll put some makeup on for the wedding," she'd said. "And don't give me that look either. I'm asking you to wear mascara, maybe some eye shadow, not carve out your kidney or anything. It doesn't have to be a lot. You could bring it with you, and we could all help you with it."

Melanie and Lina had always made unlikely friends. They were polar opposites; Melanie, with her pale blond hair, blue eyes, and voluptuous build was soft spoken and dainty, the perfect portrait of feminity, while Lina—athletic and long legged, with no bust to speak of and a sharp tongue to match her attitude—had always been a tomboy. Yet friends they had remained for nearly twenty years now, and Lina didn't have the heart to refuse Melanie on her wedding day.

However, she also didn't have the heart to sit in an antechamber at the church while her friends fussed and flitted around her, cosmetic brushes and tubes in hand, like she was some kind of life-sized Barbie doll. She knew how to apply makeup. *There's a big damn difference between not knowing how to do something and simply not wanting to do it.*

"I'll be in the bathroom," she told Brandon, darting down the hallway, eager to escape his attention, as he hadn't cut his eyes from her once since she'd come through the door.

Twenty minutes later, Lina decided she looked like a hooker. "Goddamn it," she muttered to her reflection in the mirror. She looked down at the eyeliner pencil in her hand. *Dusky amethyst, my ass,* she thought, because that was what the label had said. *This is Barney-the-Dinosaur purple if I ever saw it.*

And it was too late now to just dunk a tissue into some Vaseline and scrub the entire mess from her face. She had forty minutes to finish dressing, grab Brandon, hail a cab and make it to the church. The wedding wasn't until six o'clock that evening, but there were photographs to be taken in the meantime. As a dutiful bridesmaid, Lina was expected to flutter about Melanie while the photographer took shots of them readying for the ceremony.

"Goddamn it," she muttered again, wriggling out of her T-shirt, trying to be mindful of her hair. She grabbed a package of pantyhose off the back of the toilet and bit the corner with her teeth to rip them open. She shook them out, a wrinkled and pathetic mess of sheer nylon, and danced clumsily from one foot to the other as she yanked them on. Just as she wriggled the hose up toward her waist, she felt her finger punch through, tearing them. "Goddamn it."

She pulled the hose up and looked in dismay at the wide runner that had shot from the hole and careened down the outer contour of her thigh. "Goddamn it," she muttered, reaching for her dress, jerking it off the hanger against the back of the bathroom door. She shrugged her way into it and gritted her teeth as she craned her arm backward, groping for the zipper. The dress had been altered supposedly to Lina's measurements, but she still thought there was enough free space through the bustline to park a small minivan. She frowned, tugging at her bra straps, hoping vainly to summon some inkling of cleavage to help fill the top of the gown. "Goddamn it."

She looked in the mirror when she was finished. *I look like a hooker,* she thought unhappily, surveying the messy splay of her hair, the garish eye makeup and plum-colored lipstick, the glossy purple satin ruffle that seemed to explode off the right shoulder of her dress. *Or a drag queen. And not a very good one either way.*

She reached for her shoes, a pair of sandals dyed to match the dress, tucked in a box atop the toilet seat. She stepped into them one at a time, and felt herself wobble for uncertain balance. She hated high-heel shoes. Already, she could feel the straps of the sandals digging into the sides of her feet, and she began to take a mental account of all of the spots in which she could expect to find blisters by the time the ceremony was finished.

"Goddamn it," she muttered, opening the bathroom door and tromping outside.

The Dolce and Gabbana suit was gone from her bed. Brandon had dressed quietly and without her notice. She hoped to God the suit fit him OK, and Jude's shoes, as well. *If they don't, we'll both just go barefooted—screw it,* she thought, shaking her head as she teetered down the hall-way. *We'll make a hell of a couple.*

Brandon sat reading again, but looked up when he caught sight of her approach out of the corner of his eye. He rose to his feet, his brows raising, and Lina drew to a sudden halt.

Wow, she thought. Her mother had an old saying she was fond of: "Life is not measured by the number of breaths we take, but by the moments that take our breath away." *This is definitely one of those moments,* Lina thought, immobilized in the doorway.

Had she ever thought Jude had worn that suit well? The lengths of dark wool draped and hugged Brandon's form as if they had been custom tailored to fit him. He looked immaculate, the white shirt and dove-gray silk tie beneath crisp and striking complements to the black planes of the suit. He'd combed his dark hair back, tucking it behind his ears, leaving wayward strands to droop loose and lay against the high arches of his cheekbones.

My God, he's a beautiful man, she thought.

She realized she was gawking at him, and to judge by the way he was staring at her, he was aware of it, too. She forced herself to tear her eyes away, to blink across the room toward her television set, the empty fish tank in the corner, anywhere else. "I . . . uh . . . it fits," she said. "The suit, I mean. The shoes, too?"

He blinked, giving his head a slight shake, and at last, cut his eyes away. *Yes,* he signed, miming a nod with his fist. *The shoes were a little big, but I shoved paper towels in the toes. It will work.*

He kept stealing curious little glances in her direction, and feeling self-conscious, Lina crossed her arms over her bosom, frowning slightly. "What?"

He shook his head again and motioned toward his face, drawing his fingers in a counterclockwise circle. *Beautiful,* he said. He gestured again, pointing to her, then turned his palm first outward then in, finally letting his fingers sweep around his face once more. *You look beautiful.*

She couldn't remember the last time a man had said that to her, not with the earnest candor she saw frank and apparent in Brandon's eyes. Lina felt her face flush all the more, and she smiled, caught off guard and utterly charmed. *Thank you, Brandon,* she signed.

"Where in the world did you find him?" Melanie's maid of honor, Sonia Woodford, whispered to Lina, poking her head out through the antechamber door and peering into the church vestibule beyond. Brandon sat patiently out there, as few, if any, other guests had yet to arrive. He dropped pleasant nods and polite smiles to family members, bridesmaids, and groomsmen as they filtered past.

Lina bit back the urge to tell Sonia, *I found him in my brother's bathroom, stripped naked and dripping wet, as a matter of fact.* "I told you. He's one of Jackie's former students. He's just visiting."

Each of the bridesmaids had taken turns peeking at Brandon since he'd arrived with Lina. One by one, they had lined up at the door, knocking shoulders and jockeying for position as they looked outside. "Stop already," Lina said, hooking her hand against Sonia's arm and pulling her away from the door.

"How's he going to know?" Sonia asked, flapping her loose. "He can't hear us. You said he was deaf."

"And mute, too, right? How sad," said another bridesmaid, a doughy-faced girl named Dawn, her expression softening as if Lina had just told them Brandon was dying of cancer or something.

"Who wants to carry on a conversation with him anyway?" Sonia asked, laughing. Bottles of champagne had already been uncorked, and several members of the wedding party, including Sonia, were already feeling giggly. "I just want to . . ."

There was more, but Melanie, the bride, caught Lina by the arm and pulled her aside, causing her to miss it. Melanie, too, was slightly into her cups, and she leaned toward Lina, speaking in a forced stage whisper. "I just wanted to tell you I'm sorry about the whole Jude thing, Lina."

Which whole Jude thing? Lina thought of asking, but didn't. *The one where I dated him in the first place or the one where you invited him to your wedding even after he'd dumped me for another woman?*

"Look, you know how I feel about him, on account of everything he did," Melanie said. "I'd like to nominate him for the Asshole of the Year award, but he and Joel are golf buddies, and he really helped Joel out that one time with the civil case after his car got totaled." She shrugged, looking somewhat sheepish. "It was Joel's idea to invite him and I didn't argue about it because I didn't want to fight about the guest list."

"It's alright," Lina said, even though it really wasn't, and she was admittedly pissed not only at Joel for inviting Jude, but with Melanie, too, for allowing it to happen. *It's your wedding day, too, Mel,* she thought about pointing out but kept mum.

"You probably won't even see him," Melanie said, hopefully. "There's going to be three hundred people here today, and he'll be lost in the crowd. But if you do, promise me you won't make a big deal out of it, OK? Just don't pay any attention to him or what's-her-name if he brings her along. I want you guys to have fun today—all of us to have fun, OK?"

"OK," Lina said, because Melanie looked really anxious about the whole prospective situation and Lina figured she had enough on her mind without that particular worry nagging at her. Jude would make a point to find Lina, be it a crowd of three hundred or three million, of that she had no doubt. He'd walked up to her on the street only the day before; nothing was going to stop him at the wedding.

Melanie smiled brightly and leaned forward, kissing Lina's cheek. "Thanks, sweetie," she said. "I knew I could count on you." She started to walk away, then paused, turning to Lina again. "Your makeup looks so pretty, by the way. Did you do it all by yourself?"

"Yeah, imagine that," Lina replied. "No training wheels or anything."

Melanie laughed, and Lina laughed with her, wishing like hell all the while that they'd never shared jump ropes in third grade or sat together in homeroom, so that she could have avoided the entire damn day.

Chapter Ten

By the time the ceremony was over, Lina's feet were screaming in pain. She managed to keep upright on them for another hour thereafter, forcing wide smiles while the photographer took shots of the wedding party. When that was finished, she stepped out of her sandals and limped toward the back of the church where Brandon waited for her.

He'd sat patiently through the ceremony, even though she knew he had to have been bored out of his mind. Because so much of the vows and readings were offered at a distance, or out of his direct line of sight, he hadn't been able to do much lipreading, and without that, she imagined he was pretty much clueless as to what was going on. But he'd tried to take his cues from the other guests, and stood when appropriate, bowed his head when required. At one point, however, he'd left, slipping quietly from the pew and stealing out the back, and she'd been worried about him. He hadn't returned until the ceremony had ended, and a majority of the crowd had filtered out of the church nave.

He smiled as she approached, rising from his seat against the pew. *Are you OK?* she signed to him. *I saw you leave during the service.*

He nodded, offering a sheepish shrug. *Just a headache,*

he signed to her. *I'm better now. Are you finished?* he asked, holding his hands up toward his face and turning his palms out in a quick, flipping gesture.

"Not hardly," Lina replied. "There's still the reception." He looked briefly puzzled at this, and she added, "You know, dinner, cake, liquor, dancing. The whole nine yards."

He still looked at a loss and she realized he had no idea what she was talking about. She didn't know what weddings were like among his family. On the cab ride from her apartment, Brandon'd only cryptically offered that they were "nothing fancy," which had surprised Lina, considering how wealthy they were.

She smiled, slipping her hand against his arm and turning him about, steering him toward the door. "Come on," she said. "You'll see."

By the time the ceremony was over, Brandon's head was screaming in pain. He'd been fighting a pretty persistent headache the last several days, a recurring, throbbing ache that had bothered him ever since he'd fled Kentucky, but that afternoon, as he sat in the church surrounded by several hundred wedding guests, it had felt like his poor skull would simply split open like a rotten melon.

He'd felt a maelstrom of thoughts whispering and whipping through his mind, coming at him in a relentless and overlapping flow as his telepathy had somehow picked up on fleeting, fluttering fragments from everyone around him. They'd flooded his head, causing what had only been a dull ache to that point to blossom into a full-blown, shuddering pain behind his eyes, in the recesses of his sinuses. It had scared the shit out of him.

I don't know what that was, but I hope it doesn't happen anymore, Brandon thought, as he held a cab door open for Lina while she ducked inside. Ever since he'd left the great house, it felt to Brandon as if his mind was coming unglued. He'd spent his entire life there feeling as though he'd carried some kind of heavy cowl within his mind, that his telepathy had been weak and worthless, like the Grandfather and Caine had always told him. The Wellbutrin had always helped with that as well, keeping even his modicum of ability in check. But now, all of a sudden, it seemed as if it was growing, coming upon him in waves that grew stronger and stronger with each incident.

As they rode in the cab for the wedding reception, he reached for his inside blazer pocket, where he'd tucked an emergency Wellbutrin. Lina watched him tear open the square of foil he'd wrapped the pill in and slip it into his mouth. "Your hands are hurting you again?" she asked, her expression softening with gentle sympathy.

He swallowed the tablet dry and nodded.

"Do you want to go home?" she asked. "We don't have to—"

He shook his head. He wasn't quite sure what a reception entailed, but it seemed like an important part of a wedding, and Lina was expected to be there. Besides, he wasn't so sure he was ready for the day to be over. He hoped to enjoy some time with Lina at the reception; that she wouldn't be distracted all the while with the wedding party. She looked absolutely stunning; when he'd first caught sight of her at the apartment, he had lost his breath in amazement. *My God, she's beautiful,* he'd thought then, and as she smiled at him in the taxi, reaching out and draping her hand against his, her dark eyes filled with concern, he thought it again. *You're beautiful, Lina.*

To his disappointment, Lina left him again once they reached the reception hall. "Only for a little bit," she'd promised him, and she'd rolled her eyes. "I'm supposed to make some sort of 'grand entrance' with the rest of the wedding party. Save me a seat?"

He'd smiled for her and nodded, watching her walk away. An open bar had been set up at the back of the ballroom, and apparently the liquor was all offered for free to wedding guests. Brandon had brought along his brass-plated notebook for the occasion, and wrote out an order—a shot of bourbon. He took his drink in hand and tucked himself into a far corner, hoping the liquor might help numb his mind. The crowd, whose thoughts had so accosted him in the church, had reconvened in the ballroom, and he'd been terrified from the moment of this realization that the stabbing pain in his head would renew. He downed the bourbon, shuddering slightly as it burned a path down the back of his throat and into his gullet. *So far, so good,* he thought.

He didn't quite understand the pomp and circumstance of weddings among humans. He'd seen the ceremonies portrayed on television, but they'd always struck him as being rather bizarre, extravagant, and unnecessary. Among the Brethren, marriages were arranged by mandate of the Elders, who dictated them based on careful and rigorous scrutiny of the Tomes, voluminous accounts of each family's records, to ensure that overbreeding among particular sects did not occur. Brides were most often wed shortly after their bloodletting ceremonies and in the prime of their youths; Brethren males were wed when they were much older. Brandon, for example, was due to marry Elita Giscard one day. Elita was currently the same age as his brother, Daniel—only four years old.

There were no wedding ceremonies among the Brethren. Marriage wasn't something that was celebrated, merely accepted. Brandon remembered helping Tessa carry her belongings downstairs to the foyer of the great house, where Martin Davenant had waited for her. That was all there was to it; the lugging of heavy suitcases, some brief hugs farewell, and then the bride would be off for her new clan's home. Only Brethren sons remained in the homes to which they were born, and here, they were expected to spend the entirety of their lives, in the near-constant company of all their kith and kin.

The bar served only top-shelf selections and ironically, Brandon had been given two-fingers worth of Blood-horse Reserve, one of the bourbons his family's distillery produced. As the initial bitter flavor of the liquor settled to a sweet, somewhat breadlike aftertaste in his mouth, Brandon smiled. *My grandfather might be a son of a bitch, but he makes a mean batch of bourbon,* he thought.

"Bourbon is as clear as water before you seal it for aging," he remembered his father telling him, his lips somewhat slow and slurred in forming the words as he spoke. "Did you know that, Brandon? It gets its color and flavor from the smoked wood of the barrels. The longer you age it, the richer it tastes."

Brandon remembered being fifteen years old, sitting in his father's study one evening with a well-stoked fire aglow in the nearby hearth, both of them in facing leather armchairs with tumblers of bourbon in hand. Sebastian had let Brandon help him smoke a cigar, a pungent and admittedly shitty-tasting thing, but Brandon had shared in it eagerly, pleased by his father's invitation and feeling very grown up.

"The author William Faulkner loved bourbon," Sebastian told him. He'd had several shots of bourbon by that point, and he was drowsy from it. "Did you know that? I've heard him quoted as saying, 'The tools I need for my trade are paper, tobacco, food, and a little bourbon.' His work *The Sound and the Fury* has always been a favorite of mine. Have you read it, Brandon?"

Yes, sir, Brandon wrote on a page in his notebook. Jackson made certain that he was well supplied with an endless assortment of reading fare, and particularly, literary classics.

"Your grandfather met him once," Sebastian said. "In 1937, while Faulkner was writing screenplays in Hollywood. Presented him with a bottle of Bloodhorse and everything. You know you can't call it bourbon unless it's made here in Kentucky, don't you? Anyplace else, and it's just plain whiskey." He canted his head back, draining his tumbler dry, and Brandon remembered the play of firelight off the faceted glass, the amber-colored liquor.

"It's the limestone, you know," Sebastian told him with

a wink and a smile. "All underground, everywhere. It gets into the water, makes our horses strong and our bourbon stronger."

Brandon smiled somewhat sadly, distracted at the wedding reception by these bittersweet recollections. As much as he had always been afraid of the Grandfather, he had idolized his father. To others among the Brethren, it had seemed like Sebastian spoiled or coddled Brandon, and it was true that Sebastian let Brandon get by with offenses he might have punished his other children for; that he was more likely to make time to spend with Brandon than even his eldest son, Caine. But that evening, as they had sat together drinking bourbon and sharing a cigar, Sebastian had let his thoughts slip, his mind unguarded.

"You're a good boy, Brandon," Sebastian had told him. *If I had only been faster all those years ago, my mind more aware to sense the danger, you could have been so much more,* he'd thought. *I could have saved you from being ruined.*

On the night Brandon had been attacked, his throat cut, his head bashed, Sebastian had wished for him to die. Brandon had sensed this as plainly as if Sebastian had told him aloud. Just like the Grandfather and everyone else among the Brethren, Sebastian had held no hope or expectation of Brandon's survival. What Brandon remembered as a tender and tearful vigil kept almost constantly at his bedside had in truth been his father's penance, reparations Sebastian had offered because he felt profoundly guilty for what had happened to Brandon.

Clearly, he hadn't meant for Brandon to be privy to this and hadn't even realized that Brandon had sensed these thoughts. He hadn't as much as averted his distant, distracted gaze from the fire as he'd harbored them.

Brandon had flinched as if he'd been slapped; he sat rigidly in the chair, stripped of his breath, stunned and heartbroken. Sebastian had no idea that he'd known; when he'd turned his gaze back to his son, he had smiled with the same gentle adoration he'd always shown Brandon. "I think it's bedtime for us both," he'd said, leaning forward and slipping the tumbler from Brandon's hand, while Brandon had struggled to keep his face a stoic, unstricken mask.

Brandon watched the crowd of wedding guests suddenly turn their attention toward the main ballroom doors, where the bridal party began entering to delighted applause. His expression shifted, his mouth unfolding in a smile as he spied Lina being led across the threshold on the arm of one of the groomsmen. She was beautiful, her hair a corona of dark ringlets about her head, her café-au-lait-colored skin aglow as she smiled broadly, radiantly. Just the sight of her was enough to drive away the painful, poignant memories of his father and the heavy sorrow that had settled on his heart at the recollection. He watched her cut her eyes about the room, scanning the crowd, and when she saw him, her gaze settling upon him, her smile widened, leaving a warm, tremulous sensation to spread through him.

After she had been promenaded around the dance floor, and the bride and groom had officially made their entrances, Lina waded through the ballroom to reach him. Somehow, she'd come to have a flute glass of champagne in her hand. "Is your head hurting again?" she asked, her brows lifted in concern. "You're over here all by yourself."

He smiled and shook his head. *No, I'm fine,* he signed. *I just don't know anybody except you.*

She laughed and shook her head, grasping him by the arm. "Come on, then," she said, tossing her head back and downing her champagne in a single, deep gulp. Although the entire prospect of the wedding and her participation in it had seemed a major source of stress for Lina, all at once, she seemed at ease to Brandon's observation. He suspected the glass of champagne had most likely not been her first. "They're about to set up the buffet for dinner. Sit with me and I'll introduce you to everybody."

He let her lead him across the room and to a formally

set dinner table. Lina offered introductions all around
to the other bridesmaids and Brandon smiled awkwardly
under the unexpected weight of their sudden, curious
gazes. As he lowered himself into a seat, politely waiting
for Lina to sit first, a chorus of whispering voices—the
bridesmaids' thoughts—fluttered through his mind.

One of her brother's students, one of them thought, a redheaded, slightly overweight woman who cut her gaze
along his form slowly, as if eyeing a dessert tray. He recognized her dimly from one of the photographs at Lina's
apartment. *Damn, I could teach him a thing or two . . .*

Mm, honey, thought another, a willowy blonde who
smiled at him as she took a sip from a half-empty glass of
champagne. Like the redhead, she, too, seemed familiar
to him, distantly recalled from one of Lina's photographs. *Wrap that up . . . I'll take him to go.*

Deaf and mute, Lina said, thought another, a mousy-
haired young woman with heavy cheeks and round,
melancholy eyes. *Such a shame. He's so handsome, too . . .*

Brandon pressed the heel of his hand against his
brow, closing his eyes for a moment. *God, stop it,* he
thought, struggling to close his mind, to somehow control whatever portion of his telepathy had suddenly, unexpectedly stirred. *Get out of my head.*

"Brandon?" Lina asked, touching his shoulder.

He opened his eyes and looked at her. The voices were
gone, his mind his own once again. *But for how long this
time?* he thought. He didn't know what was triggering
the episodes, much less how to prevent them.

"Are you alright?" Lina asked, and he nodded, forcing
a smile for her.

The rest of the meal went without incident. The bride
and groom had arranged for an expansive dinner buffet
for their guests, followed by helpings of Italian cream
cake and dancing. The ballroom lights dimmed to near
black, and a dizzying, sparkling array of strobe lights and
neons flashed above the dance floor. Brandon watched
with curious interest as people abandoned their tables

and began to dance, raising their hands skyward and gyrating to music he couldn't hear. The bass was loud enough to feel in the air, faint vibrations he felt through his chair, in the tabletop beneath his palm, and could see against the surfaces of ice water and coffee in cups near his place setting.

The bridesmaids and their respective dates left the table to join the growing throng on the dance floor. By now, a majority of those remaining had been drinking steadily and heavily over the course of the past several hours, and the entire ballroom had shifted toward a decidedly raucous atmosphere. Brandon glanced at Lina and found her leaning over in her chair, her leg crossed, her right foot propped against her left knee. She'd kicked of her sandals and slowly massaged her foot. He could see dark weals along the top, where the sandal straps had pressed too long and hard against her skin.

She looked up at him and smiled. "The hazards of being a woman," she remarked. She was thinking about leaving. He could sense it, and see it in the way she kept letting her gaze wander around the room, as if she was looking for someone. Jude Hannam, the man they'd met outside of the Chinese restaurant, the man in the picture she kept hidden in a frame at her apartment, was supposedly at the reception somewhere, and clearly Lina didn't want to run into him. He knew she would rather leave than risk seeing him, and this left Brandon admittedly disappointed. Aside from the freak incidents in which his telepathy seemed to swell uncontrollably, he'd actually been having fun. Neither one of them had touched much of their dinner, content to laugh and talk together in sign language, enjoying the fact that no one else at the table could tell what they were saying.

He liked being with Lina. The past two days had been wondrous for Brandon, as if he'd been able to somehow step beyond the confines of his life—who and *what* he was—and become someone else in her company. Some-

body different, better; somebody unafraid of his future
and unencumbered by the past.

She said something to him, catching him by the hand
and startling him from his thoughts. He blinked at her,
puzzled, her comment lost to him, and she laughed.
"Dance with me," she said again, leaning forward and
playfully exaggerating her pronunciation. She kissed
him when she was finished, awarding him a quick, light
peck on the lips that left him wide eyed and startled all
over again.

"Come on," she said, rising to her feet, tugging against
his arms, and it didn't matter if she'd just suggested they
go trudging barefooted against a bed of molten rock. He
would have followed her willingly, gladly.

I can't dance, he signed to her as she led him onto the
dance floor.

"Sure you can," she said.

He shook his head, shying back a step. *Lina, I can't
hear the music . . .* he began to sign.

Lina laughed. "You dance with your feet, Brandon,
not your ears," she said. "It's easy, a slow song, even. All
you do is step from side to side."

She drew her arms around him, her fingers settling
lightly against the back of his neck, her body pressing
suddenly, wondrously against him. "Put your arms
around my waist," she said, looking up at him.

He did, sliding his hands around the slim margin of her
waist, the satin of her dress cool and slick against his skin.
He touched the small of her back, where the outward
swell of her buttocks began its shapely descent to the
strong, lean lengths of her legs. Touching her, standing so
close to her, caused his body to react; he felt sudden heat
stir powerfully in his groin, and all at once, his gums tin-
gled, beginning to swell. He could smell her, perfume and
lotion and lipstick and champagne; he could smell the
heady scent of her blood beneath all of these.

He stepped back quickly, his eyes wide, his hands jerking away from her. *I can't do this,* he signed.

"Yes, you can," she said, catching his hands against her own, smiling at him.

He glanced around as she tried to step against him. *People are watching,* he said, feeling foolish. He could see Lina's fellow bridesmaids as they swayed and danced with their partners. They watched out of the corners of their gazes, smiling softly, with the same sort of piteous charm typically reserved for watching a toddler try to climb a steep flight of stairs. *They'll laugh at me—*

Again, she caught his hands, staying them in mid-motion. "No," she said. "They won't."

She slipped her arms around his neck again and there was no escaping her. He closed his eyes for a moment, the fragrance of her body and blood having more powerful, immediate impact on him than any shot of bourbon or glass of champagne. *Christ, she feels good,* he thought.

"I'm going to tap my hand to the beat," she told him, patting her left hand against his shoulder demonstratively. "All you need to do is step with me in time to that. OK? I've taught plenty of people to dance—including Jackson. And he's a big, clumsy ox compared to you. So you can do this, alright?"

She grinned at him, her cheeks glowing with bright, champagne-infused cheer. He was helpless against her, and relaxed in her embrace, relenting. He let his hands slide around her waist again.

"Here we go," Lina said, patting his shoulder lightly. She moved to her left, and he moved with her, stepping abruptly onto her foot. She sucked in a hissing breath through her teeth and he stiffened, trying to pull away, his eyes round and sheepish. "It's alright," she said, tightening her arms around him. She smiled for him and shook her head. "Forget about it. Try again." She offered him a playful little shake. "Come on, loosen up, Brandon. You're as stiff as a board. This is supposed to be fun."

She moved again, and he stepped with her, feeling her body rock gently against him. Her hips swayed as she danced, undulating slowly from side to side, and the more they danced, the closer Brandon drew her against him. After a few long moments, she stopped marking the time against his shoulder with her hand, and he felt her fingertips dance lightly against the nape of his neck, twining in his hair. She was so close to him, when she lifted her face, her cheek brushed against his, and he could feel her breath against his throat, brushing against his ear. He was powerfully, poignantly aware of her heartbeat thrumming through the front of her gown and against his chest, and of the motion of her hips, the wondrous sensation as she moved against him, nearly grinding now, slowly deliberately.

God, I could do this for the rest of my life, he thought, drawing the sweet scent of her hair against his nose. *Every day, always.*

She leaned her head back and smiled as he met her gaze. "See?" she asked. "I told you . . ." He leaned toward her, letting the tip of his nose brush hers, her breath flutter against his lips as she spoke. ". . . this was fun."

Brandon closed his eyes, meaning to kiss her. He felt her hands slip abruptly away from him as she stepped back, and he opened his eyes, bewildered. He watched Lina flap her arm, a quick and angry gesture, her brows furrowed, her mouth open and moving, and he realized someone had come up to them on the dance floor and caught her by the elbow, interrupting them.

Not someone, he thought, recognizing the clean-cut, handsome black man who stood before him on the dance floor. *Jude Hannam.*

Chapter Eleven

"Get your hand off me, Jude," Lina snapped as she wrenched herself loose from his grasp. She'd somehow managed to avoid running into him all evening long, and had even entertained the fleeting and stupid notion that he had already left the reception. That, on top of several glasses of champagne, had left her confidence bolstered, and was why she'd invited Brandon to the dance floor, rather than just suggesting they leave.

That, and she'd wanted to be near to Brandon again. The champagne had left her feeling bold and somewhat reckless. She'd found herself sitting at the dinner table, her mind turning again and again to his kiss outside Joe's Wok. She'd wanted him to kiss her again, touch her once more.

Because I'm falling for him, she'd thought, as he'd leaned toward her while they danced, his nose trailing lightly against hers, his mouth so tantalizingly within kissing distance of her own. *God—hook, line and sinker, head over heels, and all of that other bullshit.*

And then Jude had come along—damn him—and ruined everything by grabbing her by the arm and practically jerking her back away from Brandon's embrace.

"What is going on here?" Jude asked, stumbling slightly and blinking at her through decidedly bleary eyes.

Terrific, she thought. *He's drunk. That's all I need.*

"Leave me alone, Jude," she said, drawing away as he reached for her. "Tell Ashlee to take you home so you can sleep it off."

"What's with you and this guy, Lina?" Jude asked, glaring at Brandon, wobbling unsteadily on his feet. He was more than drunk; Jude was shit-faced, to judge by the pungent whiff of liquor Lina could smell even from her proximity. His voice was loud and sharp, and other couples around them faltered in their dancing, cutting glances in their direction, curious about the disruption.

Lina stepped toward Jude, her brows narrowed as she slipped easily into her cool, composed police officer mode. "Jude," she said quietly, evenly. "You're drunk and causing a scene. Where is Ashlee? You need to go home. I'm not going to talk to you when you're like this."

"Ashlee is in the bathroom," Jude said. "Where she's been for the better part of the last hour, puking up all of the champagne she's guzzled tonight."

Lina blinked at him, somehow not surprised by this. *And yet, here you are,* she said, equally unsurprised. *Leaving her alone and sick as a dog, while you keep on partying.* He hadn't changed a bit; he was the same selfish prick he'd been when he'd left her, and that didn't surprise Lina either.

Jude stepped toward her, pleading with his eyes. "Remember you told me that I only fucked her for the novelty of it, and once that wore off, I'd be sorry? You were right, Lina. She's just . . . eye candy, isn't that what you said once? Something for me to show off at company functions? You were right. You were right all along and I . . ." He sighed, his shoulders sagging, his expression growing mournful. "Christ, I miss you, Lina. I miss *us*. After I saw you yesterday, all I've been thinking about was how good things were between us, and how I fucked that all up."

Lina glanced toward Brandon and found him blinking at her, bewildered and somewhat uncertain. *Brandon, do you mind?* she asked, signing. *Give me a minute, let me talk to him. He's drunk and upset.*

He looked wounded, but nodded, relenting, and she felt terrible. He turned and walked away, shouldering his way through the crowd and leaving the dance floor.

"What's with you and that guy?" Jude asked again as Lina grabbed the sleeve of his suit blazer and dragged him toward the nearest corner. "Christ Almighty, Lina, after all the shit you gave me about Ashlee, and here you are, practically humping some white boy on the god-damn dance floor—"

"Don't make this a color thing, Jude," she snapped, shoving her forefinger in his face. "Don't you dare make this a color thing—you of all people."

"Look, I just want to talk," he said, holding up his hands in supplication. "Let's get out of here, you and me. Forget Ashlee, and fuck that guy. Seeing you yesterday . . . Jesus, it tore me up inside. And today, with you here, and you look so beautiful . . ." He reached for her. All of a sudden, he looked pathetic and miserable to her, his eyes filled with sorrow, remorse, and something deeper, heavier—loneliness.

"Let's get out of here," he said again. "I've been thinking about all of the things I threw away with you—the chance for something like this, a wedding, a family. I want that back, Lina. Let's go somewhere and talk, just the two of us. Let's work this out."

"There's nothing to talk about, Jude," Lina said, ducking away from his hand. God, two days ago, she would have given almost anything to hear him say those words. Two days ago, she'd missed Jude so desperately, sometimes she couldn't breathe for her loneliness. *But that was then,* she thought. *That was before Brandon.* "There's nothing to work out."

"How can you say that?" he asked. "Three years, Lina—we gave each other three years."

"Yes, and you're the one who pissed them away, not me, Jude," she said.

"I know that," he replied. "Didn't I say that? I know I fucked up. God, Lina, please, just give me a chance to

make it up to you. I'm not saying we can pick up where
we left off, but we can try to start all over again."

"No, we can't," Lina said. She turned around and
walked away. "Go home, Jude. Sleep it off. You'll feel like
an ass about this in the morning."

She felt his hand close tightly, painfully against her
arm and he jerked her around. "Let go of me, Jude," she
warned, her brows furrowing, her hands closing into
fists. She could have dislodged him easily, but didn't
want to embarrass him, or herself, by causing any more
of a scene than they already had.

"Not until you talk to me," he said.

"I'm not dealing with you when you're drunk," she
said, trying vainly to pull her arm away. "You want to
talk? Call me when you're sober."

"Lina, goddamn it, I love you—" Jude snapped loudly,
but as he reached to grab her other arm with his free
hand, Brandon suddenly stepped into Lina's view, planting his hand firmly against Jude's shoulder and shoving
him back. Jude stumbled more in surprise than from the
force of Brandon's blow. He tripped gracelessly and
crashed down onto his ass against the floor.

"You son of a bitch . . . !" he said. He blinked up at
Brandon for a wide-eyed, startled moment and then his
face twisted angrily. "Hey, that's my suit!" He glared furiously between Lina and Brandon. "That's my goddamn
Dolce and Gabbana suit, you son of a bitch . . . !"

"Good night, Jude," Lina said, catching Brandon by
the sleeve and wheeling him smartly about, marching
him away. *I told you to let me handle this,* she signed, her
motions sharp and swift.

No, you said let you talk to him, Brandon replied, his gestures equally short. *And he wasn't talking. He was grabbing.*

I can handle him, Lina signed. *I can take care of myself.
Goddamn it, you of all people ought to know that, Brandon. I—*

"You son of a bitch, take off my goddamn suit!" Jude
exclaimed as he grabbed Brandon roughly by the scruff
of the coat and wrenched him around in a floundering

semicircle to face him. His free hand was cocked back, balled into a fist, ready to swing. "Take it off, I—"

Brandon reacted, his fist whipping out reflexively, even as Lina cried out his name to try and stop him. He punched Jude in the face, and Jude flew backward off his feet, crashing to the ground, landing sprawled against the polished tiles of the dance floor.

The crowd fell quiet. The music continued to blare overhead, the strobe lights flashing, but everything else drew to an abrupt and eerie stillness as Jude groaned and sat up slowly, pressing his hand against his nose.

"Jude, are you alright?" Lina asked, hurrying toward him. He blinked at her dazedly, and she drew back to see blood seeping between his fingers.

"My nose," Jude said, only the words came out in a strange, pinched tone: *mah node*. He moved his hand momentarily, and it didn't take a genius to figure out his nose was broken. Already, it had started to swell; it looked puffy and slightly off-center, the tip of it mashed and bloody. Jude blinked at the blood on his fingertips and then toward Brandon. "He . . . he broke my goddamn nose." *He bote mah goddamn node.*

Brandon looked at Lina, stricken. *I'm sorry,* he signed. *I'm sorry, Lina. I didn't mean . . .*

Lina stepped back as several of the groomsmen came forward and helped Jude to his feet. They led him off the dance floor, and he moaned the entire way. "My nose . . . ! Jesus Christ!"

Lina met Brandon's aghast gaze. *I'm sorry,* he signed again, and she walked toward him, taking him by the arm.

"Come on," she said. "Let's get the hell out of here."

She waited until they were outside the reception hall waiting for a taxi before bursting into laughter. She laughed until she doubled over, whooping for breath, tears smarting in her eyes. She stumbled about, her sandals in her hand, her nylons ripped to shreds on the coarse pavement beneath her feet, and she laughed her ass off. She thought she might piss her panties.

Brandon watched her uncertainly. Whenever he could catch her gaze long enough, he'd rub his fist in a circle against the lapel of his jacket: *I'm sorry*. Which would only make Lina laugh all the harder.

She knew he was upset, and she was only bewildering him, so at last, she struggled to control herself. She hiccuped for breath and dabbed at her eyes with her fingertips, trying to spare the damnable mascara she was so unaccustomed to wearing. She stepped toward Brandon just as he moved to sign in apology again, and caught his face between her hands. She rose onto her tiptoes and pressed her fingertip against his lips. "Hush," she said. "Stop apologizing. I could kiss you right now, do you know that?"

His eyes widened slightly in surprise, the corner of his mouth lifting in a hesitant smile, but before anything more could come of the moment, their cab pulled up to the entry and honked its horn.

On the ride home, they sat in silence, neither saying anything for a long time. Lina gazed out the window at the cityscape rolling by and replayed the delicious moment when Brandon had knocked the shit out of Jude over and over again. At last, she reached out, touching Brandon's hand and drawing his gaze.

"Jude is my ex-boyfriend," she said. "He dumped me for the blond woman we saw with him yesterday. You did me a favor back there tonight. Something I have wanted to do personally for three months now. So, thank you, Brandon."

Brandon studied her for a long, nearly quizzical moment before raising his hands. *You're welcome*, he signed. *I think.*

Chapter Twelve

When they arrived back at Jackson's, it was well after midnight. They had stopped by Lina's apartment building along the way, and she'd left Brandon to wait in the cab while she ran up to throw together a change of clothes and grab her toothbrush. He felt badly, disrupting her life as he had, and told her so. *Disrupting, hell,* he'd thought glumly, remembering the looks on people's faces at the wedding reception—Lina's friends, all wide eyed and shocked—after he'd laid Jude out on the floor. *More like* ruining *her life.*

I'll get a hotel room tomorrow, he'd begun to sign, but she'd caught his hands.

"No, you won't," she said. "Jackie said it was fine. You could stay at his place as long as you'd like. And he asked me to keep an eye on his plants, so it's like killing two birds with one stone. It's no big thing, really, Brandon."

He sat on Jackson's sofa while Lina went into the bathroom to wash her face and brush her teeth. He looked out the eastward-facing windows at the nighttime city skyscape, the looming silhouettes of neighboring buildings dotted with pinpoints of light. He forked his fingers through his hair and sighed heavily, jerking against the knot of his tie, loosening it from around his neck.

Not my *tie,* he thought. *Jude's tie. This is Jude's suit. I punched the hell out of him, and here I am, wearing his goddamn suit.*

He shrugged his way out of the coat and stood, pulling his shirt tails loose from his pants and unfettering the gold cuff links. *How the hell did Lina sleep on that thing last night?* he thought, frowning as he glanced down at the couch. He hadn't sat there for more than a moment, but it had been long enough to feel a persistent loose spring poking him in the ass. No matter how he'd fidgeted or shifted, its sharp point had seemed to find him. *That's it,* he thought, kicking off Jude's too-big leather loafers. *She's sleeping in the bed tonight, and I'll take the floor. I may have ruined her life, but I won't ruin her spine, too. Christ, on top of the kitchen counters would be more comfortable.*

Lina walked into the living room, wearing a fresh T-shirt and sweatpants as pajamas. She had washed her face, scrubbing away any hint of the makeup she'd worn for the wedding. Her headful of curls bounced with each step and she tucked wayward tendrils behind her ears before hopping over the back of the sofa. "How are you doing?" she asked, sitting comfortably, looking up at him.

Brandon sighed wearily and sat next to her on the couch. He squirmed slightly, frowning as the wayward spring point found his ass once again. *I'm alright,* he signed.

"Look, stop worrying about Jude," she said, patting her hand against his thigh. "He's an ass when he's sober, and when he's drunk, he's even worse."

I shouldn't have punched him, Brandon signed.

"No," she replied, smiling wanly. "You should have kicked him in the balls." He laughed at this, and she leaned against him, resting her cheek comfortably against his shoulder. "So we're good now?"

At the moment? he thought, glancing down at her, feeling her hair tickle his mouth and nose. *I'd say we're just about perfect.*

He settled for nodding, and she signed to him: *Good. Because I was thinking we could get your car back tomorrow.*

His good mood, brought upon by her proximity and the sweet fragrance of her hair, immediately withered. *I can't afford it,* he replied.

I'll pay for half, she said, and when he lifted his hands to offer protest, she sat up from his shoulder, shaking her head. "Come on, Brandon, we'll wind up spending it anyway on cab fare at this rate," she said aloud. "And those tow companies will only keep the cars a few days before they try to track down the owner. If they trace it back to your grandfather, he's going to know you're here in the city—if he hasn't reported it stolen already."

He hasn't, Brandon signed. Her comment had caught him off guard. He'd never thought about anyone connecting the car to the Grandfather.

"How do you know?" she asked.

Because he wouldn't take that chance, he thought, but said nothing to her. *He'd rather write the car off as a loss than have the police out looking for it—looking for me, risking anyone finding out who—and what—I am.*

But Lina was right. If the tow company was able to run the car's license plate, then the Brethren would know where to find him. It was an inevitability anyway, and only a matter of time, but frankly, Brandon had enjoyed the time he'd spent with Lina—more than anything or anyone's company in a long time—and the idea that he would have to leave the city, and her, left him dismayed. *I'm not ready yet,* he thought, looking at Lina. *I don't want to leave. I've fallen in love with her.*

"We'll get your car back," she said. "And then we'll go see a friend of mine. He was my partner on the force until last year. He's got a lot of money, and he knows a lot of people. I'm going to see if he can hook us up with an attorney, someone who can help you."

Brandon blinked in surprise. *I don't need an attorney,* he said.

"Brandon, come on," Lina said. She reached for him,

draping her hands against his. "I'm not stupid. I know you're in some kind of trouble. I don't know if it's something to do with money—"

I told you it's not, he said, pulling his hands back and signing sharply. *I told you I don't give a shit about my family's money.*

"Well, then it's something else," Lina said. "I don't know what, but I know it's something, because Jackie's scared to death of them finding you, and so are you." He tried to turn away, but she caught him firmly by the chin, forcing him to look at her, to watch her mouth as she spoke. "Tell me what's going on. I want to help you. I'm a cop. Maybe there's something I can—"

No, Lina, he signed, ducking his head away from her. *Look, I know it's your job, but I don't—*

This doesn't have anything to do with my job, Brandon, she signed back, slapping his hands aside, her brows narrowed. *That's not why I want to help you.*

He blinked at her, meeting her gaze and suddenly realizing. He didn't even have to open his mind to her to understand. He wasn't a little boy to her anymore, one of Jackie's students, the teenager whose hair she'd ruffled after a hard-fought game of basketball five years ago. She saw him differently now, just as he saw her, too, and she wanted to help because she cared about him.

Brandon touched her face, brushing his fingertips lightly along her cheek, settling his palm against her. Her heart trembled at this, its tempo quickening, and he sensed it; his touch pleased her. He leaned toward her, holding her gaze, and when he canted his head slightly, she tilted hers up to meet him. He drew her near and closed his eyes, letting his lips brush lightly, gently against hers.

He'd waited the last five years of his life for that moment, that opportunity, having imagined kissing Lina a thousandfold in countless adolescent fantasies. The reality was so much sweeter, by far more wondrous than anything his mind could have fathomed. Her lips melded against his own, pressed in perfect complement, and when the tip of her tongue brushed against him, he opened his mouth, whimpering soundlessly. He moved his free hand to her face, and pulled her against him, tangling his tongue against hers, kissing her deeply.

He felt the intake of her breath against his mouth, could sense the eager, hammering cadence of her heartbeat in his mind. He could smell the hot musk of her blood as it raced suddenly, wildly in her veins; and his body reacted. He felt a tingling warmth in his gums, a tightening in his groin, and he leaned toward Lina, pressing her back against the couch until she lay beneath him, enveloping his hips between her thighs. She clutched at his hair as he drew his lips away from hers. The tips of their noses brushed; her breath fluttered against his lips and she whispered his name, fully aware of the hardening length of him, the swell of his growing arousal pressing through his pants against her.

For a moment he hesitated, uncertain and frightened that he would forget himself, that his body would forget the difference between bloodlust and desire, and that he would hurt her. He could feel his canine teeth throbbing, wanting to drop, his gums aching, and he drew back, breathless and alarmed.

I can't do this, he thought. *Oh, Christ, I can't . . .*

Lina reached for him, touching his face with her hands. "Brandon . . ." she breathed, and he abandoned any reservations at this simple, poignant plea. He kissed her again, trailing his lips to her neck. She craned her head back, guiding him with her hands, leading his mouth to the frantic measure of her pulse beneath her throat. His lips settled there, his tongue drawing against her in slow, deliberate circles. Her fingers tightened in his hair and she writhed beneath him, undulating her hips against him, and forcing the strain against the fly of his pants to grow nearly unbearable. His mind clouded with a wondrous heat and he lost himself, succumbing freely, touching her, tasting her with the same intense passion that had seized him the day before.

His hand moved to her breast, and her nipple hardened

eagerly against his fingertips. He let his mouth follow his hand, sliding his tongue against her through the thin fabric of her T-shirt. He hooked his fingers against the neckline and jerked, ripping seams loose of their moorings, tearing open the front of the shirt. She wore no bra beneath, he drew her nipple lightly between his lips, teasing her with the tip of his tongue, making her clutch at him urgently.

He explored her with his mouth, every wondrous curve and lean muscle between her breasts and belly and upward again to her throat. He reached between them, touching her through her sweatpants, caressing her amazing heat through the confines of the fabric. She guided his hands with her own, shifting her weight, raising her hips so he could slide his hand beneath her waistband, the hem of her panties, and she gasped as he kissed her mouth, as his fingertips brushed through the soft nap of tightly curled hair between her thighs. He touched her further, his fingers delving between her warm, wet folds, and he moaned soundlessly to slip inside of her, to slide first one finger and then another into her wondrously tight sheath. He moved his hand against her, sliding his fingers slowly in and out, venturing deeper with each thrust. Lina moved her hips in time with his hand, and faster still, urging him to match her pace. He drew his lips away from hers and looked down at her, watching as she closed her eyes and rocked against his hand, moving toward a powerful release he could feel coming upon her, tightening through her entire body.

"Stop . . ." she whispered, grabbing his wrist, trying to stay him. She trembled against him, opening her eyes, and he tried to move his hand again, to bring her to the pleasure he knew she wanted desperately. "Stop," she said again, holding him still. He blinked at her, confused, wondering if he'd done something wrong. "Do you have anything?" she asked, and when his confusion only deepened, she smiled. "A condom, Brandon. Do you have a condom?"

He shook his head. He drew his hands reluctantly away from her and sat back somewhat to sign. *I've never . . .* he began, feeling foolish. His fingers hesitated, then moved again, his right index finger tapping his upturned left thumb. *This is my first . . .* he started to sign, but still he couldn't manage the humiliating admission.

Lina caught his hands, drawing his gaze. "Hush," she said, smiling gently at him. She pulled against his arms, drawing him toward her again. "Come here."

She caught his face between her hands and kissed him deeply, settling him against her once more. She reached between them, unfastening his fly, pushing the slacks away from his hips. For a moment, they laughed together, nose to nose as they wriggled and shrugged their way out of their clothes, and then she smiled at him again, kissing him, using her hands and her long, lean thighs to guide him inside of her. Brandon gasped at the sensation of it, her wet, amazing heat enveloping him. She urged him deeper, her fingers hooked against the small of his back, and then deeper still by opening her legs farther, allowing him greater access. She showed him how to move, the pace to set, the rhythm that pleased her, and he met it gladly, eagerly.

He started slowly, but with her hands to guide him, her quickening breath against his mouth to encourage him, he began to move more quickly, driving himself into her. His mouth abandoned hers, and he took her hips between his hands, lifting her from the couch, pulling her against him to meet each thrust. He looked down at her, and she was beautiful to him, her body glossed in sweat, her hair a thick mess of curls spread about her head, her eyes closed, her hands clutching at the sofa cushions, her breath hiccupping as again, he drove her to the brink of release. *God, I'm in love with this woman,* he realized.

This time, she didn't beg him to stop, and he delivered her. Her entire body went rigid, her muscles tightening against and around him and she arched her back, crying out. That powerful, wondrous, gripping pressure coaxed his own shuddering climax, and Brandon gasped sharply, crumpling forward, shocked by the intensity.

He tucked his head against her shoulder and trembled, breathless and exhausted. Lina stroked his hair gently; he felt her lips settle lightly against the crown of his head. *This is what I want,* he thought, closing his eyes. *Right here, all of this. I want to be with Lina. I want a life that's just like this.*

But then the tip of his tongue accidentally brushed against the sharp, elongated tips of his canine teeth, and he stiffened, his eyes flying wide, his breath caught. His teeth had lowered at some point during their lovemaking. He brought his hand to his face, his fingertips against his lips and could feel them. They hadn't dropped all of the way, thank Christ; his sexual release had likely stopped their descent, but they were long enough now to be noticeable to Lina if she saw his mouth.

Oh, God, he thought, as she tucked her fingertips beneath his chin and tried to coax him into looking up at her. He pressed his lips together in a firm line and peeped up at her, keeping his chin pressed against her bosom, his mouth somewhat hidden against the side swell of her breast.

"You OK?" she asked. Her cheeks were flushed in the aftermath of her pleasure, the caramel of her skin deepened to dusky hues along the apples of her cheeks. She smiled at him and he smiled back, keeping his lips together as he nodded. He cupped his hand by her belly to draw her gaze, and rolled it slightly outward, away from her in a quick sign: *Tired.*

She laughed. "Me, too. That . . . that was something else." *You're something else, Brandon Noble,* she thought, and he heard her plainly in his mind.

God, you don't know half of it, Lina, he thought, sliding sideways off of her, letting his feet hit the floor. He stood, heading quickly for the bathroom before she noticed his mouth, his newly elongated canines. He motioned behind him as he walked away. *Be right back.*

Chapter Thirteen

Lina watched Brandon walk toward the bathroom. She felt breathless and tremulous, her heart still racing. She had never experienced an orgasm like that in her life; pleasure had swept over her, pounding into her in heavy, shuddering waves, over and over, leaving her spent and stunned, unable to move, much less think. *And that was only his first time,* she thought, admiring the play of light from the kitchen against the curves of his buttocks, outlining the lines and muscles in his back and legs as he disappeared down the hall. *Imagine what he could do with some more practice.*

She giggled at this, wrapping her arms around her middle and lying back against the couch cushions again. The day had been disastrous, the wedding ruined, the confrontation with Jude every bit as horrible as she'd dreaded. She'd spent the day forcing smiles, half-blinded by camera flashes, her feet aching, her face caked in makeup and now Melanie—whom Lina had considered her friend since childhood—would damn likely never speak to her again. *But I'd do it all again,* she thought with a smile. *God, every last moment of it.*

She closed her eyes, still able to smell Brandon, his fragrance against her skin. She tried not to think too long or hard about what she'd done, but rather, tried to revel in the simple, residual pleasure of it for a moment or two longer. She knew once that wore off, and reality hit her, she was going to feel ashamed of herself.

And let's not even consider what Jackie's going to do to me when he finds out, she thought, pressing her lips together to stifle a groan. *Christ, what a night.*

She was actually charmed and more than a little flattered that Brandon had wanted her as his first lover. She'd never been anyone's first at anything before; even hers had come at the hands, mouth, and hips of a man far more experienced than she. *He chose me,* she thought, a wonderful warmth spreading through her at this realization. *Brandon chose me.*

She sat up, leaning over to pick up her sweatpants. Her T-shirt still lay draped over her shoulders, the front of it ripped open. She fingered the torn edges of fabric and giggled again. *He ripped my clothes off me. Just like in a movie. Jesus, no one's ever ripped my clothes off before.*

She stood, stepping back into her panties and drawing the pants over her hips. Her overnight duffel bag rested in a chair nearby. She dug out a fresh T-shirt and pulled it over her head. She glanced over her shoulder toward the hallway, wondering what was taking Brandon so long. After a curious moment, she followed him, stealing into Jackson's bedroom and over to the bathroom doorway. She found him leaning over the sink basin, examining his reflection closely in the mirror. He had his upper lip pulled back from his teeth, the way a person might if they were checking for food bits. He caught sight of her through the mirror and jumped, his dark eyes wide as he swung toward her.

"Everything OK?" she asked, and he nodded. "You sure?"

He nodded again, but she had the distinct impression he was lying. He was acting too skittish and uncertain around her now; she didn't miss the way he took a hedging step back toward the toilet, as if he didn't want her drawing too closely to him. She felt a dull but distinctive ache in her gut.

Oh, shit. Here we go—the brush off. Just like with Jude, only worse. This time, it only took one night, not three years for him to get sick of me.

Brandon blinked at her, his face softening, as if he'd somehow read her mind or sensed her sudden anxiety. He stepped toward her, surprising her as he caught her face between his hands and kissed her. His mouth settled firmly against hers, his lips parting, his tongue delving deeply, as if he had every right and reason in the world to do so. He walked her backward, guiding her toward the bed, and when her knees struck the mattress and she sat, he pressed her down against the bedspread. *You're beautiful, Lina,* he signed, sweeping his fingers in a counterclockwise motion in front of his face.

He placed his hands on either side of her and leaned over, kissing her again, making her smile. Whatever had happened, whatever had upset him, it was over now. *Really* over, to judge by the sudden, hardening heat she could feel pressing against her through her pants. She giggled against his mouth and he smiled for her.

Let's leave these off for a while, he suggested, sitting back, and then he reached for her hips, tugging against the waistband of her sweatpants.

Lina laughed. *Sounds good,* she signed in reply.

Several hours later, Brandon woke with a start, his eyes flying wide in the darkness, his mind snapping instantly from sound sleep to sharp clarity. He had been dreaming of moonlight flashing against dark water, of kneeling along the banks of an anonymous river and ripping the throat out of an old man in tattered clothing who thrashed beneath him.

He lay spooned against Lina, his arm draped over her waist, her fingers twined through his, and her nude body was soft and warm, molded perfectly to his own. He lifted his head from the pillows, peering past her toward the digital bedside clock. It was nearly four o'clock in the morning.

Jesus, he thought, sighing heavily and closing his eyes. *Just a dream.*

He'd never had a nightmare as vivid or horrifying before; in it, he'd been seized with the bloodlust and unable—not to mention unwilling—to resist it. He'd felt it within his mind, swollen, hot and heavy, clouding his senses, making him focus on nothing else but the urge to feed, the need for blood. The smell of it racing through the old man's veins as he'd struggled in terror had left Brandon ravenous, and he'd dreamed of wrenching the man's head back by the hair and sinking his fangs, fully extended and ready, deep into the meat of his neck.

A shivering sensation prickled his skin and danced through the fine hairs along his forearms, at the nape of his neck, and at this, Brandon sat up fully, drawing his arm away from Lina. She stirred somewhat, squirming briefly beneath the sheets before settling herself comfortably and falling still again.

Brandon tried to forget about the dream and looked around the shadow-draped room, studying the play of moonbeams and streetlamp light coming through the window off the floor, furniture, and doorways. He sensed something within his mind, a peculiar whispering sound, like distant static on the radio. His head was throbbing again, the dull ache rekindled inside his skull and he frowned.

He wasn't immediately alarmed, or at least, not as he'd been when Lina had left him alone in the cab the day before in front of that strange building, when he'd experienced a similar sensation. It had been weaker then, much weaker than now, but it had proven a false alarm, and he'd panicked for nothing. *It can't be the Brethren,* he thought, climbing out of bed. He reached down and grabbed his jeans, stepping into them. *They can't have found me, not yet. Even if they followed me to the city, they can't have found me here. Jackson isn't listed in the phone book. They won't know how to find this place.*

Besides, his telepathic abilities had been going nothing but bug-shit and out of his control ever since he'd left Kentucky. For all he knew, he could be picking up sensations from miles away, halfway across the city, or even just one of the neighboring apartments.

Or it could just be my imagination, he thought, as he padded slowly toward the bedroom door. *Something left over from that weird-ass dream. My nerves are all on edge.*

He glanced over his shoulder once as he finished buttoning his fly. Lina was sleeping, curled on her side, her body gracefully draped in pale bed linens. For a moment, he didn't move; he remained poised in the doorway watching her sleep.

God, she's beautiful, he thought. He still couldn't believe she'd let him make love to her—not once or twice, but repeatedly, and for hours. They had only just succumbed at last to exhaustion an hour or so earlier.

He wanted to return to her, to strip off his jeans and duck beneath the sheets again. Not just to make love to her, although the simple thought of that left dim heat stoking in his groin, but to hold her, to draw the sweet fragrance of her skin and hair against his nose, and feel the heat from her body seeping into his own. He wanted to snuggle against her and forget about the strange whispering in his mind, the horrible nightmare that had wrenched him from sleep.

The monster I dreamed I'd become.

That strange whispering, tickling sensation shivered through his mind again, and he turned to look down the corridor toward the living room beyond.

Nothing here, he thought, his brows narrowing. *There's nothing here. It's just my imagination.*

Nevertheless, he walked down the hallway, his footsteps light and cautious, his gaze sharp. He cut his eyes around the broad expanse of the living room, studying all of the shadows carefully. Jackson's towering assortment of tropical plants cast irregular swatches of darkness everywhere. The ceiling fan had been left on, and the breeze stirred palm leaves and fern fronds, making shadows dance in constant, distracting motion.

There's nothing here, Brandon thought, following the kitchen wall, glancing over the breakfast bar into the empty room beyond. In a nearby corner, Jackson had stowed an umbrella stand. Aside from a few umbrellas, plus some hand-carved walking sticks from Peru, Jackson kept his *katana* there; an exquisite, tempered-steel Japanese sword housed in a simple, wooden scabbard. Brandon curled his hand around the unadorned grip and slowly, quietly lifted the sword from the stand. He'd only used the blade a time or two in his youth, under Jackson's tutelage and close watch, but he'd practiced plenty of times with its solid-wood counterpart, a *bokuto* sparring sword.

There's nothing here, he thought again, but he wasn't about to take that chance. Not with Lina asleep in the next room. He drew the *katana* free from its sheath, watching light filtering in through the windows gleam along the polished length of its blade. He set the scabbard aside on the breakfast bar, gripped the sword hilt between his hands and stepped forward into the living room.

He crossed to the patio doors, then returned toward the kitchen. There was nothing but the bobbing, fluttering shadows of plants moving in the fan's breeze—and that faint, prickling sensation that let him know he was not alone. He glimpsed a flutter of light against the flat of the *katana*, a reflection of sudden, swift movement, and then something plowed into his back. He staggered forward with the force of the blow, startled and knocked off balance, and his sharp gasp of surprise cut short as a strong, slender arm snapped suddenly beneath the shelf of his chin, crushing against his windpipe.

Hello, Brandon, his sister Emily seethed inside his mind, as her fingers closed fiercely in his hair, and her long legs coiled viselike around his waist from behind. *It's so good to see you again. We've been—*

Brandon reacted instinctively, ducking forward, tucking his chin. He grabbed her by the arm and threw her forcefully over his shoulder. He didn't hold back or offer her any restraint; he threw with all of his might, and she sailed across the living room, clear over the breakfast bar and into the kitchen. She smashed headlong into a row of cabinets and then crumpled beyond his view to the floor.

Shit! Brandon thought, his heart pounding, his eyes flown wide in panic. *How the fuck did she find me?* He scrambled backward, the sword still in hand, but when he stumbled against someone standing behind him, he whirled, wide eyed with new fright.

We followed your scent, little brother, Caine told him, his hand clamping against Brandon's throat and shoving him back. Caine slammed him into the wall with enough force to crush the drywall beneath him, to rattle the wits from Brandon's skull, and make him drop the *katana* to the ground. *The stink of your weakness clings to you—pathetic and unmistakable.*

Brandon drove the heel of his hand mightily into Caine's face, smashing his nose and sending his brother floundering back in surprise. The moment Caine's hand was loose from his throat, Brandon struggled to recover. If he hesitated, he was dead, and he knew it. He swung his hand around and down, slamming his fist into the side of Caine's head, staggering him anew.

Fuck you, Caine! he yelled in his mind, his brows furrowed as he threw another powerful, sweeping, diagonal punch at his brother's face, and then another, and another; a relentless volley that sent Caine retreating, backpedaling and stumbling. *I'm not going back! You can tell the Grandfather that! Have him do his worst—let all of you come! I'm not going back!*

The Grandfather is no longer interested in what you have to say, Caine seethed, grabbing Brandon by the arm as he swung another punch. *And neither am I.* He head-butted Brandon, seizing hold of him by the hair and jerking him forward. Their foreheads smashed together and

Brandon staggered back, dazed and reeling. He crumpled to his knees, struggling to clear his head.

Caine recovered more quickly and again closed his fist in Brandon's hair. He wrenched Brandon's head back and forced him to his feet. Brandon's fists had bloodied Caine's mouth, but Brandon could see those wounds healing, the bloody fissures in his lips closing. He'd fed recently, then, and well. Nothing accelerated their already-heightened healing abilities like an overindulgent feeding, and Brandon thought of the nightmare he'd suffered, the dream in which he'd imagined tearing open the old man's throat and gorging himself on blood. *Not me,* he thought, horrified. *Then it was Caine. It must have been. I sensed him somehow, even in my sleep!*

"Did you think you could hide?" Caine said, grasping Brandon's throat again, hoisting him into the air and holding him aloft. "Did you really have such pathetic hope, Brandon? Abandon it, then. You're—"

He turned to look over his shoulder, his hand falling away from Brandon's neck, sending him crumpling to the floor. Brandon clutched at his throat, whooping momentarily for breath, and looked up, trying to see what had distracted Caine. *Oh, no,* he thought in dismay. Lina stood nearby in a T-shirt and nothing else beneath, her pistol clasped between her hands, aimed directly for Caine. *Oh, Christ, no, no, please, no . . . !*

Lina! he signed, his hands frantic, his palms swatting past one another. *Run! Run, Lina! For the love of God, run!*

Lina didn't know who in the hell the tall young man with the waist-length fall of heavy, dark hair was, but as he walked boldly, swiftly across the room toward her, she leveled the barrel of her nine-millimeter squarely at his chest. "I said, *freeze,* asshole!" she shouted.

She'd awoke with a frightened start at a terrible clatter from the kitchen and living room, as if someone was chucking Buicks by catapult headlong into the cabinetry.

She's managed to jerk on a T-shirt and snatch her gun from the bedside table before darting out of the bedroom, and that's when she'd discovered the long-haired man throttling Brandon.

"You smell like sex," he told her as he approached, not slowing his gait in the least, despite the gun trained at him. She shied back, uncertain all at once, unnerved by his boldness. "You were fucking him, weren't you? His stink is all over you."

"Get back!" she cried, pulling the trigger, feeling the gun buck against her hand. The man didn't have a weapon that she could see, and he hadn't raised a hand against her, but she'd felt immediately, distinctly threatened all the same. It was as if he marked the leading edge of some encroaching thunderstorm, and the air all around him literally trembled.

The bullet slammed into his chest, near the vertex of his shoulder, and he stumbled, his eyes widening as if in surprise. He halted momentarily, bringing his hand to his wound.

"Put your hands up," Lina told him, her voice quavering. "I'm a police officer. You're under arrest."

When the man drew his fingertips back, they were spotted in blood, and his brows narrowed, his dark eyes seeming to punch clear through Lina's skull. "Bitch," he said, his voice hoarse with sudden fury. "I will bleed you for that."

She didn't know what the fuck *that* meant, but it sounded bad and she decided she didn't want to find out. "Put your hands up," she snapped. When he ignored her completely, and began to move again, marching toward her, she shied back. "I said put your goddamn hands up!"

She shot him again, the roar from the pistol deafening in the confines of the corridor. He lurched, plowing into the wall, crying out as he clutched at his opposite shoulder. He glared at her from beneath furious brows, and then he shambled toward her again.

Oh, shit, she thought, backing away.

"You bitch," he hissed, and then he shook his head once, twice. She cringed at a horrible, sodden sound, the cracking of bone, and then she shrank back again as he turned to her, opening his mouth wide. His canine teeth had suddenly become enormous, long and hooked, jutting down from his upper palate like something out of a B-grade vampire movie. The snapping she'd heard had been his lower jaw wrenching out of socket, widening the circumference of his open mouth in order to accommodate those horrifying teeth.

Oh, shit . . . !

She couldn't see the whites of his eyes anymore. It was dark in the hallway, and she was frightened, nearly frantic, so it might have been her imagination, but she could swear that his eyes had turned black, the dark pools of his irises spreading out, engulfing the surface of his corneas.

What the hell is he? she thought, because those black eyes met hers and held her fast; just as Brandon's gaze had seemed to reach out and somehow physically restrain her the day before, so, too, did this man's. His dark, featureless eyes suddenly bore into her, and she could feel him *inside of her head,* a cold, slithering shadow creeping behind her eyes, seeping through her skull, immobilizing her.

Oh, my God, what the hell is he?

Brandon caught the man from behind just as he came within three steps of Lina. He seized hold of the man's arm and whirled him smartly about, slamming him back against the wall, and Lina saw a wink of pale light against silver—her brother's Japanese sword, clenched in Brandon's hand. He rammed the blade through the long-haired man's gut, punching in one side of his torso and out the other, shoving so forcefully, the leading edge of the blade speared out of the man's lower back and into the wall, puncturing the drywall and pinning him in place.

Lina screamed in shocked horror, the gun wavering, nearly tumbling from her hand. When Brandon reached for her, holding out his hand in mute, desperate beckon, she drew back, shaking her head. "How . . . how did you do that?" she whimpered. *He drove that sword through a man's gut—and clear through the wall. No one is strong enough to do that.* "How did you do that?" she cried. "What the hell is going on?"

Brandon's fingertips brushed against the front of her shirt, grabbing hold. He jerked her toward him in stumbling tow, and she shrieked as the long-haired man impaled against the wall snatched at her, pawing at her arms, yanking at her hair. He snapped at her like a deranged, rabid hound, his horrifying mouth lolling wide on its dislocated hinges, his teeth snapping in the open air scant centimeters from her face.

"Oh, God!" she cried, as Brandon tried to shield her, swinging his fist around again and again, pummeling the man until his hands fell away. "Oh, God, let go of me! Let go of me, goddamn it!"

"There's no place you can hide!" the man screamed at them, thrashing against the sword, struggling to free himself as Brandon pulled her past. "We'll find you! We'll come for you!" He grasped the hilt in his hands and strained to jerk it loose. Lina watched him in horrified disbelief, even as Brandon hooked his arm around her waist and hauled her forcibly for the front door. "We'll never stop coming for you, you bastard!"

Brandon reached the door and fumbled frantically with the deadbolts and chain. A blur of movement caught Lina's gaze, and she turned, screaming as a woman launched herself over the breakfast bar separating the kitchen and living room, leaping at Brandon. Like the man in the hallway, her mouth was flung impossibly wide, and her teeth were horrifically long. Lina only had a fleeting, split-second glimpse of her eyes, but they looked black, too, with no discernable irises. The woman screeched, her voice piercing, inhumanly shrill, and her shag-cropped, dark brown hair splayed crazily around her face.

"Brandon—!" Lina screamed, and he pivoted, his eyes widening. The woman slammed into him, smashing him against the door. The wood splintered on its hinges at the impact; only the deadbolts kept it from collapsing out into the corridor.

Brandon crashed to the floor, with the woman atop him, her fists flying, a furious garble of inarticulate sounds shrieking from her mouth. He managed to draw his leg up between them, to plant his foot against her belly, and heaved mightily, punting her off him. She sailed across the room as if she were made of no more than linen; she smashed down atop Jackson's glass-and-brass coffee table, shattering it beneath her. When she sat up, her face was blood streaked from dozens of cuts. Her brows furrowed and she scrambled to her feet, rushing at Brandon again. Just as she leaped in the air, meaning to pounce at him, Lina remembered the nine-millimeter dangling heavily in her hand. She jerked her gun arm up and out, squeezing the trigger once, twice, three times, firing more from instinct than aim. Two slugs struck the woman's torso, and she jerked violently. The last punched into her forehead, sending her brains scattering out of the backside of her skull and across Jackson's polished, pine floors. She crumpled to the floor like a runaway marionette with its strings abruptly severed.

From behind Lina, the man pinned to the wall howled shrilly, hoarsely. "No!" he screamed. "*Emily, no! No!* Oh, you bitch, I'll kill you for that! *I will bleed you dry, you bitch!* I'll rip your goddamn heart out through your mouth and shove it up your goddamn—"

There was more, but she didn't hear it. Brandon scrambled to his feet. His hand closed viselike around Lina's wrist, and he jerked open the remaining locks, shoving the broken door out into the corridor. He stumbled over it and began to run, dragging Lina in tow, leaving the man to scream in protest behind them.

Chapter Fourteen

Lina didn't remember much after that for a while. She had dim recollection of Brandon leading her down the street, both of them barefooted and running down the cold, deserted sidewalk. At some point, he hailed a cab, and she vaguely recalled sitting in the backseat beside him. He'd elbowed her, needing her to talk to the driver. *Hotel,* he'd finger-spelled at her. *Lina, please, tell him to take us to a hotel.*

If the driver had been disturbed by their appearance— Brandon beaten up and blood-spattered, dressed in only his blue jeans, and Lina in a T-shirt, her legs and ass flapping in the breeze—he said nothing that Lina could remember. *Hell, he's probably seen worse,* she thought, sitting on the edge of the hotel room's full-sized bed. *We were probably typical fare for this time of the night.*

This time of the night was now almost six in the morning. The cabbie had delivered them to the Bluebell Inn, a musty, seedy motel in a rundown section of town. Thankfully, Brandon had his wallet in his jeans pocket, so he'd covered the cab fare and the room. Like the driver, the clerk at the hotel had said nothing to them at all. *Maybe couples come in here all the time like this,* Lina thought, looking down at herself. *Brandon in no shirt, and me in no pants. Well, at least between the two of us, we can throw a whole outfit together.*

She snickered slightly, her shoulders jerking. Her eyes swam with tears and she blinked down at her lap, struggling to compose herself. *I'm in shock,* she thought, trembling. *That's all. I've got to pull myself together. Just a few deep breaths, that's what I need.*

Brandon genuflected in front of her, offering her a paper cup filled with water. She took it from him, her hands shaking, slopping water over the rim and against her thighs. She took a few sips and then cradled the cup between her hands. "What . . . what the fuck happened back there?" she whispered, her voice hoarse and tremulous. She looked up, meeting Brandon's gaze. "Who were those people?"

He drew his fist against his cheek and then brought his hands together in front of him, holding his index fingers extended outward, parallel to the ground. *My sister,* he said, and he finger-spelled her name. *Emily. And my brother, Caine.*

Lina stared at him, her stomach twisting in a horrified knot. "Sister?" she breathed. *Oh, my God. I just . . . I just shot and killed his sister.*

"But they . . . their faces," she said. "I saw their faces, and you . . . you stabbed him, Brandon. You pinned him to the wall with a sword. And their faces . . ."

She'd seen suspects so hyped up on methamphetamines or crack that repeated jolts from a stun gun hadn't as much as slowed them down. She'd once seen a speed freak so out of control and delusional, it had taken six cops—all strapping grown men—to subdue him. She'd seen her fair share and then some of some freaky-ass shit, but she had never in her life witnessed anything like she had that night. *Their eyes turned black,* she thought, a chill shivering through her at the memory. *Their jaws had broken open, and their teeth . . . !*

"They weren't human," she whimpered, her tears spilling down her cheeks. "They . . . oh, God, they weren't human!"

Brandon pressed his hand against her face. He shook his head, his eyes sorrowful, as if to say, *No, they weren't*.

Brandon left her to take a shower, and she listened to the sound of running water from the hotel room's cramped, dingy bathroom. When she was satisfied that he was occupied, she leaned across the head of the bed, reaching for the telephone.

Rene answered the line on the fifth ring, just as she was about to give up. "Hullo," he said, his voice husky and hoarse.

"Rene?" she said, closing her eyes in abject relief. *Oh, thank Christ.* "Rene, are you awake? I really need to—"

"Lina, *chère*," he interrupted, sounding pleased . . . and something more. She glanced at the clock. It was six-fifteen in the morning. It wasn't even dawn yet, and Rene was already wasted. "How was the wedding? I'm awake, yes." She heard a rustling as he turned away from the phone and then groaned. "I don't think I've even been to bed yet. I've been . . . busy."

She heard a woman's muffled giggle filter through the line, and felt new, frustrated tears well in her eyes. "Damn it, Rene," she whispered, trembling.

"What?" he asked, the good humor in his voice faltering as he at last realized something was wrong. "Lina, what is it?"

"Couldn't you just be sober for once?" she asked, her tears spilling. "I . . . I just . . . goddamn it, Rene, I really needed you this time."

She hung up on him, setting the receiver back in its cradle. *I really needed you to tell me I'm not crazy,* she thought, and she clapped her hands over her face, bursting into tears.

Brandon stood in the shower, his eyes closed, feeling the stinging spray of hot water pelt the crown of his head. It spilled down, following the contours of his face and neck, streaming down his body in thin, fast-moving rivulets. He felt it dripping from his lips, the tip of his nose, sliding into his ears. It helped to disguise his tears, though not the hitching of his chest, his soft, occasional, anguished gasps.

He wanted to call Tessa. He'd never wished for anything so badly in his life. He felt frightened and lonely, scraped suddenly raw inside, and God, he wanted to curl up against her, to tuck his head against his twin sister's shoulder, as he had when he'd been a boy, and feel her arms around him, comforting him.

Once upon a time, Brandon and Tessa had been amazingly close, and she'd always been able to sense when he was hurting, frightened, or upset. That had been before her bloodletting. After that, everything between them had been different, even though she'd tried to tell him it wasn't.

He'd known she would come on the day he'd ran away from the farm, the morning of his bloodletting. He'd been alone in his room, staring out the window at the rolling hills of the horse farm. He could feel the morning chill creeping in through the thick planes of glass. He saw Daniel and Emily playing together in the yard. Emily chased him, her hands outstretched, threatening to tickle.

You let a child go in your place because you're a coward. Caine's words had echoed in his mind as he watched Emily reach out, tagging Daniel lightly with her fingertips, her mouth open in laughter. *You're weak and pathetic, a goddamn coward hiding behind Father and his pity for you.*

And then he had known Tessa was there, hovering in the doorway behind him like a shadow. He sensed her, a prickling sensation within his mind, and turned. She regarded him cautiously, moving her fingers through her dark hair, tugging a shank off her face to tuck behind her ear.

She didn't come immediately toward him. There seemed to be something besides the silence separating them, and he realized sadly it was because she really was different now, despite all of her protests. Things had changed between them because she had changed; she looked at him through different eyes and he knew a part of her regarded him the way Caine, Emily, the Grandfather, and everyone else did—coldly, contemptuously.

Tessa held her pointe shoes in one hand by the tangled ribbon lacings. The pink satin toes had long since worn grey and split open, and the layers of moleskin carefully tacked over wore away with alarming frequency. She loved ballet. She was an extraordinarily talented dancer. Just as their father had paid for Jackson to come and tutor Brandon, he'd hired the most expensive and exclusive instructors to come and teach Tessa ballet. He'd built a large studio on the third floor of the great house just for her, and before her bloodletting, before she'd married Martin and left, Tessa had spent hours every day practicing and performing. Brandon wondered if she'd ever dreamed of fleeing the farm like he did, of making a life somewhere among the humans for herself as a dancer.

"I was hoping to get some practice in upstairs," she said, smiling awkwardly, shyly at him. "I thought maybe you'd want to help me with some lifts, like we used to, but then I . . ." She laughed. "I can't get my feet in the shoes. They're too tight."

Her whole angle of conversation bewildered him; he'd been sure she was going to talk to him about the bloodletting, offering him more false reassurances of how she'd be there with him, help him through it. He brought his hand up to his forehead and then out in front of his chest, folding his three middle fingers inward to his palm: *Why?*

"My feet are swollen," she said, smiling at him mysteriously, pressing her hand lightly against her stomach. "My ankles, too. I . . . I'm pregnant, Brandon."

He blinked at her, dumbfounded, and she nodded. "I'm going to be a mommy."

He forgot about the bloodletting, his plans to flee,

and how she'd been a stranger to him for the past three years. In that moment, his heart softened and he rushed to her. He drew her into his arms in a warm embrace, and when her arms wrapped around his neck, he lifted her from her feet, spinning her gently, making her laugh against his ear.

Oh, Tessa, that's fantastic! he signed after setting her down. *Congratulations! How are you feeling?*

"I'm OK," Tessa said, still smiling. "A little sick, but only if I eat anything in the morning. Or anything really greasy. Or anything with milk in it." She laughed, then added, "Or anything other than chicken soup."

He smiled at her. *What does Martin think?*

Her face clouded for a moment, nearly imperceptible. A stranger, or someone else in the family even, might not have caught the dark look, but Brandon still knew his sister, despite the differences and distance that had come between them, and didn't miss it.

"He's excited, of course," she said at last, smiling brightly, a forced and strained effort.

How far along? Brandon asked. He took her by the elbow and led her toward the bed.

"Not much. Three months, maybe a little more." She drew to a halt and laughed. "Brandon, what are you doing?"

Shouldn't you be sitting down or something? he asked.

She laughed again, flapping her arm to shake him loose. "I'm fine, Brandon, really." She reached up and touched his face briefly, fondly. "Do you want to feel it? It's tiny, but it moves sometimes and I can sense it, its little heartbeat. It's like this bright, wonderful little patch of warmth in my belly. And it's growing every day."

She reached for his hand but he shied back, shaking his head. *I can't, Tessa,* he thought. *I don't know how, and my telepathy is—*

"I'll help you," she said. She pulled her shirt up, pressing his palm against her stomach. "Open your mind, Brandon." He did, and was immediately aware of the baby somewhere inside of her; it was as if he could feel the fluttering, persistent rhythm of its heartbeat from deep within her uterus against his hand, and see it within his mind, a pinpoint of light, something golden and glowing.

He blinked at Tessa in stupefied fascination and she laughed, grinning. "Pretty cool, huh?"

It's amazing, he thought. She sat down on his bed, lying back, letting her long legs dangle over the side. He stretched out beside her, and they rolled over, facing each other, as they'd always done as children.

"I'm sorry about Gallaudet . . . and your hands," she whispered, nearly nose to nose with him. Her dark eyes, so much like his own, were round and sorrowful. "Are you better now?"

He drew his hand between them, waggling his fingers demonstratively, making her smile. In that moment, in his room, on his last day at the farm, she had been the old Tessa again, *his* Tessa, but now she was gone. He'd never see her again, and if he did, it would be because she'd come for him, to bring him back to Kentucky, to deliver him to the Beneath.

Oh, God, I couldn't fight her, he thought, anguished. *I . . . I could never hurt Tessa.*

He thought about Emily, and his heart ached. *She was too young for the bloodletting. Caine's right. She went too soon, and it was my rightful place.*

Like Tessa, Emily had changed after her bloodletting, but her transition had been even more noticeable. In childhood, Emily had played often with Brandon and Tessa. It was though a part of her had broken when she'd killed for the first time. Something in her mind had changed, turning spiteful and feral, and she'd never recovered.

It was because she was too young, he thought. *It's my fault, what happened to her. All my fault that she's dead.*

As he stood in the shower in the dingy hotel bathroom, Brandon clapped his hand over his eyes and shuddered with silent sobs.

* * *

When he stepped out of the bathroom, swatting at his dark hair with a towel, he realized Lina was asleep, curled on her side on the bed. She'd been waiting for her turn in the shower, and slept with a towel wrapped around her torso. Her T-shirt lay in a rumpled pile on the floor beside the bed. Brandon went to her and knelt, lifting the shirt in one hand and brushing the cuff of his knuckles against her cheek with the other. *I love you, Lina,* he thought, wishing desperately he could have one moment of voice, no matter how fleeting, so that he could wrap his mouth around those precious, wonderful, poignant sounds and let her know.

He drew the T-shirt over his head and slipped on his jeans. He went to the bedside table and wrote her a quick note on a small notepad embossed with the Bluebell Inn logo, in case she woke in his absence. *Gone to buy clothes. Be right back.*

He pocketed the key and left the room. He'd noticed a Dollar-A-Rama store just up the street from the motel last night from the cab. He hoped like hell that they'd be open that early in the morning, and tried not to pay attention to the fact that the pavement beneath his bare feet was cold and damp. He walked briskly, his hands shoved in his hip pockets, his shoulders hunched against the chill.

He caught sight of a pair of young men watching him from beneath the motel's entrance awning as he cut across the street. A couple of quick glances over his shoulder revealed they followed his progress with undisguised interest, and he could sense their attention in his mind, feel their dark eyes trailing in his footsteps. He found himself suddenly growing anxious, his throat and chest tightening to think of Lina, alone and asleep in the room.

She'll be fine, he told himself, his brows narrowing. *She's still got her pistol, and at least one bullet left. She knows how to take care of herself.*

The Dollar-A-Rama had just opened when he arrived, and he found himself the solitary customer inside. He didn't bother with a basket or cart, because he didn't plan on browsing. He draped two pairs of sweat pants and two oversized, zipper-front hoodies over his arm. He grabbed a package of plain white T-shirts, and two pairs of plastic flip-flips.

The clerk eyed him somewhat warily as she rang up each item. She folded the clothes neatly between her hands, pressing each down into a large, yellow plastic bag. "You been in a fight?" she asked, and Brandon nodded, handing her two twenty-dollar bills. His face remained battered and bruised from his battle with Caine; it would be a few days at best before the telltale discoloration faded altogether.

The clerk made change in the same, slow, damn-near grating fashion that she'd used to pack his bag, and he snatched it from her hurriedly. He could feel her watching him as he tromped away, tucking the bag under his arm and hurrying back toward the motel.

Lina was still sleeping when he slipped back into the room. It was just as well, he realized. *I can't stand good-byes.*

He'd made up his mind in the shower that morning, although somewhere in the back of his mind, he'd known all along—from the moment he'd first realized who she was, as she'd pinned him against Jackson's bed two days earlier. She would be in danger as long as he was with her. The Brethren were never going to stop looking for him. They would come again. That it was Caine and Emily who had found him first—two relatively young and inexperienced members, little more than pups compared to some of the more seasoned veterans among the Brethren—still shocked him. He'd been able to hold his own against them, but only barely, and not without Lina's help.

Brandon had spent his life around Thoroughbreds. He understood the concept of *track odds*—and he knew that his would be significantly less, bordering on abysmal, if one of the more venerable Brethren, like his father or uncle, came for him.

Lina had killed Emily, but without Brandon to draw them, the Brethren would never find her again. Caine's shrieking vows of vengeance, no matter how passionate, wouldn't amount to shit if the Brethren didn't know where to look. They didn't know who she was; they had no way to trace her. *Not if I leave now,* he thought, standing beside the bed and gazing down at her, feeling his chest tighten, his throat constrict, his breath fade. *Not if I get the hell out of this city and take them with me.*

He didn't have enough money left to get the car out of tow, but he had enough for a bus ticket. He didn't know for sure where he meant to go, but the opposite end of the country sounded good in his estimation. *The farther from Lina I can draw them, the better.*

He knelt beside the bed, leaning over the nearby table and writing again on the motel stationery.

Dear Lina,

Please forgive me for getting you involved in this. None of this is your fault. It's all because of me, and I'm going to try and fix it somehow. No matter what Caine said last night, they won't come for you again. I'll see to that. I'm leaving—someplace far away, and they'll follow me. They'll forget about what happened, and if they find me, then they'll punish only me for it.

Being with you these past two days has been like a dream for me. It's what I've always wanted. If I could keep my life just like it was yesterday, being with you, making love to you, I would. Every day. Every moment. You made me feel alive inside and real.

You made me feel human, he thought, the point of the pen hesitating against the page as he closed his eyes, drawing in a soft, pained breath. *I love you,* he wrote at the bottom of the page. *With all of my heart, everything that I call my own, Lina. To the last of my days.*

He rose to his feet, leaned over and lightly kissed her cheek. She didn't stir, not at this, not at the sound of his soft footsteps as he stole toward the door, or the soft click as it fell close behind him, locking in his wake.

Brandon walked down the sidewalk, his hands tucked into the deep pockets of his new hooded sweatshirt. A light, cold drizzle had started to fall from the swollen gray skies, and he drew the hood up over his head. His flip-flops slapped against his feet, the plastic thong cutting uncomfortably between his toes. *Mental note,* he told himself. *Stop and get some* real *fucking shoes before leaving town.*

He didn't know where a bus station might be in the city. He thought about getting a cab; he'd grabbed one of the notepads and a pen from the motel room and carried them tucked in his pocket so he could communicate more easily, but it was early on a rainy, cold Sunday morning, in what appeared to be a rundown, shitty area of town, and there was precious little traffic on the streets at all, much less taxis. He thought about looking up a bus station in a phone book, but so far, in the twenty minutes he'd walked away from the motel, he'd come upon four payphones—none with a phone book.

Goddamn it, he thought, frowning, and then he paused, glancing over his shoulder. The sidewalk behind him was empty. A low-slung, late-model sedan rolled through a crossing intersection, disappearing from his view, and a lone, orange tabby cat darted into a nearby alley. Otherwise nothing. And yet, he'd had the feeling he was being watched.

It's nothing, he thought. *My imagination, that's all. And even if it's not, it's not one of the Brethren this time. I can feel that for certain. Anything else, I can handle.*

He walked again, groaning inwardly as the drizzle shifted, growing heavier, turning into a full-fledged rainfall. He hunched his shoulders all the more and quickened his stride, jerking the drawstrings of his hood beneath his chin, pulling the fabric snugly about his face. He tucked his head down, his chin toward his chest and hurried along. Within moments, his sweatshirt was soaked, and his T-shirt beneath. The morning chill seeped into his bones, and he shivered miserably.

He kept his eyes trained on his feet, watching helplessly as his toes grew numb with cold, exposed and constantly splashed with water ponding on the sidewalk. He wasn't sure where he was going, but didn't give a damn. *Anywhere's better than here,* he thought, because he'd inadvertently wandered into some kind of old, rundown industrial district, and there was nothing around him but dilapidated warehouses and abandoned storefronts.

He felt a tickling sensation, as if light fingertips caressed against the back of his neck, and he drew to a halt, his eyes wide, his gaze snapping up from his feet. He looked around, puzzled and wary, and saw a dark, granite-faced building looming above the old turn-of-the-century low-rises around him. *That place,* he thought, frowning. *I know that place. I've seen it before. That's where Lina stopped the day before yesterday.*

He cut across the street, walking briskly in the rain toward the building. He didn't know what it was, or why he felt so drawn to it, but he did just the same. The closer he came, the more insistent that prickling little sensation became, and the more he kept glancing around him on all sides, convinced he was being watched. *I can feel it,* he thought. *Eyes on me, like from everywhere. I can sense it.*

Within moments, he found himself standing at the entrance in front of the security box Lina had used to try and page whoever was inside. *Her partner,* he thought, struggling to recall. *Didn't she say her partner?*

He thought about pressing the button, ringing in to whoever Lina had been trying to reach. He eyed the red button for a long moment, hesitant and uncertain. *This is nuts,* he thought. *What am I doing? I've got to go. Whoever's here, he's not one of the Brethren—if it was one of us, he'd be all over me right now, dragging my ass back to Kentucky.*

He sighed, jerking his hood back from his head. It wasn't doing him a damn lick of good, anyway; the rain had soaked through the fabric, drenching his hair. He forked his fingers through the wet, tangled mess and shoved it back from his face. *Goddamn it. I need to keep moving.*

He ducked back out from beneath the entry overhang and its momentary reprieve from what had turned into a downpour. Just as he passed in front of the dark, open mouth of a deep alleyway between the black granite building and its older, crumbling neighbor, Brandon felt a hand hook against his sleeve, jerking him backward. Another hand, large and heavy, clapped over his mouth, and he was forced into the alley in stumbling tow. He grunted soundlessly as he was shoved against the cold, wet brick wall.

He didn't react at first. Although startled and alarmed, he knew it wasn't the Brethren, or his extrasensory ability to sense them would have kicked into frantic overdrive. He felt a strong arm plant against his back, holding him pinned to the wall, while another hand patted fervently against him, slapping and pawing at his clothes, fumbling for his pockets. He felt the hot push of breath fluttering momentarily against his cheek and ear as someone spoke to him, harsh sounds he couldn't hear that expelled air forcefully against Brandon's skin.

I'm being robbed, he thought, in stunned disbelief, as he felt the prodding, fumbling fingers jerk his wallet from his back pocket. *Holy shit, I'm being robbed!*

His brows narrowed and he rammed his elbow back, striking the man in the gut and forcing him to stagger away a breathless, stumbling step. Brandon spun around, his feet automatically slipping into a ready fighting stance, his hands curling lightly, reflexively into fists. The man stumbled, nearly doubled over, and looked up at

Brandon. "You . . . you fuck . . . !" he gasped and Brandon recognized him—it was one of the young men he'd seen watching as he'd left the motel earlier. Brandon drew the heel of his free hand back and smashed it into the man's face. *He's followed me all this time. That son of a bitch! He must have meant to rob me all morning!*

He broke the man's nose with his punch but didn't stop there. He launched himself at the man, swinging his fists, driving them again and again into the man's face and head, knocking him to the ground, forcing him to draw his hands up in a futile, feeble effort to protect himself. *You son of a bitch!* Brandon thought. Something in him had snapped; some deep-seated, desperate rage. He'd been through too much in too little amount of time, and his mind abandoned him, yielding to fury. *You son of a bitch! You stupid fucking son of a—*

Brandon felt a sudden, bright pain explode from his right shoulder as something slammed into him from behind, back in the shadows of the alley, plowing into him with enough force to knock him forward. He remembered then—and all-too late—that there had been *two* men standing outside the hotel that morning.

He stumbled over the fallen robber, and crashed to his knees. He caught himself with his hands, and gasped in breathless amazement at the sheer and exquisite pain that ripped through his entire body, originating from his shoulder at the effort. The strength in his arms was immediately stripped from him, and he pitched, face-first against the cold, wet ground. He felt something hot pool almost instantly beneath his face, spilling from that center point of molten agony in his shoulder. *Blood . . . !* he thought, dazed, bewildered. *I . . . I'm bleeding . . . !*

He felt it rise suddenly in his throat in a thick, terrifying flood, and all at once, he couldn't breathe. He whooped desperately for breath and choked on the blood. He felt it spew out of his mouth, spurt from his nose.

He didn't realize what had happened, that he'd been shot until the second man stepped toward him, his shoes settling in front of Brandon's face. Brandon felt the cold press of a metal gun barrel against his temple and smelled the pungent, powerful stink of pistol smoke lingering in the air.

Oh, God . . . ! he thought, moving his hand weakly, his blood-smeared fingers scratching in the dirt as he struggled to reach up, defend himself somehow, push the gun away. *No . . . please . . . !*

There was no measure of healing preternatural or accelerated enough to counteract a gunshot wound to the head—as evidenced by his sister, Emily, the night before. A bullet in the head was a bullet in the head, and it didn't matter if you were a goddamn *Nosferatu* or the pope.

Please, Brandon thought, closing his eyes, shuddering with terrified anticipation, and then the gun was gone, the barrel moving away from his face. He opened his eyes a bleary half-mast, his consciousness waning from shock and pain, and watched the two men dancing clumsily about, flapping their arms and thrashing their legs. They were being attacked by birds—not one or two, or even a dozen, but a hundred at least, all swarming around the robbers in a thick cloud of constant, furious motion.

I . . . I'm dreaming . . . Brandon thought, as another swell of pain wracked through him, making him writhe against the ground. *Oh, God, he must have shot me . . . I must be dead . . .*

He tried to drag in a mouthful of air, but there was nothing but blood. His throat had constricted down into a tight little pinhole, and Brandon fainted, his mind dragged mercifully into shadows.

He felt the terrifying, panicking sensation of drowning and dreamed about before, of trying desperately to suck in air because his lungs were shrieking, burning for it. He'd been so young then, only five, and the great house had seemed enormous to him, like a city. If someone had told him that years later down the road he would feel claustrophobic there, trapped like the wolves at the zoo, he wouldn't have been able to believe it.

He remembered.

It had been late, after midnight, and the corridors and rooms of the great house had long since fallen dark and silent. Tessa had crept into his room, sneaking silently on tiptoes and holding the long hem of her nightgown in one hand to keep from tripping over it.

They had pulled the covers up over their heads and laid in his bed, side by side and facing one another, whispering, giggling, playing silly, secret, long-forgotten games. Finally, she was ready for sleep, and curled next to him, snuggling close. "Brandon," she whispered. "I forgot Balloo."

"So?" he whispered back, but he knew what was coming. Even in the darkness, underneath the sheets, he could see her face and her large brown eyes, round and imploring.

"Go get him for me," she said.

"You go get him. He's your teddy bear."

"No, you go," she insisted, adding in a hush, "I'm scared to go down there by myself."

He'd slipped out of his room, careful to hold the door steady with his hand to keep the hinges from squawking too loudly. His parents' bedroom was a ways down the corridor, and the Grandfather slept on the next floor up, but Caine was right across the hall, and he would tell on Brandon gladly if given the opportunity.

Like right now, Brandon figured, stepping lightly down the hall until he reached the stairs. He looked back and saw Tessa peeking out of the bedroom, watching him. He motioned to her: *Go back!* and she ducked away.

He tiptoed down the main staircase, watching his shadow play long in front of him in the moonlight filtering through the enormous picture window on the landing. He reached the foyer and stepped cautiously onto the floor. The polished hardwood creaked, but only barely under his slight weight. He crept toward the study.

Earlier that evening, their father, Sebastian, had read to him and Tessa. They had snuggled up on either side of him so they could both get good looks at the pictures. Brandon loved Sebastian; the way his father smelled, the way his voice rumbled deep down inside his chest, like a cat purring. He liked the way Sebastian always seemed happy to have him around, and the way his hands were large and soft and warm when he would touch Brandon's face or tousle his hair. Brandon especially loved story time with his father, when Sebastian's deep, baritone cadence would soothe him, nearly lulling him to sleep.

That night, Sebastian had read one of their favorite stories aloud, *Where the Wild Things Are,* and that was where Tessa had said she'd forgotten Balloo, in the seat of their father's leather armchair.

Brandon was almost to the doorway of the study to reclaim it when he heard a soft, tinkling sound, like breaking glass, and someone hissing, "Shit!"

Puzzled, he paused, wondering if his father was still up or maybe his uncle Adam. He poked his head into the study, and froze, his dark eyes flying wide. There were two people in the study—a man and a woman, each holding pillow cases in their hands. They were busy riffling through drawers and scattering books and papers quickly about, stuffing silver ash trays and candlesticks down into their makeshift sacks.

"Leave that, just leave it," the man snapped to the woman when she reached for something. Brandon recognized him. He didn't know the man's name, but he remembered seeing him working in the stables, feeding the horses and raking fresh straw into their stalls. He wasn't one of the Kinsfolk, but one of the humans that the farm manager, Diego kept close to him at all times. He was one destined to be bled dry by the Brethren; what the Grandfather referred to as *cattle.*

The woman glanced up and saw Brandon in the doorway. Her eyes widened. "Pedro," she gasped. *"En el puerto— un niño!"*

The man jerked around and saw Brandon. Frightened, Brandon backed away, meaning to bolt for the staircase. Someone grabbed him from behind, and a rough, calloused hand clamped down hard over his mouth. Brandon panicked and began to struggle. He was hoisted off his feet and dragged into the study. He cried out around the muffling hand.

"Shut him up," the man from the stables said. "Jesus Christ, Manuel, shut that fucking kid up before he wakes up the whole goddamn house!"

Manuel dragged Brandon toward the fireplace and grabbed one of the cast-iron pokers out of the nearby stand. He shoved Brandon to the floor and swung the poker mightily, smashing it into the side of Brandon's head.

"He's still crying! Do it again!" Pedro snapped. "Hurry up, man! Do it!"

Manuel raised the poker and brought it down again. And then again, and again. At some point, Brandon lost most of his consciousness, but he was still dimly, dazedly aware when suddenly all of the sound in the room—Manuel's harsh, labored breathing, the soft, melodic sounds of his family's stolen belongings knocking together inside the pillow cases—all of it abruptly cut off, like someone had severed the wires to a stereo speaker. The sounds were all gone, and all that was left was a strange, fuzzy emptiness, like static on an open TV channel.

He was still semiconscious when Manuel yanked him up and shoved his arm around his neck, choking Brandon in the crook of his elbow. Dazed and bewildered by the sudden, overwhelming silence, Brandon tried to open his eyes. The pain in his head was unbelievable. He could feel blood running down the sides of his face from his scalp. He saw moonlight wink through the windows against something metallic, and then Manuel dragged the edge of a hunting knife beneath the shelf of Brandon's chin, cutting open his throat.

Brandon fell to the floor, crumpling onto his side. He watched with strange, detached fascination as his blood began to spill out across the Grandfather's 250-year-old oriental rug, ruining it. The pool began to widen in circumference. Brandon could feel blood bubbling and gurgling against his throat and chin. He couldn't breathe. His lungs were suddenly full of blood, and he realized he was drowning. He tried to struggle, to claw at his throat, but his arms felt leaden, heavy, and cold.

And then, the most terrifying thing Brandon had ever seen had occurred, something that would haunt and terrorize him for the rest of his life, burned into his brain like a branding scar. His father and uncle, Adam, burst into the room, leaping through the air like tigers pouncing. Their eyes were black, the irises so swollen and distended, the white corneas were completely obliterated. Their mouths hung open in wild, twisted snarls, snapped open unnaturally on dislocated hinges, their canine teeth dropped in twin, hooked fangs that forced the leers.

Sebastian was on Manuel before he even had time to react. Brandon watched his father tear the man's throat wide open with his bare hands, nearly ripping the man's head all the way off his neck. Manuel didn't even have the chance to scream before he was dead. Next, Sebastian launched himself at Pedro, seizing him by the collar of his chambray work shirt and flinging him across the room. Pedro flew like a rag doll, slamming into the far wall and crumpling to the floor. Sebastian darted after him, moving with impossible speed. Brandon could see Pedro's head shaking back and forth, his eyes bulging in wild, frenzied terror: *No, no, no, no, no, no . . .*

Everything was silent.

Sebastian fell on top of Pedro, sinking his fangs into the side of the man's neck. Pedro shrieked and thrashed beneath him, kicking and slapping, until Sebastian tore his throat out, sending blood arcing toward the ceiling in a violent, sweeping spray.

Adam, meanwhile, had caught the girl by her hair and slammed her face-first into the mantle. When he pulled her back, her face was bloodied and shattered. He slammed her against the marble again, and then jerked her head back, craning it on its axis, hyperextending it to the point where her neck must have snapped.

Brandon was drowning. He tried to scream as Adam buried his face in the girl's throat, ripping her open. He tried to scream at Sebastian, at the horrifying monster his father had become, but all he could suck into his throat was blood.

He remembered Sebastian looking down at him, and his mouth and eyes were normal again, with blood smeared all over his face and neck, staining the front of his pajama shirt. Sebastian wept, his tears cutting streaks through the gore on his cheeks, and his hands were hot, blazing against Brandon's face. "Brandon," he cried, over and over again, but to Brandon, his mouth had moved soundlessly. "Brandon, oh . . . oh, God, Brandon!"

Daddy, Brandon had wanted to plead. *Daddy, please I can't breathe . . . it hurts . . . !*

He remembered his father gathering him into his arms, and pain had lanced through him. As Sebastian rushed upstairs, clutching Brandon against his chest, Brandon had seen Tessa cowering in the doorway of his bedroom, her eyes enormous and frightened, threatening to swallow her entire face.

He'd passed out then, his entire body screaming for oxygen, his lungs straining for air. He didn't remember when he'd been able to breathe again, as his young healing ability had slowly kicked in, but he remembered waking up in a strange and alien world where there was no sound. It was a world where his parents would smile at him and talk to him soundlessly, their mouths opening and closing, pushing words mutely at him that he couldn't understand.

A world from which he would never escape.

Brandon woke with a start and the world was pitch dark. There was something cold and damp on his face, over his eyes and the bridge of his nose and he panicked. He twisted sharply, his hands darting to his face, shoving it away from him. As soon as his fingers touched the nap of the fabric he realized. *A washcloth . . . it's just a wet washcloth.*

There was a stabbing pain in his shoulder as he moved, and Brandon sucked in a ragged, gasping mouthful of air.

I can breathe again, he thought. He forgot everything else for that second and closed his eyes, reveling in the ability to freely draw breath again. His chest felt strangely heavy, but he could breathe once more and nothing else in the world had ever felt nearly as good.

He opened his eyes again and tried to get his bearings. *Where am I? What happened to me?*

He lay in a large bed framed by towering wrought-iron posts. There was a shadow-draped, vaulted ceiling high overhead and a tangled network of pipes and conduits dripped gracefully down toward him. He rolled carefully onto his side, whimpering silently as fresh new pain speared through him. He was bare chested, but didn't remember what had happened to his shirt. He brought his hand up to the front of his shoulder, touching gingerly. The entire right side of his chest, from the plain of his belly to the swell of his bicep and up toward his neck was a mess of brutal, dark bruises, a colorful corona with the lightest hues around the outermost edge, and a ragged, raw, open sore at his collar line. His fingertips came away spotted with blood, and when he looked down at the tousled bed sheets upon which he'd been lying, he saw a large bloodstain.

What the hell . . . ?

He remembered, like being hit by a freight train— leaving Lina at the motel, trying to find a bus depot and instead feeling drawn toward the dark tower, the strange and somehow familiar black granite building. He remembered being grabbed as he'd walked past an alley-way, the bullet that had punched through his chest and the cold stink of gunmetal as the barrel of a pistol had been shoved against his brow.

Birds, he thought dimly, pressing the heel of his hand against his forehead. *I thought I saw birds . . .*

That part of his recollections seemed murky and jumbled. He'd been in tremendous pain, struggling vainly to breathe, and nothing he'd witnessed returned clearly to him.

Brandon swung his legs slowly around until he felt his bare feet hit the cold, smooth floor. Somehow, he'd come to be in a pair of baggy grey sweatpants instead of the blue jeans he seemed to recall having worn. Bewildered and frightened, he tried to stand, leaning heavily against one of the black bedposts for support. His shoulder and back hurt unbearably and he stumbled weakly, reaching out and catching himself against the foot of the bed. Pain swelled through his arm and shoulder girdle at the impact, and he cried out mutely.

I have to get out of here, he thought, forcing himself to his feet again. *I don't know where the fuck here is, but I have to get out. They'll be coming for me again. God, I can't let the Brethren find me like this.*

There were drapes around the bed, long, flowing sheets of white, opaque silk, and Brandon stumbled through them with his hands near his face reflexively, timidly. Once beyond, he found himself stumbling across an enormous room, some kind of open, expansive warehouse loft. He saw a wide, hulking fireplace in the center of the space, with a broad brick mantle and stone hearth. Antique furniture had been scattered around the fireplace, reminding Brandon vaguely of the Grandfather's study—all of it very old and very well preserved. Undoubtedly very expensive.

Directly in front of him, toward the center of the loft, was an old-fashioned iron streetlamp that spilled soft, warm light around in a small circumference, the only point of illumination in the room that Brandon could see. His head swam, and he staggered, feeling his knees buckle. He nearly fell across a settee, but caught himself before crumpling. More pain welled through his shoulder, and Brandon gritted his teeth, sucking in a hissing breath around another soundless mewl.

There were no walls in the loft. To his right, another set of drapes partitioned off another area, marking the boundaries of a makeshift room. These were fashioned out of heavy, blood-colored velvet. As soon as Brandon saw them, that peculiar, tremulous, tickling sensation slithered along the nape of his neck, just as it had outside. *Someone's there.*

He limped toward the drapes, his shoulder throbbing, his head reeling. The closer he drew, the more his pain-dulled senses discerned. *Blood,* he thought, salivating unconsciously, the gums around his canine teeth beginning to ache. *That smells like blood.*

He hooked his fingers against one edge of the velvet drapes and pulled it aside. He saw a woman and man in bed making love. Both were facing him, their eyes closed; the woman was on her hands and knees on the bed, while the man stood behind her, cradling the generous swells of her hips between his hands and driving himself into her with a powerful, vigorous rhythm. Her large breasts bounced, and her dark auburn hair spilled over her back in a glossy tumble of curls. Brandon could see her neck, the small, almost careful marks on the swell of her throat and the thin, dark trails of drying blood standing starkly against her ivory skin. He could smell her, a wondrous, musky fragrance, the coppery scent of her blood.

She opened her eyes and looked directly at Brandon, her face flushed, glossed with light sweat.

Oh, God, he thought, shying back clumsily, his eyes flown wide.

"Hey," he saw the woman say. "We've got company. Come here, baby. You like to watch?"

The man's eyes flew open, his expression puzzled and somewhat aggravated. His low brows furrowed over sharp, narrow eyes, and the corners of his thin mouth turned down in an imposing line. "What . . . ?" he began, and then he, too, saw Brandon. His brown eyes widened, and he immediately jerked away from the girl, moving to hurry around the bed toward Brandon.

He was lean and strapped with muscles, and Brandon was in no condition to fight him. Plus, he was getting all kinds of strange scents and sensations from him, things he didn't understand. Brandon stumbled backward gracelessly through the heavy drapes. He was back in the loft, but didn't know where to go from there. He looked around wildly, but didn't see anything that looked even remotely like an exit.

He staggered across the room, tripping over the up-turned edge of a rug. He fell, spilling across a large coffee table, and one of the corners smacked into his wounded shoulder. He screamed silently, collapsing to the floor.

He felt hands against him, someone touching him, and he panicked, trying to pull away. The pain in his shoulder was immense now, however, overwhelming and immobilizing him. He looked up, his vision blurred with tears and saw the man kneeling beside him, a robe lashed loosely around his waist. He had disheveled, shoulder-length, dark blond hair and a scraggly shadow of beard bristle outlining his sharp jaw. The intimidating severity in his face was gone and his features had soft-ened with kindness that Brandon didn't understand. He reached for Brandon, sliding his arm beneath the younger man's shoulders.

"Here now, *petit*," he said. "You don't need to be out of bed yet. Come on."

Brandon felt him slip his other arm beneath his legs and lift him off the ground. Sharp pain ripped through the entire left side of Brandon's body at this, and he arched his back, crying out mutely; a ragged, choked gasp.

"I know . . ." he saw the man say as his mind faded, suc-cumbing to the pain. "I know that hurts."

Brandon was semi-lucid as the man carried him back to the bed behind the white, gauzy drapes. *Who . . . who are you . . . ?* Brandon tried to sign as the man lay him against the mattress again, forgetting in his daze that the man wouldn't understand him.

"It's alright," the man said, smiling, gently easing Brandon's hands back down. "You're safe here, *petit*. Nobody's going to hurt you. Sleep now."

You're like me, Brandon thought, as his eyelids fluttered closed. *You . . . you're one of us . . .*

Chapter Fifteen

When Lina woke, she was alone in the motel room. She sat up in bed, groggy and disoriented. The light from outside, seeping through the drawn draperies was bright and pale, no longer early morning. She glanced at the clock and found it nearly noon.

"Brandon?" she called, her voice hoarse. *Brilliant, Lina,* she thought, pushing her hand through her hair. *Give a shout out to the deaf guy.*

She rose slowly, realizing she still had a white, terrycloth towel wrapped around her torso. She'd been waiting for him to get out of the shower so that she could take a turn. The light was now off in the bathroom, but she peeked inside anyway. He was gone. There was no sign of him, and she felt a tremor of panic flutter through her.

Where did he go? Oh, my God, what if they found him again? Followed us somehow? What if they . . . ?

She saw a yellow plastic bag on the bed, and picked it up, puzzled. Inside, she found T-shirts, sweatpants, a hoodie, and some flip-flops, along with a receipt from a nearby Dollar-A-Rama store. Brandon had bought clothes for her. She could tell from the sales slip that he'd bought some for himself, too, but of the second hooded jacket and sandals, there was no sign. *He left again,* she thought. *He went and bought these, then brought them back. He left again, but for where?*

She frowned thoughtfully, and as her eyes cut around the room, she saw the note on the bedside table. She felt another tremble of anxious fear, and leaned over the bed to grab it. *Oh, Brandon,* she thought. *Don't tell me you went and did something chivalrous and stupid. Please don't . . .*

But she read the note and realized that he had, and crumpled the page in her hand. His words—the sweetest anyone had ever offered to her—had been meant to comfort and reassure, but instead, left her filled with terrified dismay. "Goddamn it!" she cried, throwing the note across the room. She sat down heavily against the bed, her eyes swimming with tears. *God, they'll kill him,* she thought. *If they find him, they'll kill him, and he's all alone against them now.*

She pressed her fingertips against her mouth and struggled to compose herself, to force herself into a clinical frame of mind—to think about things like a cop. She felt raw and unraveled, as if she'd been ripped loose at the seams. *I need to pull my shit together,* she told herself firmly. *I was imagining things last night. That stuff about their eyes, their mouths . . . their teeth . . . all of it imagined. I was half-asleep and frightened, still buzzing from the champagne, and they were both strung out on meth or something else—something worse. They were crazed.*

And I shot one of them.

That realization shuddered through her. She had shot and killed a woman last night; had sprayed her brains out of the backside of her skull in the middle of Jackson's living room. She knew that the apartment had to be crawling with cops now—homicide detectives, crime scene investigators, the medical examiner's crew.

If Brandon's brother, Caine, the one he'd impaled against the wall with a *katana* blade, had survived, he could easily identify Lina as the one who'd shot the girl, Emily Noble. And even if he hadn't, it was only a matter

of time before she was pinpointed as a suspect. Her
brother's home was the crime scene, and she had ready
access. Even if none of the neighbors had seen her and
Brandon fleeing the scene the night before, her bullets
were all over the place, buried in both victims. It
wouldn't take long before investigators put two and two
together.

I need to turn myself in.

She wasn't necessarily concerned about the legal ram-
ifications of doing this. She'd acted in self-defense. However, she figured the Nobles would go after her like a
starving wolf against a ham bone, all claws unfurled and
fangs bared. She didn't want to think about the clout
their kind of money commanded or the cut-throat
lawyers they could afford. *Christ, when they're finished with
me in civil court, I'll be lucky to have anything left of my pen-
sion, much less my paychecks.*

She tried not to think about what Brandon's brother,
Caine, had shrieked at her as he'd thrashed in the corri-
dor, struggling to wrench the *katana* blade from his gut.
I will bleed you dry, you bitch!

Compared to that, the prospect of a lawsuit sounded
nearly bright.

I need to turn myself in, she thought again, rising to her
feet. She went to the bathroom and flipped on the switch,
flooding the small room with bright, stark light. She
blinked in shock at her reflection in the mirror; her hair
hung in a dull, disheveled mess about her face. Her eyes
were swollen with tears, rimmed and ringed with exhausted
shadows. She had dark smudges peppered and smeared on
her cheeks, forehead and neck; closer examination revealed it was blood, contact spray from where she'd shot
Brandon's brother and sister. She felt her stomach hitch
at this realization, her gullet heaving, and she stumbled
sideways, grasping the rim of the toilet bowl and leaning
over as she vomited. She retched violently, her stomach
heaving again and again, tightening with each bout into

painful knots. She knelt on the floor and huddled against the toilet bowl, spitting feebly and shuddering.

I have to find Brandon, she thought, closing her eyes and reaching up, pawing blindly until she hit the commode handle to flush. *He needs me. He can't be alone against these people.*

She limped to her feet, grimacing at the bitter taste left her mouth, and spitting again into the toilet. She turned on the shower, opening the hot faucet as wide as it would go, and then stood under the pelting, stinging spray. *Caine may not be dead,* she thought. The wound had been gruesome, but not immediately fatal, and if he'd been rushed to the hospital in time, he could have well survived Brandon's sword strike.

And if he did, Lina thought, ducking her face beneath the shower's relentless spray, scrubbing with her hands to get the dried blood off her skin. *If that son of a bitch survived, he and I are going to have ourselves a little talk. He's going to tell me what the fuck is going on, and then he's going to help me find Brandon.*

Lina blinked in admittedly stupefied surprise when the cab pulled up in front of Jackson's apartment building. Instead of the flurry of activity she'd been expecting—crime scene vans, marked and unmarked police cars, ambulances, all with lights flashing and illegally parked—there was absolutely nothing. No cops on the street, no service vehicles, no curious crowd of onlookers. Nothing. It looked like absolutely any other ordinary, mundane morning, as if nothing in the world was unusual or awry.

She frowned as she paid the driver, using a twenty dollar bill Brandon had left for her. He'd tucked fifty dollars, neatly folded, in the shopping bag with her clothes, and although she knew he'd meant it for this— cab fare to see her home again, she'd still sat on the edge of the motel bed, her stomach taut, her throat constricted, her eyes stinging with fresh tears. She'd felt momentarily, heartbreakingly like a whore, like he'd paid her for the lovemaking they'd enjoyed the night before. *No better than a hooker,* she'd thought, even though she knew it wasn't true. It had still hurt her, though, and for that moment, her carefully reassembled cool had withered once more, and she'd cried.

She felt her composure faltering again, this time in mounting bewilderment, as she walked into the apartment building, and took the stairs to the eighth floor. She found Jackson's door unguarded. A tall piece of plywood had been placed over the ruined remnants of his threshold, secured in place with a pair of padlocks. There was nothing besides this; no crime scene tape, no painted stenciling ordering trespassers away by edict of the police. Lina stood, her hands on her hips, blinking stupidly at the board and feeling absolutely dumbfounded.

"Oh, Angelina, thank goodness it's you!" she heard someone exclaim from behind her, and she turned to find Sun Ying, Jackson's middle-aged, rotund, Korean landlady coming down the hallway toward her. Sun carried a large, loaded key ring in one doughy hand, and the keys rattled noisily together as she moved. "I've been trying to call you all morning at the number Jackie gave for you, but no answer!"

"I . . . I've been out," Lina said lamely, clumsily.

"You won't believe it," Sun said. She stopped beside Lina and began to sift through the keys. "Some kids trashed Jackie's apartment last night! The police think they broke in somehow, had some kind of wild party and just junked it!"

"Kids?" Lina asked, watching in stunned, numb disbelief as Sun unlocked first one padlock and then the other. She pried by the metal hinges and then wrestled with the heavy plywood plank.

"Help me with this," Sun said, and she and Lina shoved it aside, propping it against the wall. "See for yourself," Sun said, nodding past the threshold. "They made a mess. Everything broken and busted up, holes in the walls, the kitchen cabinets all wrecked. Goddamn kids." She shook her head. "Mrs. Nuñez across the hall said she even heard gunshots last night. So did Mr. Trapper downstairs—that and a lot of banging. They both called the police right away. I tell you, if I ever find out who did this, I'll plant my foot up their asses."

But what about Emily? Lina asked, walking hesitantly, uncertainly into the apartment. *I shot her in the head. There should be blood everywhere.*

There should have been, but there wasn't. Lina looked around in shock. Everything was just as they'd left it. The coffee table was shattered; the kitchen trashed. But the floor—which should have been doused in Emily Noble's blood and brain matter—was absolutely spotless.

What the fuck . . . ?

Lina darted for the hallway and switched on the overhead light. She could see the crunched section of the wall where Brandon had shoved Caine; she saw the slim, black hole in the drywall where the *katana* blade had punched through. In fact, the *katana* lay on the corridor floor, its long, narrow blade flashing in the sudden, yellow light.

There was no sign of blood anywhere. Not on the floor, not on the blade, not along the edges of the hole in the wall. "What the fuck . . . ?" Lina whispered, brushing her fingertips against the ragged edges of the hole. They came away white from drywall dust, but nothing more.

"I know," Sun said, standing behind her, folding her arms over her ample bosom. "The police told me maybe whoever did this had been staying here all this time with Jackie gone. I told them no, that's not possible. You've been coming and going, taking care of things for him, watering his plants." She shook her head. "I hope they didn't go and piss in any of his plants. You know how he loves those things. And piss will kill them dead at the roots in nothing, no time flat."

I don't understand, Lina thought, rising to her feet again. She'd heard of organized crime hits, professional jobs, where specialists came in afterward and cleaned up any trace of evidence. *But how in the hell could anyone have gotten in here and cleaned this up so thoroughly so quickly? There's no way. Sun said two of the neighbors heard gun shots and called the police. They would have been here in no more than ten minutes, tops, after Brandon and I left. How the fuck is this possible?*

"Did you see what they did to the front door?" Sun exclaimed. "My insurance adjuster is coming this afternoon to take a look at the damage to that and the wall, but Jackie's going to have to take care of anything with his furniture and what-not himself. He—"

"I'll call him," Lina murmured, turning on her heel and walking down the hall into Jackson's bedroom. The bed was still unmade, the sheets rumpled and swept aside in the aftermath of the lovemaking she'd enjoyed with Brandon, and for a moment, she stood frozen in the doorway, her heart hesitating, her breath bated, her self-control slipping. Then she shook her head and forced herself forward.

"You know what I think?" Sun said, following closely behind her. "I bet it was some of his students from that school. Deaf or not, they can still be hoodlums. And they've got to know he's out of town. Shame on them, that's all I have to say. This is the last thing he needs, what with your mother and all."

Lina knelt beside the bed, slipping the straps of Brandon's oversized duffel bag against her hand. She hoisted it onto the bed, rifling through the contents quickly, curiously. She planned to take it with her, to tear it apart back at her own place, in a desperate hunt for anything that might help her. *Brandon said he was going someplace far away,* she thought. *He doesn't have enough cash to get that Audi out of impound, so that leaves him with a bus or a plane. Those are as good a place to start as any.*

"I'm going to take this with me, okay?" she said to Sun, turning around, hefting the duffel bag by the shoulder strap. She reached down, lifting Brandon's beige barn jacket in hand, too. "And this."

"Sure, I . . . I guess," Sun said, sounding surprised and puzzled.

Lina had left her cell phone on Jackie's nightstand, and she jumped, startled, as it suddenly rang. She snatched it in hand and flipped it open. *Please let it be Brandon,* she thought. *God, just let him call me so I can go and help him.*

"Finally," Jude said when Lina answered, and she bit her teeth against a groan. "I've been trying to reach you all morning."

Not now, she thought. "Jude, this is not a good—" she began.

"Time? Yeah, fine," he snapped in reply. His voice sounded hoarse and flat, like he spoke while pinching his nose closed. "Tell me about it. I won't keep you long, trust me. I just have a message for your little goddamn boyfriend. My nose is broken, the caps on my front teeth are cracked, and his sorry ass is going to pay to get them fixed. Plus some compensatory damages like pain and suffering. Not to mention humiliation."

Lina frowned. "Jude, you were drunk last night," she said. "If you're humiliated about what happened, it's your fault, no one else's."

"You're wrong about that, Lina," Jude said. He was really angry, his voice edged with sharp malice. "I didn't bust up my own face. Your boyfriend, Brandon Noble, did that."

"Because you . . ." she began, and her voice faded in surprise. Jude chuckled humorlessly at her pause.

"Yeah, I know his last name, and who his goddamn family is. I figured that out real quick, Lina. One of Jackie's old students? Who else could it be? I remember

you both talking about Brandon, about the whole damn
Noble family."

"Jude, I don't know what you're—"

"Bloodhorse Distillery," Jude said. "Triple Crown
contenders. Thoroughbred horse breeding. Any of that
ring a bell? And goddamn deep pockets, you'd better
believe that. Tell Deaf-and-Dumb he just made the
biggest mistake of his fucking life. I wouldn't be surprised if his grandfather doesn't cut him out of the will
for this. Believe me, he was pretty pissed off to hear
about it."

Lina felt her stomach suddenly twist into a knot.
"What?"

"I'm a lawyer, Lina," Jude said with a laugh. "I know
how to follow the money. As soon as I got home from the
hospital last night, I tracked down the Noble family's attorney and gave him a ring. Told him what had happened, that I'd been to the emergency room and I had
the bills to prove it. I also told him Brandon Noble had
stolen a thousand-dollar suit from me. That's a goddamn
felony, if I decide to pursue it. He was very accommodat-
ing—forwarded me right to Augustus Noble's cell
phone."

Oh, my God, Lina thought, closing her eyes. "What
have you done?" she whispered. *That's how they found us
last night. Jude told them where to look.*

"You stupid son of a bitch," she said.

"Stupid, hell," Jude shot back. "I'm about to be a very
rich son of a bitch, Lina. I should thank you for—"

Lina hung up on him, snapping the phone closed.
She uttered a furious little cry and hurled the phone
across the room. From the doorway, Sun jumped, startled, as it smacked against the wall.

"Who was that?" the landlady asked in a small, hesitant
voice.

"Nobody important." Lina grabbed her overnight bag,
the one she'd brought from her apartment a seeming
eternity ago. She marched across the room and stooped

long enough to snatch up her phone again. Then she turned, brushing past Sun. "I'll call Jackie and let him know what happened. I'll try to get a hold of his insurance company, too. Thanks, Sun."

She paused in the living room, reaching down and grabbing Jude's rumpled suit from the floor where Brandon had left it the night before. She shook loose any shards of glass from the broken coffee table, and draped the clothes across her arm. "I'll be taking these, too," she said to Sun, snatching Jude's shoes and cufflinks off the floor and sparing her a glance as she left the apartment.

Her first stop was Jude's apartment building, an old and expensive Victorian condominium complex. The building had brass-plated elevator cars, a marble foyer and a deskman on duty at all times. He looked up, immaculate in his crisp grey uniform and cap, as Lina marched through the revolving front door.

"May I help you?" he asked.

"Yeah," Lina replied, and she threw the Dolce and Gabbana suit, watching the jacket, slacks, shirt, and tie scatter across the polished floor. "You can ring the son of a bitch in 4-A and let him know his fucking suit's downstairs."

Next, she pitched the Italian leather loafers across the foyer, followed by the gold cufflinks. "Tell him I'd cram it up his ass, but then he wouldn't be able to breathe."

She turned and stomped away, her hands closed in furious fists, her mouth twisted in a wicked smile.

Lina stopped by her apartment long enough to change clothes and reload her pistol. While she was there, she turned the contents of Brandon's duffel bag out against her bed and listened to her cell phone messages.

"Lina, *chère, où es-tu*?" Rene asked. *Where are you?* He'd called her cell within moments of her hanging up on him at the motel, according to the time stamp on the message. She frowned to hear him, despite the obvious concern in his voice. He only spoke French in lieu of English when he was drunk or stoned on his painkillers—or both— because he'd forget himself. He'd told her once that that was a Cajun thing, lapsing periodically into French in the course of a conversation, or worse, interspersing French words into his English dialogue. She'd once found it charming, but now, she found it grating, because it meant he was wasted. *And apparently indulging in a little casual fuck, too,* she thought, her frown deepening as she remembered the high-pitched, irritating woman's laughter from his end of the line that morning. Not that this bothered her. What grated on Lina's nerves was that Rene had a fondness for vacuous, bleached-blond, centerfold types with enormous—and obviously fake—breasts and absolutely no appreciation for multisyllabic words. *Just what a man with more time, liquor, and money than sense needs.*

She deleted his message without even bothering to listen to the rest of it. The next was from Melanie, and she winced to hear her friend's voice. "Look, we're on our way to the airport, but I'll call you when we get back from the honeymoon," Melanie said. "I want to talk about this, Lina. About last night. I want to hear your side of things, find out what happened. We—"

No, you don't, Lina thought, erasing the message. *Trust me, Melanie.*

The last message came from Jackie, from less than an hour ago. Although he preferred his keypad phone, where he could type in his messages himself, he also relied on a vocal-relay service to communicate with people who weren't hearing impaired. "This message is from Jackson Jones," said a female operator, reading aloud as Jackie had typed to her on his TDD. "Call me, Scarecrow. Where are you? How is Brandon? You haven't forgotten about my plants, have you?"

"Sorry, Jackie," Lina murmured, snapping the phone

closed and hanging up on his message. "I've got other things on my mind."

As she sifted through Brandon's things, she found a photograph tucked beneath a pair of jeans; a wrinkled four-by-six image of Jackson and Brandon. Brandon was a boy in the picture, sixteen years old if a day, and Jackie had his arm draped fondly around his neck. Both of them grinned broadly at the camera.

With the photo, she found a prescription bottle of medicine. She frowned, reading the label. *Jackson Jones,* it said. *Wellbutrin (bupropion hydrochloride), 75 mg. Directions: Take two tablets by mouth every 12 hours as needed.*

As needed for what? she thought, puzzled. *What the hell are Jackie's pills doing in Brandon's bag? And what are they for?*

She opened the bottle lid and recognized the little lavender pills. She'd seen Brandon take two in the cab yesterday. He'd carried them wrapped in aluminum foil in his pocket, and had told her they were for his hands. *Was he lying to me? These aren't painkillers. I've seen this shit advertised on television. It's to help you quit smoking, I think.*

Why the hell is my brother's name on the label?

"Maybe I need to give Jackie a call after all," she murmured, frowning. She'd shrugged Brandon's barn jacket on over her fresh T-shirt, pausing long enough to close her eyes and momentarily draw the scent of him from the thick, coarse fabric and against her nose. She tucked the photograph down inside the front pocket, then checked the clip on her nine-millimeter, locking it home. She thumbed the safety on and holstered it at the small of her back, against the waistband of her jeans. She clipped her badge to the front of her pants and then headed for the door. *Time to get to work,* she thought.

Chapter Sixteen

Here, petit.

Brandon stirred, feeling something press between his lips, a small, bitter-tasting pill. He winced, trying to spit it out, but felt gentle fingertips push it insistently against his tongue.

It's for your pain. Take it. It's alright.

He sensed a man's voice, soft and gentle, a lulling, comforting, warm sensation resounding inside his mind. He felt a hand slip against the back of his head, raising him somewhat, and then the rim of a cup touched his mouth. He drank, swallowing the pill. He was parched; his mouth and throat felt dry and scraped raw, and he gulped greedily at the water until he choked. Water spit down his chin, splattering against his chest as he whooped for breath.

Easy now, the man said. *Not so fast,* petit. *We've got plenty more.*

Brandon opened his eyes as the man drew a washcloth against his mouth, wiping at the spilled water. He blinked dazedly, the man's features dimly familiar to him. *"Bonjour,"* the man said, speaking in French, a language Brandon didn't know but recognized vaguely because Tessa had spoken it. It was the language of ballet.

Brandon moved his arms, grimacing at the effort. His

right shoulder felt stiff; a glance told him the open wound he'd seen earlier, the horrific bruising were now all tucked beneath a heavy wrapping of bandages. The man tried to ease him back down against the bed, but Brandon frowned, pulling away from him. He motioned with his hands, holding one palm out flat and pretending to write against it with the other.

"Cat got your tongue, *petit*?" the man asked. He reached forward, brushing his fingertips lightly beneath the shelf of Brandon's jaw, tracing the scar along his throat. "Maybe so."

Brandon turned his head away, his brows narrowing. Again he motioned with his hands, wincing as the effort sent pain through his shoulder. He felt the shift in the mattress as the man stood, and saw him chuckle out of the corner of his eye. "Alright," he said. "Hang on."

He ducked around the silk drapes, walking away. Brandon noticed he moved with a slight, barely discernable limp. He was gone for a few moments, long enough for Brandon's mind to fade wearily again, and when a spiral-bound notebook and ballpoint pen dropped unceremoniously against his belly, he jerked awake, his eyes flying wide.

"*Voilà*," the man said, standing above him, folding his arms across his chest.

Brandon moved slowly, turning back the cover of the notebook taking the pen in hand, grateful that it was his right side that was veritably crippled for the moment and not his dominant left. *Who are you?* he wrote.

The man looked at him for a long moment, his brow raised, his expression somewhat hardened and cool. It was nowhere near the level of ferocity Brandon had seen when he'd stumbled upon him fucking the redheaded woman, but it was still less than kind and more than a little unnerving.

I'm deaf, Brandon wrote. *And I'm mute. I can read lips, but . . .*

The man draped his hand against Brandon's, staying him in mid-sentence. "I know you're deaf," he said. "Mute, too. I figured that out pretty quick. Seemed a

strange thing you didn't cry out any, what with a bullet
having gone straight through you."

Brandon glanced down at his bandages, and then
back toward the man. He spoke funny; his lips formed
words in an unusual fashion Brandon was wholly unaccustomed to, and had mild difficulty understanding. *He
spoke French to me,* he thought. *Is that it, he's French? He's
speaking with an accent?*

He tapped the pen against the notebook, pointing to
his original inquiry. *Who are you?*

The man arched his brow and smiled wryly, affecting
a quick little bow. "My name's Rene Morin. At your service, *petit.* And you are . . . ?"

Brandon Noble, Brandon wrote. He looked at the man
for a moment, troubled. *Are you Brethren?* he asked, because he'd never heard of any Brethren by the clan
name of *Morin* or who lived outside of the compound,
much less alone in the city.

"Brethren?" The man, Rene, shook his head, looking
puzzled. "What's that?"

But you're like me, Brandon wrote. His vision blurred
slightly as his head swam, and he frowned.

"I am, yes," Rene replied, the corner of his mouth lifting. "Fifty-seven years I've walked this earth, Brandon
Noble, and I've never met anybody else like me but my
daddy . . . until today. Where did you come from?"

Brandon moved to answer, but his head spun again.
He closed his eyes momentarily, drawing in a deep
breath, feeling a strong wave of vertigo sweep over him.
What did you give me? he wrote once it had passed, not realizing his handwriting began to loop lazily.

"Percodan," Rene said. "I know you're hurting. I've
been there." He glanced over his shoulder, as if a sudden
sound attracted his attention. "Anise is still here," he said
to Brandon. "The redhead you saw earlier. I pay her
good, and she doesn't mind what she thinks is no more
than kinky shit. You need to feed. Let me . . ."

No! Brandon's eyes widened, and he struggled to sit up,

despite the sudden pain that cut through his injured side. He'd forgotten himself and tried to sign. He reached for the notebook and scrawled two large, block letters: *NO.*

Rene blinked at him, bewildered. "But you're hurt," he said. "It will make you heal faster. It—"

No, Brandon thought, writing again, scribbling madly to keep up with his frantic thoughts. *No, I don't do that— I'm not like that not like them I'm NOT—*

Something in his mind snapped, like a bright flash of light searing through his skull, and Brandon jerked in bed, his hands darting toward his face. At the same time, Rene floundered back from the bed. He cried out sharply, clutching at his head, his fingers hooked through his hair in claws. He crashed to the floor, sitting down hard and nearly falling back through the drapes. *"Viens m'enculer!"*

Brandon lowered his hands slowly, trembling and stunned. *Oh, my God,* he thought, watching as Rene gritted his teeth, wincing, and struggled to stand again. *Oh, my God, what was that?*

"What . . . what the fuck . . . ?" Rene said, staggering. He caught one of the bed rails and clung to it, trying to catch his breath. He looked at Brandon from beneath severely knitted brows, his thin mouth pulled down in a frown. "What the fuck just happened here?"

Brandon picked up the pen and notebook, writing quickly. His hand shook, his letters scrawled and crooked. *You're a police officer.*

Rene stared at the note for a long moment and shook his head. "Not anymore, *petit,"* he replied. "How . . . how do you know that?"

I saw it in my mind, Brandon wrote. *Oh, God,* he thought, as he replayed those fleeting, astonishing moments. *I saw you in my mind, Rene.*

He looked up at the man, stunned. *I could hear you.*

He awoke some time later, his mind emerging from out of the murky, shadowy depths into which he'd succumbed.

He blinked up at the ceiling, feeling leaden and stiff. He had been dreaming, wonderful dreams in which he had relived those brief few seconds when he had somehow gained access into the private world of Rene's mind, his memories.

Brandon remembered the sounds, beautiful, magical sounds, things he had forgotten about or had never known—*music*, a wondrous, jubilant, exuberant cacophony Rene knew as *zydeco* . . . something slower and more visceral, nearly melancholy called *blues* . . . something somewhere in between, *jazz*. Clifton Chenier, Wayne Toups, Etta James, Lou Rawls . . . trilling melodies from Ravel and Vivaldi . . . fast paced, nearly staccato beats from Elvis Presley and Jerry Lee Lewis . . . all of it playing, echoing, overlapping in his mind.

Voices. A woman with yellow-blond hair named Irene, her laughter, sweet like music: "Rene, goddamn it, I said stop tickling me!" An older woman Rene knew as *Mamere*, with a heavy, lilting accent: "Rene, I swear, boy, I am gonna swat you 'cross that backside if you don't stop that running through my house . . . !"

Ordinary sounds, like Rene's shoes on the hardwood floors of his loft. The soft whisper of a match head sliding across a strike pad and the hiss of the flame. The melodic clink of a bottle lip tapping against the rim of a crystal tumbler, the quiet burble of vodka spilling down, filling the glass. The patter of rain against the sidewalk, the growl of a car engine revving, the redheaded woman, Anise, whimpering in Rene's ear, her breath growing quicker, mewling as she climaxed during sex.

It had felt so good, so glorious to Brandon to spent those fleeting moments in Rene's mind, even though it had caused Rene pain. Brandon didn't know what had happened, and obviously Rene didn't either. *But he has to know,* Brandon thought, puzzled. *He's the one who caused it. I couldn't do that, nothing like that. There's no way.*

He sat up slowly, cradling his right arm against his belly to avoid putting weight down on his injured side. He stood, limping beyond the drapes, looking cautiously around him. He had no idea how much time had lapsed since he'd been shot, or even since he'd last passed out. There was no way to judge; he didn't see a clock anywhere in the entire loft, or any windows, either, for that matter. Only the pain in his shoulder was a gauge, the bruising evident on his torso a rudimentary timeline. He was still hurting enough, the contusions visible beneath the edge of his bandages dark enough, to show he hadn't been out for long, hours at best, and not days. *Good then,* he thought. *I can still make my way out of the city and head west, draw the Brethren away from here—and from Lina.*

He didn't necessarily want to leave so soon, not after what had happened, after he'd somehow been able to hear again through Rene's mind. But he knew that no matter how wondrous or unbelievable it had been, he couldn't take the risk of remaining. *If the Brethren find me here, they'll go after Lina, too. I've already put her in too much danger. I can't let that happen.*

He looked around for a phone. *I could call a cab,* he thought, but then shook his head. *I don't even know where the fuck I am. I don't even know where I was when I got shot, and Rene could have carried me twenty blocks away from there, for all I know.*

Then another realization occurred to him. *My wallet . . . !*
He ducked back beneath the white silk drapes, looking for his clothes, but there was no sign. He felt his heart seize in dismay. *Oh, Christ, those guys who shot me . . . one of them grabbed my wallet out of my pocket.*

He stumbled around the bed, looking vainly in the dim light for his jeans and hooded sweatshirt. *God, please tell me they didn't take it with them. Please—that was all of my money, everything I had.*

He tangled his fingers in his hair. *Fuck me.*

He limped out into the loft again, looking for Rene. He peeked beyond the heavy velvet drapes toward the bed where he'd discovered him earlier, but it was empty. The woman was gone, too, but the scent of her—a combination of musk and flowers, underlain with a darker, headier fragrance, *blood*—still lingered in the air, trapped in the narrow space between the drapes. *I wonder what he did with her body,* Brandon thought.

Toward his right as he left the second bed area, Brandon saw a kitchenette. It was built on floor decking raised about two feet above the rest of the loft, but like everything else, had no other indicated boundaries. Brandon walked up a small flight of steps and stood against a granite-tiled floor. He blinked around at the stainless-steel stove and refrigerator, the broad sink basin with a slim fluorescent bar hanging over it, casting a stark, pale glow. Cabinets had been installed by anchoring them to exposed beam studs rising from the floor decking. Brandon had never seen anything like it in his life. *Christ, what does this guy have against walls?*

Beside the sink stood a cluster of alcohol bottles, mostly expensive varieties of vodka, most of them empty or nearly so. These were flanked by a bevy of bright orange prescription pill bottles, and Brandon lifted them in hand, reading the labels. *Percodan, Tylox, Paveral, Ambien . . . What the hell is all of this stuff?*

Brandon left the kitchen, walking toward the living room area and the expansive brick fireplace. The loft was filled with antiques, like stained-glass Tiffany floor lamps—the genuine variety, and not inexpensive knock-offs—and oriental rugs, mahogany armoires, barrister-styled bookcases, chocolate-covered leather sofas and chairs arranged, like the draperies around the beds, to lend the illusion of perimeters. Brandon's father, Sebastian, had been a lover and avid collector of antiques, and through him, Brandon had gleaned his own appreciation for the hobby. *He's got a small fortune invested here,* Brandon thought, admiring a black enamel writing desk with etched gold filigree detail that he estimated to be from the early eighteenth century. *Who is this guy?*

For all of the wondrous and lavish appointments, there was nothing personal in the apartment at all that

Brandon could readily see, outside of the vodka and medicine bottles in the kitchen. Rene looked no older than his mid-thirties at most, but he'd told Brandon he was in his late fifties.

Fifty-seven years, I've walked this earth, Brandon Noble, and I've never met anybody else like me but my daddy . . . until today.

Yet, Rene had no photographs or sentimental effects out on display, no scrapbooks or albums. It was as if he had no past—or at least, none of which he particularly cared to be reminded of regularly.

Beyond the fireplace, the open space of the loft continued onward, but Rene had neither furnished nor lit this broad space. Brandon stepped around the hearth, peering curiously into the heavy darkness beyond. Closer to the circumference of light cast by the iron streetlamp, he could distinguish boxy, shadowed objects, other pieces of furniture that Rene had yet to incorporate into his existing decor and that waited for him, draped in bedsheets and plastic drop cloths. Brandon walked into the darkness, his footsteps hesitant, his uninjured arm outstretched warily until his vision adjusted. When he at last grew accustomed to the shadows, he saw a faint hint of bluish-white light at the far end of the room, a narrow beam of illumination spilling down from the ceiling. In its soft glow, he could see a spiral staircase leading upward.

The further he drew from the well-tended bank of coals in the fireplace, the colder Brandon became. A damp chill permeated the air as he approached the staircase. He was still barefooted and shirtless, and goosebumps raised along his skin. His breath frosted in the air before him, hanging in an ethereal cloud about his head as he looked up toward the light.

He climbed the stairs, moving slowly, having no desire to take a tumble and add to the misery of his gunshot wound. He could feel the staircase trembling beneath him, shivering with his weight. It looked old and rusted, tenuous at best. He reached the top and drew to a breathless, wide-eyed halt. A portion of the roof had collapsed here on the upper story of the building, leaving a wide, gaping hole that awarded a spectacular view of the sky beyond and the surrounding cityscape. The broken, twisted remnants of steel I-beams and joists protruded from the opening, visible in silhouette, along with draping, snaking coils of wires and broken conduits. Night had fallen, and the rain clouds had cleared enough to allow in a spill of moonlight, the pale glow that had drawn Brandon's notice. The air had cooled quickly, and yet remained moist, and a light, hazy mist hovered, luminous and eerie.

Rene stood beneath the tear in the ceiling, bathed in moonlight. He stood with his head canted backward, his arms outstretched. The air around him was alive, filled with hundreds of birds—pigeons, sparrows, starlings, and doves, all of them flapping and fluttering and circling around him, darting and diving, moving in sweeping, spiraling groups.

Oh, my God, Brandon thought, motionless with wonder. He remembered from when he had been shot—birds had swarmed down upon his attackers, driving him away, saving him from taking a bullet to his skull. *The birds . . .*

Rene lowered his eyes from the sky and caught sight of Brandon at the top of the stairs. "You shouldn't be up and about, *petit,*" he said. As if this flipped some invisible switch, immediately, the dance-like procession of the birds ceased. They scattered about the rooms, swooping into the rafters, chattering and squawking. Brandon ducked, drawing his hand toward his face in reflexive fright as they darted past him, leaving downy tufts of feathers floating down from overhead.

When they were gone, he lowered his hand and blinked at Rene, incredulous. *How did you do that?* he thought, because the man's mind was open to him; he could feel it.

Rene smiled, but he still studied Brandon warily, the way a man will eye a dog that has snapped at him in the past. "Do what, *petit?*" he asked innocently.

Call the birds, Brandon said as Rene approached. *Make them fly around you?*

Rene shrugged. "I don't know," he replied. "I've always been able to, ever since I was a little boy. I just open my mind to them, and once I sense them, I just . . . push myself into them. I see through their eyes, sense through their senses. I don't know how to describe it otherwise. Why? You can't?"

Brandon shook his head. *My telepathy isn't very strong,* he thought.

Rene laughed. "Says who, *petit?*"

My family, Brandon replied, puzzled by his reaction.

Rene chuckled. "Then they lied to you," he said. He patted Brandon's shoulder, heading for the steps. "Come on. Let's go downstairs, back in front of the fire before we both—"

Wait, Brandon thought, catching his arm. Rene paused, glancing down at Brandon's hand and then up at Brandon's face. His brows narrowed slightly, just enough for Brandon to glean his unspoken, disapproving message and Brandon turned loose of his sleeve. *Wait,* he thought again. *Please tell me what you meant. You said they lied to me.*

"I don't know why someone said you're weak, *petit,*" Rene said. "I've never met anyone but you and my daddy with the power, but yours is sure as hell strong. A lot stronger than his—more than anything I've ever felt before. You damn near split my skull open downstairs earlier, from the feel of things."

What? Brandon thought, bewildered. *No, that wasn't me. It was you, Rene.*

Again, Rene smiled innocently, almost mysteriously. *Says who,* petit?

"You don't believe me?" he asked aloud. When Brandon shook his head, hesitant and uncertain, he nodded toward the exposed rafters overhead. "Try calling the birds, then. See for yourself."

Brandon didn't know what kind of game Rene was playing. *No. No, I can't.*

"How do you know?" Rene asked. "You haven't even tried." He held out his hand and Brandon watched, fascinated, as a pigeon fluttered down and settled against his palm. Rene noticed his interest out of the corner of his gaze and smiled, giving his hand a shake, scaring the bird aloft again.

Alright, Brandon thought. *OK, fine. But you're wrong about it. You're wrong about me.* His family couldn't have lied to him. True, his telepathy had seemed to be growing ever since he'd left the great house, swelling beyond his control at times, but that still didn't mean his family hadn't told him the truth about his potential. *Father wouldn't have lied to me. Neither would Tessa, not before her bloodletting. Caine and the Grandfather, everyone else might have, but not Father or Tessa.*

He thought about what Rene had said. *I just open my mind to them, and once I sense them, I just . . . push myself into them. I see through their eyes, sense through their senses.*

"You just can't try too hard is the thing," Rene said. "It doesn't take much. Their thoughts are really innocent, simple, you know? They don't love or hate. They just eat, shit, and make baby birds."

Brandon looked up at the ceiling. He couldn't even see the birds, much less call them. He concentrated, trying to open his mind, extending his senses beyond sight, smell, touch. *This won't work,* he thought. *I know it won't. I'm not strong enough to do this. I've never seen anyone in the Brethren call to birds like that. I'm not strong enough.*

After a few moments of nothing but Rene's gentle but unwavering scrutiny filling his mind, Brandon sighed, disappointed and frustrated. He threw his hands up demonstratively: *See?*

"It takes practice, that's all," Rene said with a shrug. "We can try again later."

We can try all you like, Brandon thought. *It's still not going to work. You're wrong about me, Rene.*

Chapter Seventeen

Why do you call me that word? Brandon wrote. *Petty? Pity? I can't understand what you're saying.*

He sat shivering against one of the leather sofas facing the fireplace. Rene took a seat in a chair across from him, slouching comfortably, crossing his long legs at the ankles. He'd closed his mind to Brandon, forcing their conversation into the open. He'd carried in a bottle of vodka from the kitchen, and Brandon watched as he poured some into a cut-crystal tumbler.

Brandon ripped off the sheet and leaned forward, offering it to Rene, who smiled as he read the note. "It's *petit*," he said, eliciting only a wide-eyed, bewildered look from Brandon. Rene laughed, shaking his head. He pressed the tumbler to his lips and tilted his head back, draining it dry in a single swallow. "I was born in Louisiana," he said. "My family is honest-to-shit Cajun, and when you're honest-to-shit Cajun, Brandon Noble, you speak French. At least every other word, if you can help it. *Petit* is a pet name, a term of endearment offered to someone smaller or younger than yourself. It's not *petty* or *pity*." He reached out, plucking the pen from Brandon's hand and writing the word in the notebook. When he was finished, he leaned back and poured himself another dollop of vodka. "*Petit* means *little*, like in *little brother.* Which, for all I know, you damn well could be to me. The world is a mighty small place at times."

I don't think we're related, Brandon wrote. *But I'm not sure. I don't know much about our history. The Elders keep account of all of that in the Tomes.*

Again, he ripped the page out and offered it to Rene. This time, Rene frowned as he read. "Tomes? Elders?" he asked. "What is all that? You asked me before if I was a part of something—*Brethren,* you called it." He leaned forward in his chair, his brows raising in sudden interest. "Are there more of us, then? More where you came from?"

Brandon nodded. *Two hundred and twenty-three,* he wrote. *And soon to be twenty-four,* he thought, his mind turning momentarily, and with melancholy, to Tessa and her unborn child.

We live in Kentucky, he continued. *The Brethren own farms there, thoroughbred horse racing farms, and a bourbon distillery.*

"Bourbon?" Rene smiled. "I like them already."

Don't, Brandon wrote. *The Brethren live on about 1,750 acres split among four families—the Nobles, the Davenants, the Trevilians, and the Giscards. Nobody bothers us there. It's very secluded and isolated. No one coming or going. We live our whole lives there—born, married, dead, and buried.*

Rene held this note in his hand for a long moment, his gaze somewhat distant. "If that's true, *petit,*" he said, cutting his eyes toward Brandon. "Then what are you doing here? It's a long walk from Kentucky."

Brandon hesitated, the point of the pen pressed against the page. He hadn't been able to reveal the truth about himself, much less his circumstances to Lina, and it had still nearly seen her killed. He wasn't certain he could— or should—trust Rene Morin. *I ran away,* he said simply.

Rene read the statement and looked at him for a long moment, his eyes sharp. He wanted to press Brandon on the matter; Brandon didn't need to read his mind to realize this. He could tell it in Rene's face, the tenseness in his posture. From the moment he'd learned that there were others like him among the Brethren, his entire body language had changed, from relaxed and comfortable to tense and charged, filled with taut, anxious energy. *He's spent his whole life looking for others like him, while I've spent mine struggling to escape them.*

Rene wanted to ask Brandon why he'd run away, but remained silent. After a moment, he sat back in the chair again, lifting his glass in hand and draining it dry.

I need to go, Brandon wrote. *You've been very kind to me, but I can't stay here.*

"What?" Rene said, frowning. "Why not?"

They're looking for me, Brandon said. *They'll be angry when they find me.* He closed his eyes momentarily as Caine's words echoed in his mind. *We followed your scent, little brother. The stink of your weakness clings to you—pathetic and unmistakable.*

He thought of Lina's horrified reaction to Caine's transformation from man into monster, how she'd screamed to see his eyes blacken over, his jaw snap loose of its moorings, his teeth fully extended.

His teeth . . . Brandon felt his heart suddenly shudder, and his breath stilled. *Oh, Christ,* he thought, remembering what he'd forgotten—for far too long, he'd forgotten it now. *My pills. Holy shit, my pills are at Jackson's apartment.*

He glanced at Rene and then quickly wrote again, *I need to go.*

What do you mean, you got the prescription for him? Lina typed to Jackson. She'd returned to his apartment under the pretense of informing him about the "break-in," and Sun Ying, the landlady, had only been too happy to let her inside. *What the hell is that stuff, Jackie, and why does Brandon need it?*

She had gone to the bus station and airport already, showing as many attendants and ticket agents as she could find both the photograph of Brandon she'd found in his bag, and her police badge, if only to further prompt their memories. Nobody had recalled seeing a young man even remotely resembling Brandon. She'd gone back and forth between the two sites periodically, quizzing the same employees over and over again, hoping she was somehow simply crossing paths with Brandon, missing him along the way, but still no luck. He hadn't been to the bus depot or the airport. She'd even called the company who had towed his car, but the Audi remained present and accounted for—and as yet, not paid for—in their impound lot.

Where could he be? she thought, desperate with worry. She'd gone back to the Bluebell Inn and tried to retrace his steps from there, walking to neighboring businesses and stores, showing his picture, asking if anyone recognized him. It was as if Brandon had stepped out their motel room door and simply vanished off the face of the earth. That his family might have found him, intercepted him somehow, was a horrifying yet all-too-real possibility—one that Lina refused to consider for too long.

If they have, I will kick Jude's ass, she thought. *He won't walk without a goddamn limp ever again—I swear to God.*

She hadn't told Jackie any of this, much less that Brandon was gone and his apartment had been trashed. She'd only said she'd discovered the pills in Brandon's knapsack and wanted to know what was going on. She didn't know what else to do, what other course to follow. She had nothing to go on—absolutely nothing, except for those pills. She hoped like hell she might be able to squeeze an answer out there somehow.

I'm trying to help him, Jackson typed back. *It's an antidepressant, Lina, and I got the prescription for him because Christ knows he needs it, living at that place, that godforsaken farm. You don't know his family, what it's like for him there.*

"Oh, I'm starting to get a really good idea, Jackie," Lina muttered under her breath.

I had the Rx written in my name, Jackie said. *Sent to the farm once a month. Brandon always picks up the mail, so I knew he'd get it. But I also knew if it was in my name, they'd*

*think it was an outdated delivery if someone else intercepted it
first, something from when I used to live there.*

Lina pinched the bridge of her nose and closed her
eyes, thinking. It didn't make sense. Brandon had been
nearly frantic to take those pills. She had a suspicion that
part of the reason he'd tried to run away from Joe's Wok
on Friday—and why he'd kissed her on such an impas-
sioned impulse—was because he'd either forgotten or
been delayed in taking them. He'd brought the pills with
him ever since, and had made it a point to take them,
even if it meant doing so in front of her, and risking her
notice. He'd lied to her about what they were for. *Why,
Brandon? What are you trying to hide?*

*Jackie, he said something to me about having broken his
hands,* she typed. *Do you know about that?*

She couldn't imagine that he wouldn't; with something
that devastating and potentially crippling to Brandon,
surely word would have reached Jackson somehow, if not at
the time of the occurrence, then certainly in the aftermath.

WHAT? Jackson typed, all caps to emphasize his surprise. For a moment, that remained stark and startled on
the screen, and then he continued, his words flying.
*What are you talking about, broke his hands? Jesus Christ,
when was this? How did he break his hands? Both of them,
Lina—hands, not hand? Jesus Christ, did that son of a bitch
Augustus Noble do something to him? Did he—*

Jackie, I don't know, she typed quickly, cutting him off.
*I don't know what happened. His hands are fine now, and he
mentioned it in passing, like it was no big deal. I caught him
taking those pills—the ones you got for him—and he told me
they were painkillers, something for his hands. He must have
been lying.*

But somehow, she knew that wasn't true. *My grandfather broke my hands when he found out I'd applied to Gallaudet,* he'd told her, and Lina understood that if she
told this to her brother, it would more than break Jackson's heart. It would see him on the first plane out of

Florida for Kentucky, where he would promptly introduce Augustus Noble head-first to his own ass.

Brandon doesn't lie, Jackson wrote. He was upset, nearly
distraught by her revelation. She didn't need to see his
face, or hear any vocal inflections to understand this
plainly. Jackson loved Brandon. He still suffered a tremendous amount of personal guilt over having left the boy
alone in Kentucky, as if his dismissal had been of his own
choosing, and he'd abandoned Brandon somehow.

Jackie, he's fine, Lina typed, wanting to reassure him.
*His hands are fine. Whatever happened, it's over now and
behind him.*

That wasn't true, either, and she knew it. She thought
about his brother Caine, speared to the wall, the length
of a *katana* shoved through his gut, as he'd thrashed and
screamed at them.

*There's no corner of this earth, no measure of time that can
hide you! We'll find you! We'll come for you! We'll never stop
coming for you, you bastard!*

She knew that however Brandon's hands had been injured, it would be nothing compared to what would
happen to him if his family found him again. *God help
him,* she thought. *It's far from over.*

Jackie, I need to go, she typed. She didn't know what she
would do next, but every moment she wasted being idle
was another in which Brandon could be in terrible
danger. *I'll call you later, OK? Give Mom a kiss.*

She locked the padlocks back into place over the plywood at Jackson's doorway and took the stairs down to
the main floor. She could have used Jackson's computer
to access the Internet instead of going all of the way back
home, but the idea of being alone in the apartment after
nightfall was definitely unsettling to her. It was dark outside, and the clouds that had hung low in the sky, spilling
rain upon the city for the better part of the day had at last
thinned out, allowing the bright sphere of the moon to
shine. She glanced at her watch as she walked out the

front doors of Jackson's apartment building. It was a quarter after eight.

Brandon was hiding something from her, and it had to do with those pills, the Wellbutrin, Jackson sent to him. Lina felt sure of it. *But what?* she wondered. She figured that yes, Brandon probably was damn-near clinically depressed, given what she'd seen and learned of his family, but she didn't think that was the reason he took the medicine. She wanted to search online, to find out what else Wellbutrin was used for; what else it could do. *I have a feeling Brandon is using it to control something,* she thought, thinking of his kiss outside the Chinese restaurant, of the wondrous, immense passion in his mouth. *And I'm willing to bet it's not depression.*

"Excuse me?"

Lina looked up, stumbling to a halt inches before plowing headlong into a young woman. The girl had dark hair and alabaster skin, with large, hesitant eyes and a slight, waiflike frame. "Excuse me," she said again. "Do you know what time it is?"

Lina glanced at her watch again. "Uh, yeah. It's eight-seventeen."

The young woman smiled, her thin mouth unfurling slightly, politely. "Thank you."

"No problem." Lina brushed past her, walking again, scanning the street for a cab. Caine Noble's threats specifically to her were still fresh in her mind . . .

I will bleed you dry.

. . . and she didn't particularly feel like hoofing it back to her apartment, being vulnerable and open out on the street as she was.

"Excuse me?" the young woman called after her, and Lina turned.

The girl had a scrap of paper in her hands, and she squinted to read it by the glow of a nearby streetlight. "Can you tell me where I might find twelve twenty-three Oakton?"

"Sure," Lina said. "That's it right there." She pointed to Jackson's apartment building.

The girl glanced over her shoulder and then back at Lina, hunching her shoulders and smiling somewhat sheepishly. Her dark hair was cropped evenly with her chin, her bangs worn bluntly cut across her brow to lend her face a heart shape. She wore a lightweight pea coat hemmed at mid-thigh, with a plaid skirt beneath that was short enough to show off her strong but slender legs, long like a ballerina's. She wore a pair of wedge-heeled boots that, at least to Lina's observation, sure as hell weren't made for walking. She wasn't the least bit surprised to see the girl fidgeting from one foot to the other, as if her feet ached her. *Welcome to the big city,* she thought.

"Oh," the girl said. "Oh, uh, thank you again."

"You're welcome again," Lina said, and as a cab approached, she darted for the curb, her hand outstretched. "Hey!" she shouted, and the taxi slowed, pulling over for her. *That's how you get around here, sweetheart,* she thought, ducking in and closing the door behind her as the cab drove off.

Brandon wished like hell he'd taken a cab to Jackson's apartment building instead of accepting Rene's offer of a lift. Brandon hadn't told Rene why he wanted to go, only that he needed to, and Rene had been more than happy to oblige. He'd led Brandon from the loft, at last showing him where a heavy steel door opened out onto a steep stairwell hidden in a distant corner. They rode a freight elevator down together. Brandon counted at least a dozen floors passing them en route, and he'd turned to Rene, bewildered. *What is this place?* he'd written.

Rene had laughed as the elevator rumbled to a stop. "It's home, *petit,*" he'd said, leaning over and raising the metal grate of the elevator door. He stepped aside to let Brandon exit first. "Home, sweet home."

He'd brought Brandon to an underground garage where he kept a colorful assortment of new and vintage sportscars and roadsters. He fished a set of keys out of his pocket and thumbed off the alarm on a low-slung, sleek, silver Mercedes SLK 280. "Hop in," he said to Brandon, grinning broadly.

By that point, Rene had polished off the better part of a fifth of vodka, and Brandon hesitated. Granted, in all likelihood, Rene's metabolism was as accelerated as Brandon's, and the effects of the alcohol would be short lived. Still, he felt uncertain. *Should you be driving?* he wrote.

Rene had only laughed, but apparently *should* and *could* were mutually exclusive terms in his vocabulary. Brandon wrapped his hand around the door handle and clung so tightly, his knuckles blanched. It hurt his arm, and sent stabbing pain through his right side, but he didn't have much choice. He couldn't hear the engine scream as Rene launched the car from the garage, up and out onto the city streets, but he could feel it thrumming around and within him, a deep and penetrating vibration that shuddered through his seat. Rene had dropped the convertible top, despite the chilly night air, and Brandon's hair whipped about his face in the wind.

"Some fun, eh, *petit?*" Rene asked, as they came to a stop at a light. He turned to Brandon, his blond hair windswept and disheveled, his mouth stretched in a broad, delighted grin.

Where the fuck did you learn to drive? Brandon wrote, his hand shaking.

"Louisiana," Rene replied with a wink, as the light turned green and the Mercedes rocketed forward with enough speed to snap Brandon back in his seat.

By the time they parked along a side street adjacent to Jackson's building, Brandon was ashen and shaking, his hair askew, his gut lodged somewhere between his diaphragm and throat.

"*Voilà,*" Rene said, still smiling. He forked his fingers

through his hair, sweeping it back from his face. "Here we are. Safe and sound."

That's a matter of opinion, Brandon thought with a frown, unhooking his seat belt. He sucked in a pained breath as he opened the car door and went to climb out. He glanced over his shoulder and saw Rene moving to do the same. He paused, shaking his head.

"What?" Rene asked.

Brandon had left the notebook and pen on the console in the car. Rather than sit again and reach for them, he patted his hand against his chest and then pointed to the building. *I'm going alone,* he tried to convey. Rene hadn't yet lowered his mental defenses again and allowed for communication with Brandon, but he tried anyway. *It won't take a second. Just wait here for me.*

Rene shrugged, slouching back in the seat, though whether responding in comprehension to Brandon's hand signal or thought, he didn't say. "Suit yourself, *petit,*" he said, reaching beside him and reclining his seat. He folded his hands behind his head and made a show of looking skyward, admiring the moon. "I'll be here. Don't go running off on me now."

I won't, Brandon thought, limping away from the car, following the sidewalk around to the building's front entrance. *You may be my only way out of this city, Rene—whether I like it or not.*

He ducked inside, and waited for the elevator. He was hurting entirely too much, and feeling far too weak to attempt eight flights of stairs. Rene had offered him another of the Percodans before they'd left, but Brandon had refused.

I'm OK, he'd written. *It hurts, but it's bearable.*

"That's because the one I gave you before hasn't worn off fully yet, *petit,*" Rene had warned. "When it does, you're going to be miserable."

Brandon hadn't listened, and now—especially after that deranged car ride—he wished like hell that he had.

He leaned heavily against the wall as the elevator car rode up, and closed his eyes, trembling in pain.

He didn't know what to think of Rene, or what made the man such an expert in pain management that he kept a veritable pharmacy of medicinal options readily on hand. He'd noticed Rene's limp, the way he seemed to favor his right side, and how he'd used his hands to help swing his leg into the car once he'd sat in the driver's seat. He hadn't said anything to Brandon by way of explanation, however, and Brandon hadn't asked.

He didn't know what to think of Rene, and it was obvious, Rene didn't know what to make of him either. He'd been kind to Brandon, gentle to him and uninhibited in opening his mind to the younger man, soothing him when he'd first awoke. After everything that had happened in the short time since, however, Rene had lapsed into a guarded mode, seeming far more aloof and cautious around him.

Brandon reached the eighth floor and limped down the corridor toward Jackson's apartment. He found a large panel of plywood propped against Jackson's doorway, secured in place with two padlocks and remembered that the door had broken during his fight with Emily. *Terrific*, he thought, staring at the locks in dismay. *Just what I needed.*

He reached down, pulling at the bottom of the plywood, easing it back. He was able to pry it enough to squeeze through by crouching on his hands and knees and wriggling. He had to twist and shimmy, and in doing so, barked his injured side any number of agonizing times. By the time he made it through, he lay against the floor of Jackson's entry way in a fetal coil, shuddering and breathless with pain.

Finally, he staggered to his feet and looked around. He could see moonlight streaming in through the windows, glittering and winking off of broken glass from the shattered coffee table. The blood was gone, the grisly mess left after Lina had shot Emily in the head, but

Brandon wasn't surprised. The Grandfather and the Brethren Council might have sanctioned Caine and Emily's departure from the compound, but they would have done so only with a strict caveat—*remain unnoticed*. The Brethren lived in constant fear of discovery; that Brandon had been gone for nearly a week now, roaming on his own, had probably left them in a panic. He wondered what they would say if they realized that Caine and Emily had indulged in a little bloodlust smorgasbord before attacking him. They'd both fed like gluttons the night before; Brandon had smelled it on them, seen it in the way they'd healed so rapidly. He'd also seen the daily newspaper before leaving Rene's loft—two bodies had been found that morning along the riverfront, a pair of homeless men whose throats had been torn open, and whose bodies had been drained nearly dry of blood.

So much for keeping under the radar, Brandon thought, following the corridor down toward Jackson's bedroom. The police were swarming all over the incident like a monkey on a cupcake, with speculations of ritualistic murder, devil worshipping, and vampire cults. *And they don't know the half of it.*

He stopped in the bedroom doorway, his eyes widening in surprised dismay. His duffel bag was gone. *What the hell . . . ?*

He looked on the opposite side of the room, then endured more pain as he dropped to his knees, teeth gritted, and peered under the bed. There was no sign of it—his duffel bag, his coat, all of his belongings. Everything was gone. *My pills . . . !*

He looked up toward the bedside table and realized not everything was gone. His notebook, the one with the gilded brass cover and chain his father had given to him, sat there, waiting for him. In Kentucky, he hadn't been able to go a day without the damnable thing, because it had been his only way of communicating. He'd been spoiled in Lina's company—and more than this, he'd been comfortable with her, and the notebook—once as much a part of him as his hands or feet—had been all but forgotten. The bitter irony that it was apparently all that remained of his personal possessions wasn't lost upon Brandon and he threw it across the room, sending it smashing into the wall. *Goddamn it!*

He sat against the mattress and tangled his fingers in his hair. Caine must have taken his bag with him when he'd moved Emily's body. *Terrific.*

It was only a matter of time before the bloodlust came upon him again, and without the Wellbutrin, Brandon would be helpless against it. For the moment, his pain and the residual effects of the painkiller Rene had given him seemed to be enough of a distraction, but Brandon knew that wouldn't last. The bloodlust would come, and when it did, he'd be driven to feed, to kill.

No, Brandon thought, his brows furrowed as he stood. *I'm not like that. I'm not like them—not like my family or Rene. I'm not a monster, some fucking killer. I'm not. I won't let myself be like that.*

He crossed the room and leaned over, picking up his brass-plated notebook. He looped the chain around his neck, and tucked it beneath the zippered front of the leather jacket Rene had loaned him. He walked back down the hall, steeling himself to leave Jackson's apartment in the same agonizing fashion by which he'd entered.

As soon as he stepped off the elevator at the building's ground floor, his extrasensory awareness kicked in, raising the hairs along the nape of his neck. He stumbled to a halt, looking around, wide eyed and apprehensive. The entry-way was empty; it was after eleven, and most residents were home for the night or in bed, but still he could sense somebody nearby—someone not human. Someone like him.

Goddamn it, Rene, I told you to stay in the car, he thought, because there was no way it could be Caine or one of the Brethren. Even they weren't skilled enough hunters to have tracked him by his scent to the apartment that quickly. And they had no reason to stake out the building in the hopes he would return.

He walked down the front steps outside the building, looking around for Rene, because the sensation of his presence had grown even stronger. He cut to his left, hurrying in the direction of the car, ready to just go back to the loft, cut his losses, drop a painkiller, and sleep. The pain in his shoulder had grown unbearable, radiating throughout his entire body. He didn't know what he was going to do and all at once, he just didn't give a shit. He was exhausted, shell-shocked, hurting, and weak.

I'll worry about it tomorrow, he thought. *I know where Rene keeps his cars now. I'll just steal one if I have to. I hate to do that, but if I stay here, they'll find me—and worse, they might find Lina, too. I just don't—*

A hand fell against his sleeve, reaching out from the shadowed alcove between the staircase and the side of the building.

Oh, Jesus, one of the Brethren—!

He whirled, his right hand snapping out reflexively, catching his would-be assailant roughly by the throat. He slammed the person back against the wall of the apartment building, gritting his teeth against a swell of molten pain that ripped through his side at the motion, the impact. He reared his left fist back, ready to let it fly, and then he found himself staring into two large, dark, frightened eyes, framed by dark hair—a young woman's face, terrified and terrifyingly familiar.

"Brandon . . . !" she hiccuped, gulping breathlessly against his hand. She pawed at his fingers, struggling to dislodge his throttling grasp. "Brandon . . . please . . . !"

He let her go and staggered back, his eyes enormous with shock. She clutched at her throat, gasping. *Oh, God, no,* he thought, anguished. *Not now, not tonight . . . Jesus, not ever! Please not this—not her.*

I can't fight my sister!

His twin, Tessa, reached for him, still panting. "Brandon," she said. "Please . . . listen to me. Please. I . . . I'm here to help you!"

Chapter Eighteen

Rene and Tessa hit it off like a soaking wet cat introduced to a dog with a burr up its ass.

"Here, *petit,*" Rene said gently, leaning over as Brandon sat reclined in the Mercedes' passenger seat. Brandon was semi-lucid, his eyes heavily lidded, his mind groggy with pain; grabbing Tessa had been the last injury atop far too many insults that evening. Rene tucked his fingertips between Brandon's lips, easing a pill against his tongue. "*Je suis désolé* . . . I'm sorry. You're going to have to choke it down dry."

Brandon nodded, grimacing at the bitter taste of the pill, and struggling to work up enough saliva to wash it down his throat.

"What is that you're giving him?" Tessa asked, leaning forward from the backseat and into Brandon's line of sight. Her dark eyes were round with worry. "What did you just give him? What happened to him? Why is he in so much pain? What—"

"You always ask so many goddamn questions at once, *pischouette*?" Rene asked, frowning irritably at her.

Tessa's eyes flew wide. "Get your hands off of him," she snapped, shoving Rene roughly back in his seat. She leaned over Brandon, reaching for the buckle of his seat belt. The hem of her short plaid skirt rode up to the swell

of her buttocks as she did this, awarding a fleeting peek at
her panties that Brandon noticed Rene didn't miss. "I
don't know who the hell you are, mister, but we don't
need your help." She leaned even farther, standing up in
the backseat now, trying to reach the passenger side door
to open it. Rene cocked his head slightly, keeping his gaze
fixed with interest upon her bottom, and she glanced over
her shoulder, catching him in the act.

"You asshole," she said, frowning, slapping him in the
head, immediately darting back into the seat. She
climbed out the side, stepping over the folded convertible top, and opened the door from the sidewalk. "Come
on, Brandon," she said, squatting and taking Brandon by
the arm. "We're leaving."

"No, you're not." Rene caught Brandon's other arm
and pulled him back into the car.

Tessa glared at him, her cheeks flushing with sudden,
angry color as she tugged against Brandon. "Yes, we are."

"No, *pischouette*," Rene said, his brows narrowing as he
yanked Brandon back. "You're not. And you keep tugging on that bum arm of his, you're liable to see him laid
up for longer than he's already going to be."

Brandon shrugged them both away, shaking his head,
flapping his hands to shoo them. *God, I don't need this,* he
thought, grimacing.

Tessa leaned over him. *Brandon, what happened?* she
asked in his mind. *Who is this asshole, anyway? Look, I've
got a car. It's parked just a few blocks away. We can walk there
right now. You can lean on me. Trust me—won't you please
trust me? We've got to—*

This asshole's the guy with a car right here. Rene's
thought's interrupted her as he opened his mind for the
first time in hours. *Your* frère *doesn't need to be walking anywhere at the moment. What are you, blind? Now get that sweet
little ass of yours back in the car if you're coming, so I can get
him the fuck out of here and to bed where he belongs.*

Tessa backpedaled from the car, her eyes round and
shocked. Brandon hadn't had the chance to explain to

her yet, to offer more than perfunctory introductions between them. She hadn't realized Rene wasn't human; she might have been able to sense his presence, but had obviously dismissed this as sensing Brandon. She stumbled against the curb, wobbling on the wedge heels of her boots, and sat down hard against the damp sidewalk. She blinked between Brandon and Rene, her mouth agape. "You . . ." she gasped. "He . . . he just . . . he's . . . !"

Rene smiled at her, broad and disarming. "That's right, *pischouette*," he told her mildly. "I'm like you. It's a small world after all, no?"

Brandon had restless dreams. In the first, he imagined himself standing outside of an apartment building, some kind of restored, subdivided Victorian. He felt tremulous, his heart racing, his breaths coming short, ragged, and rapid. The bloodlust was upon him, flushing his skin, warming him from the inside out against the dank chill of the night.

He looked up at the mostly darkened windows, scanning along the outer building facade. He inhaled deeply through his nose, and a myriad of scents and fragrances came to him. One in particular caught his interest and attention, and he turned his face in that direction, sniffing again.

He dreamed of following the scent, of using the nooks and crannies among the bricks and stones of the building's walls to tuck his fingers and toes as he climbed slowly, steadily toward the fourth story. He was utterly heedless to the danger, the potential to fall; his body felt strong and sure, infused with preternatural potency from the rising bloodlust.

He climbed almost to the roof, where a turret flanked with windows awarded a panoramic view of the surrounding neighborhood, the street far below. Two of these windows had been left ajar, raised in their sashes to allow the cool breeze to filter inside. The scent that had drawn him from the street was coming from here, somewhere inside the room past the windows. Brandon dreamed of easing one open, shoving it up quietly in its frame and then slipping inside, wriggling over the sill and into the dark room beyond.

He knelt on the floor for a long moment, feeling the bloodlust surging through him now, infusing his muscles, making his nerve endings scrape and sing. His mouth was throbbing, his gums aching as his canine teeth descended completely, and the shadow-draped room seemed to lighten as his pupils spread wide, swallowing his irises, filling his corneas, drawing in every scrap or hint of illumination discernable.

He could see a man sleeping in bed ahead of him, a black man, naked from the waist up, with a blond woman stretched out beside him. Brandon looked to his left and found the source of the intoxicating scent that had lured him that far—a dark suit coat and slacks laid out against a wing-backed chair, a white shirt draped atop.

I know this man, Brandon thought, moving silently toward the bed. *I know his smell, I know his face. I've seen him before. It's Jude Hannam, Lina's ex.*

He glanced into the mirror hanging above a chest of drawers as he passed. To his surprise, it was not his reflection he saw, but his brother's. He dreamed that he was Caine, that Caine had somehow tracked down Jude Hannam by following his scent.

Not his, Brandon realized, his stomach tightening with sudden horror. *Not Jude's scent, but mine. It's all over that suit.*

Caine clamped his hand firmly down against the blond woman's, mouth, and her eyes flew wide in startled fright. She uttered a feeble, muffled mewl, and Caine tore her throat open, burying the hooks of his canines deep into her neck. She thrashed against the bed as he ripped back a broad flap of flesh and then gulped greedily, noisily at the blood that gushed from the massive wound. Her struggles woke Jude, and he sat up, his eyes wide.

"Ashlee . . . ?" he began, sleepy and bewildered, and then he uttered a choked, startled cry as Caine reached across the bed and caught him by the throat.

"You're not Brandon," he purred, blood smeared around his mouth, spattering from his lips as he spoke. Ashlee lay still against the mattress, uttering soft, sodden, gurgling sounds as she bled to death atop the Egyptian cotton sheets.

Jude gargled for startled breath as Caine hoisted him out of bed. He threw Jude across the room, sending him crashing against the mirror, shattering it in a spray of moonlight-splashed shards. Jude crumpled to the floor, dressed only in a stark-white pair of boxer shorts. He looked up at Caine, wide-eyed, bewildered, and frightened.

"Who . . . who are . . . what do you . . . ?" he whimpered, shaking his head, holding out his hand as Caine closed in on him. He squealed when Caine caught his throat again and hoisted him aloft, slamming him back against the wall. "Oh . . . oh, Jesus . . . what are you?" Jude wheezed in terror.

"You're not Brandon," Caine said again, and then he lunged forward, his jaw snapping unhinged, his teeth poised to strike.

The dreamscape shifted, Brandon's mind drawing him from that disturbing scene and into something much sweeter. This time, he dreamed of Lina. He could see her at a computer desk in her apartment, her arms crossed over the keyboard, her head resting against them. She had fallen asleep while surfing the Internet. He could see beyond her shoulder to the computer screen, a Google search results page with a list of Web sites about Wellbutrin.

Why are you looking up Wellbutrin, Lina? he thought, puzzled, but it didn't matter. All that mattered was that he was with her again and he didn't feel frightened or anxious of discovery, that Caine or the Brethren would come upon them again. He stepped close to her chair and leaned over, brushing her hair aside and sliding the tip of his nose, his lips against her throat.

She stirred and when he leaned against her, nuzzling her ear, drawing his arm around her middle to caress her breast through her shirt, she tilted her head back against his shoulder. *I miss you,* he thought, his fingertips settling against her nipple, stroking it until it hardened into a fine, rigid point.

She reached up, touching his face, twining her fingers in his hair, and opened her eyes. She blinked sleepily at him and smiled. *My God, you're beautiful,* he thought.

"Brandon . . ." he watched her murmur. He touched his lips to hers, and she opened his mouth, kissing him deeply. His tongue circled against hers, mimicking the motions of his fingers against her nipple. He slid his other hand down her stomach, reaching beneath the waistband of her sweatpants. She arched her back, giving him more access, and her breath fluttered against his tongue as he slipped his fingers between her thighs, sliding against her warm, slick folds.

He found her core, the sensitive nub at her apex, and her breath sharpened against his mouth as he moved his fingers, circling against her here. Her grasp tightened in his hair, urging him on. He could feel himself growing hard, the crotch of his jeans becoming uncomfortably tight. He could feel his gums swelling, his teeth wanting to drop, but it didn't matter. He didn't care. All that mattered was Lina; all he cared about was making love to her.

He slipped his hand from beneath her pants and drew her to her feet. He turned her toward him and kissed her face-to-face, shoving the chair between them aside. His shoulder didn't hurt him here; he could move freely and unabated, and he tangled his fingers in her hair, pulling her near, kissing her deeply. *I love you,* he thought, as he felt her hands between them, tugging at his jeans, unbuttoning his fly. *I love you, Lina. God, more than anything. I love you.*

She shoved his jeans down and they danced together clumsily as he stepped out of them. He pushed her sweatpants, her panties away from her hips, and she kicked them free of her feet. Brandon clasped her buttocks in his hands, and lifted her; her legs wrapped around his middle and he pushed her back against the nearest wall, kissing her. She was lean and lithe in his arms, and he supported her slight weight easily against him, feeling her breasts, the hardened points of her nipples press into his chest, the flat plain of her belly mold to fit his own.

Her legs were spread wide, with nothing between them or preventing him, and he sank deeply into her incredible warmth. He slid back slowly and then entered her again, gripping her buttocks, sliding in and out. He took his time with her, setting a slow, deliberate pace at first, delving deeply. She clutched at his shoulders, growing impatient with need, her body trembling against him.

He increased his rhythm, pushing himself into her again and again, until finally, they moved together with enough pounding force to send things clattering from cabinets and across countertops in the adjacent kitchen. When she climaxed, her legs tightened about his waist, her fingers coiled in his hair, and she arched her back away from the wall, throwing her head back, gasping his name in delight. Her innermost sheath constricted against him in sudden, rhythmic waves, drawing him to his own abrupt release. He pushed himself into her, one last powerful thrust, and cried out soundlessly.

When it was over, he held her, remaining inside of her, loathe to leave her. She touched his face, kissing his brow, his eyelids, his nose, his lips, whispering his name to him, her eyes glossed with tears. "Brandon," she pleaded. "Where were you? I . . . I've been looking for you. I've been so scared."

Please don't cry, he thought, but she did anyway. She clung to his neck, clutching at him, her breath shuddering against his skin. *Oh, God, Lina, please don't. You'll break my heart . . .*

He came to with a start, his eyes flying wide, his body jerking reflexively. For a moment, he was disoriented, forgetting where he was and what had happened to him, but then pain lanced through his wounded shoulder, and he grimaced, remembering abruptly and all too well.

He found Tessa sitting in a chair beside him. They were in Rene's loft again, and he lay in the bed surrounded by white drapes. Of Rene, there was no sign, and Brandon winced as he tried to sit up, looking for him.

"You should rest," Tessa said, rising to her feet and trying to ease him back again. He frowned and shrugged away from her. He still didn't know what the hell she was doing there, or how she'd found him. Outside Jackson's apartment building, she had told him that she'd come to help him, but that didn't necessarily make Brandon inclined to trust—or believe—her.

What time is it? he signed. Despite the Grandfather's strict and stern mandate, Tessa and their father, Sebastian, had learned a modicum of sign language; enough, at least, that he'd been able to sign with them in simple conversation.

Tessa glanced at her watch. "A little past seven in the morning," she said. "You slept through the night." She tried to stroke his hair, but he ducked away from her again.

Where's Rene? he asked.

Tessa frowned. "Last I knew, he was sitting by the fireplace," she said, apparently deciding that she would rather risk Rene overhearing by her speaking aloud than having him privy to her thoughts. She cut her eyes warily over her shoulder and leaned toward her brother. "I don't like him, Brandon. He frightens me. We don't know anything about him, and—"

He's one of us, Brandon signed, and Tessa shook her head.

"No, he's not," she said. "He might have some kind

of extrasensory abilities, like a psychic or something, but he—"

He feeds, Brandon signed, cutting her short. Her eyes widened, and he nodded. *I've seen him do it. And he's long lived. He's fifty-seven years old, he told me. He—*

"It's not possible, Brandon," Tessa whispered. "There can't be any other clans. The Council would have known about them. The Brethren would have sensed them."

She reached for him again, meaning to hold his hand, but he drew away. *What are you doing here, Tessa?* he signed.

She blinked at him, looking wounded. "I came to help you."

Brandon smirked without humor. *Since when?* he thought.

She heard him, and the pain in her face only deepened. "Please don't do that," she said. "Whatever you think about me, whatever you think has come between us, Brandon, please . . . it's different now. I'm different now. You know that." She pressed her hand against her belly, her eyes mournful. "I . . . I want something different for my baby. Another life—a better one—than what I've known. You were right, what you told me at the great house, the day that Emily and Caine were tormenting you, after . . . after your hands . . ."

After the Grandfather and Caine broke my hands, Brandon signed, his gestures forceful and angry, making her hunch her shoulders, her eyes swim with tears. *They broke my goddamn hands, Tessa,* he told her in his mind. *The Grandfather beat me senseless and then he and Caine took turns crushing every bone in my hands because I applied to college. That's it, Tessa—that's all, my horrible crime. I wanted to get away from them.*

Her tears spilled and her shoulders trembled. He might have left her alone then, but didn't. He felt years' worth of bitterness and hurt welling up inside of him, ready and eager for release. *He hates me anyway—they all do. They all wish I'd died that night of the burglary. You think*

I don't hear their thoughts? See it in their eyes? They're ashamed of me, and they wish I'd died. Even Father—

Tessa's eyes widened, and she shook her head. "Brandon, no," she pleaded. "No, Father loves you. He—"

I've seen it in his mind! Brandon cried, making her flinch. He crumpled back against the pillows, exhausted, hurting. *You're ashamed of me, too.*

"No," she said, shaking her head again. "That's not true."

Who sent you to find me, Tessa? Was it Father? The Grandfather? Or Martin, your husband? They figured Caine and Emily couldn't pound me into compliance, so they'd try to capture me next with kindness?

"Caine and Emily?" she asked. "They were here?"

Brandon nodded. *Night before last, they found me at Jackson's apartment. They attacked me.* He thought of his dream, of how he'd imagined he was Caine. How he'd dreamed that Caine was hunting for him. *Emily is dead,* he said.

Tessa shrank back, her face draining of color, her eyes widening with horror. "What?" she said, her hand fluttering to her face. "What . . . oh, my God, Brandon, what have you done?"

Nothing less than what the Grandfather had planned for them—and you—to do to me, he replied.

This time, his words angered instead of wounded. "The Grandfather didn't send Caine or Emily to find you," she said. "Or me, either, Brandon. He wouldn't send us—practically children. He's petitioned the Brethren Council and they've agreed—the Elders are the ones coming, Brandon."

All at once, Brandon's throat constricted, his breath drawing still. *The Elders?*

The Brethren Council was comprised of nearly one hundred adults from all of the clans, married males who had undergone the bloodletting. Among the Brethren, democratic power was not awarded to the women, and the Brethren Council was responsible for dictating and enforcing a majority of the rules and laws governing the clans.

Brandon had expected the Council to unleash some of its more venerable members to track him down and return him to Kentucky; adults like his father, uncle Adam, or Tessa's husband, Martin. But the Elders were even older and more expert than these adults; these were the Brethren members of the Grandfather's generation, ten altogether, each with centuries of experience in perfecting the art of the hunt. They had absolute and final say over all Brethren matters; omnipotent and utter control over all other members of the clans. These were Brethren with strengths the likes of which Brandon had never fully seen unleashed; twice as strong as Brandon's father, and probably twice that again his own meager merits.

"They don't know where to look," Tessa told him. "Not yet. But it won't take them long to figure it out. I remembered that Jackson Jones had moved here, so I tried to beat them. I looked in the phone book, found all the deaf schools and hit them one at a time until I found him. They said he was out of town, but I used my telepathy to trick them into giving me his address."

Brandon blinked at her, stricken. He'd never considered this, that anyone would think to track him through Jackson or the school. *Oh, Christ, if she can, what's to keep the Elders from doing it, too?* he thought.

"The Grandfather never would have let Caine and Emily go," Tessa said. "Oh, God, they must have followed me. They must have been watching me. They must have . . ."

She reached for him, touching his hand, and this time, he didn't pull away. "I came to help you, Brandon," she said. "To warn you about the Elders. We have to leave here." Her voice choked, and her eyes filled with tears again. "The Grand-father doesn't want to see you banished to the Beneath, Brandon. You defied him. You ran away. He'll see you answer for it—in blood. He . . . he wants the Elders to kill you."

* * *

"We have to get out of here," Tessa had pleaded, and Brandon had agreed. He made her wait for him while he crept beyond the white silk drapes and went to speak with Rene. Tessa had a car; she'd taken her husband's Cadillac. The Brethren wouldn't report it stolen anymore than they would the Grandfather's Audi, but it was back at Jackson's apartment building. Rene would have to take them to get it.

Brandon didn't want to leave Rene behind. There were still too many unanswered questions for both of them. But he knew he had no choice. *I've already gotten Lina involved in this,* he thought. *I can't get Rene, too. Especially not against the Elders.*

The living room portion of the flat was empty, so Brandon limped toward the red velvet drapes marking Rene's bedroom. He drew the edge of the heavy fabric carefully aside and peeked within, finding Rene sitting in his boxer shorts, his legs hanging over the side of the bed.

Or rather, his left leg hanging over the side of the bed. Brandon drew back in start to realize that Rene's right leg was missing, amputated at mid-thigh. The sleek, skeletal-like frame of a prosthetic leg rested beside him against the bedspread, slender beams of black metal fused together, converging at a hinged knee joint. Beside this was an opened cigar box filled with papers and photographs. Rene had apparently been perusing through these mementos, one of which he held in his hand. At the sound of Brandon's sharp intake of breath, Rene looked up in surprise, the photograph falling to the floor.

"Oh, *bonjour, petit,*" he said, his mouth unfolding in a smile. "You are awake, no? Good. How you feeling, better now?"

Brandon waggled his hand from side to side: *So-so.* He walked hesitantly toward the bed, staring at the open space where Rene's leg should have been. He knew it was impolite, and painful besides, having been the recipient of such gawking attention before for his own handicaps, but he felt ridiculously helpless to prevent himself.

I had no fucking idea! he thought in amazement. *I mean, I'd noticed a limp, I'd seen a glimpse of some of his memories, but I never in a million years thought . . . !*

Rene noticed his attention and cocked his head to draw his gaze. Brandon lowered his eyes, feeling abashed color stoke brightly in his cheeks. *It's alright,* petit, Rene thought, opening his mind to Brandon. *You can look. It's something else, huh?*

He patted the prosthetic beside him. *This one is, too. It's got all kinds of microchips and shit in it. It's smarter than me, that's for sure. I put my weight on it and it knows to flex the knee. As close as you can get to flesh and blood in titanium.* His smile grew somewhat forlorn. *The best money can buy,* petit.

Even with Rene's permission, Brandon felt awkward looking at his leg. He genuflected, lifting the fallen photograph in hand. He blinked at it in new surprise; it was a picture of Rene surrounded by a group of five other young men, all of them in Army green fatigues and helmets, all standing arm in arm, grinning and laughing, with military tents and palm trees visible in the background. He glanced up at Rene, his brows raised, and Rene smiled gently.

"Vietnam, 1967," he said. "Ninth Infantry Division, Company E, stationed at Dong Tam in the Delta. We were a long range reconnaissance patrol platoon. I served with them until the spring of '69."

Brandon glanced quizzically at Rene's leg, and Rene chuckled. "No, that's not where that happened. My legs came out of the deal just fine." His eyes grew momentarily distant. "That's when I found out, you know, *petit.* What I am, I mean. I took a couple of rounds in the stomach and got left for dead. Nobody's fault, really. Hell, I thought I was dead, too." He smirked. "I could see my guts coming out of me. They were all over the ground, and I was lying there, in shock, trying to scoop them all back in again. *Ça fait mal!* And then, just as I've got my hands full of my own *boyaux,* here comes this little Viet Cong boy, no more than eight or nine, all dressed up in his black pajamas with an M-16A1 assault rifle in his hands."

Brandon stared at Rene, dropping to his knees and resting on the floor before him like a young child enthralled by a bedtime story. "He looked at me," Rene said. "And I looked at him, *petit*, and then he pointed that rifle square at my head, just about like this . . ." He mimed with his hands, pointing his index finger at Brandon's nose. "And then it hit me. This heat just came over me, filling me head to toe, and I leaped at him. I moved so fast, he couldn't even squeeze the trigger. I knocked him backward and beneath me and I bit his neck. I could smell his blood. That's what made me go crazy. Not the pain from my gut, or the shock of it all, or even fear when he stuck that rifle in my face. I could smell his blood. And suddenly, that's all I wanted in the world. I ripped his throat out and I drank it. He didn't even have time to scream."

Rene looked one last time at the photograph and tossed it back into the cigar box. "I lost my leg last year, *petit*, when I was shot again, this time by some *bon rien* son-of-a-bitch drug mule toting a half-kilo of cocaine in his gullet." He sifted through the pictures and papers in the box until he found something, which he handed to Brandon—a police badge.

Brandon cradled it in his hands. He'd seen this in Rene's memories earlier, that he'd been a police officer, but had nearly forgotten about it since. *I wonder if he knows Lina,* he thought.

"I was shot in the knee," Rene said. "Blew it all to hell. It might have healed on its own, but you can't go telling that to doctors. Not the human sort, anyway. So off the leg went." Rene took the badge back and dropped it into the cigar box once more. "Anyway, when I got out of the Army back in 1969, I went back home to my grandparents in Bayou Lafourche in Louisiana, where I'd grown up. I never knew my mother. She died just after I was born. I'd never known my father until then. He came to find me. He told me who I was, who he was and what we both were. Said we were the last of our sort, and that I'd live a long, long time. He was one hundred and fifty-three years old, he told me, and he'd had himself enough. Two days later, I read he ate the bitter end of a shotgun at a hotel in New Orleans. He left me everything. He was a very wealthy man, *petit*, and now . . . so am I."

He flipped the weathered lid of the cigar box closed again. "I've never forgiven myself for that little boy, though," he murmured. "Of all the things I've done in my life, all the hurt I've helped caused along my way, that one keeps with me the most." He reached for his prosthetic leg. "I never killed anybody since."

Brandon jerked as if Rene had slapped him. *What?* He reached for the notebook around his neck as Rene began strapping the titanium limb back into place. *What do you mean, you never killed anybody since?* Brandon wrote hurriedly. *Since that boy in 1969?*

That can't be right, he thought, ripping the page out and flapping it in the air until Rene slipped it from his hand.

"Yeah," Rene said with a nod. "I probably would have killed that drug muling *salaud* who blew my knee to fuck, but my partner took care of that."

But I saw you feeding, Brandon wrote. *Yesterday, there was a girl here, a redheaded girl, and I saw her neck . . .*

Rene looked down, following along as Brandon wrote. "Anise," he said. "Yeah, I told you. I pay her a little something extra, and she doesn't mind. She just thinks I'm kinky, that's all." He dropped Brandon a wink. "In her line of work, *petit*, trust me—she's seen stranger."

He stood up, drawing sharply against the straps of his prosthetic leg, securing it. He sat again, reaching for his jeans.

He doesn't kill to feed, Brandon thought, dumbfounded. *How is that possible? How can he control the bloodlust enough? How does he get enough blood to sustain himself?*

Questions flew, rapid-fire, through his mind. He forgot about leaving, his promises to Tessa that they would go. He forgot about the Elders, and his own imminent danger. He began to write, scribbling excitedly, glancing up only as Rene leaned past him for his bedside table to pick up a cordless phone.

"Hey, *chère*," he said, smiling as he answered a call. "*Comment ça va?*"

Brandon wrote again, trying to get all of his questions in some semblance of logical order. When Rene tapped his fingertip against the notebook, Brandon blinked up at him, startled. "Why don't you wait for me in the living room, *petit?*" he said. "See what that sister of yours might like by way of breakfast. I need to take this."

Brandon nodded, rising to his feet. He felt vaguely light-headed at the motion, and stumbled, catching himself against Rene's bedpost. "Go get one of those Percodans in the kitchen," Rene told him, cupping his hand against the handset's mouthpiece. "It's time again for one, or close enough, I think. Don't let yourself get to misery again, *petit*. Trust me."

Brandon nodded again, but didn't immediately go for the kitchen or the proffered medicine as he left Rene's bedside. He returned instead to his own bed behind the white silk drapes. "Will he take us?" Tessa asked. She'd been sitting against the side of the bed, but stood now, her eyes wide and anxious.

Brandon shook his head. *We're not leaving yet*, he signed.

Chapter Nineteen

"Rene, are you drunk?" Lina asked with a frown. She glanced at her bedside clock. *Christ, and it's not even eight thirty in the morning yet.*

"No, I'm not," he replied with a laugh. "You keep asking me that, *chère*, and getting pissed at me besides. You hurt my feelings. And here I was just thinking all fondly of you a minute ago."

"I need to borrow one of your cars," she said. She'd already been up for hours, and had gone for a run. She'd needed to clear her head when she'd awoke that morning. She'd fallen asleep at her computer last night and had the strangest, most dream in which Brandon was there. He'd come to her apartment somehow, and had made love to her. When she'd come to, she had still been seated at her desk—not pressed against the wall, her legs twined around his midriff, as she'd been in her dream—but her body had still felt warm and flushed, her nipples and groin acutely sensitive, as if she really had just achieved the wrenching orgasm she'd imagined.

She'd covered her face with her hands and struggled vainly not to cry. *Goddamn it, I miss you, Brandon,* she'd

thought, frustrated, lonely and frightened. *Where are you?*
Please, God, please be alright.

"Of course, *chère,*" Rene said. "Come and take your
pick. If you hurry, you can have breakfast with us. I've
met some—"

"No, thanks," she said, frowning. The last thing she
wanted to do was meet Rene's latest fuck-of-the-month.
And apparently, from what she'd overheard as he'd ad-
dressed this anonymous girl, she had a sister, too. *Terrific.*

"Look, I'll be there in a couple of hours, how about
that?" she said. "I've got some things to do first, then
I'll be over."

"Sounds good, *chère,*" he said. "I'll see you then."

She planned on recanvasing the neighborhood over by
the motel again that day. It was close enough to Rene's
building that she could take care of that while he and his
bimbos had breakfast, and then she could swing by when
she'd finished to pick up a car. She wanted to hit the airport and bus station again, but the cab fare was beginning to take a real bite out of her wallet. She hated asking
Rene for a loaner—because he had nothing in his garage
that cost him less than $100,000 to buy, and that left her
sick to her stomach just to consider—but she had no
choice. She knew he wouldn't refuse her, and—best yet—
he wouldn't ask her too many questions. He knew her
well enough to just turn her loose sometimes with whatever she needed from him, and she loved him for that.

After she hung up with Rene, she left her bedroom
and returned to her computer. She'd watched the news
earlier that morning, and seen a segment on a pair of
bodies discovered yesterday along the waterfront—two
transients, both of them with their throats mauled, both
drained almost entirely of blood. Lina had flinched as
if someone had slapped her when she heard this; she'd
stared at the TV screen, her eyes enormous, her breath
stilled.

"Preliminary autopsy investigations indicate that yes,

the wounds to the victims' throats occurred prior to their deaths," said a Metro Police spokesman in a snippet taken from a press conference the day before. A flurry of noisy questions greeted this comment, reporters demanding in overlapping voices whether a vampire cult or devil worshipping were being considered.

Vampire cult, Lina thought, remembering Caine and Emily Noble's teeth, the long, wicked hooks of their canine fangs. *Maybe I wasn't imagining things after all.*

"At this time, we're investigating every possible scenario," the police spokesman said on TV. "We're asking for the public's help in identifying leads in this investigation."

Lina Google searched for *vampire* in the metropolitan area. She'd found nothing in her searches the night before for any new information on Wellbutrin, instead turning up only page after page of what she already knew. The drug was prescribed to treat mild-to-moderate depression. In lower doses, it was also used as an effective smoking cessation treatment. Side effects included irritability, increased anxiety, weight loss, dizziness, and impotence. None of which particularly applied to Brandon—especially the latter—and none of which gave her any hint as to why he might be taking the medication.

Now she wondered if Brandon took it for depression, after all, and if Jackson's original suspicions about the Nobles and their neighboring families wasn't more on the mark than she'd first believed. *I think they're part of some kind of cult,* he'd told her.

A vampire cult, maybe? Lina thought, again thinking of Brandon's brother and sister, and those horrifying teeth.

Her search turned up all kinds of hits, and one item in particular kept appearing again and again—the Catacombs at Apathy. Apathy was a relatively new nightclub, but rapidly becoming one of the city's most popular, particularly for fans of alternative lifestyles. It was built on the waterfront, floating against the shoreline atop three old coal barges. It included a network of interconnected dance clubs and bars, each designed with a particular fetish or theme in mind. The Catacombs, located appropriately below deck on one of the barges, apparently catered to vampire aficionados.

Jesus, Lina thought, reading through post after post on message boards, and skimming through at least a dozen articles on the place. She'd expected to find maybe a few people in the city at most with any kind of publicly proclaimed interest in vampirism, but apparently, there was a whole freak-show underworld she'd been otherwise unaware of—hundreds of people, teens and young adults mostly, who not only believed in vampires, but fancied themselves to *be* vampires.

She studied images of kids with dental bridges they could remove or insert at will, with elongated, vampire fangs affixed. Others were even more drastic, having their canine teeth filed down to pointed nubs or topped with fang-like crowns. She read about vampire parties and blood bars, where people would bite and cut one another open, drinking blood. *Like a goddamn Tupperware party from hell,* she thought, shaking her head. *This has got to be what I saw at Jackie's apartment. Brandon's brother and sister— they're into this shit, and they were wearing prosthetic teeth.*

And since those were precisely the kinds of people who frequented the Catacombs at Apathy, Lina figured it would be as good as place to look next as any. *I may not find Brandon there, but I have a feeling I might run into Caine—or at least someone who knows him, someone he's holing up with,* she thought. *He's got to be laying low somewhere. I shot him twice, and I've called every hospital in the city, with no sign of him. He's my last chance to find Brandon before anyone else in his family can—so what better place to look for a freak than a freak show?*

Chapter Twenty

"He's lying," Tessa said with a frown, folding her arms across her bosom and sparing a dark glance toward Rene. "He can't possibly feed without killing someone. It's impossible. He's lying."

She and Brandon sat across from one another at a small dinette table in Rene's kitchen area. Rene stood nearby at the stove, stirring at a skillet of eggs with a wooden spatula. He turned at this, his brows arched in challenge.

Oh, God, Brandon thought. *Here we go again.*

"Your confidence in me is flattering, *pischouette,*" Rene said to Tessa. "Almost as goddamn endearing as your mouth."

"Stop calling me that," Tessa said, her frown deepening. "What is that, anyway? What does it mean?" The icy malice in her eyes clearly imparted: *And it better not be anything bad.*

"It's French," Rene replied. "It means *little girl.* I think it's fairly apt in this case."

"That's not French," Tessa said. "I speak French, *merci beaucoup,* and I've never heard that word before."

"It's *Cajun* French, not your high-falootin' sort, *pischouette,*" Rene said. "Straight out of Bayou Lafourche."

Enough already! Brandon thought, flapping his hands at them. *Jesus, will you both stop?*

"It doesn't matter anyway," Tessa said, turning back toward her brother. "Brandon, he's lying. You can't just turn the bloodlust on and off like a light switch. I know you've felt it, even if you haven't succumbed to it yet. You know I'm right. It doesn't work that way."

"I've been alive longer than the both of you put together," Rene said, scraping the eggs from the pan, dividing them among three plates on a nearby countertop. He glanced over his shoulder, glowering at Tessa. "I been called a lot of things in that time, but a liar isn't often one of them. You told me yourself, Brandon— you've seen me feed. I'd be glad to call Anise and have her come over for a visit, let you see she's alive and well."

"Stop putting these ideas in his head!" Tessa snapped. "That's not how we've been taught! Our people have survived for millennia by doing things certain ways— specific ways, and that's a lot longer than you've been around!"

"So is your way of things to lie to your brother, too?" Rene asked. "Suppress his telepathy and feed his head full of bullshit about being weak and unworthy?"

"Suppress his telepathy?" Tessa said.

Brandon wrote quickly, ripping the note loose and flapping it in the air. *Rene, you don't know that they were doing anything like that.*

"What do you mean, supressing it?" Tessa asked, snatching the note first. "What the hell is he talking about, Brandon?"

Brandon shook his head. *It's nothing,* he signed. *Something happened earlier, before we found you. He thinks I did it somehow, but I didn't.*

"What?" Tessa asked.

Rene poked at another skillet where he had sliced sausages sautéing. "The way I see it, it seems like a damn funny thing that Brandon didn't seem to have any telepathy to speak of the whole time he was in Kentucky with your family, *pischouette*. A damn funnier thing is that the minute he's away, he's suddenly got it in spades. Stronger than you or me—or the lot of your Brethren, too, I'd bet." He glanced at her pointedly as he transferred the sausage from pan to plates. "Sounds to me like someone knew it, too, and either wasn't too happy about it, or was scared of him. They tried to block up his mind."

"They did not," Tessa said. "You're full of shit, do you know that? Nobody blocked Brandon's telepathy. He was hurt when he was a little boy—he lost his hearing because of it, and he can't talk now, either. That's when it happened, when his telepathy was damaged."

"All I know is your brother got inside my head, *pischouette*," Rene said. "He did it without even meaning to, and he punched past any kind of defenses I had to keep him out. It hurt like hell, and I don't have any other explanation for it."

"Brandon, you can't believe that," Tessa said. "Not even the Grandfather would do such a thing, try to restrain your telepathy. Rene doesn't know what he's talking about. He's feeding you all of this crap, and he doesn't know about us, or the Brethren, or our lives. Who is he to question anything? We—"

"Seems to me, *pischouette,* that I'm not the one who's questioning stuff," Rene said. He walked toward the table, two plates in his hands, and dropped one unceremoniously in front of her. "He is."

He nodded toward Brandon, setting the second plate before him. "I don't think Brandon wants to kill anybody—your way of things or not—and that's why he ran away from that little pony farm of yours in Kentucky. I also think your grand-daddy was scared of him, of his power and that maybe other folks might start getting ideas in their heads like Brandon's, that killing to feed is wrong. So he stifled Brandon's telepathy, made him—and everyone else—think he was weak. Like I said, I can't find any other explanation." He spared her a glance. "But if you do, *pischouette*, then please feel free to share."

Tessa had been staring at her eggs, a stricken and de-cidedly ashen look on her face. She rose abruptly to her feet, shoving her chair back from the table so hard, it toppled behind her. She clapped her hand to her mouth and pushed Rene aside, darting from the kitchen and rushing for the bathroom on the far side of the loft.

Rene looked after her for a moment, his brow arched thoughtfully, and then he looked down at Brandon. "I'm going to try real hard and not take that personally, *petit*," he said.

She didn't mean it, Brandon wrote. *She doesn't under-stand, that's all.*

"Yeah, well, I hate to be the one to put a knot in her panties, but she had it due," Rene said. He'd crossed back to the counter and returned, carrying his own plate of breakfast. He speared a forkful of eggs and popped it in his mouth. "She's a beautiful girl, *petit*, but she's got a way about her that could curdle milk."

It's not her fault, Brandon wrote unhappily. *She's not always like that. I think it's because she's pregnant.*

Rene blinked as Brandon handed him the note. "*Quoi?*" he asked, visibly startled. "She . . . she's what? *Viens m'enculer.*"

She's not far along, only a few months, Brandon wrote. *You can't tell to look at her.*

Rene shoved his fingers through his hair, his brows fur-rowing. "Christ, I'm an ass." He moved as if he thought to follow Tessa, but stopped short, swung around, and began to pace. "I should say something to her, apologize."

It's not your fault, Rene. You didn't know, Brandon began to write, but Rene shook his head.

"My grandmother raised me a gentleman," he said. "And I've been anything but to your Tessa. *Mamere's* probably turned sideways in her grave."

He turned his head suddenly, his eyes widening.

"There's the doorbell. Hang on, *petit*. That's my partner, come to borrow a car. Why don't you see if your sister's OK? Bring her out here so I can tell her I'm sorry."

While Rene went to answer the door buzzer, Brandon retreated to the back of the loft, to the bathroom. Like everything else in Rene's private corner of the world, the bathroom was surrounded by drapes, not walls. Brandon drew aside a panel of heavy fabric and peered beyond, finding his sister kneeling on the floor beside the toilet, her hands over her face, her shoulders trembled as she wept.

Brandon knelt beside her, touching her shoulder gently. *It's alright,* he signed. *Please don't cry, Tessa. Rene's sorry. And maybe he's wrong, anyway. I don't know. It's not—*

Tessa shook her head. "What if he's not?" she said. "What if he's not wrong at all, Brandon?" Her words dissolved inarticulately as this only prompted her to cry all the more. He leaned toward her, cradling her cheeks between his palms and pressing his forehead against hers.

Please don't cry, he thought.

I'm sorry, Brandon, she said. *At the great house, after my bloodletting . . . it's like you always tried to tell me, but I never believed it. I never saw it. You told me I was different, and I was. I let you down. I left you alone. I knew how it was for you there, with Caine and Emily and the Grandfather, but I . . . I left you there. Now look at what's happened!*

She leaned back, touching his face. "The Grandfather hurt you," she whispered, anguished. "Maybe he did block your telepathy. God, it would make sense, wouldn't it? I should have sensed it . . . should have known. And now you're hurt again. You . . . you've needed me, Brandon, and I haven't been there to help you. I'm sorry. I . . . please, I'm sorry."

Brandon pressed his fingertips against her lips and shook his head. He felt the sudden sting of tears in his own eyes. *It's not your fault, Tessa,* he told her. *None of this is.*

* * *

"Hey, *chère*," Rene said to Lina, answering the front door to his building himself, instead of simply buzzing her in.

"Hey, Rene," she said, as he stepped aside so she could walk past him. The ground floor of Rene's home had once been a bank, built during a postwar construction boom in the 1940s, and his foyer was the main lobby, a broad expanse of charcoal-colored granite floors, marble pillars and long panels of teller stations flanking either side. Vacant offices kept a stoic vigil as he led her toward the elevators. Through several of these empty doorways, she could see that the bank's enormous safes remained, their doors permanently ajar, their steel bellies empty.

She very seldom got to see Rene's home. As a general rule, he picked her up at her place on those occasions when they did anything socially together. And when she came to his building, she couldn't peep through any of the ground floor windows, because he'd had most of them covered with stainless steel plates. Those that remained had thick, polarized, shatterproof glass in them, tinted so dark, she'd never been able to make out anything beyond them.

She found herself gawking around like a wide-eyed child at the shadow- and cobweb-draped fixtures, listening to the echo of their overlapping footsteps bouncing back at them from the vaulted ceilings. *It's like a tomb in here,* she thought, shivering slightly.

He didn't say much as she followed him to the elevators, and as he pulled the brass gate shut and threw a switch, sending the car upward with a slight lurch and an occasional wobble, she noticed that he seemed distracted, troubled somehow. "Rene?" she asked. "You OK?"

He blinked at her, as if snapping out of distant thoughts. *"Quoi?* Oh, yes. I'm fine, *chère."* He smiled for her, thin and forced.

"Why are we going up?" she asked. He kept his cars in the basement garage.

Rene shook his head, sighing heavily. "Because I'm a dumbass," he murmured. Lina had the distinct impression he was talking about something else entirely, but he didn't elaborate and she didn't press. She'd had no luck canvasing the surrounding neighborhood, looking for Brandon, and she needed to get the car and be on her way. She had to report for work that afternoon at four thirty, and her patrol began at five. That didn't leave her much time for lending her friend a sympathetic ear. *I'm sorry, Rene,* she thought, feeling crummy. *I'll make it up to you, I promise.*

"Well, while we're here . . ." Rene said, as the elevator came to a halt. "Why don't you come into the loft a minute? I've got some company and we were just sitting down to a late breakfast."

"Oh, Rene, I . . . I really can't . . ." she said, but he was already drawing open the elevator gate. *I don't want to meet this girl of yours, Rene, or her sister either.*

"Come on," Rene said, stepping off the elevator. "*S'il te plaît.* Please, Lina. It won't take five minutes. Besides, my keys are all up in the kitchen. I forgot to grab a set for you."

She sighed, hunching her shoulders, following him. "Alright, Rene."

Rene's loft reminded her of a television studio or some kind of theatrical set. He lived with everything out in the open, with drapes instead of walls, everything centered around the fireplace in an otherwise unadorned, unbroken expanse of space. He used strategically placed, warm lighting and the deliberate arrangement of furniture to lend the illusion of intimate perimeters, but to Lina, it still felt stark and lonely; his life on display, and yet hidden from the world at the same time.

There was no apparent sign of Rene's latest bimbo, for which Lina was immensely grateful. *Maybe I can get out of here without having to go through that bullshit after all,* she thought, watching as Rene mounted the steps leading to his kitchen.

"You want some eggs and andouille, *chère?*" he called as he sifted through a drawer.

"No, thanks," she replied. "Just the keys, please, Rene. I've really got to get going."

"No problem," Rene said. He held up his hand, dangling a pair of keys on a small ring at her. "You want to drive the Jaguar, *chère?*" He held up a second keying in his other hand. "Or the Lexus?" He glanced beyond her shoulder, and she bit back a groan as his expression softened. Somebody was behind her; she could hear their footsteps, and tried not to grimace.

Terrific, she thought. *The fuck-of-the-month.*

"Hey, good timing, *petit,*" Rene said. "Here's someone I'd like you to meet."

Here we go, Lina thought as she turned, her shoulders stiff, her posture rigid, her smile forced. '*So nice to meet you . . . Bambi, is it? And my goodness, what gigantic tits you have! What are those, triple-D's?*'

She froze, her eyes widening, her heart suddenly shuddering to a halt. "Oh, my God," she whispered when she saw who approached from behind her, who Rene's houseguest was. "Brandon!"

She flew across the room, grinning broadly, her eyes flooded with sudden tears. He blinked at her, shocked, and then she plowed into him, throwing her arms around his neck. She leaped against him, wrapping her legs around his waist, staggering him momentarily, and felt his arms encircle her, his hands slipping against her buttocks to support her, as he had in her dream. "Brandon!" she cried, her face buried against his neck. She kissed him, taking his face between her hands and pressing her lips over and over against his cheeks and brow, his nose and mouth. He smiled, kissing her back, but there was pain apparent in his eyes, the sudden lift of his brows, and in the ragged intake of his breath against her lips.

"What is it?" she asked, alarmed, dropping her feet immediately to the floor and drawing away from him. He stumbled, his knees buckling, and she got an arm around to support him. "Oh, my God, Brandon!" she gasped. "What is it? What's wrong?"

He shook his head, holding up his index finger as he tried to reclaim his breath. *Give me a minute.*

Lina looked over her shoulder at Rene. "What happened to him? What's wrong?"

"You two know each other?" Rene asked, walking toward her. He smiled somewhat wryly. "I take it so, *chère.* I'll be damned. This world just keeps getting smaller by the minute."

"Oh, my God," Lina whispered, shocked, as she drew back the last of the bandages covering Brandon's wound. She looked into his eyes, at the pain that was still visible and obvious there. "We have to get you to a hospital."

At this, Rene shook his head. The girl who had come out of the bathroom, introduced as Brandon's twin sister, Tessa—who Lina had met of a sort the night before outside of Jackson's apartment building—shook her head.

"No, we don't, *chère,*" Rene said, just as Tessa had opened her mouth to speak. "He's going to be fine. He just needs to rest."

Lina stared at him, her eyes wide. *Is he drunk?* she thought. *Is he out of his goddamn mind?* "He doesn't need to rest, Rene—he's been shot!" she exclaimed. "A bullet punched through his chest!"

She and Brandon had been sitting side by side on a couch, but she stood now. "Come on, Brandon. I'll take you."

To her utter astonishment, he shook his head. *No,*

Lina, he signed, and his brows lifted, his dark eyes imploring. *It's alright. Please don't be upset. It will be healed in a couple of weeks. It's already much better today. You don't understand—*

"You're right—I don't," she snapped. "What the hell is the matter with you—all of you? Bullet wounds don't just heal in a couple of weeks! You . . . you could get an infection! You could have fragments left in there, or internal bleeding, nerve damage—God only knows what!"

No, Lina, Brandon signed, his expression gentle. *I'm not like you. That won't happen to me.*

She blinked at him, stricken, something about his words, the look on his face, sending a creeping chill along her spine. *I'm not like you.*

"What are you talking about?" she whispered.

"If you take him to the hospital, *chère,* they'll just make it worse, like they did for me," Rene said.

She turned to him, wide eyed with shock. "Rene, they saved your life. Is that what this is about—your leg? I'm sorry you lost it. I know it's eating you up inside, and it breaks my heart for you, but you can't do this to Brandon. You can't fill his mind with that shit, make him afraid to get help. He could *die,* Rene. He could—"

Lina.

Her voice cut abruptly short as she heard a soft voice in her mind—a voice that was not her own. It was a man's voice, quiet, deep, and gentle. She'd never heard it in her life, and yet it was suddenly, poignantly familiar to her. She turned, staggering in surprise. "Brandon . . . ?" she gasped.

He rose to his feet. *Lina, listen to me,* he said inside of her mind, his mouth motionless, his lips lifting softly in a smile. *I'm not like you. None of us are.*

Chapter Twenty-one

"You're all crazy," Lina whispered. She'd sat again, watching as Brandon had signed to her, telling her things that he called the truth—about himself, his sister, his family, and even Rene. Things that made her head spin to consider; her gut ache to even think about. *Things that sound too fucking nuts to be possible.*

She blinked against stunned tears and shook her head. "You can't honestly expect me to believe this. That you're all *vampires,* like . . . like something out of a comic book or . . . or a goddamn horror movie?" She stood, her brows furrowed. "You're all crazy."

She started to leave, to storm toward the door, but Brandon rose to his feet, catching her by the hand. Again, she heard his voice in her head, pleading and plaintive. *Lina, please . . . !*

"Stop that!" she cried, jerking loose of him. "Stop doing that! *How are you doing that?*"

He reached for her, but she shoved him away. Again, he reached for her, brushing his hand against her cheek, and she pushed him. *Lina, I love you,* he signed, folding his hands against his heart.

He touched her again, caressing her cheek with the cuff of his knuckles and she tried to turn away from him. *I love you,* he finger-spelled with his free hand, leaning toward her, kissing her softly. His lips lingered, the kiss deepening, his tongue slipping gently, sweetly against hers.

I love you, he finger-spelled again as he drew away. His hand left her face and he signed. *Among my family, there's a rite of passage called the bloodletting. It's where we feed for the first time—when we kill someone for the first time. I was supposed to have my bloodletting five years ago, on the night Jackson took you to the casino boat in Indiana. My family wanted me to kill you.*

Lina recoiled at this, gasping in shock.

I couldn't, Brandon signed. *I don't want to kill anybody. That's why I got Jackson to leave the farm with you. Then I hid in his house all night until the ceremony was over, and the bloodlust had faded within me.*

The bloodlust. *This is insane,* Lina thought. *I can't believe I'm standing here, listening to this.* But the more he explained, the more it made sense. She remembered the night Jackson had brought her to Indiana to gamble. Neither of them were particularly enthusiastic about the prospect, but had gone anyway. *Brandon gave me three hundred bucks for it,* Jackson had told her on the drive north. *Said his father wanted me to have it. They're having some kind of big party there tonight.* He'd spared his sister a wry smile and a wink. *Must not have wanted us around.*

My grandfather had Jackson fired to punish me, Brandon signed. *After that, my dad was able to keep me from the bloodletting for awhile. I started taking Wellbutrin—Jackson helped me get it—to help control the bloodlust, because it could dampen it, keep it from growing inside of me.*

Oh, God, Lina thought, blinking against new tears. *That's why he was taking the medicine?*

I knew I wouldn't be able to get away with it forever, Brandon told her. *So I came up with a plan to get out of there. I applied to Gallaudet. Jackson helped me with the enrollment. But my grandfather found out last year, and that's when he broke my hands.*

Lina stared at him, stricken. *He told me once they were healed, I would go through my bloodletting,* Brandon said. *He was going to make me kill someone, Lina, whether I wanted to or not. That's why I ran away. You saw Caine and Emily, what happens to us when the bloodlust takes over. I don't want to be like that . . .* His hands trembled. *A monster, like them.*

Lina looked over his shoulder toward Rene and Tessa. "If that's true," she said quietly, her voice hoarse and unsteady. *And I can't believe it is,* she added mentally. *I can't, oh, Christ, I just can't!* "If what Brandon's told me is the truth, then you're both murderers. You . . . you kill people so you can feed on them." She glared at Tessa. "Illegal immigrants your family tricks into working on their farms—like they're goddamn cattle to you."

Tessa's dark eyes swam with shame, glistening with sudden tears, and she blinked down at her feet. "It's not her fault," Rene said, draping his hand against her shoulder. "She didn't know any better than what they told her. Her whole life through, she heard that's the way it's supposed to be. I never had anyone to tell me all that. I had to figure out everything about who I am—what I am—on my own."

"So you've never killed anyone?" Lina challenged, locking gazes with him. She'd never stood against Rene, not in all of the years she'd known him, and for a moment, his face clouded, hurt.

"I can't say that, *chère,* no," he said quietly, and then his brows narrowed slightly. "But then again, neither can you. Nobody here's got themselves a guiltless life. Do you want to sit and split hairs all afternoon or do you want to do something to help your boy? Because out of all of us, *chère,* you're the only one who can."

No. Brandon shook his head. He finger-spelled it. He signed it, snapping his two forefingers closed over his

thumb. He jerked back the cover on his brass-plated
notebook and wrote it in big, block letters: *NO.*

"Brandon, do you want to be laid up here for weeks,
as feeble as a kitten, waiting for these Elders of yours to
coming sniffing around?" Rene asked, frowning at him.
"Lina says thanks to 'Jude Law,' they're probably well on
their way, and from what I understand from *pischouette*
here, they don't sound like they'll be coming to pay you
a friendly sort of visit."

"They'll kill you, Brandon," Tessa said. "It's not a question of *if* they find us. It's *when.*"

Then I'll go, Brandon signed to Lina. *Tell Rene to give me
the goddamn car keys, and I'll leave, head west—California,
Oregon, something. That's been my plan all along.*

"You can't leave, Brandon," Lina said. "Not like this—
you're hurt."

"You need to heal, *petit,*" said Rene.

I don't have time to heal, Rene, Brandon wrote angrily in
the notebook. He ripped the page out and thrust it forward, holding it out so Rene could read.

"I know you don't," Rene replied. "That's why you
need to feed."

Christ, here we go again, Brandon thought. *No, no, no,* he
wrote. *I'm not going to do it, Rene. I know you can—you can
feed without killing, and that's all well and good, but I can't!
And I can't ask that of Lina, besides. She already thinks we're
all fucking nuts!*

"I'll do it," Lina said quietly, within Brandon's line of
sight. He blinked, jerking as if she'd physically struck him.
"I'll do it," she said again. "If everything you've told me is
true, and it will help you, make you strong again, I'll do it."

No, Brandon signed. *No, absolutely not, goddamn it, no!*

"Brandon," Lina said, catching his hands, staying him.
"I love you." He blinked at her, startled, and she smiled
gently at him. "I love you," she said again, reaching up
with one hand to caress his face. She leaned toward him,

kissing him, settling her lips lightly, gently against his own. "I love you," she said as she drew away.

I'm scared, Brandon thought to Tessa.

She smiled at him, brushing his hair back from his brow. *I know*, she said. *It will be alright. Just keep your mind opened to Rene. Listen to him. Learn from him.* Her eyes grew sorrowful. "I wish I could help you through this," she said.

He drew her against his uninjured shoulder, hugging her fiercely. *You already have, Tessa*, he thought, closing his eyes against the sting of tears. *More than you know.*

She stepped aside, retreating to the far side of the loft. Brandon knelt on a large oriental rug spread out in front of the fireplace. He struggled not to grimace as he did this, hoping if he could just prove he wasn't in nearly as much pain as he was, that Lina would abandon the entire idea. It didn't work. She was already kneeling on the rug facing him, and he could tell by the way her brows lifted, crimping with worry, that she'd seen the pain in his face.

"Brandon," she whispered, and he tried to smile at her in clumsy reassurance.

"Here we go," Rene said, leaning between them and handing them each a tumbler half-filled with vodka. He lifted a third one—filled significantly higher—from a nearby coffee table and raised it in hand. "*À votre santé*," he offered in toast.

"What's this for?" Lina asked, giving it an experimental sniff.

"Liquid courage," Rene replied. "And besides, it must be happy hour somewhere, no?" He tilted his head back, draining the glass dry.

Lina glanced at Brandon, then swallowed her own shot. *What the hell*, Brandon thought. He leaned his head back, downing the vodka. He choked slightly, blinking at the sudden backwash of heat that stung his eyes and nose.

It had been more than a full day since Brandon had last taken his Wellbutrin, and his metabolism had completely eradicated any of its subduing effects on his system. When he scooted toward Lina, touching the side of her face and leaning toward her so that he could nuzzle her throat gently, it stoked an immediate and powerful arousal in his mouth. He felt heat seep into his gums as they swelled; the sockets of his canine teeth ached.

He was afraid he would hurt Lina. She was afraid of this, too; he could feel it in the way her body stiffened against him, the way her breath grew sharp and anxious. *There must be something in our saliva, what do they call it? An analgesic,* Rene had said. *Anise tells me she feels pressure when I bite her, but nothing that hurts. And I know there's something in us that makes their blood clot faster when we're finished with them, otherwise they'd bleed to death for sure.*

Brandon kissed Lina's throat, his lips drawing lightly against her skin, and the taste of her, the sudden, maddening awareness of her pulse beneath her flesh, its fluttering rhythm, and the smell of her blood made him dizzy. He could feel his teeth dropping from the roof of his mouth, beginning a slow but certain descent.

Will this make me like you? Lina had asked. *If Brandon bites me, won't that make me a vampire, too?*

Only in the movies, chère, Rene had replied.

Brandon felt it when his lower jaw slid reflexively out of socket; a dull, popping sensation beneath his ears. *That's so you can get your mouth wide enough to bite in the right place,* Rene had explained. *So you can sink your teeth in at the right angle to hit the carotid artery.*

He could feel the bloodlust rising in him, immediate and urgent, as it had come upon him on the day he'd met Lina, outside the Chinese restaurant. Then, he'd kissed her, his mind confusing one lust for another, but this time, with her throat so tantalizingly within his reach, with his fangs fully extended and poised against her trembling flesh, he knew there'd be no such mistake. He could feel her blood surging through her body, racing through her carotid artery, pulsating just beneath the delicate surface of her skin. He drew the tip of his tongue against her pulse point, and she flinched, hooking her fingertips against his shoulder.

Go ahead, petit, he heard Rene said quietly in his mind. *It's time.*

Brandon closed his eyes, feeling a warm, flushed wave wash over him, dragging him under, just as it had done on the sidewalk outside of Joe's Wok. *The bloodlust.* It seized hold of him, and he moved on instinct, settling his mouth against Lina's throat, opening his lips wide. He pressed the points of his canines against her flesh, and she stiffened against him, her breath jerking in a gasp as he bit her. He felt his teeth punch through her skin, sinking into the firm meat beneath, spearing past ligaments and tendons and sliding into her artery. He felt her blood suddenly surge into his mouth, spurting with the force of her heartbeat, shooting against the back of his palate. He nearly choked, but felt Rene touch the back of his head gently, holding him in place, keeping him fixed against Lina's throat.

He swallowed, sucking down a thick mouthful, tasting the coppery, musky flavor of Lina's blood against his tongue. With every thrumming beat of her heart, blood filled his mouth; he hardly had to suck against her at all. Again and again, he swallowed, and the more he drank, the more urgent his need seemed to become. He leaned against Lina, easing her back against the rug, pressing himself atop her as if he meant to make love to her. Her fingers twined in his hair, her other hand splayed against her shoulders, and she drew him near, moving her body beneath him, slowly, rhythmically, as if she lay beneath a lover. He swallowed frantically, his mouth pressed against her throat, his mind consumed with heat, bright and searing, the bloodlust in full, unbridled release.

Brandon, Rene said, his hand falling against his shoulder. *That's enough. Let her go now.*

Brandon's eyes snapped open and he drew abruptly back from Lina, his mouth still full of blood. He stared down at her, stricken and aghast. Her eyelids fluttered momentarily, and she smiled dazedly at him.

Are you alright? he thought to her, and she nodded.

"I'm fine," she murmured. "Rene's right. It . . . it didn't hurt . . ."

Brandon rolled off of her, taking her by the hands and helping her stumble to her feet. The wounds in her neck still seeped, even though, as Rene had promised, the violent measure of bleeding was already ending. She staggered against him, pressing her hand against her head as soon as she was upright. Brandon watched in horror as her eyes rolled back, and then she crumpled, her knees failing her.

Lina! he cried in his mind, catching her in his arms. He knelt, lowering her to the floor again, grimacing as pain speared through his injured shoulder. He looked up at Rene, frightened and panic stricken. *Rene! Help me! Oh, God, what have I done?*

It was a very fine line between feeding and killing. Rene had made that sternly clear to Brandon. *A human can only afford to lose a pint or so of blood, maybe two, at best,* he'd said. *So you can't get greedy, no matter how you might want to—even if you feel you need to. Because you don't have to bleed them dry to kill them.*

Rene leaned over, reaching beneath Lina's hair and pressing his fingertips against her throat. He met Brandon's eyes and smiled. "She's okay, *petit,*" he said. "She's just fainted, that's all. Her pulse is strong, and keeping steady. She'll need to rest a little bit."

You're sure? Brandon asked, still unconvinced and frantic.

Rene clapped him on the shoulder. *I'm positive,* he

replied. *She's no worse off now than if she'd donated at the Red Cross. It's just the shock of it, that's all. Sometimes they pass out. How about you? How are you feeling?*

Brandon touched his shoulder gingerly. It still pained him as much as ever—more so, even, from having borne Lina's sudden and unexpected weight. He blinked at Rene, confused. *I don't feel any different,* he thought. *Nothing at all, Rene. I feel just the same.*

"Don't worry. You will," Rene said, with a wink. "It takes time for your body to process the blood. Trust me—a few more hours, and you'll be flying. It's almost as good as making love. Almost." He cut his eyes across the loft, in the direction Tessa had followed, and his bright expression faltered. "I'll carry Lina to your bed, *petit,* how about that? Then, if you'll excuse me for a moment, I still owe your sister an apology."

I can't leave now, Brandon thought. He'd curled up alongside of Lina on the bed behind the white silk drapes, her back against his belly, her buttocks tucked against his groin. He slipped his arm across her waist and twined his fingers through hers. She rested comfortably, her breathing deep and slow, and he closed his eyes. He could still taste her in his mouth, the coppery flavor of her blood against his tongue.

I can't leave now, he thought again. He was tired of running, so wretchedly exhausted of being afraid. Before, that had seemed like his only option; running, the only escape he might find from who and what he was. But now he realized that wasn't true.

Rene was right. I don't have to kill to feed. I don't have to try and drug my bloodlust into submission. I can control it.

And if he could control it, Brandon realized he could have the kind of life that Rene enjoyed—the kind he had so desperately wanted for so long. A life among humans—unnoticed, undetected.

A life with Lina, he thought, the fragrance of her hair, light and sweet, like baby oil, against his nose.

If he ran again, it wouldn't be for the last time, and Brandon knew it. The Brethren would never give up. The Elders had been unleashed. The Grandfather had promised him no place on earth or measure of time would keep him safe, and Brandon believed him. He couldn't bear the thought of never being able to stay in one place for too long, of having to constantly make and break friendships as he fled, leaving people behind.

I can't leave Lina, he thought. *I can't. I love her.*

If he couldn't keep running, it left only one other alternative. He would have to stand his ground against the Elders—and the Grandfather. He would have to fight them.

Lina stirred against him, rousing. She rolled slightly, looking over her shoulder at him and smiled. "Hey, you," she said, reaching up and touching his face. "Did it work?"

He shook his head and her smile faltered. *Not yet,* he thought to her. *But it will, and soon. Rene said it should take a couple of hours.*

Lina rolled some more, turning onto her back. She moved as if to sit up. "I . . . I need to be at work by four-thirty," she said, scowling groggily. "What time is it?"

Brandon caught her by the shoulders, pulling her back down against the pillows. *There's time,* he signed to her. He leaned over and kissed her, drawing her tongue into his mouth. He felt his groin tighten at this, the warmth of arousal stirring, and he reached for her breast, kneading her through her shirt.

"Is there now?" she asked, as his lips parted from hers slightly, briefly. He nodded and she smiled, the corner of her mouth hooking wryly as she reached between them, unfastening his jeans. "Time for what?"

That was all it took—the barest scrape of her fingers against the bare skin of his belly beneath his waistband, and that mischievous smile, and he was hardened in full, urgent measure. He shoved his jeans away from his hips, and then jerked at hers. She was already wet and eager for him; he speared all of the way into her with one deep thrust.

Within moments, she was writhing beneath him, approaching release, and he folded himself over her, taking her breast in his mouth, encircling her nipples with his tongue each in ravenous turn through her shirt. She coiled her fingers in his hair and jerked with climax. The force with which she tightened against him drove him to his own instantaneous release, and he gasped, plunging into her.

He lay against her, breathless and trembling, feeling the shuddering rhythm of her heart through her shirt against his face. After a moment, he sat up, keeping her thighs wrapped around his waist. She smiled at him, and he caught her hand, sliding her fingers between his.

I love you, he finger-spelled with his free hand, making her smile widen.

She was drowsy again; their lovemaking had been too much, too soon, and he watched her eyelids sleepily droop. "I love you, too, Brandon," she murmured. Her eyes closed, and she rested for a moment, her fingers slackening against his. Then, all at once, they tightened again momentarily, and her eyes opened. "Will you stay with me?" she said, even though he'd made no move to leave. "Please, Brandon. Just . . . just for a little while."

He nodded and she smiled, her eyes fluttering closed again. He stretched out beside her, holding her hand, watching her sleep. *I'll stay with you, Lina,* he thought, leaning over and kissing her. *I swear to you I'll never leave again.*

Chapter Twenty-two

"You look like hell," Lina's partner, Larry Turner, said as they walked out of the precinct debriefing room together, ready to begin their shift.

"Thanks, Larry," she replied with a scowl, quickening her stride to try and beat him to the patrol car.

"I mean it, Lina," he said, hurrying after her. He caught her arm, staying her momentarily. "Are you feeling OK? Because you look—"

"Like hell. Yeah, you've mentioned. I had a rough weekend, that's all." She pulled her arm away, and while he was within reach, snatched the car keys from his hand. "I'm driving."

Larry had a wife, two small kids, a mortgage, a balding spot, and a paunch—things Lina knew nothing about. Which was about the same as she could say for her partner, even though they'd been assigned to work together for the last ten months, ever since she'd returned from administrative leave following the shooting. She'd never made much effort to get to know Larry, although he tended to chatter rather incessantly and inanely about whatever household project his wife was currently nagging him to complete, or which kid had puked or shit the weirdest color that week.

She climbed into the driver's seat of their squad car

and fastened her seatbelt. As she turned the key in the ignition, she wondered if she really ought to be driving. She'd passed out after Brandon had fed from her. Rene had explained it was no different than feeling woozy after donating at a blood drive. She'd had a snack when she'd awoke, a bit of orange juice, and she was no longer feeling quite so sluggish or dazed. She still felt tired, however; wretchedly so, and the events of the afternoon seemed to linger behind the dim drape of fog in her mind, hazy memories that seemed more like dreams. *The man I've fallen in love with is a vampire*, she thought, as Larry thumbed the radio mike and reported them as *10-41*, ready for duty. *Brandon is a vampire, and today, I let him drink my blood so he could heal himself from a bullet wound.*

"And tomorrow, I'm off to the nut hatch," she muttered, looking behind her as she backed the car out of its parking slot in the garage.

"What?" Larry asked. His brows raised slightly, and he reached for her. "Hey, what happened to your neck?"

She swatted his hand away before he could touch the bandage against her throat. "Nothing," she said. She dropped the car into gear and drove toward the exit. "Cut myself shaving."

He shook his head, chuckling. As soon as they hit the street, he was rambling. Something about pressure washing his deck to get ready for summer. The wife had apparently been bitching for months to get him to do it. Now she was threatening to withhold sex. Which apparently, to Larry, was no incentive whatsoever to see the task completed.

"I work nights, for Christ's sake," he griped. "I want to sleep in the daytime, and trust me, that's hard enough with a goddamn two- and four-year-old running around the house nonstop, screaming and bawling. The last thing I want to is waste my shut-eye time spraying bird shit and mildew off the goddamn . . ."

There was more, but Lina tuned him out. She zoned out the chatter on the radio, a steady relay of codes and dispatch calls between operators and officers. She had other things on her mind.

They responded to two domestic disturbances, one minor traffic collision, helped a woman jimmy the lock on her car door so she could retrieve her keys, and busted two subjects for public intoxication, one of whom had a bench warrant outstanding for failing to pay his child support.

By the time they'd dropped this latest and greatest off at the precinct drunk tank and resumed their patrol, it was fast approaching midnight. "I need to make a detour," Lina told Larry, driving toward the riverfront.

"Fine with me," Larry replied, slouched in his seat. He cracked his window and lit a cigarette, drawing a sideways glare from her. "What? I brought Febreeze. I'll spray."

Lina bit back a nasty reply. Larry wasn't supposed to smoke in the car. Not only was this a department rule—and one that she'd get in trouble for breaking right along with him, whether she was the culprit or not—but it was also a personal pet peeve. She hated cigarette smoke. She imagined that was a big factor in why she'd never felt more endeared to Larry; the stink of stale smoke remained permanently trapped in his clothes and hair, surrounding him in a distinctive, malodorous cloud.

Lina pulled the patrol car to a halt in a fire lane facing the waterfront wharf where the floating nightclub complex, Apathy, was anchored. It might have been a Monday night, but the place was hopping, to judge by the packed parking lot nearby, and the throngs of people milling about the docking ramp, waiting to enter.

"Dispatch, this is unit fourteen forty-two," Lina said, using the radio mic clipped to her shoulder. "We'll be ten-seven for the next thirty minutes on a signal four. Do you copy?"

"Standby, unit fourteen forty-two," the dispatcher replied, his voice squawking fuzzily over the radio.

"Hey," Larry said, blinking at her, straightening in his seat. "What are you doing?" She'd called them in as going out of service on a meal break. This was something Larry took even more seriously than an officer-down call. And with no food in hand, and no drive-through window in apparent sight, her call had obviously alarmed him.

"Relax," Lina said, glancing at him. "This will only take a few minutes."

"Why are we here?" he asked, frowning out the window at the bar.

"I need to check out something," Lina murmured, as dispatch came back on the air.

"Unit fourteen forty-seven, what's your ten-twenty?"

"I'm at the waterfront, the Fourth Street landing," Lina replied.

"Ten-four," the dispatcher replied. "You're clear."

"Why don't you go on over to Chelsea's Diner?" Lina told Larry, unfastening her seat belt and opening the door. "I'll radio you when I'm finished and you can swing by and pick me up on your way back."

Lina had a suspicion that if Caine Noble wasn't hanging out in Apathy that night, someone there would know where to find him. In either case, she didn't feel like having Larry, the wonder suburbanite, tagging along for the ride. If it had been Rene riding shotgun with her, she would have insisted he come. But it wasn't Rene; it was Larry, and Lina had doubts that Larry could find his ass with both hands, a flashlight, a map, and a week to try sometimes.

"Sounds good," he said, climbing out of the car. "You want me to bring you back anything?"

"No, thanks," she said. "I don't have much of an appetite tonight."

He traded places with her, settling down in the driver's seat, and leaned out before closing the door. "So does this have something to do with your rough weekend?" he asked, a hint of glee in his eyes.

If only you knew, Lina thought, forcing a strained and insincere smile. "Yeah. Something like that."

She walked toward the steel boarding ramp as the

squad car pulled away from the curb. She could hear the pounding, thrumming rhythm of heavy dance music spilling out of the nightclub, shuddering through the night air. She checked her side arm reflexively, settling her hand momentarily against the butt of the nine-millimeter strapped faithfully to her hip, feeling comforted by its presence. *Bullets can stop them,* she thought. *Bullets can kill them. Brandon said a bullet to their heads will kill them just as sure as anyone else.*

She didn't want to kill Caine Noble, but, depending on his reception, she might be forced to. The gun was leverage, her ace in the hole. *But I'm going to try to win him over with my charming personality first,* she thought with a smirk, as she ducked and shouldered her way through a heavy tangle of young people waiting in line. They were dressed in ridiculous fashion, some head to toe in black, with jet-black dyed hair, alabaster white faces, ebony lipstick. Others wore hot-pink and electric-blue wigs, stood on platform heels that hoisted them a good—if not precarious—foot and a half off the ground and shiny vinyl pantsuits or miniskirts. She passed by at least a dozen whose sex she couldn't clearly distinguish based on outward appearance alone. *Thank Christ I made Larry wait in the car,* she thought. *If he'd tagged along, he couldn't have kept his damn mouth shut—and we'd both be killed before we hit the lobby.*

Lina wanted to talk to Caine, to reason with him. Tessa had explained that people called the Elders were coming for Brandon; that more than just a mandate to bring him back to Kentucky and punish him, they were under direction to kill him. The Elders were the most powerful among Brandon and Tessa's people—the *Brethren,* they'd called them. Tessa suspected that Caine was acting outside of the Brethren's control; that he'd followed Tessa from Kentucky to try and find Brandon. The Elders hadn't found their way to the city yet, but they would. They were hunters, Tessa had explained. *That's all they know. It's what they do.*

If Lina didn't find a way to diffuse the situation—and fast—then Brandon was going to leave. He and Tessa had apparently been preparing to do exactly this when Lina had arrived at Rene's building that afternoon. Lina might have been able to persuade him to change his mind, but she hadn't tried. He'd been sleeping when she left, and she hadn't wanted to disturb him. Rene had told her rest would help him heal from the bullet wound in his shoulder. She also hadn't wanted to beg him to stay. *Because he would, if I asked him to,* she thought. *He would stay for me, and the Elders would find him, kill him. I can't let that happen.*

She didn't know how to get in touch with the Elders—and most specifically, with Augustus Noble, Brandon's grandfather, under whose orders the Elders operated. She didn't have Jude's connections; she couldn't just come up with the man's phone number with a few quick calls. *But I bet I know another way,* she thought. *Caine knows how to get in touch with his grandfather, and whether he likes it or not, I'm going to ask him to help me.*

"May I help you, officer?" the bouncer at the end of the ramp asked. He was an enormous man, at least a foot taller than Lina, and outweighing her by a good seventy pounds of nothing but sheer muscle. His bald head gleamed, and his brows narrowed warily at her. "Several of you've already been out here today, and we told you— we don't know nothing about those murders. We don't let freak cases like that get in here."

Ah, Lina thought. So homicide investigators had followed her own line of thinking—and their search had delivered them to Apathy, as well.

"Yeah, I can see you have a closed-door policy for freak cases," she remarked dryly, with a pointed glance at the nearest pink-haired, seven-foot-tall, platform-booted transvestite. "I'm looking for a man."

The bouncer raised his brow and offered a little snort. "Hope you like them in skirts," he said. "It's the Queen-for-a-Night pageant in the drag lounge."

"The guy I'm looking for is probably more interested in the Catacombs," Lina said. "His name is Caine Noble. He's about six-one, six-two, lean build, about my age. White guy with dark eyes and black hair, really long, down to the middle of his back."

The bouncer looked thoughtful. "Hang on a sec," he said, reaching for a shelf on the podium beside which he perched. He picked up a handheld walkie-talkie. "Let me call down there and see."

He turned and walked a few paces away from her, holding the radio up to his ear like a telephone to hear and be heard over the din of the music. After a few moments, he returned. "You know what?" he said. "Phil said there is a guy matching that description down there. Been coming in every night the last few or so. A real lady's man."

Yeah, I bet, Lina thought, remembering how his eyes had rolled over black and how he'd shaken his head like an enraged dog shuddering off a dousing of water, snapping his jaw out of socket to accommodate his growing canine teeth.

"He said to send you on down," the bouncer said, side-stepping to allow Lina past.

Lina walked aboard the crowded nightclub. She stepped off the gangplank onto the main deck, where colorful neon signs offered her a number of venue options. She followed the doorway marked *Catacombs,* descending down a narrow flight of steel stairs. The air smelled funny, filled with the peculiar, stale odor of dry ice used to create a mist effect on the dance floor. The driving beat of dance music was deafening, thrumming through the stairs beneath her feet, trembling in the walls. The nightclub was packed and dark, with multicolored strobe lights flashing violently in time with the music. She smelled the stink of cigarette smoke, sweat, and beer, and as she stepped off the bottom riser, she was immediately surrounded by steaming, perspiring, scantily-clad bodies in heaving, gyrating motion.

Jesus, she thought, scowling as she shoved her way forward. She planned to make her way to the bar. Even in the poor light, she could tell she was going to need help in finding Caine among the throng. To her perfunctory observation, everyone in the Catacombs had long, black hair, dressed head to toe in black and clearly had ambitions of being vampires when they grew up.

She was frightened. She hated to admit it almost as much as she hated feeling that way in the first place. Lina didn't like being intimidated. She'd never taken to it well, but she knew she was placing herself in a very precarious and potentially dangerous situation, and only an idiot would be in her place and not feel apprehensive. She didn't know what Caine's reaction would be. She hoped that, vampire or not, the sight of her uniform would keep him somewhat reasonable. Brandon had told her they'd been raised on a horse farm, not the moon; surely Caine could appreciate that he couldn't do anything to a police officer in a public place.

She frowned, sidestepping as someone shoved roughly into her. Someone else jostled her from the other side, and she yelped, ramming her elbow back angrily. "Watch it!" she snapped. She stumbled as someone else bumped her and then another, and another, until she felt hands all over her, grabbing and pushing, forcing her along, shoving her forward. They stared at her, cutting dark glances around black-rimmed, heavily shadowed eyes in her direction, and she realized this wasn't an accident. *Oh, Christ, it's like they're herding me!* she thought, the anxiety she'd felt stirring mounting suddenly, swiftly to panic.

"Get your hands off me!" she cried, but the pounding bass from the dance floor swallowed her voice whole. She tried to backpedal, to fight her way to the stairs again, but there were too many people, all wedged too closely to her. She felt fingers fumble against her clothes, pawing at her hair, and she danced clumsily, balling her hands into fists, swinging at them. "I'm a police officer!" she yelled. It was too tight a space, too confined, and she couldn't fend them off with her aikido. Each time she'd drive someone back with a wrist lock, another would surge forward to grope her in their place.

"Goddamn it, I'm a cop!" she shouted, reaching for her pistol, her one comfort, her emergency escape. Her eyes widened in bright alarm when her hand brushed against the open mouth of her holster; someone had stolen the gun. *Oh, fuck me . . . !*

All at once, the crowd drew to an abrupt halt. They unfolded from around her, leaving Lina staggering backward into a suddenly broad, empty circumference of space. The music continued playing, blaring around them, but nobody moved. A crowd of at least two hundred people—their faces white, their lips and eyes painted black—stared at her, leveling dark, menacing glares, watching her as they might have a beetle pinned by sunlight focused through a magnifying lens.

"I'm a cop!" Lina yelled, her voice hoarse and shrill. Without her gun, she felt as good as naked against them. *Maybe they didn't take it,* she thought, her mind whirling desperately, struggling to find some escape. *Maybe it fell on the floor while I was being pushed around and all of this is my imagination. Just my goddamn imagination . . . !*

Her heart pounded, her breath hiccupped frantically. She still had her shoulder mic; she could call for emergency backup. *But, oh, fuck, these kids can do a world of hurting to me in the time it would take for that to get here,* she thought.

"I'm a police officer!" she cried again. "Stand aside and clear a path for me to the stairs—all of you! Right goddamn now!"

Or what, Officer Jones? she heard a man's voice purr inside of her mind. It was the second such time in her life when a stranger's voice had infiltrated her thoughts—only this time, she knew it wasn't Brandon.

Oh, Jesus, she thought, turning slowly. She still had pepper spray clipped to her belt, and she reached for it now. *Oh, Jesus, oh, Christ, oh, holy fuck . . . !*

The crowd had been herding her, alright. She turned

in full and found herself facing a lounge in the back corner of the nightclub, a semicircle of cushioned leather sofas with a black lacquer coffee table in the middle. Caine Noble sat against the sofa immediately in front of her. His long hair was unfettered, draped over his shoulders in thick, glossy sheaves. He was impeccably dressed, black from head to toe, with his long legs outstretched before him, crossed at the ankles. He was flanked on either side by a bevy of beautiful young women, all of them more naked than clothed.

"Why, Angelina," he said, cradling a tumbler of what appeared to be whiskey in his hand. He took a long drink and smiled at her, revealing that his canine teeth had lowered somewhat, the tips curving downward over his bottom teeth. "What a pleasant surprise. While I'd certainly have liked to see you again, I couldn't have hoped for such an opportunity quite so soon."

He knows my name, she thought, shying back, feeling her chest tighten. *Oh, fuck, how does he know my name?*

Because I'm not a fucking idiot, Caine told her in her mind, making her flinch, crying out in startled, frightened reflex. He chuckled at her, turning his glass this way and that in his hand, admiring the play of lights from the dance floor against the liquor. He glanced at Lina and winked. "You told me you were a cop two nights ago," he said. "You say that a lot. You must like to. Does it make you feel powerful?"

He rose to his feet and walked toward her, his gait slow and leisurely. "I figured out real quick that the apartment you used to hole up with Brandon belonged to your brother," he said. "Brandon's nigger teacher from the farm. From there, it didn't take much to track you down—a nigger bitch cop with the last name of Jones."

Lina blinked as if he'd slapped her. *Did he just call me and Jackson niggers?* She moved her hand from the pepper spray and curled her fingers in toward her palms in light, ready fists. *Oh, goddamn it, that was a mistake.*

She swung at him, her fist flying forward, the heel of

her hand aimed with brutal velocity for his nose. She didn't hope to incapacitate him, but if she could stun him enough, catch him by surprise, she might be able to duck back into the crowd, to fight her way to the exit. Caine caught her punch, his hand darting up to intercept the blow so quickly, it was a blur in her peripheral vision. His fingers folded against her hand, crushing, and Lina cried out, crumpling to her knees. She screamed hoarsely; when Caine released her, she huddled at his feet, cradling her injured hand against her belly, gasping raggedly for breath.

Oh, God, she thought, terrified now, plain, stark, and overwhelming. She could hear footsteps approaching—lots of them—and looked up to find the crowd closing in on her again, drawing near, like something out of a horror movie. *Oh, God . . . !* she thought as they reached for her, dozens of hands, all outstretched and groping. "Oh, God . . . no—!" she screamed.

Brandon awoke to find himself alone in bed. He sat up, groggy and bewildered, and winced as he rested his weight inadvertently against his sore shoulder. He pressed his hand gingerly against his bandages, wondering dimly if Rene had been wrong about feeding accelerating his healing ability.

He was naked; his clothes still lay in a tumble on the floor. Lina's were gone and of her, there was no sign. She'd told him she had to work that night. *She must have left already,* he thought, as he stepped into his jeans, drawing them back over his hips. *What time is it?*

He smelled something wondrous and spicy and felt his stomach grumble hungrily. He ducked around the silk drapes and saw Rene and Tessa in the kitchen. Tessa sat at the table, looking through what appeared to be some kind of scrapbook, while Rene stood over the stove. Both looked toward him as he approached.

"Bonjour, petit," Rene said, grinning broadly. "How are you feeling?"

Brandon shrugged to convey *OK, I guess,* and pointed toward the stove, his brows raised inquisitively.

"Hoppin' John," Rene replied. "An old family recipe straight from the bayou. I thought I'd fix us a late supper. *La pischouette* was getting hungry."

Brandon blinked at Tessa in surprise. *You sure?* he signed to her. Since scrambled eggs had been enough to roll her stomach only that morning, he was surprised that she'd consent to eat anything Cajun.

I'm OK, she signed in reply, laughing. She stroked a light fist down her chest: *I'm starving, in fact.* She motioned to draw him near. *Look at this, Brandon. It's Rene's family tree.*

Brandon stepped closer to the table, peering curiously over her shoulder. It was indeed a scrapbook she was looking at, filled with yellowed postcards and ancient photographs. She'd drawn a piece of brittle, aging paper from the book and carefully unfolded it against the table top. Sure enough, it was a family tree, recounted in elaborate detail, recorded in tiny, tight, sloping handwriting.

Who did all of this? he signed to Tessa. He and Tessa knew next to nothing of their own family's genealogical history, particularly for generations preceding the Grandfather. The Elders kept all of the family Tomes under closely guarded lock and key because they used them to determine which clans would intermarry and which generations would wed into one another.

"Rene's grandmother," she replied aloud. "Isn't it amazing? And look at this . . . ." She pointed to one entry, which Brandon had to lean over and squint at to read. "This is Rene's great-grandfather, Remy Morin. This says that he married Marguerite Davenant in 1782. *Davenant,* Brandon, as in Martin's last name. And now mine."

Brandon blinked in surprise, glancing toward Rene. If he was the least bit interested in Tessa's discovery, he didn't show it, busying himself instead with stirring the pot of black-eyed peas and rice.

"He really is one of us," Tessa said, hooking her hand against Brandon's arm to draw his gaze. Her eyes were bright, her cheeks flushed excitedly. "The Brethren have always married clans into clans—no outsiders. So the only way Rene's great-grandfather could have married a Davenant is if he'd been in the Brethren, one of the clans."

But his name is Morin, Brandon said, finger-spelling it.

"I know," Tessa replied, nodding. "There must have been another clan once—one we don't know about now, that the Elders don't tell us about. Maybe more than one. Maybe *a lot* more. Something must have happened to make them leave, and now the Elders don't want any of the rest of us to know about or remember them. No one but the Elders are allowed to see the Tomes—the recorded histories for each of the clans. How do we know there aren't more like Rene out there in the world? Whole clans out there, missing all of these years?"

We don't, Brandon thought, looking again toward Rene.

"I wish we could get into the records at the great house somehow," Tessa murmured. "The Elders keep all the clan Tomes stored in the Grandfather's library, I know it. I'd love the chance to see—" She jumped, startled, her eyes flying wide. Rene turned around simultaneously in surprise. "My cell phone's ringing," Tessa said with a laugh, as Brandon held up his hands, waggling them slightly: *What?*

She reached across the table for her purse, a small, leather clutch. "It's probably Martin," she said with a frown, fishing the phone out. "He keeps calling and leaving me messages. I meant to turn it off last night . . ." Her voice faded and her frown deepened at the number displayed on the phone.

Brandon leaned over the table again, studying the chart that Rene's grandmother had made. *What did your family do that was so horrible, Rene?* he thought. *Why would the Brethren try to wipe out any evidence or memory of your clan's existence?*

Curiously, the reference to Marguerite Davenant was

the only such tie to the Brethren clans—and the last
entry made for the paternal side of Rene's family. Rene's
maternal history, however, was tracked in far more
detail, and for far more generations. Something about it
seemed odd. Brandon couldn't put his finger on it at
first. When Tessa rose, abandoning the table, he slid into
her chair, looking down at the family tree, puzzled.

When it hit him, he blinked as if he'd been slapped.
Rene's maternal family tree traced back more generations, but not necessarily more years. His father's side
was documented back to the early 1600s, when Remy
Morin was born in France. That only accounted for four
generations, however—Rene, his father, his grandfather,
and Remy. His mother's side went at least twice again
that many generations back to reach the same time
period, as if the people there had lived only a fraction of
the time as Rene's paternal kin.

They lived human lifespans, Brandon realized, his eyes
widening. *Jesus Christ, Rene's family is half-human!*

Tessa, he signed, closing his hand into a fist and folding his index finger over his thumb in the letter *T. Tessa,
you're not going to*—

His hands faltered as he looked up. Tessa stood, holding her cell phone to her ear, her eyes wide and stricken.
All of the eager color in her cheeks that had bloomed so
brightly only moments before had drained in full, and
she blinked at him, ashen and shaking.

Rene had noticed only seconds before Brandon, and
crossed the kitchen toward her. "Who is that on the
phone, *pischouette?*" he asked, his brows narrowed,
crimped over the bridge of his nose, his mouth turned
down in a frown. He held out his hand. "Give it to me."

Tessa? Brandon thought, rising to his feet in alarm,
opening his mind to her. *Tessa, what is it? What's wrong?*

Rene reached her first, snatching the phone out of
her hand. Brandon watched the furrow cleaving his
brows deepen as he shoved it to his ear. "Who the hell is
this? Hello?"

Tessa, Brandon said, taking her by the arms. She looked like she was about to faint, that at any moment, even a slight nudge would topple her. He helped her to a chair and eased her into a seated posture. *Tessa, what happened? Who was that on the phone?*

She blinked at him, her eyes glossed with tears. "It . . . it was Caine," she whispered, and he drew back, startled. "He knows I'm with you. He . . . he wanted me to tell you . . ." Her voice faltered, and she looked down at her lap, shuddering.

What? he signed, grasping her by the arm to draw her gaze. *What, Tessa?* he finger-spelled, and then her tears fell.

"He said he has Lina," she said. "Oh, Brandon, he said he'd kill her if you don't come!"

"I'm going with you," Rene said, slamming a loaded clip home into the butt of a pistol. He'd produced the gun from a drawer in his nightstand and tucked it now in the waistband of his jeans as he turned.

Brandon shook his head, standing just within the perimeter of velvet curtains marking Rene's bedroom boundaries. *No, Rene,* he wrote. *It's too dangerous. You don't—*

Rene caught him firmly by the hand, startling him. "I'm going," Rene said again, his brows furrowed so deeply, his eyes were draped in heavy, menacing shadows. "Lina was my partner, and I owe her my goddamn life. I'm not going to sit here sidelined, like some pimple-faced, fat girl at the high school dance while you—"

There was more, but he stormed past Brandon, ducking past the drapes, and Brandon could no longer read his lips. Brandon frowned, turning and following. *Rene, listen to me,* he thought, reaching out and grabbing the older man by the sleeve.

Get out of my head, petit, Rene warned, his frown deepening.

You can't go, Brandon said. *Caine will kill you. Even if the Elders aren't with him yet, he'll kill you.*

"I'm not planning on giving him that chance, *petit,*"

Rene said, jerking the gun from his pants and wiggling it demonstratively under Brandon's nose.

You don't understand, Brandon thought, and he shoved the gun out of his face. *Will you listen to me? You're different—I've sensed that from the start, and so has Tessa. Caine will, too, and he—*

"You think I give a shit if he figures out I'm not part of your little goddamn family tree?" Rene said. "I'm not planning on giving him *that* chance, either."

He started to turn, but again, Brandon grabbed him, staying him. *It's not just that.*

Let go of my arm, petit, Rene thought, glancing at Brandon.

Brandon hadn't wanted to bring this up. He couldn't be sure if Rene was aware of his heritage. All Brandon knew was that if Caine or the Elders caught wind of Rene, they would realize the human blood in his veins and kill him for it. They'd consider him an even greater disgrace to their species than Brandon. *They'll think he's an abomination.*

Rene, it's not just that you're not of a recognized Brethren clan, he thought. *It's more than that. The Elders can sense things—easier than I can, or Tessa, or even Caine. And if they're with him, if they've got Lina, then they'll . . .*

He hesitated, and Rene's expression shifted with bewilderment. "What?" he said. "They'll what, *petit?*"

Brandon glanced at Tessa, who was sitting on a nearby sofa, still trembling and stricken. She didn't know about Rene's heritage, either; Brandon hadn't told her, and she'd been so excited about the discovery of a Davenant ancestor on Rene's family tree that she hadn't yet realized on her own. He didn't want to take a chance on her overhearing his thoughts, so he reached for the notebook hanging around his neck. *Rene, your mother was human,* he wrote, underlining the word *human* for emphasis. *I saw it in your family tree.*

Rene blinked at him, seeming all the more puzzled for having read this. *"Et alors?"* he asked. "So what, *petit?*"

Brandon blinked in surprise. Rene knew, then, but still

didn't understand the danger into which this birthright placed him. He didn't comprehend, and Brandon didn't have time to explain it to him. He abandoned the argument and wrote again, the point of his pen flying against the page. *I need you to stay with Tessa,* he said. *If something happens to me, I need to know I can count on you to take care of her. They know she's with me—that she's helped me. She can't go back to the Brethren. They'll kill her. They'll kill her baby.*

He thought that might work—had hoped for it—and saw in the immediate softening of Rene's face that it had. For whatever reason, the baby was a point of tremendous concern for Rene; his entire demeanor toward Tessa had changed since Brandon had told him about her pregnancy.

Promise me you'll look after her, Brandon wrote. *That you'll keep her safe, Rene.*

Rene glanced toward Tessa, and the hardness in his brows, the line of his mouth faded. He looked torn. *I'll get Lina back,* Brandon thought to him, drawing his gaze. *Whatever it takes, whatever they want from me, I'll give it to see her free and unharmed.*

Even if that means they kill you, petit? Rene thought in reply.

Brandon looked away, closing his mind abruptly so that Rene couldn't sense his fear and trepidation. *Yes,* he wrote instead. *I'll die before I let anything happen to Lina.*

He blinked down at his toes for a moment, and then Rene tapped his shoulder, drawing his gaze. *Here, then,* he thought, offering the pistol butt-first to Brandon. *This is a Sig Sauer P228 double-action nine-millimeter with aluminum frame and steel slide. Her trigger's tight, but she's got a light recoil and a thirteen-shot clip up her ass. You might need the company.*

Brandon slipped the gun into his hand, feeling the heft of it settle against his palm.

You ever shoot one before, petit?

Brandon looked up at Rene, shaking his head. Rene smiled thinly, and with little humor. "Safety's here," he said, pointing. "Thumb it off. Point her and squeeze the trigger. Don't worry—she'll take care of the rest."

Chapter Twenty-three

Lina came to slowly, the same heavy, pounding beat of dance music that had refused her the respite of deep unconsciousness all along at last stirring her fully from a semi-lucid doze. Her head ached; her shoulders felt strained and sore. She lay on her belly, her arms drawn together behind her back. It took her a dazed moment before she remembered. *I went to Apathy, down to the Catacombs looking for Caine Noble . . .*

Caine!

Her eyes flew wide, her momentarily forgotten terror returning in full. She found herself on a leather couch in the lounge area of the Catacombs where she'd found Caine earlier. She didn't see any sign of him, but as her eyes adjusted to the murky gloom, the staccato flashes of strobe lights and the dim haze of dry-ice fog, she could see the nightclub and dance floor were still packed to capacity. She heard people talking and laughing, their voices overlapping.

Lina snapped her eyes shut again. There were people immediately around her, sitting near her, standing behind and around the couch; she'd heard them. No one had seemed to notice her rousing. *Maybe I can run for it, then,* she thought. *Catch them by surprise, at least for a few moments, cut and run for the stairs.*

That would be easier said than done, judging by the pain in her body. Her hands were bound against the small of her back with handcuffs undoubtedly taken from her own uniform belt. She'd been pinioned like this long enough for the sockets of her shoulders to feel strained and sore, and her legs felt stiff, leaden from where she'd been prone. *What other choice do I have, though?* she thought. *Jesus Christ, I have to try. I can't just lie here and wait for that son of a bitch to kill me—and Brandon!*

She held her breath, her brows furrowing. *Alright, then,* she thought. *On three, I'm doing this. Swing my legs around, get my feet on the floor, sit up straight, and take off running. On three. One . . .*

She flexed her legs, stretching the long muscles in her calves and thighs, poised to move.

Two . . .

She pursed her lips and let her breath out slowly.

"Three," she whispered, and then she was in motion. She drew her knees beneath her, kicking her feet around and to the floor, sitting upright as she did. Using the strength of her legs to leverage herself, she scrambled to her feet. She bolted away from the couch, charging headlong for the crowd, amid a scattered chorus of startled yelps and surprised shouts from behind her.

She ducked her head and plowed into the throng. Her broad, frantic stride immediately slowed, but she shoved and shouldered her way forward. The cohesiveness of the crowd that had so worked against her upon her arrival was gone; they'd expected her then, and had been able to herd and hinder her. No one had realized she was even conscious again, much less anticipated that she'd run, and she had that element of surprise to her advantage. It took the clubgoers in the crowd a moment or two to realize that she wasn't one of their fellows knocking past them, and by then it was too late; she was already out of their reach. She heard voices behind her shouting out to catch her, stop her, but they were dim, nearly drowned out by the pelting backbeat from the dance floor.

God, just let me make it, she thought. She could see the staircase ahead of her through the sea of shoulders and heads; the bright glow of the large, neon exit sign. *Let me get out of here, please, oh, Christ, please, just let me—*

She felt a large, strong hand clamp against her arm, jerking her backward in mid-stride, and she screamed. "No! No, goddamn it, no!"

Another hand clapped over her mouth, cutting off her cries to muffled mewls. She thrashed and kicked, shaking her head furiously, pinwheeling her feet in the air as she was dragged back toward the lounge. Here, she was shoved unceremoniously to her knees on the floor.

"You son of a bitch!" she shouted, her voice hoarse and shrill. She tried to scramble to her feet again, but the man who'd caught her forcefully shoved her back down.

"Now, Officer Jones, that's hardly any way to behave," she heard Caine say. She turned, looking toward a group of men and women gathered closely around one of the couches, all standing hunkered, with their backs to her. Caine turned, breaking away from the group to walk toward her, his handsome face softened deceptively with a smile. There was something dark smeared all over his mouth and chin.

"It's too early to leave," he told her gently. "The night's still young, and I'm only just now getting my second wind."

She saw the crowd pull apart behind him, stepping aside to reveal what had been the center point of their attention. *Oh, my God . . . !* Lina thought, her stomach tightening.

Her ex-boyfriend, Jude Hannam, was there somehow, sprawled and lifeless against the sofa. He wore only his underpants, and his dark skin gleamed eerily in the light from the nearby dance floor. His head lolled to one side, his eyes wide open and unblinking, his mouth somewhat agape. His throat had been torn open. The front of his chest, the slight paunch of his belly glistened with blood. The people around him had been taking turns leaning over him, pressing their mouths to the ruin of his neck and sucking greedily, noisily at the blood.

As she watched a girl with platinum blond hair cut in a short-spiky style do exactly this, Lina's gut heaved and she buckled forward, vomiting. She retched until her stomach knotted, empty and aching, and then she blinked up at Caine in stricken horror. "You . . . you bastard," she whispered, shuddering. *Oh, God, Jude,* she thought. *You poor, stupid son of a bitch . . . you forgot there's hell to pay when you try to bargain with the devil . . . !*

Caine wiped his mouth absently with his fingertips. "Funny how he had my brother's scent all over him," he said, and Lina realized. "Or at least, his clothes did."

The suit, she thought, aghast. *Oh, God, I led Caine right to him!*

"I figured he must know Brandon, could tell me where he is," Caine remarked, reaching out and brushing her cheek with his hand, smearing Jude's blood on her. She recoiled in frightened disgust. "Then I find out he has no fucking clue—but he did call my grandfather." He shook his head, clucking his tongue in mock scolding. "So you see, now I'm in a bit of a hurry. If the Grandfather knows where Brandon is, he and the Elders could be here at any moment, even as we speak. I can't afford to keep trailing Brandon all over a goddamn city of this size anymore. Because now I've run out of time."

He grabbed her by the hair, jerking her head back, making her cry out. "You've saved me a lot of trouble coming here tonight, officer," he said. "And for that, I thank you." His other hand darted for her throat, ripping loose the square of bandages taped over her wounds from Brandon's feeding. Caine met her gaze and smiled wickedly, any pretense of kindness or good humor gone. "I'll show Brandon what it really means to feed," he said.

* * *

Brandon gave the cab driver a pair of twenties when they arrived at the Fourth Street landing on the river-front. He could see the floating Apathy nightclub complex to his right as he climbed out of the taxi. To his left, across the street and beyond a broad parking lot, he saw a thick, silhouetted line of trees framing the outermost perimeter of Water Tower Park, the place where he and Lina had visited only days earlier, where she said she'd gone as a kid to day camp, and had earned the nickname "Hoops." That carefree afternoon felt like a million years ago to Brandon now, little more than some wondrous dream.

Brandon had Rene's nine-millimeter pistol tucked beneath the waistband of his jeans, but he didn't know the first thing about guns, and found it more disconcerting than soothing. It was almost two o'clock in the morning, and the scene at the club was apparently winding down for the night. There was no line waiting to cross the steel gangplank, only a bored-looking bouncer leaning heavily against a podium, a cigarette dangling from his hand.

"Hey," he said, nodding once in greeting as Brandon approached. "I need to see your ID, kid."

Only the Elders and older members of the Brethren had anything resembling what the Grandfather called "human frailties," like bank accounts, social security cards, birth certificates, driver's licenses—all fake, of course, but official looking just the same. The younger members had no need for such frivolities, as he was apt to say. Brandon didn't have a driver's license. His father, Sebastian had taught him the basics, letting him practice driving his pick up truck around the narrow, winding lanes bisecting the horse farm, but that didn't make Brandon legal by any means.

He blinked at the bouncer for a puzzled moment. *Why the hell would Caine call me here if he knows I can't get in?* he thought. He patted his hands against his T-shirt and jeans briefly, demonstratively, then shrugged.

"No ID?" the bouncer said. He pinched his cigarette between the pad of his thumb and the tip of his middle finger and flicked it across the landing. "What's the matter? You can't talk?"

Brandon shrugged again and the bouncer smiled. "How old are you, kid?"

Brandon held up his hand, two fingers extended first, and then only his forefinger. *Twenty-one.*

The bouncer motioned toward the gangplank. "Go ahead," he said. "We close in two hours anyway. Knock yourself out."

Brandon flipped him a wave in thanks and started across. *The Catacombs.* That's where Caine had told Tessa to have Brandon go. *The Fourth Street Landing, down on the riverfront, a floating nightclub complex called Apathy. Go aboard and below deck, a bar called the Catacombs.*

"He said he'd be waiting for you there," Tessa had whispered, looking ashen with fright.

Apathy's main lobby opened onto several doorways, all leading to different clubs. The lobby was relatively empty, with the exception of a few women—who on closer glance, turned out to be men in drag—sitting sprawl legged against the floor, leaning together, as lifeless as corpses, too drunk to stumble any farther. Brandon stepped over them, heading toward the doorway marked *Catacombs,* and jerked in surprise as one of them grabbed him by the leg of his jeans.

"Hey, beautiful," the young man said, blinking up at Brandon from beneath heavily applied, bright blue eyeshadow and at least three sets of fake eyelashes. He smiled dazedly up at Brandon, still slumped against his unconscious neighbor. "You got ten dollars? Everybody's gone home and we gotta get a cab. Come on, baby, please. I'll suck you for it, right here. For fifteen, I'll even swallow. I—"

Brandon danced back, jerking himself loose from the

man's grasp. He turned so he didn't have to lip-read any more of the drunk man's disquieting proposition. He felt the man's fingertips pawing insistently at him again, and he hurried away, ducking down the staircase for the Catacombs.

The party might have been dwindling upstairs, but below deck, things were still apparently pretty lively. Brandon could feel the bass line of a dance music track thrumming in the steel steps beneath his feet, and through the iron piping handrail. It was dark, the shadows punctuated by the bright, fluttering flashes of strobe lights. By the time he reached the bottom of the stairs, Brandon could see that the club was still very much packed. The air was stifling, hot and thick with humidity, stinking of sweat and musk, and something else, bittersweet and metallic that caused Brandon's gums to immediately ache. *Blood,* he thought with a frown. *I smell blood.*

He still had not begun to feel any of the aftereffects from his feeding, despite Rene's promises that he would. His shoulder still hurt like hell. He still felt weak and somewhat unsteady. He knew that facing Caine in his current condition could damn well be the most stupid decision he'd ever made in his life—but he had no choice. *Lina is down here somewhere. I have to find her.*

The only consolation Brandon could conceive of was that if he was still feeling this way from a single gunshot wound, then maybe Caine—who'd been shot twice by Lina and punched through with a sword to boot—might still be feeling like shit too.

As he eased his way through the crowd, he noticed people glancing at him, peeking over their shoulders, stopping in mid-conversation, nudging one another, and pointing. They'd see him and step deliberately aside, allowing him to pass. They were all human, but their faced were painted ghastly white with makeup, their eyes ringed in black shadow, their lips tinted black. Some of them slipped Brandon little smiles that sent shivers across the nape of his neck; some had filed their teeth into jagged points at the tips, while others wore fake canine teeth in place of their own—exaggerated and elongated to look like a vampire's.

What the hell is this place? Brandon thought. The paradox that he—a vampire who wished he could be human—was making his way through a crowd of humans who apparently wished they could be vampires, was not lost upon him.

He stepped out onto the dance floor without even realizing it until he was about halfway across. The music abruptly stopped, the air drawing still, and the crowd immediately shrank back from him on all sides, opening up a broad, empty circumference around him. Brandon froze, wide eyed, glancing around him as they moved. His hands closed reflexively into light, wary fists. *Oh, shit.*

The dance floor was an old, disco-tech sort, and when it lit up beneath him, bright golden light spilling up from under his feet, he scrambled back in surprise.

Hello, Brandon. Caine's thoughts slid through his mind, cold and slithering, like a centipede through soft loam. Brandon pivoted and saw his brother come forward, moving out of the crowd as people obligingly moved aside to allow him passage. Caine stepped onto the dance floor and into its bath of yellow light. *I see Tessa was able to relay my message to you. Good. I'll be sure to thank her, because when I'm finished with you, I'll be going after her sorry ass too.*

Where's Lina? Brandon asked, stepping carefully back from Caine's approach, keeping a cautious distance between them.

Your nigger-cop girlfriend? Caine asked, the corner of his mouth hooking. *She's here. She's just tied up at the moment. Tell me, Brandon, did you really fuck her? I can't believe even you would stoop so low as to sully your dick inside a human's orifices. And a black bitch, at that.*

Where is she, Caine? Brandon demanded, sending his thoughts sharply to his brother. His fists tightened reflexively and his brows furrowed. *I'm here, you son of a bitch, just like you wanted. Let her go.*

"You're here, indeed," Caine murmured with a conciliatory nod. He locked gazes with Brandon and smirked. "But that's not all I wanted."

He motioned with his hand, and the crowd behind him moved, parting to reveal Lina, stripped to her bra and panties, handcuffed to a metal post. She'd been gagged, a piece of fabric tied roughly around her mouth, and when she saw Brandon, her eyes flew wide, her mouth moving inarticulately around the gag.

Lina! Brandon stepped forward, unable to breathe, the strength nearly abandoning his legs. He glared at Caine. *Let her go!*

No, Caine replied. *Not yet. I'm not finished with her.* He waved his hand again, and the crowd moved, closing in around Lina, obscuring her from Brandon's view. *What do you think of my new friends?*

Some friends, Brandon thought. Every time he moved, stepping toward the edge of the dance floor, wanting to go to Lina's aid, the throng stepped closely together, blocking his way. He turned to Caine, his frown deepening. *How are you controlling them all at once? Not even the Grandfather can do that.*

Caine laughed, canting his head back. "I wish I was controlling them," he said. "But I'm not. They've opened their minds to me freely, and when I ask them favors, they oblige. They want to be like us—can you believe it? Even the least among them has more Brethren merit to them than you, Brandon. They're more than willing to please me—they beg for the chance."

He stepped closer to Brandon, arching his brow. "Maybe you weren't so wrong to leave the Brethren after all," he said, and he began to gather his heavy sheaf of hair back against the nape of his neck, securing it with an elastic band he wore around his wrist. "To their eyes, I'm little more than a child, but here—in this place, this world, to these humans—I'm a god."

You're fucking nuts, that's what you are, Brandon said. *When the Grandfather finds out what you've—*

"The Grandfather will be down on his goddamn knees singing my praises when I deliver your head to him, ripped loose from your neck!" Caine shouted. "I'll be a god among them too—I found you before even the Elders! I'll kill you—stop your pathetic blight upon us—and then bring them the goddamn human bitch that butchered our sister!"

No, Brandon said. The Brethren would slaughter Lina; they'd rip her limb from limb, open her wide and scatter her viscera to the wind because of Emily. He shook his head at Caine. *No, Caine, let her go. I'm here. You've got me—I'm the one the Grandfather wants. They'll praise you enough for that alone. Let her go.*

He stepped toward his brother. *I'm begging you,* he said. *Whatever you want from me—anything, Caine. I'll give it to you. Just let her go. I won't fight you.*

Caine laughed. "But Brandon," he said, his eyes blackening, his fangs extending in full. "That's exactly what I want."

He hooked his hand against the collar of his shirt and yanked, ripping the fabric wide open. He shrugged his shoulders, tossing aside the shredded remnants and stood bare chested before Brandon. His torso was smeared with dried blood; he'd fed recently, and well, too, given the copious amount. His skin was glossy with a sheen of sweat, the muscles in his chest and abdomen standing out in sharp, etched detail in the bright light of the dance floor. Brandon could clearly see fading coronas of bruising at each of his shoulders from the bullets Lina had pumped into him; a thin, ragged scab bisected the lower quadrant of his gut—the healing wound where Brandon had run him through.

I'm going to break you, little brother, Caine said inside of Brandon's mind. *Mind and body, both broken when I'm through. I'm going peel your flesh back from your bones and see you choke on the meat of your own marrow.* He shook his

head once, furiously, whipping his jaw violently out of
socket to accommodate the length of his bared fangs.
He opened this newly hideous, gaping maw at his
brother and screamed, a scraping, shrill, inhuman
sound that Brandon heard in his mind.

Caine charged, leaping into the air and hurtling
across the dance floor. The crowd immediately swelled
back, broadening the space around them, giving the two
brothers more room. Brandon jerked himself sideways,
feeling the whip of wind against his face as Caine flew
past him. He whirled, just as Caine charged him from
the other direction, and caught the blur of movement
out of the corner of his eye as Caine swung at him. Brandon's hand snapped up reflexively, catching Caine's
proffered punch against his palm. He folded his fingers
against Caine's hand, and swept his hand around and
then upward, hyperextending Caine's wrist.

Caine's eyes widened with sudden pain and surprise,
and he whipped his other first around to pummel Brandon's face and loosen his grip. Brandon caught his other
hand and again, wrenched it around and up, craning it
at an abrupt, unnatural angle that left the two brother's
dancing together, face-to-face and damn near nose-to-
nose.

Caine reared his head back and then forward, head-
butting Brandon, ramming their foreheads squarely,
brutally together. Brandon let go of Caine's hands as he
stumbled back, reeling, tiny pinpoints of light and
shadow suddenly sparkling before his dazed eyes. He
crashed backward, tumbling onto his ass, but recovered
before Caine could seize upon the momentary advantage. He punted his left foot out, driving his heel mightily into Caine's knee. Caine crumpled to the floor,
screaming soundlessly to Brandon's perception, his
hands clutching his wounded leg.

Brandon rolled back onto his shoulders and then forward in a kip-up, kicking with his legs and arching his
back to lend himself the momentum to spring immedi-

ately upright. He landed on his feet and scrambled backward, putting distance between himself and Caine again, watching warily as Caine limped to his feet.

Brandon's shoulder throbbed with pain. *Christ, I can't do this,* he thought. He glanced behind him and realized the crowd had withdrawn enough to leave a clear path between him and Lina. She stared at him, straining her hands desperately against the handcuffs, her face twisted with fright and pain. *I've got to get her out of here. I've—*

Movement out of his peripheral vision and he turned his head, just as Caine tackled him, slamming into his chest and knocking him back. Brandon slammed against the floor, the impact, and Caine's tremendous weight crushing the breath from his lungs. The pistol slipped out of his waistband in the fall, and went skittering across the floor.

Caine glanced at it, and then stared down at Brandon, straddling his hips and catching him by the wrists to pin him. *And what were you going to do with that, little brother?* he asked. *Did you really think you could stop me with it—that you could stop me at all? You're a fool, Brandon. A goddamn fool, and I—*

Brandon swung up his legs, locking his knees around Caine's neck, and throwing him off. He rolled as Caine fell and wound up on top of his brother as they tumbled together. Caine reached up, shoving his hand toward Brandon's face. Brandon had a bewildered half-second to realize he held a slim black canister of some sort against his palm, and then something wet and abruptly searing sprayed against his face, almost directly in his eyes.

Brandon screamed mutely, pitching sideways off of Caine, writhing on his side against the floor. He clapped his hands over his face, shoving the heels of his palms against his eyes as molten heat, horrible and agonizing, ripped through him. It felt as though Caine had just shoved handfuls of burning coal into his eyes, up his nose. He felt his nasal passages immediately swell shut;

tears streamed from his eyes and he couldn't as much as begin to force his eyelids open. He gagged for breath, feeling the chemical mist scorch his tongue, his throat.

Caine's hand closed roughly in his hair, jerking his head back. *Consider that a parting gift from your girlfriend,* he said inside Brandon's mind. *A little blast of police-issue pepper spray.*

He turned Brandon loose, and Brandon crumpled, covering his face with his hands again, gasping and shuddering helplessly. He struggled to open his eyes, knowing that if he didn't, he was dead; if he didn't find some way to fight back, Caine would kill both him and Lina. He pried his eyelids back a faint margin, but the pain was so immediate and excruciating, it was all he could bear. *Oh, God,* he thought in a terrified panic. *Oh, God, I'm blind!*

See no evil, Caine purred to him, and Brandon felt something press against his temple; the cool, round end of Rene's Sig Sauer P228. *Hear no evil, speak no evil. Now you've got it right, Brandon.*

Brandon closed his eyes fiercely, his teeth gritted, every muscle in his body tensed and poised for that horrific moment of heat and pain, the fleeting seconds of awareness that passed between the pulling of the trigger, and the scattering of his brain against the floor.

And then he remembered.

How did you do that with the birds? Brandon had asked Rene. *Call them like that, make them fly around you?*

I don't know, Rene had replied. *I've always been able to, ever since I was a little boy. I just open my mind to them, and once I sense them, I just . . . push myself into them. I see through their eyes, sense through their senses. I don't know how to describe it otherwise.*

Brandon opened his mind, struggling to summon his telepathy, to force it outward beyond the club.

It takes practice, that's all, Rene had told him.

Oh, please, Brandon thought. *Jesus Christ, please . . . !* All at once, he sensed the birds in Water Tower Park, a hint of them in his mind—hundreds of them roosting in the trees—and seized up on it. He focused on the fluttering, whispering sensation of them.

I don't know why someone said you're weak, petit, Rene had told him. *I've never met anyone but you and my daddy with the power, but yours is sure as hell strong. A lot stronger than his—more than anything I've ever felt before.*

Please . . . Brandon thought, pushing with all of his might, reaching out desperately to the birds. *Oh, God, please . . . !*

That's it, Brandon, Caine whispered in his mind. *Beg me for mercy.*

It takes practice, that's all, Rene said in Brandon's memory, and he felt the birds stirring in the treetops, taking to the skies, a dizzying whirlwind of images flashing through his mind—leaves and branches silhouetted against the sky; stars overhead with faint inklings of clouds, luminous in the moonlight; the sudden thrill of flight, of looking down and seeing the outline of the nightclub barges below, its decks peppered with lights that flashed against the surface of the water.

Maybe I'll let you live long enough for your eyes to heal . . . Caine said.

When the birds swooped down, plunging toward the barges, Brandon felt the whip of wind against his face. He watched the bright lights of the deck suddenly swell into view, and then the birds swept aboard the nightclub, flooding into the lobby like the leading edge of some massive, swift-moving wave.

I'll let you watch me tear your bitch's throat out with my hands, Caine hissed to him. *I'll let you watch as I drain her—*

The birds rushed through the doorway leading downward into the Catacombs. Brandon could see through hundreds of tiny pairs of eyes as they swooped over the dance floor in a sudden, frenzied cloud. Immediately, the humans frighted and panicked, staggering about and screaming, flapping their hands, and plowing into each other, knocking one another down and underfoot as they tried to escape. The birds were everywhere, clawing and pecking, talons tangling in hair, tearing at faces, hands, and eyes. When they surged toward Caine, Brandon saw it through them; he watched his brother's eyes widen in bewildered shock and then they were upon him, forcing him back, driving him away from Brandon.

Brandon staggered to his feet, hunching his shoulders reflexively, even though the birds cut and dove around him, giving him a broad and deliberate berth. He couldn't open his eyes, but in his mind, he could see what the birds saw; flashing, overlapping, rapid-fire images from all around him, a panoramic view of the entire club. He turned until he could see Caine in his mind, and then limped toward him. The birds cleared a path for him, guiding his way.

Caine's eyes were closed, his hands drawn toward his face as he swatted and screamed at the birds. They were tangled in his hair, ripping and pulling, stabbing their beaks into the meat of his shoulders and chest. He couldn't fend them off; for every one he drove back, ten more darted forward in its place. He still had the gun in his hand, and when Brandon reached for it, it was as if he watched it on television. Through the birds' eyes, he could see himself, as well, and when he closed his fingers around the barrel of the pistol, twisting it suddenly and sharply out of Caine's grasp, he saw his brother open his eyes, blinking in surprise.

"You—!" he began, and then Brandon closed his free hand into a fist and sent it flying, smashing his knuckles into Caine's temples, crumpling him to the floor. Brandon had expected his shoulder to scream in protest, but all at once, as his fury grew and his adrenaline surged, the pain was forgotten. The burning in his eyes and airways was forgotten and he could see again; through a veil of fading tears, the world around him swam again into sudden, murky focus. He felt a new heat sear through his body; something invigorating and wondrous. His gums throbbed and his canine teeth began to drop. Rene had told him that feeding would accelerate his inherent healing ability, and that when its full effects came upon him, he'd know it. *You'll be flying,* he'd said. *It's almost as good as making love . . . almost.*

Get up, Brandon thought to Caine. He tossed the pistol away, sending it clattering across the floor. He stepped back, motioning to Caine in beckon. *Get on your feet, bastard.*

"You . . . you're dead," Caine hissed, raising his head. Blood streamed from his nose, and he choked, spitting out a mouthful. "Do you hear me? You're dead! You and the goddamn bitch!" He pressed his hands against the floor and staggered to his feet. He glared at Brandon, laughing. "I'll bleed her dry right in front of you. I'll open her goddamn throat."

Brandon hooked his left fist around, driving it into Caine's nose and cheek. Caine didn't even see it coming in time to draw his hands up; his head cracked sideways on his neck, and he sprawled to the floor again, landing hard, gasping for breath.

Get up, Brandon hissed again. Caine huddled against the floor, whooping in mouthfuls of air, laughing as blood choked him again. He drew his knees beneath him and stumbled, rising clumsily. He turned his face and spat; a tooth flew in a spray of bloody spittle from his lips, making him laugh all the harder.

"She's a carcass," he said, and he swung his right fist toward Brandon's face. Brandon ducked his head toward his left shoulder and drove his left fist around again, battering into Caine's cheek, sending him reeling. Caine recovered his footing and charged again, slamming his knuckles into Brandon's gut. Brandon gasped, buckling slightly, and then he lashed out with his foot, hooking against the back of Caine's heel, punting his leg out from beneath him. Caine toppled to the floor, and Brandon danced away from him.

"A . . . a goddamn human whore . . ." Caine hissed,

grinning at Brandon as he limped to his feet again, his lips and teeth smeared with blood. "And when she's dead, I'll rip her head off and bring it back to the Grandfather along with yours."

He swung at Brandon. Brandon canted back, arching his shoulders and spine away from the blow. As Caine's fist darted at his face, he raised his hand, catching the punch squarely against his palm. He wrenched Caine's arm, hyperextending his wrist, and Caine cried out hoarsely, staggering. Brandon drove his free fist around, pummeling Caine's face. He kept hold of Caine's arm and drove his fist again and again into his brother's head, shattering his nose and cheek, pounding teeth loose of their moorings.

Caine collapsed to his knees, his face bloodied, and Brandon backed away from him, opening his hands and flexing his fingers, closing them deliberately into fists again. *Get up*, he said.

Caine sprang from the floor, leaping unexpectedly. He tackled Brandon, knocking him off his feet, and the two of them crashed to the ground, rolling together. Somehow, Brandon wound up on top and reared back, sitting up and letting his fists fly, driving them again and again into Caine's face. Caine screamed and fought beneath him, trying to punch him, to ward off his blows.

Brandon struck him, his knuckles slamming into Caine's cheeks, temples, his brow, his eyes, nose, and mouth. Blood sprayed in wild arcs every time his fists connected; every time he drew them back on the fulcrums of his shoulders and drove them forward again. He beat Caine until his knuckles shattered, the bones in his hands that had only just healed crumpling anew, cracking with the force of each furious, brutal impact. He beat Caine until his brother's struggles beneath him waned, and his hands abandoned their feeble efforts at protest.

Brandon beat Caine until his face was gone, bashed beneath Brandon's fists, a bloodied, battered ruin. He beat him until he was oblivious to everything but the marks of his aim as he drove his fists downward. The room around him faded and there was nothing but help-less, anguished rage—rage for the years he'd spent living in terror beneath his grandfather's roof; for the shame Caine had always inflicted upon him; for the hopeless-ness that had time and again made Brandon's heart and mind turn to escape—any escape, even death—if it meant freedom from the Brethren. The rage welled inside of him and he unleashed it against Caine.

When he was finished, when Caine lay motionless be-neath him, Brandon fell still, gasping for breath. The nightclub had emptied quickly; the birds had driven the humans away. Some still remained, but only because in their panic, enveloped in swarms of birds, they'd been unable to reach the exit. Brandon staggered to his feet, holding his injured hands against his belly, blinking in dismay at the swollen, crippled mess that had once been his knuckles.

He stumbled toward Lina. She knelt against the floor, her cheek pressed against the pole, her hands cuffed on either side of it. She was weeping, her entire body wracked with sobs. Brandon had inadvertently knocked Rene's pistol in her direction, close enough so that she'd been able to kick her leg out, hook it with her foot and draw it near. She clutched at it now in her bound hands, grasping it so tightly, her hands shook, as if it was a life preserver to her.

She'd managed to jerk the gag away from her mouth and cried his name as he approached. He fell to his knees before her and touched her face, unfurling his broken fingers to caress her cheek, ignoring the terrible pain the effort caused.

"Brandon . . . !" she gasped again, and when he leaned toward her, tucking his forehead against her shoulder, she shuddered, weeping and kissing his hair.

It's alright, he thought. *It's alright, Lina. It's over now.*

He sat back and managed to smile for her. She raised

her hands and strained to reach him, touching his blood-smeared, battered face. New tears welled in her eyes and he leaned toward her again, kissing her. *Where are the keys to the cuffs?* he asked her in his mind.

She glanced over her shoulder. "There," she said, her lips trembling uncontrollably. "There, near . . . near those couches . . . my pants pocket."

Brandon nodded, rising again. His shoulder and eyes might have felt better, restored at least in part from the aftereffects of feeding, but he'd traded old injuries for new ones and tried not to grimace, because he knew it would frighten her. She saw anyway and her tears spilled. He limped toward the nearby lounge area she'd indicated, a cozy arrangement of leather couches and arm chairs. A dead man lay sprawled on one of the couches, clad only in his underpants, his arms and legs outstretched. It was Jude Hannam. His throat had been ripped open; Caine's gruesome handiwork.

Jesus, Brandon thought, shivering. He saw Lina's uniform lying in a pile. Rather than attempt the excruciating act of shoving his broken hands down into her pockets, he settled for the less painful effort of simply picking them up and carrying them to her.

You'll have to help, I'm afraid, he thought to her as he approached, stepping over Caine's fallen body, unable to look at what remained of his brother's face—the brutal damage he'd caused. Instead, he locked gazes with Lina, offering her a feeble smile. She still clung to the pistol tightly, with such desperate fervency he wondered if she'd be able to let it go. *My hands are in pretty bad shape. I don't think I can—*

Her eyes flew wide, and her mouth opened in a silent cry. He watched her scream his name—*Brandon!*—and then she raised her hands, jerking the tether of her cuff chains up the metal pole, aiming the nine-millimeter straight at him. His eyes flew wide and he ducked, throwing himself sideways as Lina's index finger flexed inward against the trigger.

He didn't hear the gunshot, but as he landed hard against the floor, catching the brunt of his fall against his hip and shoulder, he saw a sudden burst of blue-gray smoke surround the muzzle of the pistol. He whipped his head around to look over his shoulder. Caine was still alive; his face was monstrously damaged, a bloodied mess of pulp and meat, but he'd managed to shamble to his feet as Brandon had passed him. He'd lunged at Brandon, meaning to tackle him from behind, but Lina's bullet had caught him in the shoulder, sending him staggering back.

The first one, anyway.

Again, Brandon didn't hear the pistol fire, but he saw Caine lurch, wheeling clumsily to his left as another bullet slammed into his chest. A third struck his groin, nearly doubling him, and the fourth—the last shot— punched into his skull, throwing him back and off his feet, crashing to the ground.

Brandon blinked, shocked and ashen at Lina, but she didn't tear her wide, stricken gaze away from Caine. She kept the gun leveled in his direction as a tremor started in her hands and worked it way up through her arms to her shoulders, shuddering eventually through her entire, slender form.

Brandon stood, stumbling toward his brother. Even as he approached, he could see the dark stain of blood spilling around Caine's head in a broadening circumference, stark and apparent against the glow from the lighted dance floor. His eyes were half-open, but there was little else left distinguishable in his face—only his canine teeth as they slowly withdrew back along his gumline, shrinking into proper place.

Brandon turned to Lina. "He . . . he said he'd kill me," she said, as the pistol tumbled from her fingers to the floor. She began to weep again, clapping her hand against her eyes. "He . . . oh, God, he killed Jude . . . !"

Chapter Twenty-four

"Rene!" Lina screamed, pressing on the call-button outside his building. It was three-thirty in the morning. The street was empty, the sky black and silken. Brandon leaned heavily against her, his strength waning quickly, and she struggled to support his weight with only one arm while she punched at the intercom. They'd taken a cab; as she and Brandon had limped together from the barge to the shore, she'd heard the distant din of numerous sirens—dozens, by the sound of them—approaching fast. *Sorry to interrupt your supper break, Larry,* she'd thought grimly.

Lina and Brandon had fled. There was no way in hell she would be able to explain what had happened that night—not without sounding like a stark-raving lunatic—and so she'd wrapped her arm around Brandon's midriff and hauled him in tow. They'd stumbled together through Water Tower Park until they'd found themselves facing Memorial General Hospital. From here, she'd been able to flag down a cab. Just as before, on the night that Caine and Emily had attacked them, they didn't draw as much as a second glance from their driver. Brandon had huddled against her in the car, whatever reserve of strength that had seen him through that night thus far abandoning him, and by the time they'd reached Rene's, he'd been glassy eyed and dazed with pain.

"Rene!" she screamed again, thumbing the buzzer over and over. "Rene, please! Goddamn it, where are you?"

The heavy steel front door squalled on its hinges as it swung open, and she burst into relieved tears to see Rene there, striding forward, his hands outstretched. *"Mon Dieu!"* he exclaimed, seizing her by the back of the head and jerking her and Brandon against him in a fierce embrace. "Oh, Christ, I thought I'd lost you, *chère*," he gasped against her ear, his voice choked and ragged. "Get inside—Jesus Christ, both of you."

"Brandon's hurt," Lina said, as Rene helped her hustle the younger man inside. "His hands . . . be careful of his hands . . . !"

Tessa stood in the expansive foyer, pinned in a pale beam of light from an overhead security lamp. She cried out softly and scurried forward, her eyes round with horror as Rene caught Brandon in his arms, hoisting him against his chest. "Oh, God! What happened?" She looked toward Lina. "What happened?"

"Caine is dead," Lina replied grimly, hurrying to follow as Rene carried Brandon toward the elevators.

"What about the Elders?" Tessa asked, scurrying closely behind.

Lina shook her head. "There was nobody but Caine. Trust me—he was enough."

Once upstairs in the loft, Rene lay Brandon against his bed. Brandon kept trying to move his hands, to sign or write, but each time, it hurt him, forcing him further and further toward unconsciousness. He lay against the bed, his eyes closed. When Rene moved to touch his right hand gently in examination, Brandon jerked, gasping sharply for breath.

"They look broken to me," Rene said, and Tessa uttered a soft, pained sound at this, her hand darting to her mouth. Rene looked up grimly. "And broken pretty bad off, too."

"But they'll heal, right?" Lina asked. "Like before, when he was shot, he'll heal fast."

"He's not fully healed from that yet, *chère*," Rene said, drawing the neckline of Brandon's T-shirt down somewhat, enough so that she could still see the bruising along his upper torso from the bullet wound. "But yeah, he'll heal. It'll take him months—at least. We'll have to bind his hands up, let those bones knit back into place."

"We don't have months," Tessa said, stricken. "Just because the Elders weren't with Caine tonight doesn't mean they won't be coming. They could be here any *day* now."

"What if he feeds again?" Lina asked, but Rene shook his head, making her frown. "You said before it would help him, that it would make him heal even faster."

"It will, *chère*," Rene said. "But he can't feed from *you* again is my point. It's no different than if you'd just donated a pint down at the blood bank. You can't afford to lose anymore—not without throwing your body into systemic shock. He can't feed from you for at least two months."

"Two months?" Lina blinked at him, startled.

"There's another way," Rene said, cutting an awkward glance toward Tessa. "I know a couple of people . . . girls I call sometimes . . ." His voice faded and he looked decidedly sheepish. Lina could have sworn he was blushing. "You know, *chère*."

"Know what?" Tessa asked, puzzled, not understanding Rene's inference. "What are you talking about?"

"No," Lina said, shaking her head, because she understood perfectly. "No, we're not calling your hookers over here so he can feed off of them. What are they going to think of this, Rene? This is more than kinky—his hands are fucking broken!"

"Hookers?" Tessa's eyes widened, and she turned to Rene. "You feed from hookers?"

"Not many other places to find fresh blood from a willing source, *pischouette*," Rene told her, scowling. "It may not be up to your thoroughbred standards, but it serves its purpose, and no one winds up dead in the process."

"Forget it, Rene," Lina snapped. "We'll move him like he is. We'll stretch him out in the backseat of one of your cars. We'll—"

"It could kill him to move him too much, *chère*," Rene said. "Not until he feeds again—he needs the blood to strengthen him. Until then, he's weak, vulnerable, pretty much like a human would be. You get one of those bone chips that are all that's left of his hands stuck in his bloodstream, lodged in his heart or a blood vessel somewhere, and he could have a massive stroke or a heart attack and die."

"We don't have a choice, Rene," Lina said, her brows furrowing. "You heard Tessa. The Elders are coming. You didn't see Caine tonight—what he did, what he was capable of. I was there. I saw it. If these Elders are anything like Brandon and Tessa say they are—a thousand times worse—then I sure as shit don't plan on letting Brandon stay here until they come beating down your door."

"We do have a choice, *chère*," Rene said. "We let him feed. It'll strengthen him enough so we can move him more quickly—maybe by the morning, a couple days at best."

"We're not using one of your whores," Lina said. "I told you that already—no outsiders. It's too dangerous and we—"

"I'm not talking about one of my whores," Rene said coolly, patiently. "I'm talking about me, *chère*. We'll let him feed from me."

Lina and Tessa both blinked at one another in bewildered surprise. "My mother was human," Rene explained, unbuttoning the front of his shirt. "Her whole family, in fact. My only claim to the Brethren comes from my daddy, and I hardly knew him at all, much less anything about him."

He jerked his shirt tails from beneath the waistband of his jeans and shrugged it off, tossing it aside. "So I'm like you, *pischoutte*," he said, glancing toward Tessa. "But I'm like you, too, Lina. Let's hope I'm close enough to help Brandon, if only enough to get us out of here."

He sat against the side of the bed and leaned over, slipping his hand beneath Brandon's head. "Tessa, *ma chère*," he said. "Go to the kitchen and bring me a knife out of my cutting block. He's sleeping on us and we've no time to be dainty. We need to wake him up."

Brandon groaned mutely as the thick, coppery fragrance of blood filled his nose. It seeped through the heavy fog of pain clouding his mind, stirring the blood-lust within him, causing his gums to begin swelling, the sockets of his canine teeth to throb and ache. He tried to turn his head away but felt fingertips slip between his lips, smearing blood against his tongue.

Brandon, he heard Rene say in his mind. *Brandon, wake up. You're hurt,* petit. *You're bad off and you need to feed.*

Brandon opened his eyes, blinking dazedly up at his friend. *Where . . . am I?* he thought groggily. *What happened, Rene?*

Rene smiled at him gently. *You're back at my loft,* he replied. He stuck his finger in his mouth, sucking momentarily, and Brandon realized he'd cut the tip open deeply to draw blood, to rouse the bloodlust in Brandon and stir him from unconsciousness. *You kicked your brother's ass, is what happened,* petit. *Only you forgot to use your feet and wound up busting your hands.*

Brandon managed a weak laugh. *You need to feed, Brandon,* Rene told him, his expression growing solemn. *We need to get you out of here—out of the city, but we can't move you like this. We've got to jump-start your healing, like we did before, OK?*

Brandon nodded. He looked around blearily, and found Lina at his opposite bedside. She stroked her hand against his hair, and he smiled again. *You sure?* he asked her, and she glanced at Rene uncertainly.

Not Lina, petit, Rene said, drawing Brandon's confused gaze. *It's too soon for her again.*

Then . . . who? Brandon asked.

"Me," Rene said aloud, and Brandon blinked at him. "You told me yourself—my mother's a human. Her blood is in me."

But so's that of the Brethren, Brandon said, his eyes widening in horror. He glanced toward his twin for rescue. *We can't feed from a fellow Brethren—it's forbidden! It . . . it's a sacrilege . . . an abomination . . . ! It . . .*

It's the best we can do, Brandon, Tessa told him.

I'm sorry, petit, Rene said. *But it's all we've got.*

You sure about this? Brandon asked him a few moments later. Tessa and Lina had ducked beyond the drapes surrounding the bed, leaving them alone.

"No," Rene admitted. "But I figure what the hell. It doesn't mean we're going steady or anything."

He glanced at Brandon, the corner of his mouth hooked wryly, and Brandon laughed.

You've been so kind to me, Rene, he thought, closing his eyes against a swell of pain from his hands. He gritted his teeth and sucked in a long, hurting breath, riding it out. *Not just for this, I mean, but . . . but all along . . . a good friend, and I . . . I don't know what I would have done without you. You've saved my life twice . . . first that night in the alley, and then . . . again tonight . . . I used what you told me . . . what you showed me with the birds and I . . .*

Brandon, Rene thought. Brandon had been on the verging of slipping under again, his mind fading, and he opened his eyes wide, startled. Rene smiled at him. "You're welcome, *petit,*" he said aloud, then he turned his head slightly, his shoulders tensing, his brows lifting anxiously as he presented his neck. "Now shut up and bite me already, goddamn it."

Chapter Twenty-five

"Is that everything, then?" Tessa asked Brandon, as she carefully tucked his brass-plated notebook down inside his duffel bag. It occurred to him that the little pad in its ornate, gilded case seemed like a relic to him, a grim and unnecessary reminder of a past best left unrevisited.

He nodded and watched as she drew the zipper closed. She sat against the side of the bed, her hands toying restlessly in her lap. He didn't move, or say anything to her. He didn't need to.

I'm scared, she thought.

I know, he replied, sitting beside her with the duffel bag between them. *Me, too.*

The Elders were coming; the twins could both sense them in their minds, like the shadows of dusk closing in upon an unlit room, swallowing everything in darkness. The Grandfather was with them; they could sense this as well. Even at a distance, his presence was enormous—the hissing snap of electrical charge in this growing storm's leading edge.

What if they've already reached the city? Tessa asked. In her anxiety, her hands stole unconsciously to her belly, where the first hint of her pregnancy was beginning to show against her ordinarily flat plane. *What if they're clouding our minds somehow, like Rene thinks they did with you before? What if they're already here and they're coming for us?*

I don't know, Brandon replied. He still wasn't convinced that the Grandfather had blocked his telepathy in Kentucky. True, he'd been able to summon enough strength and power to command the birds against Caine, but that was a far cry from being as strong as any of the other Brethren, much less stronger. *I guess we'll find out shortly.*

They were leaving. They had agreed the night before to travel separately, with Brandon and Lina following one path southeast from the city, and Rene and Tessa following another. They hoped that doing so would cover their tracks somewhat, and hopefully keep one, the other, or both parties away from the notice of the Elders. They'd prearranged for meeting points along their way, and planned to criss-cross the country for as long as they could—however much time was needed—until Brandon's hands were fully healed, and they could risk making a stand against the Brethren—and the Grandfather.

Tessa lay back on the bed, blinking against tears as she looked up at the ceiling. "Maybe we can go back someday," she whispered. "To Kentucky, the great house. Maybe we can rescue Daniel somehow."

Brandon felt his heart tighten with sorrow at the thought of their brother, so young and innocent, trapped and helpless among the Brethren. *Maybe,* he thought, lying down next to her. *If he hasn't already learned to hate me.*

He doesn't hate you, Brandon, Tessa said. *Daniel loves you—more than anything or anyone. He always will.*

Brandon closed his eyes and said nothing. *Because I'm not so sure about that.*

The Elders will kill Rene if they find him, Tessa thought, drawing his gaze. He watched a tear steal from the corner of her eye, trailing down the high arch of her cheek toward her ear. *If not because he helped us, then because of what he is. They'll know it. They'll sense it right away—the human blood in him and they'll kill him.*

Brandon reached out with his bandaged hand, wiping her tear way. *I didn't think you'd mind for that,* he said, making her laugh despite herself. They both rolled onto their sides to face one another.

I have to admit there's a certain kind of charm about Rene Morin, she said, rolling her eyes slightly, color stoking almost shyly in her cheeks. *There have been times these past couple of days when he's been almost bearable. Sweet, even. But don't you dare go telling him I said so.* She smiled at her brother. *I haven't seen him touch a drop of liquor or one pill either, not since you and Lina came back. I think he's tryng to be different. I think we've changed him somehow.*

I think he's changed us too, Brandon thought.

When I found out I was pregnant, do you know what Martin said to me? Tessa asked. *"It had better be a son." That's it. It was like he was angry with me, that I'd done this deliberately.* A crimp furrowed the smooth, porcelain skin of her brow. *I hate him, Brandon. When he . . . he'd come to me in my room at night, I'd just lay there. I wouldn't move. I'd try not to even breathe, hoping he would just leave. But he never would. I hate him. I've hated him all along, and the Grandfather for making me marry him.*

I know, Tessa, Brandon told her gently.

She smiled at him, touching his face, stroking her thumb against his mouth. "You were right," she murmured. "About everything, Brandon, all along."

He remembered how he'd thought her lost to him—*his* Tessa, the one he'd adored, to whom he'd always turned and trusted. He remembered how a part of his heart had hardened toward her in his last years at the great house; how he'd nearly come to hate his sister. *No, Tessa,* he thought, closing his mind to her so she couldn't overhear. *Not right about everything.*

"Are you sure you want to take this car, *chère?*" Rene said, looking decidedly distraught as Lina turned the key in the Mercedes SLK 280's ignition, gunning the little silver convertible to life.

She pumped the accelerator twice, listening to the well-tuned, resonant growl of the V6 engine in response. She cut a glance toward Rene and grinned broadly. "Oh, yeah. I'm sure."

Rene stumbled back a step, looking as stricken and aghast as if he had just handed over his firstborn child. "She's got a real easy clutch on her," he said. "Don't go popping it out at every goddamn stoplight. You have to ease it gently with her."

"I know how to drive, Rene," Lina told him, rolling her eyes heavenward. "You're the one who pretty much taught me, remember?"

What? Brandon asked, as he walked with Tessa around to the passenger side of the car. He'd been smiling, but his bright expression faltered abruptly. *Oh, Christ.*

Shut up, Lina signed, laughing. *Get in.*

Brandon turned to his sister and smiled again, drawing his bandaged hands carefully around her, drawing her near. *I'll see you soon,* he whispered in promise in her mind, and she nodded against his shoulder, clutching at him, trembling with sudden tears.

Three weeks, she thought. *In New Orleans. The Hotel Maison de Ville.*

Brandon nodded. *Rene offered to give us the grand tour, bayous, backwaters, and all,* he said.

Tessa drew back from him, her eyes swimming in tears. They spilled even as she smiled, struggling to laugh. "He said if he could still find anything since the hurricane," she said. She hugged him again, pressing her lips against his cheek. "I love you, Brandon."

This he could still sign, despite the bandages. He crossed his hands over his heart and then pointed one of his swaddling mittens at her, brushing against the tip of her nose. *I love you, too, Tessa.*

He glanced over as Rene walked around the back of

the car, approaching. He motioned toward his neck. *How's it doing?*

Rene brushed his fingertips against the gauze square taped beneath the shelf of his chin, almost as if he'd forgotten about it. He laughed, arching his brow at Brandon. "You left a hell of a hickey, *petit*," he said. "But I'll live. You got those pills I gave you? And the money too?"

Rene had presented Brandon with a pair of medicine bottles, each filled to the brim with Percodan tablets. "You're going to need them, *petit*," he'd warned grimly, and then he'd tucked a thick roll of money, bound with a strained rubber band, into Brandon's shirt pocket. "There's seven thousand dollars and change there," he said, and Brandon had blinked at him, startled. "It's yours. You get in a pinch, you use it, *petit*."

Brandon nodded to Rene as they stood facing each other in the garage, and it might have been only a trick of the fluorescents from overhead, but Brandon could have sworn that Rene's eyes had suddenly grown glossy. *Thanks, Rene,* he thought, feeling somewhat choked up himself.

Rene hooked his arm around Brandon's neck, offering him a brief but fond embrace. *Take care of yourself,* petit, he thought. *And Lina, too. Tessa and I will see you soon.*

Brandon climbed into the car and sat patiently as Lina reached across him, helping him with his seat belt. When she'd clicked the buckle home, she glanced up, meeting his gaze. "You ready?" she said, her eyes wide and anxious. He could sense the fluttering, uncertain rhythm of her heart, and smell her fear like a light perfume in the air around her.

He smiled at her gently, trying to reassure. *Let's do this,* he thought.

She nodded once, seeming to draw upon the comfort he offered. Her expression relaxed somewhat, and she looked beyond his shoulder, smiling at Tessa and Rene. "You two try not to kill each other between here and Louisiana," she said.

Rene and Tessa exchanged quick looks. "I think *la*

pischouette and I will be fine," Rene said, to which Tessa only laughed, mysterious and inexplicable. "Get out of here, the both of you. *Je vous aime.*"

"Love you, too, Rene," Lina said, turning around in her seat and settling herself comfortably. She glanced at Brandon and dropped him a wink. "Ready?" she asked. "Set? Here we go, then."

Off the deep end, with both feet, he replied with a nod, and then she floored the accelerator, making the little Mercedes scream as it raced for the exit.